In The Arms Of Giants

Lily Yorke

EMMALILY

To Patti, Edward and David

Prologue

Silence? What could stop miss-chatterbox in full flow?

Ilona followed her daughter's wide-eyed stare across the shop, the young girl's rapidly flushing cheeks and slow deliberate swallow confirming her mother's fears.

Oh my darling, she thought, knowing exactly what was happening, he is indeed a gorgeous specimen of a man, but in every way far too old for you.

Please, not him.

In that moment however, Sophie, frozen by a pain she didn't understand, had decided. *Yes.*

Chapter 1

Had he done another of his disappearing tricks? It hurt that she wasn't on the list of people he would tell, but it was some consolation that the list held just one name and even she never knew when he was going or for how long.

Where?

Sophie had learnt not to ask. It brought only worry to those who might have an idea.

What?

Silence.

Her foot slid out from under her and Sophie's heart jumped. She desperately wanted to get to him quickly, every minute would be important, but the last thing she needed was to slip and spend *this* afternoon in hospital.

Thank goodness mum had insisted on the duffel coat. Already lying like an inviting, pure white, sound deadening blanket across gardens, cars and adjacent fields and now feather-kissing her face, the swirling heavy snow flakes would have soaked her. Her thin, pink cotton top, carefully chosen to suggest that she had boobs, but cleverly hide the fact that they were unfairly late arriving, would have stuck to her and achieved exactly the opposite. Her classmates' tease name of 'Eggy' wasn't funny at all. Mum's reassurance that by the time she needed breasts they would be there was all very well, but she might need them today and they were nowhere to be seen. Thank goodness for her hips. At just turned seventeen she considered them already near-weapons-grade. Men looked at her hips. Funny how no one in school called her 'Hippy'.

She clasped her hands together. Damn! They were still warm despite having been out of her pockets and held away from her body for the whole five minute walk. The chance of a passing boy thinking she was playing aeroplanes in the snow had been a risk she was prepared to take. She was almost there, she needed a plan. Yes, there it was, she stopped at the last lamppost out of sight of the house and clamped her hands on to it. The cold was immediate and painful. Would they turn blue? She didn't know, they were already numb. Just a few more seconds. She started a count to ten, got to seven and decided it was enough. She couldn't feel her fingers and her wrists didn't seem to be connected to her either. Good. Only one serious pimple today and that was on the back of her neck. Good. If he was in a position to see that then their closeness would be well beyond anything she could wish for and hopefully they would both by then be out of control.

She gave the heavy, black, iron ring of the knocker two steady, firm raps, two seconds apart, just as he always knocked with his knuckles when he visited their flat. Every time she opened the door to him she enjoyed the ritual of defending herself against his telling-off for not using the safety chain by pointing out that she knew it was him, every other visitor used the doorbell.

What if he wasn't at home? This was the sort of weather he loved to run in, he said it made him 'Feel alive'. Surely in this thick snow even Harry wouldn't be pounding cross country on one of his five mile runs with his twenty-five kilogram rucksack of weights on his back. Yes, he would. Her heart sank.

Movement. An inside door opened. Of course he was in, he never let her down.

She pulled on her straight face, she needed to look cold, distressed, sultry, not grinning like the excited teenager that was threatening to burst out of her.

The front door opened wide, her grin followed.

His almost-smile did that usual scary, but so wanted thing

that hurt her insides in a very strange way.

'Come in Sophie, you look iced through,' he said with that tone she was sure meant genuine happiness to see her. His understated flourish invited her.

'And *why* didn't you use the safety chain?' she demanded, trying to frown the crazy grin from her face.

'Because I saw you through the window and guessed I'd be safe enough.'

Not for very much longer Harry, not once I'm eighteen.

'Why didn't you put your hood up? Although... all that snow in your hair makes you look very... anyway.'

Exactly Harry.

'My hands are so frozen, I can't do the toggles. Can you undo them for me?' she whined, turning her back to him so he would have to reach his arms around her.

'Of course,' he said, gently turning her around and steering her to the centre of the lounge.

With his sleeves turned up to his elbows in neat, flat folds Sophie could see the gentle ripple of powerful forearm muscles. She was torn between watching his strong, confident hands undo her toggles and gazing into his eyes.

Keep going until every fastener on me is undone she tried hard to beam to him through telepathy.

She looked for recognition in his eyes. He either hadn't received the message or was pretending.

'There,' he said, gently peeling her coat off and hanging it over the chair, 'now let me see those hands.'

He cupped her hands between his, holding them gently. She could feel his warmth, his strength, his power, in his hands, in his voice, in his presence.

'They've got this cold just walking from the shop?' He touched the back of his fingers to her upper arm. The tingle shot through her chest and downward to her toes, caressing everything in between. 'Odd, the rest of you seems warm enough… Are you sure you didn't stop to build a snowman on the way?'

She returned his deadpan gaze with what she hoped would be a disabling smile.

'Right. Five minutes, hands between upper arm and body, wiggle fingers continuously,' he said, in what Sophie thought must be a military instructing kind of way.

'OK,' she said, scarcely able to believe the invitation, stretching her hands towards him, 'but isn't that going to tickle you.'

'*Your* hands, *your* arms, *your* sides.'

He glanced at his watch. 'We're already seven minutes behind schedule, we've got some serious cooking to do or our mothers will be having a Mother's Day dinner without any dinner.'

With her hands still not fully recovered she insisted he help with her apron and then nearly disgraced herself as he pulled her close to pass the strings behind her. She leaned in so her shoulder touched his chest. With her lips close to his throat his smell rushed through her and an animal desire to pull herself onto him and wrap her legs around his waist threatened to takeover.

She panicked, the top of the apron was pulling tightly, exposing the absence of anything of much interest inside it. Her hands made a miraculous recovery as she struggled to loosen the ties.

'Now,' he said, picking up a cook book with a cover picture of a beautiful woman in African costume, 'this is my cooking secret and I expect absolute confidentiality! Most of my best dishes are from here and I don't want anyone else getting it and competing.'

'Where did you find it?' Sophie whispered, expecting a story involving a search and a lucky find in a secret bookshop in a faraway, exotic place.

'Internet,' he said, matching her hushed conspiratorial tone, then winked and smiled and waved his phone, 'it's on here as well.'

Sophie looked at the title again, the author's surname was unusual, that shouldn't be difficult to remember. She was going to save up and buy the book and, as soon as her A-levels were over, study it from cover to cover. The way to this man's heart could well be through his favourite cook book.

'You're doing this,' he said, pointing to a luscious picture of a dessert, 'Guava and Plantain Pudding with vanilla mascarpone. I bought all the ingredients in Yeovil yesterday.' Then, with an over-the-top artistic flourish, he turned to a second yellow sticky tab, 'And I'm doing this. Lamb Jollof. The best rice dish you will *ever* eat.'

Sophie was disappointed when they completed the chopping and mixing so quickly. It had taken little more than thirty minutes and now things were either baking or simmering. She had hoped for at least a whole hour of kitchen stumbling, grumbling and fumbling (as her supposedly more experienced friends called it), but as she had expected, Harry had been super organised. Everything laid out and planned, worktops wiped after every step and utensils washed and put away as soon as they were finished with. Sophie, Harry and the kitchen were as spotless as when they started.

It had been a wonderful thirty minutes though. For the whole of that time she had been close to this gorgeous hunk and the sole object of his attention. They had laughed, chatted and helped each other. He had made the recipe instructions and measuring look simple and his speed and confidence with sharp knives was impressive, a machine-like dexterity. She decided to remember forever the moment he stood behind her with his arms around her to guide her hands and the knife to peel the plantain. She had never heard of plantains and now they would always be special. There was something seriously sexy about a man in an apron, with his arms around you.

Most of all he had treated her as an equal, an equal with considered, valued views. He, Harry, was interested in what she, Sophie, thought. And was it her imagination or had his eyes occasionally held hers for longer moments than may be expected for just good friends?

Why didn't he just kiss her? Why couldn't she just kiss him? Should she? Right now? Maybe not just yet.

She looked forward to the sixth form common room on Monday and comparing 'Eggy's' weekend with everyone else's.

'That's yours,' she said, setting his mug of tea on the glass topped Ashanti stool side table at the end of the sofa. As soon as he sat down she put her mug next to his and wriggled in close beside him. 'Now, show me your top five favourite recipes,' she said, taking the cook book from him and wriggling even closer. It was all going well. She rested her shoulder lightly against his, enjoying his muscled warmth. Her classmates had said men like nothing better than to talk about themselves (apart from S.E.X. of course) and all you had to do, if you could stand the boredom, was to discover their interests and keep asking them questions. Sophie was relieved Harry wasn't bothered with football, that would have been a test.

Africa seemed important to him, he had mentioned it several times in the kitchen and now he was giving her a brief tour of how its foods influenced the Americas. She wished she had paid more attention in geography classes, she knew where Africa was and West Africa was obviously the bit on the left, but that was the sum total of her knowledge. He had friends in a place called Takoradi, she would do an internet search tonight before bed and in her first study break tomorrow she would head for the library.

This was wonderful, they had been chatting for a good twenty minutes and she had moved closer to him under the pretence of trying to get a better view of the book resting on their touching legs. He hadn't made any effort to move her away, he must surely be comfortable with her close to him, touching. Was now the right time to kiss him? She so desperately wanted a kiss, any sort of kiss. No, apparently men didn't hold back from stealing kisses, he wasn't ready yet, he needed more time.

How had he steered the conversation to her? She hadn't even noticed and now here she was explaining her university and career aspirations. He certainly wasn't simply trying to be polite, he seemed to know a lot about business studies and asked her about the course details and how she thought she may use them. He was the first person she had told, apart from her mum, about her plans for developing their shop beyond bricks and mortar, an online business selling specialist foods and goods, promoted by a social media campaign.

She had enjoyed telling him everything she knew about setting up and running websites and e-commerce, it probably wasn't a great deal, she hadn't actually set one up yet. It didn't cost much to get started, but they didn't have any spare cash and it would need to be carefully budgeted for. Harry had soaked up every word and she had felt an uncomfortable sense of responsibility when he told her he knew next to nothing and wanted to learn.

There had been no dismissal through thinly veiled, patronising compliments packaged as encouragement. He was interested. At first she was hurt when he challenged her general assumptions on net margins, but then realised he had been assessing rather than finding fault. She wondered what sort of army job needed a knowledge of profits? (and why had he said he was in the Navy? He was a soldier).

Sophie was enjoying the sofa beyond the tingling of the physical closeness. Harry was relaxed and talking without his usual caution, there were no pauses for consideration, no carefully chosen words, no clipped sentences. She had only seen him like this on the rare occasions she had heard him speak with his mum, or his friends on the phone. Here they were now, two friends together, relaxed, alone, sharing. He had opened a door somewhere and let her in.

'I'm hoping to go to Brighton *if* I get the right A-level passes.'

His mood changed, he gripped her hand and faced her. 'You can be anything you want to be Sophie.' His eyes drilled into the middle of her brain, the intimacy thrilling and frightening her. 'If anything gets in your way go through it or around it or knock it aside, but never ever stop, never give up and never ever doubt yourself. Decide what you want and don't stop until you've achieved it.' A more gentle squeeze of her hand ended the moment.

Something new, almost overwhelming, pulsed through her. She really wanted to kiss him now, not in an unbuttoning blouse sort of way, but in a thank you, get close to a friend way. Suddenly the status of her buttons wasn't important, there was something much bigger happening to her. He had shown her a door into her own self, to a huge place until this moment unknown to her and there he was, her darling Harry, standing right in the middle of it.

'Thanks Harry,' she said quietly, returning the squeeze, pushing up against him and blinking her eyes clear.

The sixth form common room would be quiet after all, she wasn't sharing this with anyone.

He checked his watch, 'Time to add the rice and mix the mascarpone.'

******

'You didn't miss much Sophie,' said her mum, warming herself in front of the black-fronted gas fire, 'it went quiet just after you left so we closed at four sharp. I think the snow's kept everyone indoors.'

'We passed the time wondering what our lovely children would be feeding us,' added Harry's mother, 'and judging by the table we're in for a treat. Something smells good in that kitchen.'

'Well Rosie,' sighed Sophie, 'I've had a bit of a problem with your son. I've had to do most of the cooking myself, but hopefully he's getting the hang of it.'

Harry nodded. He always enjoyed the warmth of their teasing, it helped him to feel human and push dark memories aside. Outside of the military and its extended family nearly all of the close friends he had in the world were in this room. He also accepted the futility of trying to defend himself when these three women ganged up on him.

'Oh Lord, this is good Harry,' said Ilona, dishing herself another spoonful, 'I want to leave room for dessert, but I've got to try just a little bit more. It's so… comforting. Where did you get the recipe from? Is all African food this good?'

'His friend's mum in Ghana first cooked it for him and now we use the cookbook,' recited Sophie in her best newscaster tone. 'They live in Takoradi, Ghana's second seaport and now a major oil hub. Jollof Rice is served at celebrations and it's sort of an equivalent to our roast beef and Yorkshire pud. You can have it with just about any meat, but *our* favourite is lamb.' She looked at him across the table, 'Isn't it Harry?'

She took a sip of water, 'And *we* cooked this from a recipe in our favourite Ghanaian cook book. Didn't we Harry?'

Rosie sensed a new closeness between these two young people. The absence of any responses from Harry to gently, but clearly re-establish distance, said so. They had been friends for some time, but now there was a subtle shift in Sophie's tone and it was a confident young woman with a purpose, not a seventeen year old child, talking to her son. She looked at Sophie and then at Harry, he must surely have shared more about himself with Sophie in the last few hours than he had shared with her, his mother, in the last five years. 'Africa' was the most detail she had ever been allowed to have. Had Harry lowered his armour for Sophie or had Sophie spotted a chink and slipped in under his defences? Either way Rosie was happy, but worried for Sophie. Did she know about Harry's previous and probably current relationships? As far as Rosie knew they were all decent women, but all of them significantly older than him, none of them publicly acknowledged and no doubt all of an age where *he* would think emotional entanglement was unlikely.

Rosie was sure her son wouldn't use Sophie, he would never do that and it was obvious to her, even if not to Harry, that Sophie was special to him, but he may well unwittingly break her beautiful heart.

Rosie wondered what Sophie's mother, her good friend Ilona, was thinking right now.

Chapter 2

The long, hot summer holiday had been hard. Harry had been gone since April, he hadn't even said he was going. One day he was there, the next he wasn't and not even Rosie knew when he would be back.

Whilst her friends, coming to terms with their growing up, had spent the warm weeks tentatively exploring each other's new found awareness she had watched from the side-lines. OK, an occasional kiss here and there and she had enjoyed the two evenings with the young farmer Rona had introduced her to. His shyness and ready admission of lack of small-talk had been endearing and completely at odds with his relaxed confidence in everything else. Perhaps that relationship could have gone somewhere if he hadn't worked every daylight hour, which in the summer was almost every hour. Anyway, he had departed for agricultural college (at least he had taken the trouble to say goodbye) and anyway, he wasn't Harry.

Now the Christmas holidays were here. For many of her friends summer romances had developed into steady relationships and regular, non-stop kissing marathons whilst she didn't even have someone to hold hands with.

Sophie had started her New Year resolution early, to forget about Harry, to move on, to put him behind her. It was painful, but she was smart enough to know the relationship wasn't going anywhere. Sod him, if he wasn't interested in her then she wasn't interested in him. His loss. She would find someone over the Christmas holidays for sure. Sod him.

As she and her mum sat down at Rosie's table for Christmas lunch Sophie had been determined not to talk about Harry, not to ask questions, not to think about him. She was *so* over him. It was all going well and she was feeling rather brave, mature and comfortable, the three of them warm and protected from the howling, freezing gale and lashing rain that smashed against the windows. As she chewed with sheer pleasure her second mouthful of tender, Scottish Aberdeen Angus rib of beef and a good chunk of apitsi, the sweet spicy pudding she had cooked instead of yorkshires, she was looking forward to the third mouthful, as simple as that.

Sophie hoped that whoever had just knocked at Rosie's door wouldn't upset her enjoyment of this little feast of warm contentment. Who on earth could it be on Christmas day? Hopefully not someone realising they had forgotten the sage and onion stuffing and expecting them to open the shop (as Sophie knew she most certainly would). She poured a little more of Rosie's fabulous gravy over the divinely creamy mashed potato.

Her subconscious grabbed her stomach and squeezed - the door! - two hard knocks, two seconds apart.

She looked across the lounge into the hallway, gasped and poured gravy over the table. Dripping wet, bronzed and smiling, his hungry maleness filling the room, there he was, her gorgeous heartache. Harry.

Her silent tears joined the gravy on the tablecloth.

Before the four of them had finished their Christmas pud (actually Sophie's lovingly baked guava and plantain pudding with custard) Sophie had decided to delay her resolution until the traditional day and, without any control, her mouth had asked, or rather insisted, Harry escort her to the pub on New Year's eve. Her declaration that 'Both mums think you should chaperone me on my first date with my new boyfriend' had surprised everyone in the room, not least Sophie herself. It was likely her new boyfriend would have been taken aback as well, had he been there, and had he actually existed.

* * * * * *

'Hello Harry,' Mrs Pansay greeted him with a warm smile, 'come into the warm.' She stood aside and gestured to the narrow stairs leading to the small flat above the shop. Despite the harshness of the overhead hallway light Harry could see she didn't need makeup to look attractive. Even now, in her baggy, loose knit jumper and loose fitting jeans she looked good and Harry mused that the absence of a partner could only be through choice. It was easy to see where Sophie got it from. Sophie was most definitely her mother's daughter.

'Go on up. I'm sorry Harry, she's nowhere near ready. You'd think she was dressing for an audience with the Queen rather than going to the pub with friends,' she laughed.

'Take a seat,' said Ilona, pointing to the worn, mustard sofa livened up with pea-green puffy cushions. 'Would you like a drink? I've got chilled beer in the cooler downstairs… oh, no, you don't do you. You're a tea man.'

'Come on Sophie, Harry's waiting,' Ilona called from the kitchen as she clicked the kettle on, 'what on earth are you doing?'

Harry sipped his tea. 'No rush Mrs P, I'm not in a hurry. I was going to spend the evening reading anyway. I'm not particularly excited about seeing in the New Year, I don't see the point really.'

'Nor me,' Ilona shook her head, 'but I really do appreciate you going with her. She had no right to ask of course and I told her so.' She paused, wondering whether to continue. 'I know she's seventeen and needs to be with people her own age and I do try to let go, but I just worry, she's not as street wise as some of her friends and on New Year's eve there's always a lot of alcohol, egos and hormones sloshing around.' Another pause. 'When you read the stories in the papers of shoplifting gangs visiting the town and a rise in burglaries I worry for her safety. Who are these people? Although I don't know how the papers can say they're Eastern Europeans, it doesn't look like the police have questioned anyone, let alone brought charges.'

'I'm happy to Mrs P,' Harry assured her, 'I understand what you mean.' Another sip of tea. 'Sophie's a pleasure to talk to. When we find a topic we're both interested in some of her observations can be quite thought provoking.' He paused. 'Although after an evening of me policing her love life the feeling may not be reciprocal.' He smiled. 'We may never speak again.'

Sophie's mum glanced over Harry's shoulder at the sound of a door opening. 'Finally!'

'Hello Harry, sorry I'm a bit late,' Sophie sang softly, glad of her pragmatism at not drawing a sarcastic link between keeping him waiting for ten minutes and him disappearing without warning after Easter and not appearing again for eight long months and two long days. Not a single text or email in all that time. She had abandoned any hope of a social media contact a long time ago. How could a man in his twenties not have an account? For anything? In fact, after hours of searching, it appeared that, as far as the internet was concerned, her Harry Stone did not exist.

'No problem.' Harry waved a greeting without turning, his attention fixed on the bulge of red wax deciding whether to break free from the bottom of the lava lamp, 'I've got all evening and this seat's a lot more comfortable than any in the Harlequin.' He would never say so to her, he had only just admitted it to himself, but he enjoyed Sophie's company, especially when they weren't in a public place. There was something comforting about her warmth and honesty that perfectly filled spaces in his head he had been determined to keep empty. She pressed a happy-button in him. She didn't seem too worried about the difference in their ages or his limited social skills and was generous with her attention, although she must surely think him a bit of an old bore, a tolerable-family-friend character. He would be happy, would even prefer, to spend the evening with them in their small, cosy sitting room, on the very comfortable and inviting sofa, talking about anything they wanted to talk about.

The unbidden thought of enjoying being alone with Sophie made him feel guilty.

The clatter of the contents of a handbag scattering over the small, folded dining table behind him broke the silence.

'Now! Check! Door key, tissues, money – thanks mum, lippy, mascara, perfume – thanks mum, phone – fully charged,' a pause, 'breath freshener? Where's my breath freshener? Ah, got it.' Another pause. 'Just in case I need to do some serious kissing tonight,' she tried to sound matter of fact.

'Rules of engagement,' said Harry dispassionately whilst trying to imagine the fluid mechanics that may be keeping the blob of wax from its upward freedom, 'so there's no misunderstanding.'

'OK,' Sophie responded with curiosity.

'You have to remain within my site at all times, unless you're in the loo.'

'Err… O…K…' Sophie frowned.

'If you do get engaged in a tongue-tangle with some unfortunate young man I will look away, but depending on how long it goes on for I will need to do a periodic quick check. Don't accuse me of voyeurism, I'll just be fulfilling my obligations.'

'OK,' she laughed. 'Harry… you do know we're going to the pub, not hostile territory?'

'Finally,' Harry continued to drone, frustrated at the lack of progress of the wax, 'absolutely no alcohol.'

'Mu-um?' she pleaded.

Mrs P shrugged, 'Harry's in charge sweetheart.'

'Harreee,' Sophie hitched her pleading up two notches, 'it's New Year's Eve. I'll be eighteen in a few weeks. Pleeease.'

'When you're eighteen we won't need this conversation. Until then you're seventeen, the law says you need to be eighteen to drink alcohol in a pub, laws are there for reasons. No.' His tone, soft, but firm, left no doubt that this was non-negotiable.

'Hmmph!'

'OK?' asked Harry flatly.

'OK,' conceded Sophie with a sullen pout. Anyway, if the evening went to her plan not having alcohol would be a small price to pay.

'So,' said Sophie, as she cat-walked across the faded, threadbare carpet, to the centre of the room, 'how do I look?'

Harry, bored, but relieved to see a large chunk of wax finally breaking free and making its way lazily upwards as he watched, turned from the lamp to give Sophie his attention.

'Holy sh…' his jaw dropped, 'Sophie! What on earth…?'

'What? What? Wasamatter? What is it?' she panicked, trying to think what could be wrong. This was not a normal Harry reaction.

'That dress… You look… You…' Harry stumbled for words. Usually he just said nothing if he couldn't express himself, but some unfamiliar thing was bouncing around his skull and mashing his mind. 'You don't need a chaperone,' he said slowly, trying to convince everyone, particularly himself, that he was in control, 'you're going to need… a bodyguard… Christ!'

'So you like it then?' asked Sophie, with what she thought was sultry allure, a tone practiced for hours at her dressing table, and now at a level of sultriness she prayed her mum wouldn't feel the need to correct in front of Harry.

She wondered if Harry was mentally undressing her, like one of her classmates said that men often did. She really hoped he was.

Harry was in fact struggling to stop the bouncing thing ping-ponging his brain to mush.

His observation and assessment skills, endlessly practiced, tuned and honed to assist with the efficient dispatch of difficult things in difficult situations, some called it the disposal locomotive, had somehow been hijacked. It was heading at full speed into a domain he didn't understand and was sending him signals that didn't make sense.

Her soft blonde hair was casually pinned up with a wild tendril tumbling without care down one side, caressing her long, slender, perfect neck. The flimsy, thin black straps of her figure hugging black dress announced the availability of her perfect, alabaster shoulders. He tried desperately not to visualise what must surely be perfect breasts, but couldn't help himself. Yes, perfect. He was powerless to stop imagining his tongue tracing the outline of her perfect belly-button on its way to…

'You look lovely dear,' Mrs P offered quietly, concerned that Harry's silence may be an involuntary indication of disapproval, but more worried by her daughter's sudden and unexpected arrival into womanhood.

'Beautiful,' said Harry, thankful that he had snapped out of his confusing, dream-like fantasy, but worried his mouth was still not fully under his control, not filtering his thoughts, 'you look absolutely beautiful Sophie.'

Sophie, thinking that Harry's remarks were now tending towards the wrong side of the sincerity-sarcasm scale, he'd only ever complimented her academic accomplishments, never her looks, tried her last hope for his interest.

'How about the shoes?' she asked weakly. 'The girls at school call shoes with ankle straps *kiss me now shoes*,' then immediately wished she had not spoken. A very different word to *kiss* had been used and the phrase was limp without it, but she knew using *that* word now would have brought an immediate and severe sanction, regardless of Harry's presence. She felt foolish.

Then she felt stupid. Why, in heaven's name, had she said *girl...* and *school*? From her surreptitious investigations of Harry's taste in women, she knew those words did not describe any of them. She wanted him to see her as a woman. Her plans for the evening were looking more distant by the minute.

Harry hoped his *very nice* response sounded sufficiently over-sincere to mask the fact that the shoes triggered a reaction well beyond what was proper for a friend. A very different word to *kiss* was trying to force its way into his thoughts.

He felt uncomfortable. When he was working he was often at risk, often up against odds that even the most addicted gambler would walk away from. There the training, the team work, the determination, the controlled aggression took over. There his biggest dangers were the ever present thirst for adrenalin and the satisfaction of success, and he could control both. Or so he thought.

What was happening here? Why was he not able to control his reactions to this woman? How was she controlling him? He wondered if women somehow got together to share their knowledge of each man they were involved with, so with each new relationship men became more and more vulnerable, more controlled. He should really stop looking at her perfect bottom.

How had she known about his weakness for that hairstyle, his weakness for that Egyptian-look thick black line around the eyes and dark grey eye shadow and then those shoes? The quiet vulnerability of her voice as she described them, inserting the warm, wholesome 'kiss' into what was a well know carnal invitation – was she subtly suggesting one could lead to the other? He didn't understand, but he did know he wanted to get away from her, he needed to get back to his unit, back to work, where he understood everything, where he was in control, safe.

He had expected a quiet time at the bar chatting about nothing, watching over a friend, for another friend. His plans for the evening were looking more distant by the minute.

Sophie did not enjoy the twenty minute walk to the Harlequin, the pub at the bottom of the town where she had arranged to spend the evening with two other couples. Evaporated was the euphoria she had felt putting on what must be a seriously expensive dress for Harry. Someone very rich and her size had donated the dress, shoes and silk stole to the charity shop, perhaps a day or so before Sophie had gone hunting for an outfit with her limited Christmas money advance. She would love Sally's mum, Mrs Stephens, forever for calling her into the shop to look at them. The whole lot had been well within her budget and there had been enough for a seriously slinky bra and knickers. She had hovered for ages over the stockings, but decided such things should be discussed with mum first, so, tights it was. Not that any of it mattered now, the underwear was unlikely to be put to the test tonight, she might as well be wearing her dark green massive school pants.

They approached and then passed the street light where she had planned to stop, hold him and then kiss him. What she imagined would be its halo of love was now a mocking spotlight of failure. If she tried to kiss him now he was likely to turn her around and march her home.

What was he talking about? His favourite subject - galaxies, stars, percentages of inhabitable planets and some such. All millions of light-years, literally, from what she had hoped they would be discussing at this point. She should try to sound interested and made a mental note to search the internet for 'Einstein' and 'Relativity'.

What Sophie couldn't know was that *had* she stopped, kissed and held him, taken advantage of his confusion before he could fully control his thoughts, the evening would have delivered far more than she could have ever hoped for. But she didn't.

Sally and Dave, Rona and Ravi were already sitting at their reserved table, sipping their first drinks. Sophie was relieved to see Sally had remembered to save two seats side by side for her and they were on the cushioned bench next to the wall. Excellent.

After checking the others were all old enough to drink Harry brought another round then, after quietly reminding her of the rules, announced he would be at the bar if she needed him.

'Hold on,' said Sophie, 'Greg's not here yet. Please sit with me until he shows. I don't want everyone to think I've been stood up and call me Sophie-no-mates.'

In his view, he said without emotion, once it was realised she was on her own there would be a queue of young men hoping to change that situation. He shared his observation that most of the males in the pub had already covertly appraised her and many, some with partners, had carefully adjusted their position the better to glance at her, hopefully without raising suspicion. Harry shrugged and sat next to her anyway.

Alcohol lubricated tongues chattered as the background noise and music grew steadily louder. She was glad he appeared to be enjoying the conversations and her attention to him.

Then, without warning, he turned and, looking into her

eyes, pulled her towards him, leaning in close. At last! He was going to kiss her, he was ready. She closed her eyes, the better to enjoy it, her pulse quickened.

'Sophie,' he whispered in her ear, his voice tender, caring, his physical, intoxicating closeness sending her head spinning.

Her heart was pounding, this was it, finally, it. She would accept the first touch of lips coolly, perhaps with some surprise, then with curiosity, then with commitment in the unexpected realisation that this was so right. Butterflies caressed her insides, her lips gently puckered.

'Isn't that Greg in the corner, kissing that red-head?'

Crunch.

'What? No, surely not!' her surprise, if not her hurt, was genuine.

Greg had assured her he was spending the evening at the hotel at the top of town, where they were bringing in an up-and-coming DJ, and agreed to come nowhere near the Harlequin. He hadn't asked Sophie for an explanation of her interest when she had agreed his new girlfriend was indeed beautiful and pressed him to recount how they had met.

But there was Greg, tucked cosily into the corner, cooing into an eager ear. Now what? Quick thinking was needed.

'What a git!' she scowled, 'how could he do this to me? I'm just going to ignore him.' Her pout supported her theatrical affront.

Taking advantage of his closeness she pulled Harry to her and kissed him fully on the lips.

'Just for show,' she whispered. Strange, no resistance.

She dismissed his protest that a man wearing jeans and a cardigan was most unlikely to be on a date with a woman looking like a supermodel. She insisted he save her from cruel embarrassment by pretending to be her partner for the evening.

Under the table Sally's knee nudged her in congratulation.

Sophie decided she could salvage something from the evening after all. Even though he point blank refused to instigate any kissing or cuddling, he did pretend to enjoy regular pecks on the cheek and squeezes of his hand. She thought perhaps he was even making an effort to get into the swing of the charade when she found him occasionally looking at her long, elegantly crossed legs and glancing at her chest.

Sophie enjoyed the warm glow from the wine Sally had been pouring into her tonic and ice whenever Harry's attention was elsewhere. She didn't feel tipsy, just relaxed, and rather bold.

'Five minutes, five minutes,' Ravi shouted above the music, chatter and laughter as midnight drew near.

Chapter 3

Sophie finished sorting the papers and dispatched the delivery-boy then took a breather on the stool behind the counter, staring through the shop window into the cold, wet, windy darkness, the rain rattling like handfuls of grit thrown against the glass. She desperately wanted coffee, but couldn't risk going up to the kitchen and waking her mum. It had been hard enough convincing her to have a lie-in and take New-year's day off.

The shop would close at four and then Sophie would cook them a satisfying spag-bol. She needed to keep occupied – to keep her mind off of yesterday evening's disastrous ending.

It was unlikely now that Harry would keep his offer to join her in the shop after his run, to save disturbing mum if anyone wanted cigarettes or alcohol. He would probably want to keep well away from her after last night.

She put her head in her hands and struggled not to cry.

'It's no good Sophie, I just can't sleep after six,' said her mum, as she padded through the back door that came from the stairs to their flat above the shop, 'I was just lying there staring into the darkness so I thought you could probably do with a hot drink.' She was also anxious to know how her daughter's first real foray into the adult night world had gone. Sophie was a sensible girl and their close relationship had allowed many relaxed conversations about what may be advisable, particularly when it came to boys. Sometimes though you could only learn from experience and not all experiences were pleasant.

'What is it sweetheart? Why so weepy?'

She set the two mugs of steaming coffee carefully on the counter then put her arms gently around her daughter, connecting through the silence. The mother - ready to support, interpret and guide, whatever the problem, the daughter - thankful to be able to sink back into the security and surety.

'I was such a fool. I was sure he liked me and I thought if I could just get him to kiss me, properly, it would break down that barrier and we could build something.' She thought back over the kiss and how it seemed to be going so well.

'And?' her mother offered a gentle opportunity to continue.

'He's always saying you should decide what you want and go for it, so I did. I grabbed him at midnight and kissed him, a real kiss. He had his arm around my waist and I'm sure he was kissing me back, but then he stopped dead and went all polite on me, nothing, blank.'

'How did you get home?'

'He walked me home, very civil, as if nothing had happened,' said Sophie quietly, staring at the floor.

'Where was Harry? Perhaps having Harry with you put him off.'

'He walked me home, Harry walked me home,' Sophie wasn't sure she had understood the question.

'So… Can I … who… did you kiss in the pub?' Sophie's mum wasn't sure she had understood anything.

Sophie, more confused, pulled away to look at her mother's face. 'Harry. I was kissing Harry and Harry walked me home. Our… my Harry. Harry Stone.'

Sophie leaned into her mother's arms, enjoying again the warmth and the silence, and softly cried.

It was comforting to share the ups and downs of the New Year's eve celebrations, from hopeful start to disastrous end. How Greg had agreed to be her stooge, he hadn't actually known he was pretending to stand her up so that, to save embarrassment, she could appeal to Harry to take Greg's place as her companion. How Greg turning up had actually worked out well, helping her to develop the hurt and the story. Her mum had chuckled at that bit, suggesting she could earn a living writing romantic fiction. How Sally had quietly shared her wine. *Good, no reaction from mum.* How at twelve Harry had seemed resigned to giving her a platonic peck, but at the first stroke of midnight Sophie had seized the moment, quickly sitting across his lap and, cupping his face in her hands, she had made him kiss her for a good ten seconds. (She hadn't actually checked her watch, but it seemed quite a long time, certainly until after the Big Ben bongs had finished. She made a mental note to time them at noon that day). His right hand had moved quickly to her waist, she thought in a steadying action, but then his fingers seemed to splay, and as they kissed, gently moved.

Sophie decided she might have gone past the point at which neither mother nor daughter wanted to share more and it was probably not a good idea to mention that, after the kiss, nose to nose, breathing each other's breath, when she thought they were both savouring something new between them, she took his free hand and held it palm down on her thigh. She wondered if it had been the deliberate wriggle of her bottom, causing her dress to ride up to a positively indecent level, or her pushing his hand a few centimetres closer to her inner softness, or her involuntary shudder of pleasure that had been the trigger for him to draw away and suggest in a whisper she might want to sit back on the seat.

'Then he went sort of quiet. So I thought if we head off home we'd be on our own and have a chance to talk.' Ever the gentleman Harry had draped his cardigan over her thankful, chilled shoulders and steered her around the dark, shiny puddles from the earlier showers.

'He seemed to be relaxed again, comfortable. We chatted about small things, people in the pub, what we were going to do today, he even offered to come here this morning to help out.'

'Well that doesn't sound too bad an end,' said her mum, calm and reassuring.

'Then I did something really stupid,' Sophie decided she had to share, her mum needed to know, if she hadn't already guessed.

'Just before we got here... I put my arms around him and...' the words seemed to be stuck somewhere in her mouth, 'I asked him to take me back to his flat.'

There, it was out, but she didn't know if she felt better for telling her mum the truth or worse for reliving what she thought was her stupidity and now, on hindsight, her humiliation. She had offered herself to him and he had refused. Refused! She felt worthless, hopeless, ugly.

'And?' her mum managed to squeeze out, even though she had stopped breathing.

'The shutters came down, he seemed to be upset or withdrawn, and, or... I don't know... I invited him in for a nightcap or coffee, but he wouldn't. He didn't even kiss me goodnight, not even a peck. He waited until I closed the door and he was gone,' Sophie sobbed, thankful for another close hug, and relieved her mum was breathing again.

'I've never seen Harry upset before, but last night I knew something was wrong. I've really messed the whole thing up, he probably won't want to be anywhere near me now,' she sobbed again, she felt sick. 'I... I... he's so special to me mum. I...' She panicked. What if he disappeared again, as he often did, for months on end? She may never see him, let alone speak to him again.

'Don't worry sweetheart,' her mum cooed, gently stroking her daughter's hair and trying to sound relaxed, 'it will work itself out. Harry's a mature lad, he won't dwell on whatever might have upset him.' She pulled away, wondering how her darling's teenage broken heart could be repaired. She knew Sophie's biggest challenge wasn't going to be dealing with whatever did or didn't happen last night, it would be trying to understand and bridge the chasm of different life experiences between her and Harry Stone. Whatever Harry's work was, how one so young could sustain so many serious injuries, she really didn't want to know, but she did know it was gradually killing his mother with worry. Sophie and Harry lived in two very different worlds, precariously tethered together by a tentative presence in Honeyborne.

'Anyway, I think you've overlooked something,' she smiled, cupping Sophie's hands between hers, sharing her warmth, 'You *made* him kiss you for ten seconds? With his *arm* around you?' she paused for playful effect, 'Sophie my dear, I don't think *anyone* can make Harry Stone do *anything* he doesn't want to do.'

Ilona gave Sophie her usual, always enjoyed, it-will-be-OK kiss on the forehead. 'It's seven, we'd better open up,' she said walking to the door. The last of the four sturdy steel bolts clunked back and the bell tinkled its first cheery greeting of the day. 'Sophie, our first customer already,' Ilona smiled, standing aside.

'Good morning.'

'And good morning to you sir. Would you like a cup of coffee Harry?'

Chapter 4

Summer

The elation of being instructed to 'Stop writing and put your pens down' at the end of her last A-level exam had lasted less than an hour and the worry of how well she might have done partly filled the space left empty by the absence of revision. As much as she tried she couldn't stop the rest of it, by far the larger piece, being occupied by worrying when (she tried hard to avoid the *if* word) she would see Harry again.

It had been more than five months since his departure in early January and she was still furious with him for announcing, as he picked up his morning paper, that he was leaving that afternoon. He hadn't given her time to finish her preparation, to think up words and instead she had blurted out 'Be careful, think about me' and 'I'm really going to miss you'. Even worse, her carefully thought out plan to corner him in a quiet place, slip her arms around him and rest her cheek on his chest whilst telling him how special he was to her, hadn't happened either.

When he refused to wish her luck with her exams, because 'Preparation, determination and hard graft, is how you achieve objectives', she wanted to thump him, hard, but his departing kiss to her cheek and the unusually long hug, by Harry's standards anyway, melted her ability to be angry.

The emptiness had been painful, much more than from his last disappearance, and she had felt physically sick for days after. At first her emotions flip-flopped randomly between hurt, anger and frustration, but mostly missing him. Then they settled down to plain missing with occasional flurries of worry. In all those months there had been not one email, text, call, letter – nothing. For weeks after her eighteenth birthday she had rushed home from school every day. At first the 'Any mail for me' question was slipped into conversations casually, but her mum soon guessed and inserted a 'Nothing from Harry' early in the daily afternoon greeting. Not even a birthday card. On her eighteenth! Swine! Git!

It was as if he had forgotten her. How could he? Surely by now he had got the message, that she wanted more than friendship. Hadn't she made it obvious? Even Harry must have understood her touching, her constant occupation of his personal space that he never seemed to complain about, the warm whispers. She pictured him in her minds-eye and sighed, perhaps not, he didn't appear to be fully tuned in to female non-verbal communication, most men struggled with it, but Harry, Harry set the gold standard for obliviousness. Although he did seem expert at picking up signals from other women, women sometimes almost twice her age, but then even Sophie had spotted *those* signals. The over-long touching of hands as change was given, the subtle, but intended to be obvious 'Anything else I can do for you', the blatant staring into his eyes – talk about putting it on a plate!

Still, she was eighteen now, an adult, and when she next saw him (she ignored the *if* word again) she would spell it out in words of one syllable that even Harry Stone could not misunderstand. But what if he had found someone else? Not one of those 'bed-friends' who seemed to be happy with the occasional physical sharing, they were anonymous and came and went (she enjoyed the unintended pun for a moment and then didn't). Until he was committed to her she could just about deal with those. What she tried *not* to picture was Harry introducing her to a girlfriend. That would mean, especially for Harry, a serious commitment.

Where was he right now, at six forty-five on this Saturday morning, whilst she was in the shop, getting the newspapers ready for the delivery boy and preparing for another predictable day behind the counter? Was he lying beside a gorgeous, intellectually stimulating beauty, her long dark hair tumbling over his face as she kisses him awake? Possibly, but knowing Harry, more likely they were still out of breath from their early morning run, stripping each other off before climbing into the shower for a mutual soaping and...

Damn, no, stop! Get on with the papers. She felt helpless, lost, angry, envious. Envious of a women in her imagination. Or was it intuition? Imagination! For goodness sake - Imagination!

What if he was already in a steady relationship and the visits home were a duty to his mother? Could he? No. Could he? Surely Rosie would know. Was she keeping his secret? No, it couldn't be, Rosie was like an aunt and wouldn't let her suffer like this. She would make him tell the truth. Whatever it was, Rosie didn't know.

Ah, now, Harry was an honourable man, Sophie was certain of that, some things you just knew, Harry oozed decency. He most certainly would not have been with all of those unacknowledged *friends* if he had a relationship elsewhere. Good, that was good, Sophie allowed herself to feel cheered. Although – on his last visit home, December, he hadn't been near anyone else, she was sure, he had spent most of his time at home, pounding across the common, or in the shop or with her. What did that mean? *And* he had refused her blatant offer at New Year. She had managed to convince herself his rebuff was because she had been tipsy, she hadn't thought that bit through at the time, he would never have taken advantage of her and she admired him for that. But what if that wasn't it? What if there was someone else somewhere else? She felt sick.

The clunk of the heavy steel door bolts, as in automation she slid them back, shook her from her thoughts. As she had done many times every day for the last weeks and as she knew she would not be able to stop herself from doing for many more weeks to come, she stepped out onto the pavement and looked up the road in the direction of Rosie's house. Nobody.

She tried to busy herself out of the descending grey by tidying the already tidy counter and dusting the already dust-free till and didn't look up when she heard the back door of the shop open. What was the point? Of anything?

'It's all very well saying I should lie in, but I just can't sleep with these light mornings,' said her mother, putting two cups of hot black coffee on the counter.

Ilona looked at her daughter and left the silence a little longer.

'Sophie, you know it's not you don't you? Rosie hasn't heard a word from him either,' said Ilona quietly. 'I don't know if it's his job or just the way he is, but he really doesn't communicate much when he's not at home. You can't read anything into it.'

Sophie smiled and nodded.

'Oh, I nearly forgot, Ravi popped in yesterday. Rona's cousins are visiting and he wondered if you wanted to join them all for lunch tomorrow at twelve thirty in the Harlequin? Why don't you? You haven't been out for ages and it's a Sunday, I can manage on my own in the shop. Summer stock's moving very well, I'm sure we can find a spare twenty pounds.'

******

Sophie sipped her iced sparkling spring water, glanced around the almost empty pub, leant back against the cushioned wall and regretted accepting the invitation. As much as she usually enjoyed the old, oaken interior and the cheerful light streaming through the coloured glass windows, today it contrasted unfavourably with the bright sunshine and blue skies on offer outside. Judging by the amount of charcoal, sausages and frozen steaks they had sold in the last week, she guessed half of the town were, at that moment, in their back gardens setting fire to all three. She stared at her drink, the bubbles sweeping gracefully past the lemon slice then sauntering lazily to the surface. Was Harry enjoying the same sunshine, sipping the same drink as hers, in the shade of an exotic tropical tree. Did he get Sundays off? Was he with… *which* friends was he with? She swallowed. This was not a good idea, maybe she would pretend to be unwell, go home and read, or something.

'There she is, bang on time as usual,' said Rona, hurrying to the table to give Sophie one of her really happy to see you kisses. 'It's so lovely outside we decided to walk and slightly misjudged it.'

'We're having shandies, half and half, perfect for a summer's day. Will you have one? Good. Ravi – four shandies please.' Having dispatched her man to the bar Rona stood to one side. 'This is cousin Rob. Rob this is my darling, *single* friend Sophie. Sit there beside her. Cousin Steve has been roped in to driving mum to Yeovil.'

Rona dropped herself onto the chair opposite Sophie and looked at her. 'Isn't Rob gorgeous? He's twenty two, *single*, works in Dorchester and lives *alone* in a lovely flat in Weymouth overlooking the sea.' Rona tilted her head to one side and looked up at the ceiling, 'I think that's all we need to know? Yes.'

Sophie didn't know if she was more stunned at Rona's blatant match-making or that the man now sitting next to her was actually drop-dead-gorgeous. Chiselled, tanned and toned, his dark green polo shirt accentuated those green-blue eyes that right now seemed to be looking at her lips. Those jeans couldn't have fitted better if they had been tailor-made, smooth fitting for the most part and then bulgy in all the right places. Was there a modelling agency in Dorchester? He must surely be their prize employee.

'Nice to meet you Sophie,' his treacly voice oozed all over her, 'I do apologise for cousin Rona and I don't believe for one moment you could possibly be single.'

Was that sarcasm? She thought not. It sounded like an expert compliment and she would take it as one. Very smooth. 'Well, actually I'm…' she stopped. Who was she trying to kid? As much as she tried not to admit it to herself, she was single, Harry would describe her as single. She was single. 'I'm just looking at the moment. You know – books and libraries et cetera.'

'Looks like you're both in the market for a summer short story then.' Rona winked at her.

Now Sophie regretted coming out without makeup and why on earth had she worn this baggy blouse and baggy jeans that made her look and feel shapeless and grey. Plimsolls, why had she worn plimsolls? Suddenly the outside sunshine had lost its appeal and lunch was looking like it could be interesting.

They had all ordered the lasagne, a Harlequin special and guaranteed to provide comfort on even the greyest day. Ravi had hardly said a word unless instructed to by Rona and was visibly happy to be sitting beside her, looking at her like a love-struck puppy. Rona's occasional glances and gentle touches showed the emotions were mutual. On any other day Sophie would have felt envious to the point of wanting to leave as soon as she politely could. Today was different. Throughout the first course Rob had been subtly attentive, talking to the group, but making clear his interest in her and especially, it seemed, her lips. She ignored the buzz of her phone advising of an incoming text. It was probably her mum telling her to enjoy herself.

By the time she finished her lasagne and started on her third half-pint of shandy she was feeling comforted and full, and slightly light headed. Like Rona, Sophie didn't join the men in the bread pudding dessert, even if it was another one the Harlequin was famed for.

'That looks good, I wish I had space,' said Sophie, watching Rob's first spoonful disappear, 'it's homemade custard as well.'

'Ravi,' demanded Rona shortly, leaning towards her boyfriend with open mouth. With obvious practice Ravi spooned up some pudding, gave it a token blow to cool it and fed it to Rona. Before chewing Rona puckered her lips which Ravi, with undisguised pleasure, kissed.

'Ooh, that is sooo good,' said Rona, closing her eyes, 'you should at least try it Sophie.'

Rob gestured an invitation and Sophie picked up her spoon.

'No, no, no, it doesn't work unless he feeds you with *his* spoon. There's more to it than taste!' insisted Rona.

Rob delicately loaded his spoon, held it mid-way between them and raised his eyebrows.

'Oh, well, what's a little saliva between consenting adults,' said Sophie and opened her mouth. Somewhere a phone buzzed again.

'Mmm, it is good,' sighed Sophie in pleasure. 'Damn!'

'No, no, no Sophie. You need the kiss to make it the real deal. Go on!' demanded Rona.

'Rona!' replied Sophie in mock indignation, realising the sensation in her stomach was due to more than the pudding. She turned to Rob for support in her refusal, but her excitement surged when she realised he was there ready with another loaded spoon, smiling.

Oh, what the heck, it's mid-day, no one's watching and she desperately needed to be kissed. What could possibly go wrong? With the pudding in her mouth she closed her eyes and gently puckered her lips. The situation was somehow surreal and a little bit naughty, perhaps that was why the sensation in her stomach had shifted downwards. His kiss was warm and soft and she made no effort to move away, this was a perfect kiss and she knew he was enjoying it as much as she was. It was like one of those wonderful dreams where everything felt so right and you hoped never to wake up, but why was Rona kicking her under the table and what was Harry's voice doing in her dream?

'Now that's what I call a dessert,' said Harry softly, 'but I suspect the custard's going to get lumpy if you don't speed it up a bit.'

Sophie's eyes opened wide in panic. No! It couldn't be! It was!

Harry was standing beside the table, his battered, grey canvass holdall slung casually over his shoulder, half smiling, staring at Rob and her - still joined at the lips.

She swallowed the food in one gulp, completely surprised her epiglottis and erupted into a deep, choking cough, spraying remnants of custardy pudding over everyone, but mostly over Rob.

Ravi sprang to his feet. 'Good to see you Harry,' he said, pumping Harry's hand. 'Grab a seat, let me get you a drink. Do you want something to eat.'

'No, I'm OK thanks. You guys are obviously having fun, I don't want to play gooseberry, I've just got off the train, I'll head home.'

Rona, unable to get any meaningful signals from the still gently choking Sophie, decided the least bad option was to convince Harry to stay for at least a short time and have a drink. She wasn't sure why. 'Hey, come on, we haven't seen you in months, you've got to give us five minutes. God, you're looking good Harry. Ravi – drink for Harry please.'

Sophie hoped her disappointment wasn't obvious as Harry

pulled a chair up to the opposite side of the table, next to Ravi and Rob. She knew that had she not been playing silly-buggers with Rob Harry would have walked around and sat at her side of the table and would have been cheerfully compliant when she dragged his chair close to her.

'If we'd known you were coming we would have waited,' Sophie managed to squeak out of still custardy lips.

'I didn't land until five this morning and it wasn't until eight that I was told I had three weeks leave. Then it was a mad dash across London to Waterloo and I got on the train as the doors slammed closed.' His voice dropped slightly and he looked away from her, 'I did actually call you, twice, but you didn't pick up, so I called your mum and she said you were coming here for lunch. I thought I'd just pop in and say hello.' He smiled again, 'You've probably noticed I'm in need of a shower. I haven't had a chance to wash or change my clothes in quite some time.'

Sophie scrabbled in the bottom of her bag for her phone. The bloody ringer was off! How? Why had she upgraded to this new phone? It wasn't working properly. Two missed calls from an unfamiliar number, two from her mum and one from Rosie. Damn! Damn! Damn!... Shit!

She analysed his words. Was he giving her hidden messages or was her imagination punishing her? He'd been travelling for probably twenty four hours or more, as soon as he knew he was on leave he had dashed, yes dashed, to the station. To do what? To come to see her? Harry never rushed to do anything, everything was carefully planned, delivered to a schedule. He had called her twice and then her mum. He never called before he arrived. As for hygiene, he was fastidious. Even at the end of the day, in casual clothes, he looked like the 'after' in a 'before and after' laundry advert. Yet here he was, unwashed, in what he would consider dirty clothes, looking for her.

Now she felt lost, defeated. After all these months of waiting and pining he turns up at the exact second when she is stealing a simple kiss from someone else. Surely he wouldn't care that much once she explained. It wasn't like she'd been sleeping with Rob. Oh God! What if he thought they had?

Harry turned to Rob and with a smile offered his hand. 'Hi. It doesn't look like we're going to be introduced so let me start. I'm Harry. Sophie and I are... our mothers are good friends. I'm home on some unexpected leave for a while.'

'Pleased to meet you Harry, I'm Rob. I'm up from Weymouth for the weekend, visiting cousin Rona.'

'My apologies for interrupting lunch, it looks like you were enjoying it.' Harry smiled. 'Interesting you're in Weymouth, my friend's just opened a restaurant there. Antonio-something.'

'Antonio's Pesce? You're a friend of Antonio? Wow. They opened last week and it's constantly full of celebs and seriously rich people. The reviews are really good. It's solidly booked until November though, there's no way to get a table,' said Rob, with a mixture of surprise and enthusiasm.

'I know his son quite well.' Harry didn't mention that they had served together for the last two years, been on the same overnight transport home and four days earlier, side by side, had been in a situation neither of them had expected to end well.

Only after Harry had settled Paulo on the Weymouth train, it would have been difficult for Paulo to carry and stow a bag whilst he was walking with crutches, had Harry run for his own train. He had reluctantly agreed not to travel to Weymouth, but insisted on calling Paulo's father to confirm his son's arrival time and carriage number. It had been some comfort that the train manager had leapt into action, advising his team that they had an injured serviceman as a passenger that should be fully attended to. Paulo would be seriously pissed off if he found out, which he surely would, but at least he wouldn't miss his stop.

Harry lifted his holdall onto his lap, unzipped it and took a large bundle of mail from inside, 'This is what happens when your mail never quite catches up with you. I got this lot this morning.' He separated two white envelopes and passed one to Sophie. He turned to Rob, 'If you carry on playing your cards as you were just now you might just get to eat there a bit sooner than you think.'

Sophie carefully prised open the expensive envelope and pulled out the card. '*Antonio cordially invites you as his special guest to Antonio's Pesce, Weymouth. Sophie Pansay plus one guest. RSVP*. It's for this Wednesday... You're kidding!'

'I took the liberty of confirming the reservation this morning, so if you can't make it please let him know as soon as you can. There's a long queue for those tables,' said Harry. 'It's all paid for. All you have to do is get there, eat, drink and get back.'

'You lucky thing,' Rona chimed in, 'I've heard about it, it sounds really good. Make sure you bring me back a doggy-bag!'

'Ravi Patel plus one, Wednesday,' said Harry, handing the second envelope to Ravi. 'Keep in his good books Rona and he might bring you a doggy-bag as well.'

Rona jumped up and bear-hugged the seated Harry. 'Stinky or not – you're going to have a kiss. Thanks Harry, thank you, thank you.'

Nobody noticed the pain flicker across Harry's eyes.

Ravi, his usual steady self, shook his head. 'Much appreciated Harry, much appreciated.'

Sophie looked at Harry. She knew her 'plus one' was supposed to have been for him. Typical Harry, stepping aside rather than confront. How did such a mild person manage in the army? Weren't they supposed to be fighters? Was he bullied by the rough soldiers? Why wouldn't he fight for her, not that fighting was needed, he could have her right now, any way he wanted. *Harry you bastard!* She screamed in her head.

Or… was he planning to take someone else? She started to panic. 'How about you Harry? Do you have an invitation? Who are you taking?' She asked, trying to hide her rising concern.

'I'll probably go on another day, I've got to go back to London.'

He's bending the truth, he's just said he's got three weeks leave. He's walking away, or covering his plans for another woman. 'Please pass by the shop before you go,' said Sophie, trying to sound indifferent, but adamant, 'I've got something for you.' Her eyes fixed on his chest, 'Harry… there's blood on your shirt, you're bleeding.'

'Ah, sorry about that, slight accident, not what you want to see at lunch,' said Harry apologetically, grabbing a dressing from his bag.

His calm release of a single shirt button and the deft sliding of the dressing out of sight onto the wound relaxed them. He had felt the wound pull as he had hoisted Paulo's bag onto the overhead rack and running for his own train hadn't helped. Rona's hug had given it the final pull it needed to come apart. Damage-wise it wasn't a big deal, he had been lucky, but he would have to be careful what he said to his mother. Rosie would certainly want to re-dress it, but if she saw it she would recognise it for what it was and that wouldn't be fair on her.

Harry didn't understand why he didn't need to manage the pain, he was aware of it somewhere in the distance. It had throbbed as he walked from the station, but when he had seen Sophie kissing another man, and enjoying it, everything had gone numb. He felt numb now and confused. He wanted to go back to the station and head out, to anywhere, to not be near to Sophie enjoying her close friend. Never seeing her again sounded like a good idea right now.

But he couldn't go. He had an unspoken commitment to Charles, they all did and everyone who could would be there. He would be there. He would have to stay in Honeyborne, get as repaired as best he could and be there.

He felt childish, his hurt must be nothing compared to what Charlie's family must be feeling now. Screw it! Sophie was a friend, a good friend, but she could only ever be a friend and he needed to come to terms with that. She probably wouldn't even want to talk to him if she knew the truth about him, any other options were fantasy. Forget it, move on.

'Right, I'd better be going, enjoy your lunch, although it doesn't look like you need any encouragement from me,' said Harry, forcing a smile and wink at Sophie. Pain registered as he swung his holdall over his shoulder. He didn't know if it was from the wound or the suffocating blanket of hopelessness that was tumbling over him.

Chapter 5

It hadn't been difficult for Harry to forego his usual morning paper and his daily crossword and sudoku fix. Taking his camera with him on long morning walks across the common had easily filled his puzzle-page space. The crisp, early morning light this far north had added a new dimension for him to work with, although he knew he would have to be more disciplined in deleting all but the best shots. Keeping seventeen almost identical pictures of a single, dew-glistening buttercup, as refreshing as the subject was, wasn't practical.

The short, early morning walk to the shop, his one comfort-anchor to mundane normality, was proving more difficult to replace. It was nonsense to think he was craving the daily invitation into Sophie and her mother's humdrum world, even if it did immerse him in warmth, laughter and unspoken love.

Moving Sophie to a different status of interest was proving more difficult than he had expected. Thoughts of her seemed to intrude randomly in his day. Why had he wanted to share his toast with her this morning? It didn't make sense.

Harry decided to treat her removal from his daily life as a short term objective, every day moving her further away. Once next week was over and his obligations to others fulfilled he would head back to London. He had several friends who would be only too happy to share their bed and empty his head for the rest of his leave.

Today, Friday, would still be difficult, but he was determined, he was going to get through it. Or so he thought, right up to the moment Rosie had given him a task to do.

Sophie had provided Rosie with first-hand material for an article about the stresses, strains, hopes and excitement of young people waiting for exam results and preparing for university. It had been a good piece, Sophie's help had been the foundation and there was every chance a series would be commissioned. The magazine had rewarded Rosie well and as a thank you she had arranged to take Sophie to lunch. Unfortunately today was one of those rare occasions that Rosie was ill and she had insisted Harry step in for her and deliver Sophie's treat. He had hoped for a quick, quiet something in town and only after he had agreed did his mother tell him the day was already planned with lunch at the out of town shopping centre half an hour away on the A303. Shopping, crowds and eating in a public place – *just brilliant.*

Sophie had insisted on driving and Harry was impressed with how relaxed and sure she was behind the wheel of the large, ageing hatchback. She had taken over the weekly cash-and-carry runs to get stock for the shop, to give her mother a break and, with less than twelve months driving experience, was already a proficient, safe driver. Harry could have easily relaxed and enjoyed the ride if it wasn't for… How could he spend another thirty minutes like this? He would have to say something. No, just deal with it. No, his eyes ached with the effort needed to resist, too much…

'Sophie, is it worth pulling over for a moment? To adjust your, err, hemline?'

Sophie glanced down and then at Harry and smiled. 'There are several things I'd be happy to pull over for right now Harry,' she glanced at him again, his stare was fixed on the horizon ahead, 'but the height of my dress isn't one of them.'

'It's just that it's a bit…'

He didn't want to admit to himself, let alone tell her, what those long, strong, pale perfect legs were doing to him, where he was trying hard not to imagine them being.

'Don't be such a prude Harry. I'm not a schoolgirl anymore, I'm an adult,' she said with a hint of a smile, enjoying his clenched jaw.

'Anyway, I *am* wearing knickers you know,' said Sophie matter-of-factly. 'Oh, wait a minute… you know I'm not entirely sure now. Could you do me a favour and check… No, never mind. I probably am.'

She allowed a few moments to let his imagination work overtime and enjoy his discomfort before delivering the final words of the scene she had planned so thoroughly, from turning her back on him at the door as she had collected him from Rosie's, to deciding how short the dress should be to get the necessary effect. The whole episode had played out almost word for word, now for the involuntary heavy exhalation she expected from him after her next words.

'Let me know if there's anything else you want me to pull over for, but make your mind up quickly. There are some secluded spots just ahead, but once we're on the A303 it's going to be difficult to stop.'

Harry breathed out, heavily. Now the lock on the glove compartment received his undivided attention. He scrutinised the door handle and realised driving wasn't the only thing Sophie had become proficient in, she had played him for the whole journey and he had to admit he was helpless. The effort to shut her out over the last days had come to nothing.

What were those words about to come out of his mouth? He couldn't stop them. Pull over? No! Change the subject. Change the subject!

'How did dinner at Antonio's go?' he asked, the raised pitch of his voice uncontrolled.

'Ooh, good, really good. What a lovely, warm man Antonio is, he fussed over us like we were close family he hadn't seen in years. As soon as we sat down he told us we should eat and drink until we are ready to burst, the whole evening was on him. The food was *just* fabulous. Can you imagine, sitting eating dinner overlooking the sea, with the waves crashing against the rocks, being spoilt by a loving uncle. We must have had the best table in the restaurant. He made us feel really special. All those people with serious money and people from the telly and we had the best table. They were trying to work out who we were, especially when we didn't have a bill to pay.' She stopped talking whilst she concentrated on pulling onto the side of the narrow, steeply hedged road to let a huge tractor bellow past from the other direction.

'Your friend Paulo joined us after dinner for a nightcap. Did you know he'd had an accident? He was walking with a stick and having trouble moving around. It seemed like he was expecting you to be there.'

'Miscommunication,' said Harry.

'They both say hi by the way. It's amazing how much like you Paulo is, if I didn't know better you could be brothers. The way he thinks before he speaks and only says just enough, no wasted words, the way he quietly assesses everybody and everything, like he's monitoring everything going on around him, all the time. He does that thing you do.'

'What's that?'

'I don't know how to explain, it's like I see this captivating, deep, dark pool that's full of warmth and kindness, but somewhere down in the depths there's something I know will frighten me.'

'I frighten you?'

'Not as in being scared, more like I don't understand, something's down in those deep, dark waters that's beyond my understanding. Maybe that's why you're so fanciable.' Sophie glanced at him and laughed.

'Paulo's a good man,' said Harry quietly. A wave of fear flushed through him and he couldn't stop the picture of where the two of them had been just a week or so ago. As quickly as it had appeared the fear was gone again, leaving nausea as its only marker.

'I guess it was a good job you had somewhere to stay in Weymouth with all that drink flowing,' said Harry.

Ha! He's fishing! You need better bait than that.

'Weymouth? We didn't stay in Weymouth. All four of us shared a cab there and back.' *What's your next question going to be Mister Stone?* Part of her felt guilty that he would add two and two and get a very big number, but most of her thought she had to be cruel to be kind. As she drifted along beside his hook the silence for her was syrupy, thick and sweet.

She decided to put him out of his misery and tug the line. 'I think Mum's fallen in love with Antonio, certainly his cooking. I think she'd elope with him if he asked.'

Harry started to reel in, but realised he was the one on the hook, 'You took your mum as well?'

'As well as who?'

'Rob.'

'Rob?' she paused, 'you mean Rona's cousin? Where does he come into it?'

'I thought you two were… close. I thought you'd take him. Um, something gone wrong? No, sorry, none of my business. Ignore me. I'll shut up.'

'Rob? I only met him at lunch last Sunday. I haven't seen him since and don't have any plans to see him again.' *Happy now?*

She wanted to confront him with unqualified affection, kiss his silliness away, but she let her wickedness get the better of her instead. 'He was a really good kisser though,' she said thoughtfully, 'I wouldn't say no to a bit more of that.'

Lunch was everything Sophie had hoped it would be from the moment Rosie had called two days earlier to say she was expecting to have a headache on Friday and if Sophie didn't mind she would ask Harry to stand in for her.

They had arrived at the shopping centre before most of the eating places were open so walked once around the huge triangle of shops to inspect the menus, Harry gently, but firmly moving her past shoes and clothes windows, Sophie refusing to budge unless propulsion involved an arm around her waist. As they had expected, there were no African food places, they both agreed spicy chicken didn't really count, so Sophie chose Italian (and after yesterday's thorough internet research, the restaurant with the smallest tables). She decided they should eat first on the basis that his inevitable post-shopping grumpiness would be an unwanted condiment if they ate afterwards and she wanted him at his most relaxed (and vulnerable). He had been visibly more comfortable since learning Rob was not a person of interest, but he still seemed worried about something, or was it confused?

The restaurant's modern decor, the tiny tables and their touching toes were all perfect and she had chosen to be snuggled away in a quiet corner even though at this early in the day the restaurant was only just starting to fill.

As they waited for the first course, they had both decided to skip the starter, Sophie propped her elbows on the table with her chin resting on the back of her entwined fingers. She looked directly into his eyes. She knew her thick black eye-liner would be weakening his resistance. She tried to get him to talk about himself, but as usual he expertly and seamlessly steered every topic towards her. She knew what he was doing, she didn't mind, she had turned it into flirting and he was fully engaged, with no escape, whether he liked it or not. By the time the food arrived, a little too quickly for Sophie, they both knew he had dropped any pretence of defence and was cautiously allowing himself to be probed and explored. A mouthful of lasagne provided his escape. For a few moments they ate in silence.

'Open? What do you mean, open?' he asked.

'Open and try my gnocchi with kaminwurz, it's really good.'

'I'm happy with my lasagne.'

'Open!'

Sophie held her forkful of pasta and sausage across the table, resisting the temptation to make helicopter noises.

'Oh, actually that is good,' Harry nodded.

'No, one's fine thanks,' he said seeing a second forkful on its way, but opening his mouth knowing resistance was pointless.

'Now let me try yours,' said Sophie, leaning over the table.

After what seemed to be a stream of *again* instructions, such that he wasn't sure if he had had lasagne or gnocchi for lunch, Harry was relieved when they both ordered small Americanos. No need to share them.

The sharing of food had been quite sensual for Sophie, she couldn't think of a meal she had enjoyed more, and she wondered what her regular, but innocently delivered, *let me have some more* and *put it in my mouth* requests were having on him.

After they left the restaurant Sophie pulled him close and rested her head on his chest. She bathed in the power of him as he held her, his hands on her lower back.

'That really was a lovely lunch and lovely company. Thank you,' she cooed.

'I enjoyed it too,' he said quietly, giving her a warm squeeze. She felt the animal urge rush through her.

She guessed he would be expecting a kiss, so… she pushed him away. No kiss.

'Now. Deep breath. Shops, here we come,' she said, grabbing his hand and marching down the first colonnade.

She was going to enjoy spending the next hours trying on some seriously slinky stuff and making him pass judgement on how each made her bottom, her boobs and her hips look. Thank goodness her breasts, very late to the party, had finally made a passable appearance. She doubted they would ever be man-fantasy double-D calibre, but judging by how some men had started to sneak looks at them they would do the job. For those ankle-strapped high stilettos she would instruct him to run his eyes from her thighs, down her legs to her toes and then back up again before giving an opinion.

In one large store, finding themselves *accidentally* wandering through the middle of the lingerie section, Sophie picked up a matching black bra and suspenders and held them against herself.

'You know… I'm never quite sure about stockings Harry. Suspenders or stay ups? Visualise me in both. Which do you think I'd look best in?'

Harry looked at the garments, looked at Sophie, shook his head and walked away.

Sophie smiled, she knew that even now his brain was working in uncontrolled overload embellishing the vision she had planted. It would be a long time before he would be free of it. All was to plan.

After what she guessed must have been two hours or more the aching in her feet was taking the edge off of the enjoyment of having Harry's dutiful attention and his forced appraisals of her best bits, so she was glad when he suggested sitting for a moment and running through what she had seen so far.

'Nothing?' Harry sounded astonished. 'Nothing? You've tried on eleven dresses, some sort of tube thing, an almost pornographic pair of shorts and fourteen pairs of shoes. Nothing?' Now he sounded bewildered.

'I'm sorry Harry, there were lots of nice things, but nothing that really leapt out at me.' That hadn't been strictly true, she had tried on several things she had absolutely loved, but none of them had been seven pounds fifty seven pence or less – the exact amount of money she had in her purse. 'Maybe we could come back next weekend?'

'You're looking tired. Are we done? Car?' he said with his

usual patience.

Sophie nodded. She had enjoyed every moment of the afternoon. Being with him, the sole object of his attention, laughing with him, the relaxed casual touching, being his friend. She wondered if it would be like this if they married.

'You're going the wrong way, it's quicker to the car this way,' she said. It was a bit odd, Harry seemed to have an inbuilt satellite navigation system and she assumed he always knew, within about five centimetres, his exact location on the planet.

'There's something I want to check out quickly before we leave. It'll only take a few minutes and then we can go.'

Sophie was curious. They were back in the shop where she had teased him with the suspenders. His navigations skills must have been restored to working order because he had led them directly to the rack where she had left the perfectly fitting, beautiful lapis lazuli dress. She had tried to pretend indifference, it was more expensive than she would even be able to save up for, but secretly she had so wanted it.

'This one? This is your size?'

'Yes, that's the one I tried on. I tied the hanging straps in a bow to keep them out of the way. Why?'

'I want to check something.'

Holding the dress with an outstretched arm, like he wasn't quite sure it was safe, he took her hand and led her with more urgency than she could understand back to the shoe section.

'Hello again,' smiled the sales assistant who had helped them earlier.

'Could we just see those in size five again please,' said Harry, pointing to the elegant, deep blue, stiletto heeled slippers Sophie had also tried and secretly fallen in love with earlier.

'Certainly sir. I left them and the matching bag behind the counter in case you came back, just a moment.'

'Harry! What the hell are you doing?' Sophie hissed through

gritted teeth as the assistant returned.

'These are the ones you tried earlier madam, I thought they were a perfect fit. Would you like to try them on again?'

'Um, no thanks, I'm sure they're the right size,' said Sophie.

'Good,' said Harry, taking the bag and shoes from the assistant and walking purposefully towards the nearby till point, 'Can I pay for them all here?'

'What? No,' said Sophie. She looked at the assistant who politely looked down. This was embarrassing, Sophie's fun this afternoon was having a cost now. 'Look at the prices Harry. I can't afford that, I can't pay you back,' she hissed.

'I'm buying them, they're a gift,' he said over his shoulder.

'Oh Lord. What's he doing?' asked Sophie, her embarrassment growing. What was the assistant thinking of her?

The assistant lifted her eyes from examining the carpet and touched Sophie gently on the forearm. 'It's a long time since I've been lucky enough to be in such a position, but in my experience from working here it's usually best not to stop a boyfriend buying a gift if he's intent on doing so,' she said quietly.

'But he's not even my boyfriend.'

The assistant looked at Sophie, one eyebrow raised. 'Even better,' she said, with a nod. 'And can I say that he may not be your boyfriend, but judging by how he was looking at you when you came in earlier, he really, really wants to be… he's very handsome.'

'What on earth have you done Harry?' said Sophie, grabbing his arm as they left the shop. 'That's over three hundred pounds worth. It'll take me years to pay you back!'

'For goodness sake Sophie! They – are – a – gift! A present. From me - to you.'

She started to feel uncomfortable. 'Harry, you know I didn't bring you here to get you to buy me… I would never…'

Harry interrupted, 'A gift! From a friend to a friend.' Now it was Harry's turn to feel uncomfortable. There were thoughts in his head and words heading for his mouth he didn't understand and couldn't control. 'You looked fabulous in them Sophie, they could have been designed for you. I mean you looked absolutely... Birthday. Yes, happy eighteenth.'

Harry focused hard on keeping his lips clamped tightly together. Why was he imagining his hands slowly pulling down that zipper, slipping the dress from her delicate shoulders? Damn!

When Harry didn't finish his sentences, which seemed to be happening quite a lot recently, Sophie was never sure if it was because he was bored or irritated. His eyes were glazing over again, perhaps he was wishing he was somewhere else. Maybe now wasn't the right time to offer to pay him back with sex, keep it simple, a pound a shag.

'Thanks Harry,' she said quietly, hugging him, 'You really are a special friend.'

As they walked towards the car park Sophie insisted on holding his hand. *Friends hold hands.* She was happy. Her dress, bag and shoes were fabulous, she had never owned such expensive new clothes, but it was the fact that he had wanted to give her something more than a token gift which was warming her through. This gentle, quiet, shy man, who normally only spoke when he was spoken to, had summoned the courage to give her something special. If they could only be together she would bring him out of his shell.

His hand tightened over hers. He stopped walking.

'Something's not right,' he said. 'Take the bags, go into that soap shop and wait for me. I'll come back in a minute, when I know what's happening. Do *not* leave that shop. I need to know where you are.' He saw her confusion. 'Please. I'll explain later.'

She turned for the shop, watching him stride away. People

were running from the direction he was heading in. There were screams and shouting. Instinct turned her around. If he was going to be in danger he might need her help. As big as he was she worried he was too mild-mannered to defend himself properly. She hated violence, but she would do whatever was needed to keep him safe.

Harry was a good thirty metres ahead of her already, but his pace had slowed. Then she saw why. A man, a young man, was slumped on the floor with his back against a large stone plant pot. What was that he was sitting on? Something wet. Blood? Blood! Christ!

Harry grabbed a tee shirt from a rack outside of a shop, pointed at someone cowering in a doorway and shouted something about nine, nine, nine, police and ambulance. She heard his *Do it now. Now!* clearly.

Sophie quickened her pace, she could help. Movement to the right grabbed her attention. A tall, sinewy man, shaven headed with tattoos on his neck was glowering at Harry, then he grinned. His missing teeth, stubbly face and filthy clothes just about completed the list of attributes of the type of person Sophie had decided long ago she would always get as far away from as she could. Shit! Was that…? Yes, a knife!

Her knees buckled, then she steeled herself and ran towards Harry. She needed to drag him away. 'He's got a knife,' she screamed.

Harry, kneeling beside the injured young man and pressing the folded tee shirt onto his wound, looked up at her. 'Christ Sophie! Go back, get away. Now!' he shouted. He looked and pointed directly at the man with the knife, 'One more step towards me and I will seriously hurt you,' said Harry, absolute authority and certainty in his voice.

Sophie ran on, realised she was still carrying her bags and threw them aside. 'Let me do that,' she shouted as she knelt to hold the folded shirt dressing, 'you run Harry, run, get away. Quick! He's got a knife.'

Harry looked at her with incredulity then turned to the injured man. 'Vijay, I'm Harry, this is Sophie. She's more or less harmless, completely crazy and always amazing,' he said. 'Vijay's the store detective and tried to stop our friend here nicking a leather belt. It didn't go according to plan. It looks like a lot of blood, but he's not in danger. Once the medics get here it will all be sorted. Vijay – you've got a good story to tell your girlfriends. Think of all the kissing-better that's coming your way.'

How was Harry so relaxed and more to the point why hadn't he run as she had told him to? Had he flipped? Didn't he see the knife?

Harry's head turned towards the armed man. 'One more step and I *will* hurt you,' he said loudly and calmly.

'I've got something for the bitch,' said the knife man, spreading a layer of pale yellow slime over his lips with his tongue. His hollow sunken eyes glowered menace.

Eyes locked on the knife, Harry spoke calmly again, 'Sophie, just keep pressing here. Do not follow me! This is important. I need to know where everyone is. Vijay hold her arm please. Don't let her go. Sophie, keep your eyes on his wound. Please do not watch me. Everything's going to be OK, I'm here with you. I won't leave you.'

Sophie tried hard to keep her attention on Vijay's wound, but a loud, sickening, hollow *Thunk* forced her to look up. She had never heard such a noise before, but instinctively knew it was about a body being badly hurt.

What was she seeing? It all appeared in slow motion, she didn't understand. Harry was holding the knifeman's outstretched arm by the wrist, the knife still firmly gripped high above them. Harry hit him in the stomach, almost lifting him off the ground and causing that sickening noise again and then somehow he twisted the man's arm around behind him, kicked his legs out from underneath him and slammed him face down onto the floor. Another dreadful body-impact noise. Only after a horrifying punch to what Sophie guessed must have been the thief's kidney, did the knife clatter to the floor. If not for the terrible, body-damage noises it could easily have been mistaken for a well-choreographed dance routine. Except Harry had forgotten to show any expression, his face was calm, almost bored, his eyes expressionless.

'Shit! Is your Harry a cage fighter?' asked Vijay, his own wound forgotten. 'I've never seen anything like that.'

Nor had Sophie. She was relieved Harry was safe and her body started to relax from its urgent preparation for she knew not what, but how had her gentle darling known how to deliver such efficient, overwhelming violence to another person? How?

'Can I help? I'm a first aider,' the plump female security guard puffed, out of breath, as she knelt beside Sophie and placed her latex-gloved hands on the makeshift dressing. There was something reassuring about her soft Scottish accent. 'And could you ask your boyfriend if he'd mind waiting with us until the police arrive. We can't handle that animal and it looks like your man's an expert.'

The security guard looked at the slumped store detective. 'Vijay! You bloody twit! What have I told you about not being brave, not taking this lot on, now look at you.' The guard leaned over, smoothed Vijay's tumbling black locks away from his face and kissed him on the forehead. 'Don't worry love, the ambulance and police will be here any moment,' she said quietly. 'The CCTV will have the bastard this time. He's going to jail and it'll be a long while before he sees his homeland again.'

Sophie stood up and looked across at the *animal*. His hands were bound tightly behind him with what was probably the stolen belt. Something like shoelaces were binding his ankles together. A portly security guard, who Sophie had earlier spotted standing well back, was now holding Harry's arm with both hands. Was he... Surely not. He couldn't be arresting Harry could he? No, he was pleading with Harry to stay with him.

Two policemen came sprinting along the concourse, followed shortly after by two paramedics and four more officers.

With the police in control and the medics joking with Vijay as they tended his wound the earlier chaos was gone and with Harry's arms around her holding her tight Sophie started to tremble.

'I'm with you,' he whispered, his warm lips brushing her ear.

'Excuse me sir,' said a police officer firmly, 'I believe you subdued the suspect and you both witnessed part of the event. I'm afraid I'm going to have to ask you wait here whilst we take statements.'

'My girlfriend's badly shaken by the whole thing, I'm going to take her home,' said Harry softly, as he took a card from his back pocket and handed it to the officer. 'Here's my name and address, her name is Sophie Pansay and she can be reached at the same address. Let us know when you want to send someone to talk to us.'

'I'm sorry, you will have to wait here,' said the officer abruptly, with a level of irritation Sophie thought should only be used by those that were really confident they were right.

Harry flicked open his wallet and showed the officer an ID. 'Please call this in and check before you say anything else.'

'No. You are staying.'

Harry sighed and beckoned over a man in a crumpled brown suit who had taken control of the area. They were all surprised at Harry's authoritative demand to see ID. They were even more surprised when, after establishing he was talking to a detective, Harry said, 'Please ask your officer to call in my ID or I will be forced to take his radio and shove it up his arse, because I think that's where his brains may actually be.'

After a moment of stunned silence the detective leaned forward and looked at the ID card. He stepped back with visible discomfort, as if caught by the blast from the opening door of a very hot oven.

'Carry on officer I'll deal with this,' said the detective quietly, 'now please!'

When the three were alone the detective looked at the ID again, then carefully at Harry and then the ID again, as if hoping one of them may change in the intervening seconds.

'Are you on a job? We haven't had any notifications. Is this some sort of...' the detectives confusion was turning to irritation.

Harry spoke over him, 'You know better than to ask me that officer, but no, my girlfriend and I are here for lunch and shopping.'

Harry looked at Sophie, 'Where's your bags? We can't lose those, that blue dress.' Harry's brain had flipped back to zips and bare shoulders mode.

'Oh, yes,' said Harry, dragging himself back, 'sorry detective. We just happened by. Your officer has our contact details. We'd be happy to come in any time or you can come to us, but I need to get Sophie home now, the whole thing has shaken her.'

The manageress from Vijay's shop had stood guard over her bags and the wash-room door whilst Harry helped Sophie scrub the blood from her hands and splash water over her face then clean the wall and washbasin after her projectile vomiting. The shoplifter's stare still made her feel grubby and frightened, she needed a shower. It was going to be hard to resist the urge to curl into a ball and hide under her duvet.

Sophie was thankful she had accepted Harry's offer to drive, the journey home seemed to be lasting forever. His driving always made her feel secure when she travelled with him in his old, dark matt-grey Land Rover and now there was that same comfort seeping through whatever it was she was feeling right now. He had called her his *girlfriend*, that sounded good, she smiled.

Harry's calm and gentle words of reassurance, as if nothing much had happened, were all that kept her from crying, but they also worried her. He had dealt with Vijay's wound as if it had been an everyday event and then her warm, gentle, quiet Harry had faced a huge, knife wielding thug and efficiently beaten him into stillness, in seconds. It was hard to understand how the subsequent terse and authoritative exchanges with the police had come from her mild-mannered man, it made no sense at all. His explanation had been sort of sensible, but not entirely complete – the military was into personal development and constantly encouraged you to train and gain new skills. There was no shortage of opportunities to learn and he had chosen self-defence, self-assertiveness and first aid. Even on remote bases there was always somebody to learn from. From the little he had told her about cage fighting it was obvious he couldn't be into that. Not her Harry.

It just seemed such a big transformation. What if the whole episode had frightened him and he was trying to be macho, shaking inside, bottling it all up for her sake? She needed to be strong for him, get him to talk, let him know it was OK to be upset, let him know she didn't need macho, she liked her gentle Harry just as he was. A kiss would have helped him, helped them both.

Chapter 6

Sophie planted a long, soft, warm kiss on her mother's cheek and skipped out of the shop. It was a fresh, tranquil, early summer Thursday, and mum had insisted Sophie take the day off.

Harry had confirmed that: yes, he did have ice and yes, he would fix her a tall sparkling water and lemon and yes, the deck chairs would be set up in the garden. He had to go out in the afternoon? *Well we'll see about that* thought Sophie looking at her full length profile in the mirror. Once he sees her in the new outfit she had just bought from the charity shop he may want to reconsider his plans for the afternoon (and thank you again Sally's mum for letting me know and thank you Sally for being two sizes bigger than me and thank you rich, mystery donor for being the same size as me).

The loose fitting, white silk one-piece top and shorts with a subtle, swirling red and blue pattern fitted her exactly and the white, delicate Roman sandals looked just right against her lightly tanned legs. The small, soft, just-cream leather shoulder bag finished it off.

The gorgeous outfit deserved more than any of the supermarket bling she possessed and there was no way she was going to wear her one piece of cherished jewellery, Granny's gold locket. She picked it up, kissed it and carefully replaced it in its blue velvet tray in pride of place in the centre of her tiny dressing table. Some of her school friends had beautiful pieces (carefully hidden in clever places in school lockers) that surely cost more than a week's shop takings and she was honest in her envy, but she wouldn't trade all of it put together for Granny Kovacova's precious locket. It connected Sophie somewhere deep inside to the woman she would never meet, but knew for certain each would have loved the other unconditionally.

No jewellery again today then, as usual. Anyway, as Harry would often say, to explain his almost complete silences in their mostly one way conversations, *Less is more.*

A generous, but still sensible spray of perfume completed it. Her mum had blown six months of her own clothes budget to buy Sophie the perfume, Sophie's favourite tester, because *Sophie was now a young woman and men are easily confused.* When they came into the shop mum didn't want anyone's nose making mistakes about who may be available for a date. She had been in her late teens when Sophie was born and Sophie was now old enough to understand the hungry looks some men gave her mother. Her slight East European accent apparently whetted their appetite. She often wished her mum would wear something other than her usual loose jumpers and baggy jeans and just once in a while at least consider some of those offers of dinner.

Sophie enjoyed the surprise of five pairs of eyes checking her from head to toe as she strolled out of the shadowed passageway between the red brick garage and the side of the house and into the sunshine in Rosie's secluded back garden. Had she walked into a photo-shoot for *Seriously Fit Blokes Monthly* magazine with five wonderful toned bodies, all stripped to the waist and lounging on the lawn sunning themselves? She did a quick scan for a cameraman, just to be sure.

'Wow, fabulous outfit Sophie, you look beautiful,' said Rosie, twisting round in the deckchair to smile at her. 'Sophie, these are Harry's friends. Guys, this is Sophie.'

The nearest Fit Bloke looked at Rosie. 'Harry's Sophie?' he asked, eyebrows raised. Rosie nodded. 'Harry, you luck dog,' he muttered.

Were they all dancers? They seemed to float effortlessly up from the grass then glide across the lawn as each smiled, shook her hand and introduced himself. She had never experienced such politeness in young men. She felt slightly awkward when one of them, probably the youngest and with still healing burn scars over most of his chest, pulled his tee-shirt on before sheepishly approaching her and holding out his hand, 'I'm Mike'. Another, with knobbly stitch scars across his upper arm and shoulder pulled on a long-sleeved cotton shirt.

'Iced lemon drink on its way Sophie,' Harry called through the open kitchen window.

Thank goodness she had heeded her mother's raised eyebrows and ran back upstairs to put on a bra before leaving home, the day was probably going to be very different to how she had been imagining it just a few minutes ago. Still, she was finally meeting people Harry considered friends, that was obvious from the way they were relaxed and comfortable together and their aunt-like affection for Rosie. Sophie was there, in amongst those he was close to. She had offered to leave when she learned they were assembling to go to the funeral of a *recently lost friend*, as Rosie had put it, but each of the five, in turn, had asked her to stay. How could she not?

'So you've met this lot,' said Harry, handing her a frosty glass full of ice, lemon yellow and bubbles. 'They're not much to look at, but I suppose they're OK,' he laughed.

Harry slid his phone back into his pocket. 'There will be three at the station in fifteen and the rest coming from BOB will be here in ten,' he announced.

'I'll go to the station, you stay and greet the others,' said Rosie to Harry as she levered herself reluctantly from the sleepy comfort of the deck chair.

Sophie had been happy to help with the tea, should those coming from BOB (whatever BOB was) get here before Rosie returned. Harry had put the oven on for the sausages and was given instructions on when to put the bacon in. The rolls were all buttered and the sauces were on the table.

With the house just about full Sophie wondered what her school friends would say if they could see her now, squashed in an average sized, three bed semi with sixteen beautiful, seriously fit (in both senses) men and three more on the way. These weren't the sometimes scruffy, often flabby, usually self-centred, occasionally childish, invariably noisy young men she was used to. These were quiet, confident, clean, well-groomed and perfectly mannered princes of men that young girls dreamt of with no real expectation of ever meeting. Sixteen of them!

Sophie wondered if fantasies you allowed to stay at the back of your mind, but didn't focus on and embellish, also counted as disgraceful. By any measure they were ridiculous, but none the less delicious.

'Bacon and sausage,' said Sophie above the low thrum of voices as she put one plate on the dining table and offered the other to the crowd. 'Fresh brew,' announced Rosie beside her, putting the huge, cosied, earthenware teapot on its coaster.

Sophie saw the last three arrivals come into the lounge and did a double take of the second person through the door. 'Doesn't he look like... is that...? Bloody hell! Is it? Oh God. How do I address him? I don't know how to do that bouncy...'

'He likes to be called Harry, simply Harry and treated like all the others, nothing special. Amongst this lot the only respect you get is what you've earned and he's earned it, the hard way, like every other man here. Much more than you've seen in the press,' whispered Rosie.

Sophie swallowed. She had his picture right now on her bedroom wall, looking like every girl's dream, resplendent in his dashing, black, officers uniform at his brother's wedding, standing like a beacon of gorgeousness amongst the pomp and pageantry. Now here he was, here he actually was, in the same room and walking towards her.

'Hello Rosie, it's been some time, how are you?' the new Harry smiled as they kissed each other warmly on both cheeks.

'I'm very well thanks Harry, summers on its way, the sun's shining, that's all I need.' She turned to Sophie. 'This is my good friend Sophie. Sophie – Harry, Harry – Sophie.'

The new Harry looked at Sophie and then back at Rosie. Rosie nodded.

'Pleased to meet you your... sir... pr... Harry,' Sophie stuttered. Her power of speech seemed to be deserting her. *Say something, anything.* 'Would you like a sausage sandwich?' She thrust the plate towards him. 'They're from our shop, local, organic. You like org... oh, no, that's your dad...'

The nearly superhuman effort Sophie had exerted to stop herself bobbing up and down at every third word had drained her of the will to be conscious and she considered just closing her eyes and pretending to be asleep, but then the other Harry had set her at ease. He chatted about the importance of small businesses and his admiration for the hard work that keeps them going and when he confirmed that her local sausages were far better than his dad's she wanted to hug him. Thank goodness she was still holding the sausage sandwich plate between them, even if it was chest high and empty.

As Sophie walked through the crush of bodies, collecting paper plates and reflecting how strange it was that there was not a speck of food left on any of them, things got even stranger. At her Harry's announcement that it was *eleven o'clock guys* everyone started to undress and within moments she was standing in the middle of a group of seriously fit (seriously edible) bodies, each clad only in socks and underpants. Sophie blushed and looked at the floor, but realised with horror that within her immediate vision were several fine, only scantily concealed examples of what many women considered the most (only?) interesting part of the male human form. Was this some sort of military version of a flash-mob where they stripped off rather than danced or had she slipped into one of her more absurd fantasies and things were about to get a lot more hot and sweaty.

Trying to navigate back to the kitchen using only the ceiling for guidance brought more flesh to flesh contact that only she seemed to notice, the first brush of skins sending a disarming tingle into her stomach. The second touch sent a weakness to her chest and she breathed in quickly. The third, her bare shoulder pushing against an equally bare and hard male nipple, released a whimper she was too late to control.

'I'm so sorry Sophie,' the deep voice of the really, really Fit Bloke rumbled quietly as his outstretched arm managed to find the second sleeve of his crisp, white shirt, 'my fault.'

Only after steadying herself against the cooker and noticing through the kitchen window that other semi-naked men in the garden were now pulling open kit bags and putting on shirts and suits was she relieved. …Or was it disappointment?

******

Three hired people carriers arrived in convoy, not staggered, to the irritation of her Harry. One left almost immediately with its cargo of smartly dressed men, followed a few minutes later by a second carrying both Harrys and the three men who must have forgotten to bring suits. She might have sounded a little too eager in her agreement to her Harry's request to join the third vehicle as a backup guide when he wasn't confident the third hire car driver knew where the church was.

Sophie didn't know which made her feel happier: being treated like a responsible adult, an equal, by the now suited, sombre and focused men, or the fact that her Harry had handed her his expensive and cherished camera and asked if, whilst the service was on, she would walk up the hill overlooking the church and see if she could snap a pair of sparrowhawks he had heard were resident in the area. She was moved when he suggested photographing the mourners may not be appropriate. He was so sensitive.

Quietly spoken Mike, one of those without a suit, had walked up the hill with her and settled her on Rosie's garden blanket he had placed carefully in the shade of a hedge. He sat down beside her. She thought a little closer would still have been fine. He didn't know much about birds or this area, but he did know a little bit about photography and this looked a good place. The birds may be nesting in the wooded rise ahead and to their right and she would have to be quick with the camera if they made an appearance. Sophie pretended not to understand the settings he was suggesting, but he didn't move closer, instead talking her expertly through the buttons and dials. As with Harry, Sophie couldn't read Mike's mood or guess what he may be feeling. Was it weariness or possibly a longing she was picking up as he gazed out over the endless patchwork of green fields stretching for as far as the eye could see, marshalled by no-nonsense hedges and watched over by occasional clumps of proud, indifferent trees?

He reminded her to take care framing the shots so she didn't capture the mourners who would soon be assembling below and then, after telling her to *just shout* if she needed him, he took a deep breath, sprang up effortlessly and wandered off for a stroll. She instantly liked Mike, there was a caring, open kindness about him that said *This is all that I am.* Sophie couldn't imagine how someone in their early twenties, so warm and gentle, could have got those dreadful burns and lost a little finger and half of his right ear.

After exploring the camera controls and taking a few test

shots, (Harry must surely agree the poignancy of the full frame of red-painted toes with a backdrop of fuzzy trees), she laid back against the hedge bank, camera ready, and scanned the area for wildlife. The faint, caressing breeze cleared her head of everything except the calming, green beauty that stretched out to her horizon.

Sophie was immediately irritated with the one side of a loud and angry telephone conversation that woke her with a start.

'Have you set me up you bastard?... I'm telling you there's a whole... there's a whole fucking team down there... I'm not doing it... you can have a refund... No... No. They're mindless fucking lunatics... I'm... Yea, well it's not you who's going to find yourself in the middle of the North Sea without the benefit of a fucking boat underneath you. No... You wouldn't! ... Shit, well just a couple of singles... Fuck you too.'

'Excuse me!' said Sophie tersely to whoever was standing out of sight, just behind the nearby gate to her right, 'show some respect please, some poor people are saying goodbye to a loved one down there.'

A hollow, rusty screech from the sliding gate bolt announced the arrival of a significant beer belly with an obviously expensive white zoom lens and camera perched on it. An unshaven, pink, puffy face followed, the remains of what was once a mop of curly, dark hair completed the picture.

'Who *are* you? What are you doing?' demanded Puffy Face.

'Mind your own business and... trying to take some tasteful pictures of wildlife,' she retorted, wondering if Mike was still within earshot.

'Well whoever you're working for needs to buy you a better camera than that piece of crap,' said Puffy Face. 'Who are you working for?'

'Myself,' responded Sophie abruptly.

'Freelance?' the tone softened. 'You must have some good contacts, this whole event has been buttoned down tight. Maybe we could share, I could put some work your way,' said Puffy Face, handing her a grubby, much too warm, slightly damp business card with a bottom-shaped curve in it. 'Scratch and scratch as they say.' Sophie tried not to consider what thoughts may lie behind his casual leer.

Puffy Face sat on the grass a couple of metres from Sophie, taking care not to encroach on her blanket. He somehow managed to manoeuvre his belly so he could prop one elbow on it to steady his camera as he fiddled with the technical-looking rings on the lens.

'Does anyone know you're here?' he asked casually as he peered through his camera, surveying the church and car park below.

Sophie froze. 'Why?' she squeaked. Her chest tightened. He could, just with his weight, easily overpower her. Mike could be miles away by now and the self-defence Harry had shown her was all from standing up. How could she use any of it sitting down or with a huge body squashing her. The fear in her last word had given her away. He turned and looked at her, his eyes lazily devouring her bare legs. She tried to guess how quickly he could move. If she could escape his first grab she could vault the gate and be a good way away before he opened it and got any momentum going. As heavy as he was, he had long legs, he could probably run very fast for a short distance. She put the camera on the blanket between them and readied herself.

'That's a no then,' he said, moving his gaze to her eyes. He shook his head slowly. 'Bloody amateurs! Do you realise what's down there?' he sounded irritated now. 'Enough kill-skills to overthrow a small country... in that one bloody carpark. If one of those bastards comes through your door on business and they don't think you're on their side you have a life expectancy measurable in seconds.'

He turned to stare down at the church as mourners mingled in small groups, hoping to use the tranquillity and early afternoon sun to dull their pain of loss. Sophie sensed he was chastising her for an apparent lack of care for her own well-being and relaxed a little, but maintained her focus on the *Immediate risks* as Harry had said.

'Do you know *anything* about them?' now he sounded exasperated. 'They're all in the military, but none of them are attached to anything or show up anywhere on any records. They're not special forces – those guys are normally sane and rational, the ones down there are *Logistics Specialists*,' he said the last two words with heavy sarcasm. 'That's military code for being expert in one hundred and one interesting, artistic and creative ways to kill people with their bare hands. They're certainly above the so-called-law, whatever that is now. They do government work no government wants to admit to doing. See?' he said, pointing to the dozens now gathering in the car park, 'I bet at least half of those people are military and yet not a uniform in sight. Only when they die, as they nearly all do very young, do they get returned to their unit for exit, like that poor sod who's having his special day down there. Crazy bastards.

'If you're following this lot you should always let at least two trusted people know where you are and what you're doing. It may give you a better chance of not *disappearing* if they decide they don't like you. You should call someone now, there's a signal over by the gate, you can use my phone if you can't get one. Tell them my name as well, it's on my card, Rory...'

Rory stopped mid-sentence, his tensing body sending a quiver through his belly, his hand rapidly adjusting his lens. 'That's... Shit... Shit!... There's half of... Not good, not good.' He sat bolt upright. 'Look,' he said urgently, holding the back of his camera towards Sophie, 'see, I'm formatting the card. See, it's all going, you're a witness. You should do the same. Too late to switch our phones off. That's Red Five down there, they're all fucking psychotic.' He looked nervously around him, his head jerking, sweat trickling down his neck to his quickly soaking shirt. 'Don't stand up, just text someone to say where you are. If they find us here we're in deep trouble,' he said, his voice turning to a panicked whisper.

Rory didn't seem to be an immediate threat and Sophie's fear leapt from herself to Harry, who had inadvertently got himself in the midst of a group of very dangerous people. What should she do? Would Harry answer his phone whilst he was with the mourners? Should she run down and tell him? Try to call Mike?

'How do I tell my Harry? He's down there with them. He needs to know the danger,' she said with alarm. The speed dial of her phone still confused her and her fumbling took her to the directory. 'Harry Stone, Harry Stone, Harry Stone,' she mumbled as she flicked desperately through the lists. 'Bloody phone. Oh god, where are you Harry?' Rory's abrupt silence made her look up. He was staring at her, frowning, confused.

'Did you say Harry Stone? Harry Stone? Stone is your *friend*?' he demanded, his gaze fixed between her eyes, making him look cross-eyed. 'Are you pulling my pisser?'

Sophie couldn't tell if her brief explanation of why she was there this afternoon and that the *crap camera* was actually Harry's, had relaxed Rory or pushed him to new depths of dismay. He was gabbling in half sentences to both her and his camera. His sarcastic interpretation of Harry's job in logistics as making people who are regularly vertical permanently horizontal didn't make any sense and she thought his description of Harry as *Snapper Stone* was childish. When she mentioned that three of his friends had forgotten their suits so couldn't attend the ceremony and had gone for walks, all in different directions, he appeared to be close to collapse and she was glad he was already sitting down. Why was he calling them sweepers?

'Of course they'll recognise me,' she replied, bemused at his stuttered question, 'I made them all breakfast this morning. Mike found this spot for me, he's around here somewhere, lovely guy,' she said, now not sure if she should be worried or relaxed. 'I'm looking after his camera bag, that's it next to you.'

'Mike?' Rory paused, deep in thought, 'Mike with one ear cut off?'

Sophie nodded.

'Oh fuck! No! Fuck!'

Sophie's worry now flipped back to Rory. His crab like scuttle on all fours dragging his plump bottom along the grass, to apparently escape Mike's bag, looked comical. It was his scuttle half back towards it and then his confession to it that concerned her.

'You heard me,' he addressed the bag, eyes wide, 'I didn't know it was you lot. I didn't know. I wiped the memory card. Check my phone logs, you've got all my numbers, I didn't Wi-Fi anything. I'll give her all my cards and you can check. OK? I didn't know. All that stuff I said is all common gossip, you can't blame me for that.'

Rory was frightening her again. He seemed to be talking nonsense and she started to question if she should try to get help for him. Was he suffering from an illness? Was this care-in-the-community gone wrong and which could result in her body being found in some remote wooded area months from now? But how could he have known about Mike's ear and what was all that about Harry? Had Rory been watching them? Oh god, was he a stalker? She was relieved to hear the screech of the gate bolt and see Mike's warm smile.

Although Rory's claim that he had never met Mike had been convincing there was definitely recognition between them as Mike approached the still seated, quivering and now seriously sweating Rory. Mike's laid back comfort contrasted sharply with Rory's fear as he recoiled with a squeak before briefly shaking Mike's offered hand. Mike introduced himself as one of Sophie's many very good friends here this afternoon and mentioned that it was so peaceful today Rory was unlikely to meet anyone on his way back to his car. Rory froze then levered his great bulk up and with a sideways glance at Sophie rushed off as if fleeing an angry wasp.

Despite Sophie's worries for Rory's wellness and whether he may be a risk to himself Mike assured her he was confident Rory would be OK today.

******

Sophie had asked to be dropped off at the shop whilst the return to casual clothes took place back at Rosie's. She refused to accept the signals from her subconscious that the earlier sight of so many fit, almost naked men had been anything other than embarrassing. She was sure that the images that kept popping into her head from nowhere would all be gone before she slept and anyway, no one can control their dreams and she had planned an early night ages ago.

She had felt both warmth and regret as she waved to the departing bus. Each passenger in turn had said her name and a thank you as she slid across the front passenger seat and stepped onto the pavement. She had only just met them and still didn't know most of their names yet there was a something comforting and warm between them that she had never experienced before.

Most of the men would be taken to the station for the train back to London or jump in their cars and head off, but five had asked Rosie and Sophie to join them in the Harlequin for some early evening food before they left. It was the first time she had met any of Harry's army friends and she wanted to make the most of it, even if he wouldn't be there. They were all so quiet and polite (OK, fit as well) and they just oozed care and concern (and edibility – no stop that!). It had absolutely nothing to do with the fact that it had been the gentle, softly-spoken Mike that had asked her. Somehow 'Yes' had popped out of her mouth before he had finished the question and her brain had actually processed the request. Mike was confusing her, she was worried that she couldn't think of a single question he could ask her where she wouldn't answer 'Yes'.

She had twenty minutes to shower and change before Rosie stopped by to collect her so they could walk together to the pub. She already knew exactly what she would wear – a loose fitting, short burgundy tee shirt, skinny jeans and her new (well, second hand) open toed black stiletto slip-ons. A light spray of her special-occasion perfume would complete it.

'Hi mum,' greeted Sophie softly, as she hugged her mother and kissed her cheek, as she always did if they had been apart all day. 'It's been a bit of a strange afternoon.' She decided not to burden her mum with Rory's odd behaviour. 'The guys were very quiet. I guess the funeral was for a good friend. He must have meant a lot to them.' They looked at each other in silent respect for someone neither had met, but both felt a loss for.

Sophie knew what would happen next, she took a tissue from her bag and patted the tear from her mother's cheek. She had no memories of Daddy, but she knew mum thought of him every day and funerals always magnified her pain.

'Enough silliness,' said her mum, easing herself from Sophie's hug, steadying herself and then smiling, 'you'll *never* guess who came into the shop earlier and bought out our whole stock of organic sausages!'

'I bet I can!' Sophie played back the morning's events and how she had been so taken aback she hadn't known what to say, where to look or what to do and ended up probably gibbering nonsense.

'He said he wanted to take some for *his father,* his father, you know who *that* is. And he took some of our own home made jam for his gran, you know who that is!' Without waiting for answers Sophie's mum continued, 'He walked in, no fanfare, plain as you like and said he'd been at Rosie's and you had just cooked him some sausages this morning and they were really good. I actually looked for those 'Gotcha' cameras, but when I saw the sort of people waiting outside for him I knew it was real.'

******

Sophie pulled open the pub's heavy oak, half glazed door and stood aside for Rosie. The blues, reds and greens of the leaded window just breathed 'Old' and Sophie felt a waft of reverence every time she entered.

She never understood why Thursday was a popular night, after all, Friday was still a weekday, but today she was glad there were a few people in the pub in this early evening. Mike and friends hadn't arrived yet and she didn't fancy the two of them sitting alone, waiting, there had been talk of strange visitors to the town these last few weeks. She followed Rosie to sit with Jonathan, a regular shop customer who's Tuesday would always be spoiled if his specially ordered *Man and Bike* magazine was late, and Greg (her New Year stooge) with his latest girlfriend, Claudia.

'Well Rosie, this is an uncommon event, meeting you in a pub. Are you out on the town tonight?' asked Greg with a smile. Rosie and Sophie declined the offer of a drink, explaining that they were waiting for friends.

'We're going to move off shortly,' said Jonathan. 'A couple of very unpleasant looking characters came in just now and left again. A really mean looking pair, I don't know where they've come from, but we don't want to be around if they come back, that's for sure.'

Claudia chastised Greg for suggesting to call the police to let them know there were a bunch of *bad-asses* on the prowl. Just because they were strangers with cold, expressionless faces it didn't mean they were up to no good. The police already had enough to do since the local police station had closed down and Greg probably wouldn't be thanked if he wasted their time dragging them out from Dorchester. 'Besides,' she said, her wide eyes flitting between Sophie and Rosie, 'they looked rather *interesting* in a thuggish, muscular, manly sort of way.'

'Yes, very good Claudia,' Greg retorted. 'I don't particularly want to get into a muscular, manly, thuggish fight which will have a very quick and predictable ending, I think we should finish our drinks and… oh crap!' he finished his sentence quietly. 'Don't look,' he whispered, looking surreptitiously over the top of his black rimmed glasses and through the gap between Sophie and Rosie. 'They're back, there's more of them. Look at the size of the one at the back! No! don't look.' Sophie, with her back to the door, felt defenceless. She wished Harry or Mike or any of her other new found friends were here, safety in numbers, even with gentle men. Her heart started to race, she swallowed hard and glanced at Rosie who, on the outside at least, looked indifferent to what may fast become a horrible situation.

Claudia, sitting side on to the door, turned her head slightly and looked out of the corner of her eye. Sophie glanced at her, was she ogling one of them? She was going to make any difficult situation downright dangerous if she started flirting.

'Oh no,' Greg continued to whisper, 'he's coming over, sod it, they're all coming over.' He swallowed hard. 'I'm going to apologise. Yes. We're all sorry and we're about to leave,' he practised under his breath. 'Oh god, it looks like someone's bitten his ear off.'

Greg stared directly over Sophie's shoulder, his eyes wide. The light footsteps on the polished, dark oak boards stopped just beside her. She tried to remember Harry's self-defence lessons. *The best defence is attack, shock and awe, strike to win.* She steadied herself. If this thug so much as touched her or any of her friends his testicles at least would regret it and if she could move quickly enough so would his windpipe.

Greg squirmed in his chair, swallowing hard, readying for flight. 'I'm so sorry,' he blurted out, 'we were just leaving…'

The soft voice spoke over him. 'My apologies for interrupting. Could I just speak to Sophie and Rosie for a moment please?'

'Mike?' said Sophie, screeching her chair legs over the boards as she shot to her feet and tried to suppress her relief. Or was it excitement?

What just happened? She had spoken to him probably less than an hour ago and now she had jumped up and kissed him on the cheek as if they were close friends who hadn't seen each other for months. *Kiss the others, kiss the others* she said to herself as she tried to demonstrate equal opportunity, to the quiet enjoyment of the other four.

After introductions, where Claudia decided she should also dispense five kisses, each far more generous and lingering than Sophie's pecks, Greg and Jonathan, now slightly less nervous, declined the offer to join the group to eat.

'We were just on our way,' smiled Greg as he ushered out the reluctant Claudia.

Chapter 7

Autumn

After a solid week of sardine sandwiches every day for lunch they were getting monotonous, although she would devour every last crumb. She had had to drastically cut down on her intake and was hungry. But Sophie was more worried about what she would eat once her dwindling stock of tins from their shop ran out. Her student loan still hadn't come through and she was down to the last few quid her mum had managed to scrape together so she could at least start the course. Sophie knew mum would send more money immediately had she asked, but she also knew her mum would immediately go on 'Mature-rations' until the books were balanced. Sophie smiled, 'Mature-rations' was what they called it as a joke when money was short and all they had for eating was the out of date stock from their shop. Funny how cornflakes always seemed to be in the mix. Sophie sighed, she had eaten an awful lot of cornflakes in these last years.

Sophie was determined to make the most of the late summer warmth and eat her lunch on the promenade whenever she could. She really missed her mum, especially the ritual sharing of late evening suppers, but life couldn't be all bad if you could eat your food, however humble, looking out over the Brighton pebbles to the sea and watch the gulls soaring, swooping and screeching. As a bonus she wouldn't have to share a canteen table with strangers, or even worse, eat in front of them, not just yet. She took the battered sandwich box from her free-gift, environment friendly, canvass tote bag and sat back on the bench.

Harry fluttered through her consciousness and she smiled, he loved sardines. Where was he now? Was he safe? At least his friends from the funeral would surely look after him if he was being bullied, although they looked as soft and gentle as Harry and, from what she had read, some soldiers could be rude, rough and tough.

Next time she saw that photographer, the rotund Rory, she would give him a good talking to as well. Calling her darling *Snapper Stone* with that sarcastic tone, just because he liked photography, was not acceptable.

It had been four weeks and four days since Harry had said the most recent goodbye. This time he hadn't even come to the shop, but called from somewhere very noisy using a new telephone number that went to *not in service* the day after when she tried to call it back. Since then not a word, nothing. Well, at least he had called, that was something. Wasn't it? What if he came home whilst she was here in Brighton? Would he come down to see her or drive down to pick her up for the weekend? Probably not. She couldn't afford the coach fare home mid-term, that's for sure. It could be ages before they were in the same place together again. These next months were going to be difficult. Giving up university wasn't an option, she needed it, but she felt so alone, empty in the uncertainty.

Decide what you want and don't stop until you've achieved it. Sod it! The next time they were together she would grab him, snog him and ram her tongue down his throat. She would make it absolutely clear what she wanted.

Sophie suspended her dreaming. Who was this walking towards her? Did she look familiar? Yes, from the enrolment hall. Anyone this good looking, well dressed and oozing confidence was bound to stand out and Sophie remembered probably three quarters of the males and many of the women in the hall tracking the progress of the gorgeous figure at one point or another. Some with surreptitious side glances, others with uncontrolled hungry stares, looking like they might drool at any moment.

Sophie's knowledge of fashion was limited to say the least, but she recognised expensive and quality. Suddenly she felt frumpy.

Oh no! Miss Beautiful, no, Miss Intruder, was going to sit down on *her* bench, damn!

Sophie soon realised that Intruder was not about to leave and if she was to eat her sandwiches before her next lecture she would have to start now. She would wait for this other person strolling into her space from the left to walk past, then she would dig in. She could see from her peripheral vision Intruder was watching the man intently. OK, he was good looking and the rich yellow of his polo shirt emphasised the definition of his muscled arms and his gorgeous dark skin, but staring? Really!

'Did he look clean to you? He looked like a clean guy to me.'

Sophie was taken aback, 'Um yes... very clean.'

On her way back from the bin, having retrieved Clean Guy's burger box, Intruder opened the lid. She sat on the edge of the bench examining the remnants.

'Thought so, he's only taken a few bites and the fries are still warm.' She looked at Sophie, 'Do you think it's still OK? It was only in the bin a few seconds and he looked very hygienic.'

'You're not thinking of... eating it?'

'Oh god, am I?' she closed the lid of the red cardboard box and stared out across the water, 'I... yes I am, I don't know, I'm so hungry, I haven't eaten since yesterday morning.'

Sophie was surprised at how she was warming to Intruder and didn't feel the usual clumsiness she felt with almost everyone else. Intruder had an honesty and openness or was it lack of arrogance? Nothing like some of her school friends whose well spoken, well dressed and obvious affluence often delivered with it a sense of 'You're beneath me, but I'll speak to you anyway' dismissive superiority.

'Let me guess, the same boat as me, waiting for your student loan? I'm broke too,' said Sophie, surprised at her own eagerness to talk.

'Almost, not quite, I've got some money in my account, but I can't get to it. Some bastard-shithole-dick stole my bag with all my cards, cash, phone and ID. Everything. The bank is sending replacement cards, when they get round to it, to my home address, but I don't have the money to get home to collect them. My stepmother would send me cash, but I'd rather starve than ask her. I've had it up to my neck with being told how irresponsible, sloppy and selfish I am to make my father worry. She'd just *love* this. Pop's back in the UK tomorrow, he'll pretend to be cross, but he'll sort me out.' She looked at the burger box on her lap and then back at Sophie. 'I'm sorry, I'm dumping my problems on you when you've got your own challenges. I'll shut up.' She put the box on the bench beside her, looking at it from the corner of her eye, still considering its contents.

Sophie popped the top off of her sandwich box and held it out. 'Share with me, I've got plenty.'

'No, really I couldn't, it's your lunch.'

Intruder's voice was saying one thing, but her eyes plainly said something completely different. 'Please do, help yourself, I had a huge breakfast, I'm not that hungry,' lied Sophie. 'I'm Sophie by the way.'

'Hi Sophie, I'm Victoria. They do look good, perhaps one then?' she looked at Sophie for confirmation.

Sophie nodded and pushed the box closer. Victoria wiped her hands thoroughly on her expensive designer jeans and took a sandwich, shoved a very big corner in her mouth, bit and swallowed.

'Ooh, good.' She took another bite.

'Err, it might taste even better if you chewed it a bit,' Sophie laughed. 'I'm afraid it's only sardine with chopped jalapeño, but very good for you.'

'Sardine? It's *really* nice, I've never had sardine. What is it?'

'Little fish.' Sophie used her thumb and forefinger to indicate how big she imagined a whole sardine may be.

Sophie persuaded Victoria to eat all four sandwiches and watched her drain the last cup of lukewarm coffee from Sophie's flask.

'Thanks Sophie, I feel like a bit of a beggar and I've scoffed your lunch, but I didn't realise how hungry I was. That will keep me going till Pop's back and sends me some dosh. I promise I'll make it up to you.'

'Why not come back to mine this evening? I'm cooking spag-bol. It would be nice to have company and it's Saturday tomorrow,' said Sophie, standing up, 'I'd better get moving, I've got a lecture at two.'

'Me too. Yes please I'd love to try your spag-bol, if you don't mind and I promise I'll leave some for you this time.'

They walked back together, chattering like old friends, recognising an obvious link between Sophie's Business Studies and Victoria's Advertising and Marketing and agreeing where they would meet later.

******

Sophie twisted the wonky, once chrome, now mostly brass handle, opened the door to her room and invited Victoria in. Mum would question whether inviting an almost-stranger in was wise, but Sophie didn't feel her usual self-consciousness with Victoria.

She knew Victoria wouldn't judge her by the poor repair of her room or plainness of her somewhat dowdy everyday clothes. She had scrubbed the bedsit from top to bottom on the first day. There was no way to improve the faded green and blue floral wallpaper and chipped, yellowing paint, it still looked tatty and run down, but at least it was clean.

'You have a room-mate?' asked Victoria looking at the second single bed.

'Sort of, well I'm not sure. She arrived on Monday, spent the whole night crying and then Tuesday apologised and announced she was going home. I haven't seen her since. I think she was home sick.' Sophie shrugged. 'I guess the landlord will put someone else in if she doesn't pay next month's rent.'

'How does that sort of thing work? Do you have to pay a month in advance or something?'

'A deposit and then monthly ahead. I'm not even sure how I'm going to pay next month's if my loan doesn't arrive soon. I wonder how far in arrears you can go before they throw you out,' said Sophie, trying to put the distinct possibility out of her mind. She moved to the corner where the new, shiny white table top double hob balancing on the battered fridge managed to make very clear the age of its fellow decrepit furnishings. 'Right, let's get cooking, I'm famished.'

'Me too. I've never cooked spag-bol, what can I do to help? In truth toast is about my limit,' said Victoria, with an honesty Sophie found disarming, 'but I do want to learn, really.' Victoria picked up a serving spoon from the cutlery jar, with an eagerness that showed her complete lack of knowledge of what happens in kitchens, that is, beyond working a toaster.

They spent the evening cooking, then sitting cross legged on the lumpy beds eating until their stomachs were full, then slouched and chattering non-stop. Sophie tried not to think about how this 'party' was punishing her already stretched budget, but what the heck, she was sure she could manage without food for a couple of days, this was more fun than she had had in ages.

'That… was… absolutely… delicious,' said Victoria, scraping the remaining sauce from her bowl to keep the last two pasta spirals company. 'I'm definitely going to have a go at cooking that.'

Sensing her own experiences would be considerably less interesting than Victoria's in the romance department Sophie elected to go first in the cataloguing of boy-friends. She didn't even bother trying to embellish her limited encounters, in fact she skipped through them to get to the one that was now, and had been for some time, the sole occupant of that thought-space.

Harry.

How, from the first time he had walked into her life in the shop, she had decided they must be together. She had been just fifteen and he a lot older, but it was completely clear to her, she was determined. Victoria aah'ed with real envy.

Sophie would happily be an army wife, enduring the months of separation knowing that the together-times would be intense and wonderful. She thought Harry did something about moving stuff around – logistics. He had said it was mostly boring and didn't want to waste home time talking about it. She was thankful he wasn't involved with guns and the like, she hated guns, even the sight of one petrified her and she had no idea how anyone could consider firing one, let alone shoot at someone. His job wasn't altogether safe though, he had come home several times with injuries. It stood to reason that moving equipment for the army was probably a lot more difficult and risky than working for a supermarket warehouse and the like. He was probably sent to some dangerous places where health and safety wasn't always as it should be.

His mum, Rosie, was a wonderful person and Sophie

couldn't believe her luck when Rosie volunteered to work two afternoons a week in the shop to give Sophie's mum a chance to go to the cash-and-carry and also take a half day off. In fact the two mums had become good friends. What more could you hope for?

Victoria soaked up every word of Sophie's stories of the man she was clearly besotted with. She felt a tiny bit envious, who wouldn't, but mostly she was enjoying that her new friend was happy and had found someone to love, someone who may well one day love her back. Something she, Victoria, for all the times she had been in another person's bed, or in the back of a car, or up against a wall in a dark alley, had never been able to find.

Gentle, caring, polite, modest, thoughtful, the list of Harry's attributes went on and Sophie realised she may be starting to sound like a thesaurus entry for 'Mister Wonderful'.

She couldn't help herself - Loves his mum, goes running across the common every morning at six, for forty five minutes, sun, rain or snow. Reads The Times every day – hooked on the puzzles pages, wicked sense of humour *and* laughs at my jokes, treats me like an adult, listens to what I say.

'Would you believe he can cook? Properly cook? He does these African dishes, I think he spent some time there. Mum and me sometimes go round to Rosie's for late Sunday lunch, we usually close the shop at four on a Sunday. If he's home he cooks these fab dishes, like restaurant food. My favourite's lamb jollof, you have to try it, you won't believe it,' she said, finally pausing for breath.

Sophie decided to share one of those wonderful, personal moments with Harry she so cherished.

He had come into the shop as usual at seven for his paper, on his way to an African themed cookery course he had finally managed to get on after trying to book for ages. As she reached to take his money an intense flash of lightning followed immediately by a deafening crack of thunder, froze her to the spot. She was petrified of thunder storms. Then another flash and crack, then another. Her eyes had flooded and her face contorted in fear. Her brain wouldn't work, she couldn't move, she couldn't breathe, she had imagined she was a split second from death, permanent darkness.

Harry had vaulted the counter in one light bound, putting himself between her and the window, wrapping his arms around her and pulling her whole body tightly against him. She would never forget his soft, confident words, words that tamed her fear. 'I'm with you. I won't leave you.'

In an effortless sweep he had picked her up and, cradling her close to him, had moved her away from the window. He hadn't tried to tell her, as others usually did, that it was just noise and flashes, intimating that her fear was illogical. He understood her fear, like only those who themselves had known real fear could understand. At every flash his arms, wrapped around her, engulfing her, pulled her closer. Holding her head to his chest he whispered confidently 'I'm with you, I won't leave you.' The storm had been fast moving and the crackling flashes and thunder retreated rapidly across the distant hills, the rain thrashing furiously against the window the only evidence.

They stood holding each other as she gathered herself.

'Harry,' she said quietly, her face still pressed to his chest, the feeling of closeness, trust and caring swamping her senses.

'Yes?' he whispered.

'I need to shower.'

'OK,' he had said, like it was an everyday event, 'I can watch the shop. Is the till unlocked?'

After her shower and despite her insistence that she was fine and he should go to his cooking course, he stayed with her all morning, the forecast had suggested the possibility of more lightning. When Sophie's mum finally managed to drag herself out of bed and her flu-induced semi-coma, completely unaware of the earlier foul weather, she thanked Harry. He shrugged it off with a simple, 'That's what friends do.'

Victoria's eyes started to mist. 'Oh Sophie, he *is* wonderful.' Then in mock irritation, 'Hurry up and marry him will you! So I can meet one of his friends at the wedding and fall hopelessly in love like you!'

'And toned, clean-cut, confident, calm - so damned sexy,' said Sophie, in mock anger. 'He's totally fit, I mean fit fit, not just fit, and a serious bum,' she said, nodding for emphasis.

Victoria nodded in return, she knew exactly what it all meant. She, like Sophie, was now convinced Harry Stone was indeed perfect.

Both Sophie and Victoria acknowledged the slight flaw in the current plan. Until Harry and Sophie were actually *together* and Sophie gained the status of at least army-girlfriend, which at this time she definitely was not, then the two of them were most definitely *not together*.

It was now even more complicated with her being based in Brighton for the next three years. If the university vacations didn't coincide with Harry's leave they weren't even going to be in the same county, let alone in each other's company. Not that he would accept anyway, but, she swept her hand in a wide semi-circle, how could she even consider inviting him to this.

On a slightly less positive note Sophie shared her observation that whilst he waited for her (admittedly he might not fully understand he was waiting) to get a bit older (nineteen should do it) he had passed the time in other relationships. It was disconcerting that most of these relationships involved women probably ten years older than him, so, at the moment, given that he was probably four years older than her, the age difference between Sophie and his partners of choice was at least fourteen years. One had been twice her age.

Victoria frowned in support of Sophie's concern.

'Still,' said Sophie with bravado, 'once we've kissed properly it will all be sorted out.'

'So… you haven't actually kissed him yet?' asked Victoria, trying to sound neutral.

Sophie didn't want to share the disastrous New Year event. She was trying hard to pretend it never actually happened.

'Well, only cheek kisses, for birthdays, Christmas and stuff,' said Sophie trying to hide her disappointment, 'but I know he wants to, I can see it by the way he looks at me. He's just shy.'

Victoria hadn't wanted to deflate her new, and in all honesty *only*, friend so didn't mention that in her own experience, with her public school classmates often from military families, she had met quite a few military uncles, brothers, boyfriends and friends-of-friends and shyness was a trait she had not spotted in any of them. In fact she had had to learn contact-avoidance skills very quickly.

Victoria looked at her watch, 'Ah, look at the time, it's late, damn, I'm going to have to walk home in the dark. I'd better get going, my turn to share tomorrow.'

'You're welcome to stay here tonight if you like. I've got another set of sheets.'

'Oh Sophie, thanks. That would be great. Pops should be back tomorrow and he'll sort me out. Then I'm going to insist on returning your hospitality.'

The following morning Sophie helped Victoria to double her cooking repertoire with grilled sardines on toast, whilst Sophie poured out, and Victoria soaked up, the health benefits of omega three oils. They discovered they both had a need for a 'decent cuppa' first thing in the morning if there was to be any hope of the day going well.

Victoria was relieved when her father answered the call on the third ring. 'Pops? Hi it's me, Victoria... Yes I'm fine. Listen, can you call me back on this number I'm borrowing a friend's phone... Yes, right now... I'm fine... No, I'm fine... Pops!... Pops, I'm OK!'

Seconds later the phone rang. Victoria explained her predicament, apologising to her father after every sentence for being a nuisance. 'You don't need to come all this way... You know I always love to see you, I just know you must be exhausted... I'll be sure to be back at the flat by then... No, I stayed with a friend last night... No! a girlfriend... No, really, a girl, you don't know her, Sophie... Love you too.'

'He got back late last night and he's setting off from home now. St Albans is about ninety minutes by train and then a twenty minute walk to my place so he should be here within a couple of hours. Why don't we clear up here and head off to mine?'

'You want me to come along? Don't you want time with your dad?'

'Please Sophie, do come. I've been stuck in that place for nearly three weeks on my own and I've really enjoyed these last hours. Besides, knowing Pops he'll talk for about twenty minutes and then fall asleep. He works hard all week and then spends most of the weekend unconscious. Oh, and I've got a real bath all to myself, you could have a good soak.'

Sophie wondered how much further they had to go. They had been walking briskly for a good twenty minutes and were nowhere near anything that looked like it could be student accommodation. This area was seriously up market, serious money. She imagined elegant people, in elegant clothes sitting on elegant furniture, behind the elegant curtains.

'Here we are,' said Victoria, slightly out of breath, as she turned into a short, tiled walkway leading to a large marble, steel and glass entrance. 'It's a good job I followed Pops advice to always carry my key separate to my bag.'

Sophie looked up at the five storey, obviously expensive and obviously not student budget accommodation. 'Come on Victoria, don't mess about, my feet are starting to ache and I need a loo.'

'No, this is it. Come on.' Victoria punched a code into the door keypad and it clicked open. 'There's a lift, but I always take the stairs, good exercise. Fifth floor.' She held the door for the sceptical Sophie.

Sophie only believed Victoria wasn't joking when she opened the apartment door and ushered her through. 'You live here?' She glanced around at what looked like something out of an American film involving oil tycoons.

'Yep, let me give you a tour.' Victoria mimicked an air hostess safety demonstration, 'This is obviously the kitchen, dining and lounge, up the corridor is my room on the right, the spare room on the left and a guest loo straight ahead.'

'Bloody hell. Fabulous.' Sophie didn't feel the need to disguise her amazement, or envy.

Sophie put her bag on the eight seater smoked glass dining table that separated the kitchen island from the sitting area and walked across the light teak woodblock floor to the centre of the lounge.

'I've never seen such huge sofas, they must be, what, six-seaters?'

'Four I think, but I suspect you could easily get six of us on one.'

Sophie looked at the four huge, floor to ceiling plate glass windows running the full length of the far wall. 'I've never seen such massive windows either. Do they open?'

'The middle two can slide sideways. I love having them open in the summer, it's a bit like living in the open. The place is air conditioned so in theory you shouldn't need to, but I just like to breathe the fresh air and smell the sea.'

Sophie slowly turned around in a full circle, taking in the design, the matt steel fittings, the tasteful abstract art in light pastels on the white walls, what she guessed were the window blinds that hung from the ceiling. Were those things light fittings? She couldn't see a bulb anywhere. Everything seemed stark yet sort of there, but not there. She nodded slowly.

'This is beautiful Victoria,' she whispered, 'really beautiful.' She moved towards one of the sofas, then checked herself and looked at Victoria, 'May I sit down?'

'Of course you can Sophie, you don't need to ask, make yourself at home.'

Sophie sank into the steel grey, padded soft leather, rested her head carefully on the back and ran her hand slowly over a turquoise velvet cushion.

'Lord,' she giggled, 'my feet don't even touch the floor. Beautiful.'

'Do you want to see the spare room?' asked Victoria eagerly.

'No thanks! I'm already green with envy. I don't suppose I'll ever be able to afford a place like this. Seeing more will just make it worse.'

Victoria perched herself sideways on the edge of the sofa beside Sophie and swallowed.

'Why don't you move in with me? Flat share. The other room's empty.'

'That's not fair,' Sophie admonished Victoria gently, 'don't tease. You know I can barely afford a scruffy, shared bedsit. I couldn't afford rent on something like this in a million years. I probably couldn't even afford the electricity.'

'There is no rent, or electricity or bills,' said Victoria earnestly, 'it belongs to my father and I'm living here until the end of the course. It wouldn't cost you anything.' She could see Sophie still wasn't buying into the suggestion. In the short time she had known Sophie it was obvious she would rather sleep on the street than not pay her way. 'I'm being selfish you know. It's so lonely here on my own and I really want company, but I just don't make friends easily with women. Perhaps it's my boarding school experience, I don't know, but I do know we'd be perfect flatmates. Please Sophie, at least think about it. We could have real fun together.' She stood up. 'I've got to shower and brush my teeth, they feel furry. Have a poke around, in the cupboards and draws and definitely the spare room.' She winked at Sophie.

After a short, but valiant resistance the inquisitive little girl in Sophie got the better of her and she ambled across to the kitchen. Maybe just a quick peek. She pulled open one door of the enormous, jet black, American style fridge-freezer. The fridge, apart from a mostly used litre of milk, was empty. She pulled open the freezer. An unopened bottle of vodka. The cupboards yielded little more: teabags, a tin of coffee and a bottle of ketchup. Utensils, pots and pans looked seriously expensive and unused and the ceramic induction hob pristine. A faint smear on the microwave suggested it might have warmed something at some time.

She ran her finger tips across the cool, charcoal-grey marble work tops then headed towards the guest toilet at the end of the short corridor, pointedly ignoring the door to the spare room. The yellow sticky note on it looked starkly out of place in the echoing, sparkling, precision emptiness. Sophie received more signals from her bladder and quickened her pace. The loo also appeared unused, spotless. She wondered if in fact anyone did actually live here or if Victoria camped in one room.

As she dried her hands on the crisply folded linen towel, looking at herself in the subtly lit mirror, it struck her – no dust, no dust anywhere. Someone must be cleaning. She tried to imagine Victoria with a feather duster.

Sophie stopped in front of the spare room, she might as well read the sticky. In thick black marker, in capitals:

PRIVATE! SOPHIE'S ROOM

She smiled. Well, why not take a look? It can't hurt. The heavy, silent door seemed to glide open of its own accord. As everywhere else, the room was spotless, minimal, everything in place. Sophie didn't think she had ever seen such a huge bed. She had certainly never been in a bedroom big enough to comfortably fit a massive bed *and* a two seater sofa and footstool. A full wall of floor to ceiling mirrors hid the wardrobes, with a single alcove in the middle for the dressing table. The little round things in the ceiling were probably lights.

She didn't move from the doorway, but looked slowly from corner to corner, ceiling to floor. This was far too grand a room for her, there's no way she could sleep in such a room. Certainly not. …Could she?

As Sophie sat at the dining table gazing out over the rooftops towards the sea Victoria padded barefoot from her room, towelling her wet hair.

'Coffee? Tea? I think we've got some milk, it should still be OK. No sugar I'm afraid, I ate it when I ran out of food.' Victoria giggled. 'I think it made me feel more sick than full. How desperate is that?'

'Coffee sounds good, black, no sugar please.' Sophie jumped at the buzz of the entry phone.

'Must be Pops, I bet he forgot the code.' Victoria ran across to the door and looked at the screen on the entry control. 'Yep, it's him. Hey Pops.' She released the downstairs door lock and frowned. 'I hope he's not too angry with me.'

Moments later Victoria was wrapped in her father's arms. Sophie couldn't help but intrude on their time, she knew she should look away, but couldn't. The father held the daughter close and still, resting her head to his chest. Then a gentle rocking from side to side, his eyes closed, his face relaxing, like a great pain had just been lifted from him.

Loneliness swept over Sophie as she wondered if her own father would have held her like this, loved her like this. She missed him.

Standing up straight, Victoria's father ran his fingers through his hair pushing the thick silvery locks back over his head, then held Victoria at arm's length. 'How are you? You're looking wonderful, as usual.'

'I'm fine Pops,' said Victoria quietly, 'missed you a bit.'

He turned to Sophie, noticing her for the first time. 'Oh, my apologies, I'm being rude. You must be Sophie. Hello, very pleased to meet you.' The warmth in his voice immediately calming.

'Hello Mr Bartholomew, pleased to meet you too,' Sophie smiled, enjoying the slightly formal, but warm handshake.

'It's Jason, please.' He rubbed his hands together. 'Now, I'm parched. Any chance of a hot drink?'

Sitting at the table and over steaming mugs of coffee Victoria apologised several times more for the loss of her bag and what she considered was her irresponsibility, sounding like a little girl trying to reduce the intensity of an expected serious reprimand. The earlier, confident and self-sufficient young lady was nowhere to be seen.

Her father, visibly pained, made it clear she should never apologise for being the victim of a crime and she should never hesitate to contact him if ever she needed help. The 'Nevers' were emphasised to make it a gentle instruction.

He twisted lightly on his chair and fumbled with his jacket hanging from the back. He slid a thick brown envelope across the table to Victoria. 'This should keep you going. And please… please Victoria,' his voice almost childlike, 'let me know if you need more. You don't have to prove yourself to anyone, least of all me.'

Victoria rested her hand on the envelope and pulled it a

few centimetres towards her, confirming acceptance. 'Thanks Pops,' she whispered.

The conversation soon turned to Sophie and she tried to downplay the sharing of her sardines, pasta and bed-sit with what had been a complete stranger.

Jason sat back on his chair. Resting his open arms Sphinx-like on the table he looked directly at Sophie, holding her in his stare for several seconds. 'A friend when in need,' he said evenly, 'is less common than we would like to think and a new friend very rare indeed.'

Sophie thought the expressions of thanks were a bit over the top considering the cost of sardines and pasta, but she had never actually met anyone of Jason's gravitas before so assumed some people were like this.

Over more steaming coffee they chatted and laughed. Although his questions suggested a genuine, warm interest Sophie noticed a subtle probing, as did Victoria. Sophie wondered if there was a hint of distance or an attempt to suggest a barrier whilst she, for some reason, shared more about her personal circumstances than she had told almost anyone.

'Hey Pops, I know what you're up to,' Victoria admonished, 'that's enough of your legal beagle stuff.'

'Oops. Was I? Sorry Sophie. It's very easy to become your job. I don't often get time to spend time with friends and sometimes I forget to switch off my interrogation mode. My apologies.'

His use of *friends* warmed Sophie and swept away her last remnants of discomfort.

She couldn't know that his considerable professional success was in no small part due to his ability to draw information from strangers whilst getting them to like and trust him.

Victoria cleared her throat, 'I'm trying to persuade Sophie to move into the spare room, we so enjoy each other's company. I've told her there's no rent and no bills and you'd be really pleased we're keeping an eye on your investment.' She looked directly at her father. 'Wouldn't you Pops?'

'Yes, absolutely,' he said with enthusiasm, 'it would provide me with some considerable comfort knowing it's going to be occupied for the next few years. It's a long term investment and you'll be saving me money in insurance and security services.' He looked at Victoria, her innocent smile comforting him.' It sounds like the two of you are well suited.'

He hoped he hadn't sounded too excited about the friendship. He knew how easy it was to open up to people who sucked you in then took delight in chewing you up and spitting you out. It had happened so many times to his darling Victoria that she had become a loner. Safer to have no one than to trust anyone. He was sure this had contributed to some of her disastrous boyfriend related decisions. There was a lot to be said for single-sex, private education, but it didn't suit everyone. As he sat there now, looking at his lovely, vulnerable daughter he regretted not over-riding her mother's insistence to send her to the 'Best schools' and wished instead he had sent her to the local comprehensive. Not all education came from books.

He knew Victoria's stepmother would not approve of what she would consider this common, poor new found friend and would work hard to sweep her aside. He, on the other hand, in the short time he had known Sophie, liked her. He had listened to the nuance of her answers, read her body language, her 'tells'. It was as much about what she didn't say as what she did. She had divulged more about herself than probably she realised.

Even though money had not been mentioned it was clear Sophie and her mother were in a dire financial situation and her on-going attendance at university was a major sacrifice, likely to be at best a struggle and probably impossible if they were to keep their small shop afloat. They were already living hand-to-mouth and the first semester of the first year had only just started. Yet it was clear that mother and daughter were determined and single-minded, they had purpose.

Sophie's predicament appeared almost hopeless with years of hard grind ahead of her and she knew it. He allowed himself an internal chuckle – a situation almost identical to his own at her age.

Yes, he liked Sophie. He had only known her a couple of hours, but he couldn't have hoped for a better friend for Victoria, to help her to connect to the real world.

He knew he shouldn't and Victoria would probably be furious if she found out, but his risk appetite when it came to his daughter was low, so first thing Monday he would get his best private detective to do a full background check on the family.

And what about Sophie's love interest? It sounded like a typical crazy teenage crush. She had known her man on and off for four years, five years her senior and a squaddie. From Jason's regular dealings with the military he understood how very different, and probably completely incompatible, their respective lives were. How could both girls think such a relationship was remotely viable? Apparently she had never even kissed him (Jason had pleaded to be excused further detail) and she didn't even know his regiment. He chuckled again – kids and crushes!

Something subliminal tugged Jason out of his happy father-daughter world and he thought about the gathering dark cloud in his professional life that threatened to cast a shadow over the ones he loved. Should he tell Victoria and Sophie about the risks now? Probably not yet, it could be something or nothing. No point in unnecessarily spoiling their happiness, no point in sharing the anxiety.

The police's stock response of 'not being able to take action because no crime had been committed' may tick their by-the-book, no-use-whatsoever boxes, but it made those under threat feel even more helpless, vulnerable, unprotected, alone. The sorts of crimes he was worried about had devastating, permanent impact for which there was no real redress. Subsequent punishment of perpetrators would provide no comfort at all, except perhaps to the police themselves and their career progressions, after their 'We caught these bad people and locked them up' television interviews. Having access to military people, people who understood and trained in the ways of violence, may be an insurance policy he should consider.

Just to be sure, he would get this squaddie checked out as well. If he was in logistics, whatever that was, he probably wouldn't know which end of a gun was dangerous, but he may be able to introduce him to those that had the permanent resolution skills he might need. What was his name? oh yes – Harry Stone.

Chapter 8

Spring

Rosie watched him from the damp morning shadows, a brute of a man, the source of her fears. Fears that prodded her awake in the small hours or stabbed her heart viciously without warning in the day. Grinding willpower locked away emotions, good and bad, as her steel cloak of no-nonsense dependability wrapped in disguise around her.

The grey indifference of the perfectly aligned, cold stone walls and the old, cold, heavy wrought iron brackets of the canopy competed with the refreshing hope of early morning rays of sunshine to colour her emotions of this moment. The moment for months she had both longed for and feared. She couldn't trust herself, she chose the safer, the grey.

He had called to let her know he was coming, he had never done that before. He had had an 'Accident, knocked about a bit', a cut to his face. She was used to, no, *conditioned* to, him appearing on the doorstep, after months of silence, with his warm, 'don't be cross' smile and what he called bumps and bruises. He had once turned up, after almost a year of nothing, with a leg in plaster and a gash to his arm that had been so slow to heal it had needed re-stitching. He hadn't called ahead then. There had been no smile that time, It had taken all of his energy to mask the pain. How bad was it this time, that he should prepare her?

He was here now, alive, in one piece, more or less. For the next few days, maybe weeks, he would be with her. She would keep him safe, out of harm's way. Perhaps she could persuade him to stay, or even not stay, just not disappear.

She knew Harry's automatic, meticulous planning would have put him in the carriage that stopped next to the bridge. He could be first up the steps, across to the eastbound platform, to 'Get on with stuff', queues frustrated him. Rosie squinted across the empty track and through the train window to get a first glimpse of his back as he disembarked from the other side. She guessed his was the first door opened and he would have been first up the steps. Yet the dozen or more other passengers, their hurrying feet clanging the rusty iron stair treads like muffled bells, had rushed past him by the time he started his hobble down from the top, the favour to his left leg poorly disguised.

Even the red coat that had disappeared up the steps a good thirty seconds after Harry was now several steps ahead of him. The girl, maybe nineteen or twenty, with her thick black eyeliner, charcoal lipstick and spiky hair dyed to almost match her tomato coloured raincoat was no doubt sending a message to the world. Was it indifference or aggression? Rosie couldn't tell and didn't care, but it was a statement, that was for sure. Red Coat seemed oblivious to the world as her head bobbed to the rhythm of an unheard tune and she skipped, almost danced, effortlessly downwards. Quite a feat thought Rosie, in those clumpy, heavily buckled black boots, made to look all the bigger by her black, skin-tight leggings. Rosie envied Red Coat's carefree, apparently uncomplicated world.

The girl jumped with both feet from the last step as if to hop-scotch along the platform, then stopped, her frown giving her pretty face a suggestion of aggression. She turned and looked up at Harry, who had so far managed three steps, then ran up to confront him. What was she saying? Why stand so close? Her hand, extended and then quickly withdrawn, suggested Harry had refused to release his bag. They were talking, or rather she was talking and Harry was listening, he wasn't smiling. Who was she? What did she want?

When the girl gripped the upper sleeve of his jacket and squared up to him Rosie held her breath. Should she intervene? No, even though she tried hard never to think about his work, she knew there were very few people in this world Harry needed physical protection from. Certainly not this young woman.

She watched the girl, still holding his right arm, move one step down, then wait for him to follow, then down another step and another. Rosie breathed out, Red Coat had insisted on helping him down, something Rosie would never have been allowed to do. Harry's emotional steel bubble, built as protection from his father, kept everyone at a safe distance. As far as Rosie could tell only she knew the secret doors and windows, but she seldom went through without invitation. Harry would need to be close to his last breath before he would willingly accept help from anyone. He would be irritated now, but polite enough to not show it.

As the pair left the last step Rosie walked into the warming morning sun and along the platform to join them. She caught the last part of the conversation, or was it a lecture?

'...and what if you'd fallen? What then? You'd have needed an ambulance and wasted everyone's time.'

To Rosie it was comical, this small slip of a spiky haired girl, little more than five feet tall, earnestly lecturing an intimidatingly powerful Harry, at least a foot taller and maybe four years her senior. He stood there in silence and confusion.

'Anyway,' she continued in an unseparated stream of words, 'as stubborn as you are you're down now, do you need help to get anywhere? I've got time, I'm Tabatha by the way and I'm available to join you for drinks or food or general chit-chat any evening over the next few weeks.' Her confident tone suggesting she was offering him an opportunity he would be silly to refuse.

As Harry turned to answer both Tabatha and Rosie saw the left side of his face for the first time.

'Shit,' Tabatha gasped, 'what the hell happened there?'

Rosie drew a sharp breath. She had prepared herself to not react, but Tabatha's antics had distracted her and seeing the wound had shocked the self-control from her.

Tabatha, now aware of Rosie, turned to her and then back to Harry. She opened her mouth to speak, but then turned back to Rosie again.

'Are you…' she used her index finger to draw an imaginary link between them, '… here for him?'

Rosie nodded as she watched Harry, searching his face for some indication of emotion.

'Hello Harry.'

'Hello mum.'

Dropping his bag he stood with arms open, a hint of a smile pulled lopsided by the long line of stitches protruding in regimented uniformity from his cheek. Rosie's steel cloak abandoned her. Wrapping her arms around him, she pulled him close and pressed her cheek against his solid chest. Her son, her child, here, safe in her arms. She allowed herself a few seconds to relish the contact, pushing every other thought away, her whole existence just this here and now. His warm arms holding her washed away every torture of fear, every worry of the last months.

He struggled with public displays of affection so Rosie eased herself away. 'Let's get you home,' she half whispered, 'I bet you're ready for a cuppa.' She turned with a warm smile to Tabatha, 'Thanks for watching him down the steps, you must have something special, he would never have let me do such a thing, that's for sure.'

Tabatha smiled and turned to face Rosie, ignoring Harry, 'He is a bit stubborn isn't he?' and then, in pretend confidence, 'he *is* gorgeous though.'

Rosie smiled, 'Stubborn's a good word, I can think of others.'

Tabatha hesitated, sensing Rosie, if not Harry, was comfortable with her presence. 'Is there anything I can help with?' She made no attempt to hide her hope of a positive answer.

The message was clear to Rosie, she was used to women showing interest in her son and had decided a long time ago to take a neutral stance, but there was something about this girl she liked, assertive, confident, yet warm. 'I think we'll be OK for the moment.' Tabatha's unguarded disappointment moved Rosie, 'Would you mind giving me your number, just in case?'

'What?' Harry was confused. He had accepted his place on the periphery of this exchange and now realised decisions possibly involving him were being made.

'Oh, yes, of course,' said Tabatha, more quickly than she wanted, 'I don't have a…' she fumbled in her pockets for a scrap of paper she already knew wasn't there, 'do you have…'

Rosie dipped into her shoulder bag and passed Tabatha a pen. 'And write on the back of this, it's my business card.'

'Rosie Stone,' Tabatha read from the card, 'Mrs Stone! I'm Tabatha Worthington, you looked after my little sister Chrissy when she started at the convent prep school and wasn't very happy being a boarder. We met once, before I was… quite as colourful.' She grinned as she wrote her name and number on the card and passed it back to Rosie. Then a frown, 'Oh, wait, no, damn!' She turned to Harry, 'You're Harry Stone.'

Harry nodded indifferently.

'You're Eggy's Harry! Damn!' Tabatha's face dropped.

'What?' Harry was confused again. He had only just met this young woman, yet here she was, assigning his ownership. The journey had taken its toll on his damaged and already exhausted body and he needed to sit down, with a brew. He wanted to get away from this girl before she decided anything else about his future, but he had to ask, 'Eggy who?' The question went unanswered.

'Not fair, not fair, not fair!' Tabatha muttered half to herself, not sure what to say next.

Rosie wondered if she had unwittingly provided competition for the unspoken, but obvious hopes of a good friend. No matter how improbable a relationship with Sophie was likely to be it was not for her, Rosie, to meddle. Her own relationship disaster was evidence enough of that. Many times she had tried to understand where she had got her marriage wrong, rewinding and replaying, like a poor quality recording, hating almost everything she saw. Apart from the end. The end was her Harry, standing in front of her now. The journey had been painful, but she knew she would do it all again for this moment, for this man.

Rosie moved the conversation on, to relieve the awkwardness. 'Oh yes, Chrissy, little sweetheart. Cried in my arms every evening for a week and then suddenly realised there was lots of fun to be had. The last time I saw her she was bouncing about all over the place, taking great delight in causing havoc,' Rosie smiled. 'I haven't worked at the convent for probably two years now. How is she?'

'Still bouncing… and driving every one crazy,' Tabatha shook her head in mock resignation. 'I'd best get on or I'll be late for work,' she lied. 'Please do call me if I can help.' Her eye contact with Rosie confirmed her sincerity. Tabatha turned to Harry, pulled his shoulders gently towards her to kiss his right cheek, then twisted to kiss the corner of his mouth. She let it linger long enough to be sure he knew it wasn't a mistake and there could be more where that came from.

She stepped back and stared at him with wide-eyed assertiveness, to make absolutely sure he'd got the message, then moved slightly to the right to look at the wound on his left cheek. 'Ouch,' she whispered then turned again to Rosie, 'see ya,' she sang and strode towards the platform exit.

Harry eased himself down to pick up the grey, battered canvass holdall.

'Let me take that.' Rosie held out her hand.

'I'm OK, I can manage.'

'It wasn't a request.'

'OK, OK, I give up, here it is.' Rosie's deliberate words and still outstretched arm left him in no doubt about who was going to carry it, no doubt about who, as always, was in charge in Honeyborne.

For once Harry was glad of the services of a taxi. He usually relished the relaxing walk home from the station, but today it would have been a long, painful exercise.

'Mr Roberts, could you drop me in front of the shop and then take Harry on please?' asked Rosie. She turned to Harry, 'I've asked them to save me some of those bread rolls you like, they should be in by now. Here's the spare keys and here's some money to settle with Mr Roberts. I shouldn't be more than ten minutes. I've shut Baggy in the lounge, be careful how you open the door, she gets quite aggressive if strangers come to the house, she may not remember you.'

'Yes mum,' said Harry, wondering what bread rolls she could be talking about and knowing any attempt to refuse the money would have led to a confrontation he would lose.

'Mr Roberts,' she popped her head back inside the car, 'please make sure he takes his bag from the boot.'

'Will do, Mrs Stone.'

As they parked outside of the three-bed semi Harry felt a sense of security he hadn't dared let himself think about for a long time. Here he was, on the edge of sleepy Honeyborne, a town with seven pubs, four restaurants and a steep narrow high street, breathing cool, clean air that smelt of cool green grass, trees, shrubs. No smell of aviation exhaust, no smell of laterite, that red earth that seemed to cover most of Africa, no smell of sweat, no smell of fear. No smell of death.

He eased himself upright beside the car. As determined as he was not to, as ridiculous as he knew it was, he couldn't stop himself doing a three-sixty degree scan. Isolation, or the fear of it, quickened his pulse. He was on his own, no team, no one watching his back, no one to keep safe or keep him safe. He was a long way away from the ready-bases, the snatch points, the free-kill zones, the lands of violence and no mercy that had been his existence for as long as he dared to think back. He was far away from them now, but they were still inside him, pumping adrenalin at every unfamiliar sound, every move. The bile of violence hit his throat, if he had eaten this morning he would have vomited now. This was wrong, he shouldn't be here, contaminating this calm, peaceful place.

'Take your time Harry, no rush son, it's good to see you back,' Mr Roberts spoke softly, 'looks like you've had a tough one.' He had carried Harry's bag to the front door and was watching, recognising the internal struggle, but knowing an offer of help would be rejected.

'Thanks Mr Roberts, how much do I owe you?'

'You know I'm not going to take money from you.'

'And you know that if I don't pay you I won't be able to ask you if I need you again.'

'OK, you win,' Mr Roberts shook his head and smiled warmly, 'let's compromise and call it a fiver and if you give me a penny more I'll poke it all through your letter box when you're not looking and deny it was me.' He looked at the wound on Harry's face. 'Hard contact?' he asked, his voice low.

'Car accident,' Harry tried to sound indifferent, but was struggling to lie to his old-soldier friend.

'I was in twenty two years matey, man and boy,' he reminded

Harry, 'I know the work of a blade when I see it.'

Harry shut the front door quietly behind him and closed his eyes as he tried to deal with the pain in his left leg. Tackling the foot bridge and then climbing in and out of the car had strained the repairs. Perhaps he should have stayed in hospital a few days longer as they had advised, but the last action had been brutal even by his experience and he wanted to be as far away as he could be from anything to do with it, even the hospital staff that had done their usual fantastic job of fixing him up. He wanted to forget it, all of it. He wanted to be home, away from the insanity. Thank goodness for Doctor M's psycho-babble-research friend who had persuaded the hospital 'Henrys' to discharge him. They had got it wrong of course. He had sneaked a peek at his file in one of the rare times he had been left unattended. Something about deep-rooted, chronic psychological trauma. Blah blah bollocks, total bollocks.

He had managed not to disturb Baggy and now stood in the small, bright hallway soaking up the normality. The crisp paint, the spotless carpet, the faint smell of something scented and he felt pleased with himself for resisting the urge to do a full room to room sweep. 'It's Honeyborne Harry, no hostiles here,' he told himself out loud.

A sudden vicious barking from the lounge, followed by a heavy, door-shaking thud, announced the presence of an angry dog. Scratching of claws on paint became frantic. 'Take it easy Bags, take it easy, it's only me.' The barking was immediately louder and more angry, the way she was throwing herself at the door worried him she would hurt herself. He cracked the door open a few centimetres and a snout of snarling, snapping teeth shot through the gap, trying to force the door open. She could see him now, but hadn't recognised him, not surprising after so many months. Maybe if he knelt down so they were face to face... Not a good idea. As he crouched agony shot through his left leg. It collapsed under him and he tumbled headlong through the door, onto the lounge floor.

The dog, startled, leapt backwards into the centre of the room. Harry's training took over and he automatically ran through the many ways he had been trained to deal with attack dogs. Unfortunately most of them involved him standing up and all of them involved the dog ending up dead, not really options he could consider here.

'Take it easy Bags, take it easy girl,' he cooed softly.

Baggy appeared in no mood to compromise. She lowered her shoulders to a crouch and pulled her lips back to expose her pink gums and full set of gleaming, white, formidable teeth. The growl came from deep inside her. Harry waved his arm just in front of him. If he could get her to go for his arm maybe he could grab her head at the last moment.

She sprang. Harry went into autopilot: assessment, options, action, assessment, options, action, in an endless subconscious loop. In the first loop, in just a split second, he knew he had a problem, he didn't have any options to deal with thirty kilos of really pissed off, but much loved family pet coming at him horizontally, teeth first. His hands clamped her head, but she was too strong for his already weakened body. Her claws frantically scrabbled the carpet as she tried to launch herself onto him, she wanted his face!

He shoved her head to one side and managed to get a hand on her snout just before she could sink her teeth into his nose. In a frenzied rage the dog snapped furiously, trying to grab at his hand, her paws scrabbling again for grip, forcing her writhing weight onto him. Then she stopped. A sniff, a pause, two more sniffs, then a whimper and a soft pink tongue shot out to lick his fingers. Then she was gone. Harry watched her scampering crazily in circles around the lounge, yelping with excitement. He eased himself up to kneel, ready for what would certainly come next. He didn't want to stand and have a fully grown black labrador flying at him and knocking him off his feet. Instead she knocked him off his knees.

After giving him a thorough face lick, involving what seemed to Harry like half a litre of drool, she had calmed down enough for him to push her gently off and climb into an easy chair. She had been eight weeks old when Harry had collected her and carried her home. Sitting on his lap and zipped inside his leather jacket for the four hour train journey, popping her head out occasionally so her tiny soft tongue could taste his chin, she'd had plenty of time to register his smell.

Now she was desperately trying to scramble up on his lap so Harry leaned forward to close the gap. Having this heavy, excited lump sat on him was not a good idea right now. She pushed her head into his chest and he hugged her and rubbed her back vigorously. 'Bloody hell Bags, what were you in a previous life, a lion?' he laughed. 'Good girl, yes, good girl, good girl.'

At the sound of a key in the front door Baggy gave a low growl and moved to the middle of the room, still, staring towards the source of the sound. Another low growl.

'Only me,' Rosie called out before opening the door.

Baggy relaxed, gave a soft welcoming bark and padded off to the hall, tail wagging.

'Hello you,' said Rosie looking down at her, then turning to Harry. 'Any trouble with the dog?'

'Not really.'

Rosie dropped into the chair opposite Harry, 'I'm exhausted, I've been up since five. I've got an article deadline for today, but I've finished and its sent.'

'Hey you, hop it,' she said to Baggy who was busy snuffling in the bag of shopping beside the chair. 'No Baggy!'

The dog, sensing the pleading eyes and tilted head approach were not going to get her anywhere, decide the best place for its nose, other than the shopping bag, was Harry so she shoved it in to the side of his leg and waited for attention.

'That's a deep tan you've got there, you must be feeling the cold even though it's nearly summer.' Rosie didn't expect him to tell her where he had been these last months, but she gave him an opener, just in case.

'I love this cool spring freshness,' he replied, shutting down the thread of conversation gently.

She so wanted to hold him close, to kiss his wounds better, to enjoy some physical manifestation of that unbreakable mother-son bond between them. No matter he was twenty five years old and probably nearly twice her weight, he was still her baby, her only baby.

'It's really good to have you back Harry,' said Rosie quietly. This time a comfortable silence as they both enjoyed a rare peaceful togetherness. 'Any idea how long you've got?' Again, she didn't expect any meaningful answer, but threw it out there as he knew she would.

'Well,' the undamaged side of his face smiled as best it could knowing he was about to make her happy, 'at least six weeks medical leave. I'll have to go for weekly assessments, but that should be half-day trips.' Before she could speak he added, 'And I've got several weeks leave owing after that, so probably most of the summer.'

'Seriously?' she frowned. 'Teasing's not nice Harry,' she scolded.

'Seriously, no teasing,' he assured her.

His smile, even if it was only on one side, melted her, as it always did. 'Here? In Honeyborne?'

'If you don't mind.'

'Oh, wonderful, no, fantastic,' she didn't try to control her happiness and now wanted to hug him even more. 'I made up the bed in your flat and put some stuff in the fridge yesterday.' She would have loved him to stay with her, but she knew he needed his own space and he would no doubt have female visitors. Anyway, it was just a five minute walk.

'Where will you go for your medical checks? Back to base? All the way to Plymouth?'

'HMS Heron - RNAS Yeovilton.'

'Yeovilton? What's at Yeovilton apart from the Museum and the air station?'

'A doctor apparently. I didn't ask. I must admit it sounded too good to be true when I got the order.'

'That's only twenty minutes away, I could drive you.' She gave up on self-control all together and allowed herself to gabble on, 'Oh, of course - it's Navy. Are your lot there? Could you be based there? Do they have desk jobs? Why don't you ask? Desk jobs can be challenging, you might really enjoy it.' She tried hard not to sound like she was pleading.

Harry saw where she wanted to take this and couldn't let her. 'I know there's a doctor there that expects to see me once a week,' he said simply. He couldn't tell her what he knew about Yeovilton, or what went out of there on a regular basis, or that he had been there five times in the last eight months. She would worry if she knew the reality. He also didn't tell her about the psychological assessment he guessed was coming after reading his hospital notes.

Chapter 9

'No Harry,' said Rosie firmly, 'I will not fetch your newspaper. You've been home how many days now and hardly been out of that door? The exercise will do you good.'

Ilona had already offered to have his paper delivered, but Rosie had declined, confiding in Ilona her fear for Harry's health, or rather his withdrawal into an almost silent, apparently joyless world. They agreed that if he wanted a paper he should collect it himself. They both laughed when Rosie suggested that even if she couldn't get him out of the house his need for a crossword would.

His injuries were still painful, especially in this unusually cold mid-spring, but Harry had, sometimes foolishly, never allowed pain to restrict him. Rosie knew his physical ailments would heal, the military would see to that. She was worried about the darkness that over the last three or so years seemed to be gradually draining the colour from him, stealing his sparkle. At first she had been able to convince herself it was a simple result of the physical stress and punishment his body seemed to get every time he went away. Over the last two home leaves and now this one she could see something was wrong. He was still the polite, caring, articulate Harry, always attentive to her and fussing over her, but he was different, as if he was existing, but not caring if he was alive or dead. Existing in emptiness, floating, unattached. Rosie was frightened for him.

Had it been a broken heart problem, a reaction to a romantic rejection? That had become increasingly difficult to believe when she considered the unacknowledged, but unconcealed relationships he enjoyed every time he came home on leave. Thank goodness he had his own flat.

There had never been a shortage of intelligent, articulate

good looking women eager for his attentions. She had been uncomfortable with Harry's 'live for today' relationship expectations and was pretty sure that his choosing of women a lot older than him helped him avoid emotional entanglement, at least from his side. Even now Rosie felt sorry for one of the recent ones, Lucy, the shoe-shop lady, who had been ready to commit everything to him.

Perhaps that was it. Perhaps he needed a relationship with someone nearer his age, maybe younger. Someone who would have the audacity to demand love from him, who would challenge his idea that relationships were best kept purely physical. Soldier or not, adult or not, she was still his mother and sometimes mothers knew best. Even though she had promised herself not to get involved with his relationships, she was going to make Soldier-Harry at least acknowledge the *existence* of Person-Harry.

Rosie ran through candidates that immediately sprang to mind. She could think of three and knew more would follow as her subconscious processed the challenge.

Nina, Tabatha, Sophie. Yes, Rosie liked all of them, a good start.

Nina had already made her intentions, not just her interest, quite clear after she had fixed Harry's broken filling a few days ago. After the professional niceties of sorting out the bill, making the next appointment and shaking hands goodbye Nina had opened the surgery door to let them out. At the door she whispered something in Harry's ear and then, in no uncertain terms, made it clear she expected them to meet socially before the end of the month and if he hadn't made arrangements within the next two weeks she would. True to her word and without waiting for the deadline, she had called yesterday and now Harry was meeting her in the Harlequin next Friday, then going back to her flat for an Indian supper. Rosie would refuse Harry's inevitable request to call Nina next week to apologise and say he wasn't well and couldn't come.

OK, Nina had had some personal challenges recently and her professional standing had suffered. Small minded gossips had cost her a good chunk of her patients, to the extent she had had to move from Yeovil to a practice in Honeyborne and only held surgery four days a week now. Rosie thought the whole thing a storm in a teacup and nothing to do with her, quietly enjoying the looks and frowns she got when she stopped to laugh and chat with Nina in the street. She liked Nina's refreshing, straightforward honesty although Rosie couldn't see how a relationship with Harry could possibly work. She smiled as she thought of Nina's own description of herself: 'A skinny, Asian, dentist, lesbian who doesn't know nearly enough about security cameras'.

Tabatha. Rosie could vaguely remember her from when she worked in the convent and could recall that her parents were hard working local business people, usually appearing on the edge of exhaustion, never flaunting their considerable success.

Rosie thought back to Tabatha challenging Harry on the station steps and taking control. There was no doubt Tabatha was very interested in her son. Tomato-red hair and crazy clothes – maybe a good counter balance to Harry's iron discipline, perfectly folded shirts and structured life. Rosie had Tabatha's telephone number carefully filed.

Then of course there was Sophie. Warm, young, shy, beautiful Sophie. Ilona's only child and Rosie's sometimes companion behind the corner shop counter during school holidays. Sophie didn't know how to hide her feelings for Harry, regularly asking, in what she no doubt thought was a roundabout way, how he was, what he was up to, when he was home next and always with the most attention, who his latest romantic attachment was. Sophie had had a crush on Harry ever since she first set eyes on him, probably three years ago.

Sophie was without a doubt Rosie's favourite, but she was a good five years younger than Harry and painfully shy. Although a far more confident and fashion conscious Sophie had come home for Christmas after her first semester at Brighton University, the transformation had been remarkable.

Ilona was expecting Sophie home today, for Easter, so it was likely she would be in the shop first thing tomorrow to organise the newspapers. Rosie was quite sure that was *not* the reason she wanted Harry to get his own paper from now on.

If only she had a magic wand she could wave to bring together those two young people she loved.

******

'Hey Baggy, come on, we're not going home just yet,' Harry called after the dog as she trotted towards the house, thoroughly contented after a long, early morning gambol across the common. 'We've got to collect the newspaper. Perhaps I could train you to fetch it. What do you think girl?'

In his haste to start getting back to fitness Harry knew he had pushed himself too far, his left leg was aching and beginning to stiffen. The cold morning air had tightened the scar tissue where the stitches had been on his cheek, making it difficult to talk. They should have been taken out a lot earlier.

Sophie tried to shake the sleep from her head, it had been a long time since she had been up at six in the morning. It felt good to be kneeling down, stuffing the supplements into the Saturday papers. She had been desperate to get home since her mum had told her two weeks ago that Harry was back. She had managed to stop counting days after Harry had disappeared in late September, counting months was far more mature, if no less painful, and it was something she would have to come to terms with if she was going to be an army wife. Or girlfriend. Or… no, shut up.

As much as she loved being at home with her mum and taking over running the shop, the last holiday, Christmas, had been an ache from start to finish. Despite spending ridiculous amounts of time willing it, Harry hadn't appeared on Christmas day, or New Year's day, or any other day and the return to university had been a welcomed release of sorts.

If he came into the shop today she was going to play it cool, like Victoria had suggested, smoulder, then slow-burn, indifferently available.

She was so focused on getting the papers sorted so she could straighten her hair and clothes and put on some lipstick in case Harry came in she didn't look up when the doorbell tinkled an arrival.

'Excuse me, could you pass me The Times please? I'm having trouble with my leg.'

Sophie tensed, slurred speech at this time of day probably meant alcohol, but she couldn't remember any of their regulars having a drink problem. A stranger. She couldn't smell it either. Vodka?

'Certainly sir, just give me one second.' She grabbed the paper quickly and stood up, she didn't want to be kneeling down with a drunk on the loose.

'Here we… Harry?'

'Sophie? I didn't recog mmpf…' speech, even slurred speech, became impossible now Sophie was holding his face and kissing him hard, full on the lips. Was that a tongue?

'Oops, sorry Harry,' she apologised wrapping her arms

around him and hugging, 'it's been such a long time, I've missed you.' Much considered plans for breasts pressing against chests evaporated. She just wanted to hold him, be close to him, smell his smell. 'I've missed you.' Damn! Shut up! What happened to smoulder?

'I didn't recognise you. You've... grown. Grown up. What's with the hair?'

Harry reprimanded himself. Severely. The walk across the common with the dog had relaxed him. He had allowed himself to enjoy the sights, sounds and smells of the spring English countryside and pretend for a short while that the senses from his recent life didn't exist. He found he could allow the sound of the dog snuffling in the grass to become his focus, then the inviting twitter of a small songbird, probably watching him from the security of the thorn hedge. He even managed to ignore the rattle of small arms fire his imagination had regularly conjured up over the last days.

He hadn't felt this relaxed in a long time, his pain was manageable, even without those brain-cosh painkillers and now, walking into the shop, he had allowed himself to enjoy the sight of a perfect bottom that really didn't need any help from the skin tight jeans that presented it. He guessed it was very un-PC to think that this woman's crazy coloured hair was intended to send out the signals he was actually receiving. He was amazed at how, in just a few short steps across the shop, his head had conjured up such a complete picture, in considerable detail, of how he would like to enjoy the rest of the morning with her. He hadn't felt like this since his last New year at home.

And it was Sophie!

He was ashamed.

Good, clean, honest, caring, fun, good friend Sophie. He couldn't identify when it had started, but she had gradually become his representation of all things decent, of all good people, wholesome. In part she was his justification for doing the things he did, taking the risks he took, his contribution, as his unit joked, to ensuring that there would be something on the earth worth inheriting, if the meek ever got around to inheriting it.

Now here she was, greeting him as a good friend with her arms inside his fleece, hugging him tightly and all he could think about were those wonderful breasts pressing against him and wishing away the two thin tee-shirts separating their bodies.

He was glad he had overheated from the walk and unzipped his fleece before entering the shop.

No he wasn't!

'It's a wig! Do you like it?' said Sophie triumphantly. 'Multi-coloured, cropped – all the rage in Brighton right now.'

She pushed herself away slightly so she could gaze up at him and he could see the thick, black, Egyptian style eyeliner he had once let slip he found attractive, during a very, very, long, very, very detailed discussion about the possible true purpose of the pyramids.

She searched for any sign of appreciation of the ten minutes she had spent on her eye makeup this morning. Nothing. She had come to terms with the fact that Harry had never seemed to understand she had a body from the neck downwards and she knew it hadn't registered that she wasn't wearing a bra.

Then Sophie noticed the wound on his cheek and, sucking air through her teeth, pushed back so she could see it more clearly.

'Oh Harry, I'm so sorry, that looks painful. It must hurt. What happened?' she said.

'It looks far worse than it feels. Now the stitches are out all I'll probably notice is the disapproving stares.'

'Well,' she said, smiling and running her fingertips gently across his cheek, just below the long, raised bump, 'I'm pretty confident that such a mark is only going to increase your already considerable score on the gorgeous-ometer!'

'Speaking of which,' she said, stepping right back and doing a slow three-sixty degree twirl to make absolutely sure even *he* couldn't miss the crop top and bare midriff, then shaking her head allowing her hair its own twirl, 'on a scale of one to ten with ten being total – how do I rate on the slut-ometer?'

'Err, two?' he said, with some confusion.

'Damn. Needs more work. I was aiming for at least a seven,' she said with mock disappointment.

'Good morning Harry,' said Sophie's mum, stepping out from the back doorway of the shop where she had been standing out of sight, listening to the conversation, 'would you like a cuppa? You can have Sophie's, she just going to pop upstairs to put some warmer clothes on, so she doesn't catch cold.'

'No, I'm…' Sophie recognised the very clear message in her mother's unwavering stare. 'Yes, good idea,' she said meekly, 'I'll be two minutes Harry. Don't go away!'

'Good morning Mrs P,' Harry returned cheerily.

He was grateful when Baggy, fed up with being tied up outside and with no obvious opportunity to eat or be fussed over, barked her irritation.

'Better go,' he said, waving his coins in the air before placing them on the counter, 'or she'll be grumpy all day.'

Mrs Pansay, a good friend, had made Harry feel doubly guilty. It was small consolation she couldn't actually see what his imagination was suggesting for another good friend, her daughter. He needed to get control of this. He thought forward to next Friday, perhaps Nina would help him put Sophie back on her much-deserved pedestal, although if he understood Nina's personal propensities, he must surely have misunderstood her whispered invitation to discuss fillings.

Shit! His head was more screwed than he realised.

******

Harry fought hard over the next days to put service out of his mind and focus on the here and now. It wasn't easy, his sense of duty to his unit often consumed him, as did the guilt of not being available and active. Somewhere in the back of his mind there was a hint of a question of who missed who and who was dependant on who the most. But it was too difficult to think about right now.

On his regular, but pointless walks through the town to keep himself occupied he often wondered if those people he passed in the street realised how empty their lives were without the brotherhood of a unit and the regular fire-hose drenching of adrenalin. How did they live without fear? Fear was the only emotion that confirmed you were alive and mortal fear confirmed it absolutely.

Harry moved his attention from the dog sniffing in the hedgerow and looked out across the common. In the early light the frost sparkling trees and silvery grass suggested it should be Christmas rather than coming up to Easter. He breathed in slowly, enjoying the chill on his nose and lungs from the fresh, clean, untainted air. He wondered what Sophie, just a few hundred metres east of here, was doing right now. He imagined her pulling on cold clothes over her warm, soft, sweet smelling body and trying to muster an interest in getting the newspapers ready in time for the shop to open. She would be good company now, that warm soft voice could thaw the chill in the hardest heart. He relaxed the grip on his thoughts the better to allow her in, but she wasn't there and too late he saw the grey coming for him.

'Let me just check,' he said aloud, taking the M73 compass from his jacket pocket. Shit! No, stop. Too late, the grey combat cloud swept over him again. Range, bearing, elevation, how many minutes in full assault kit to run there, how many minutes and men to set up a defence perimeter. Shit. 'For fuck–sake Harry you twat. Stop. Here, now, focus.' Baggy looked up at him, then, realising no food was involved, ignored him and continued her search.

Harry knew the only way out of this darkness was to dive in head first and fight his way back to the surface. He let his mind wander back in time. The debrief of the last operation had been painful. Like him, barely capable of talking, two others had given their account from their critical-care beds. Two more, close friends, would never give an account of anything ever again. Powerless to help, he had witnessed the brutality of their last seconds and now fought hard not to re-see them and not to throw up. The operation had achieved its objective, they had extracted what had to be extracted and delivered what had to be delivered. The politicians had labelled it a complete success. *Yes, there were losses,* but apparently *A price worth paying*. Easy enough to say, he thought, as long as your friends weren't the actual currency of the exchange.

Harry hauled himself out of the grey, back to the present. 'Come on Bags, a brisk one down to the end of the field, up into the next one and exit through the gate above the houses.' Baggy looked up at him and then ignored him and continued her search.

He didn't question how he knew it would take seventeen minutes to finish the walk, drop the dog off at the house and be in the shop picking up his paper. Best not to.

******

'Perfect timing Harry,' said Sophie's mother, as she set three mugs of hot coffee on the counter, 'you must have some sort of inbuilt radar.'

'How's your leg Harry?' asked Sophie, as she put his newspaper down beside his coffee, 'do you need to sit down?'

'No, I'm fine thanks,' he lied, not admitting to himself that he would rather stand and be close to her than sit and be further away.

'Now, let's see,' said Sophie, opening the newspaper to the crossword page. 'What was yesterday's five down? "Bailey"? Never heard of it. Did you get that? Of course you did, it's part of your business,' she answered for him.

When Harry finally left the shop, long after his coffee was finished and the offer of a second declined, he was more at ease than he had been since leaving hospital. The stocking of shelves had been therapeutic, even if Sophie had playfully mocked him for spending so much time perfectly aligning the square bottles of brown sauce. The women's quiet, calm efficiency in the daily preparation of the shop relaxed him, as did Sophie's non-stop chatter about everything from how her salmon-pink cotton blouse wasn't sitting properly on her shoulders to her speculation of software patch levels *really* necessary for their till operating system. He knew that Mrs P's occasional interjections were more of a token politeness, because she was enjoying her daughter's voice as much as he was.

He wasn't sure how he had been volunteered to go with Sophie to the cash and carry in the afternoon and then take her to the Harlequin in the evening to 'receive' a thank you drink, but he didn't care. The darkness of the early morning was gone and right now he could feel the warmth of a sun shining on him, even if it was actually drizzling.

******

Sophie fought the temptation to look over her shoulder at Harry, she didn't want him to think her over eager or needy. The barman was taking an age to produce a slice of lemon for the sparkling water. Never mind, Harry was hers for the evening. She had seated him at a small table just big enough for two, there would be no distractions for him, just the two of them, eye to eye. If she sat close enough to the table they would be knee to knee as well. She checked her blouse buttons in the mirror behind the bar, not too many undone. Tonight, after much deliberation, she had decided to be tasty, not tarty.

She picked up the two drinks and composed herself, she needed to be dead centre between eager and bored.

She took a deep breath to calm her excitement. Now, head up, turn and smile.

What? No! Who the heck is that woman sitting with Harry? How?

It looks like... it is! Tabby – Tabatha Worthington and even from this distance Sophie could see she was definitely doing tarty this evening. Sophie had willingly agreed Tabatha deserved her school nickname of *Dee Dee*, she was a walking, talking man-magnet and now here she was, almost knee to knee with Harry, filling his vision, in the exact place Sophie had carefully constructed for herself. From this angle Sophie couldn't see where Harry's eyes were, but she guessed they would be flitting leisurely between Tabatha's enviable cleavage and her bare bellybutton.

'Hi Tabby,' Sophie beamed as she sat on the chair Harry had pulled to the table as she approached, 'this is a surprise.' *Twit Harry!* She thought, you've just invited her to join us.

'Harry, this is Tabby, a sixth form class mate, we haven't seen each other in... nearly a year. Tabby, this is...'

'Harry, I know,' said Tabatha, cutting across Sophie and smiling at Harry. 'We met at the station a few weeks ago and I'm telling him off for not calling me. And don't even try to tell me you lost my number.' Tabatha's sultry pout was perfect, as was her messaging.

'It's really good to see you Sophie, I've missed you, I've missed everybody. I'm enjoying university, but I don't have any close girlfriends there.'

Tabatha turned to face Sophie and tilted her head towards Harry. 'Have you snapped him up? Is he yours? Are you an *item*?' She winked at Sophie.

'Well…' Sophie paused, trying desperately to compose a lie in real time.

'We're just good friends,' said Harry honestly, as Sophie knew he damned well would, 'really good friends. We've known each other for quite a time.' Only Sophie saw the slight nod that signalled Tabatha's intent.

'I've got some friends from uni with me for Easter,' Tabatha tilted her head towards three more gorgeous and temptingly dressed young women sitting at a table across the room, 'and I wondered Sophie, if you're not busy Friday, if you'd like to stay over. I popped into the shop this afternoon and your mum said you'd be in here this evening.'

Mum! Screamed Sophie in her head. Another one who's direct honesty was causing Sophie problems.

As much as she really did like Tabby Sophie wanted as much distance between them as possible until Harry had accepted his destiny to be with her.

'Oh no,' Sophie whined in pretend disappointment, 'I can't, I've promised to babysit for one of mum's friends.' Sophie congratulated herself, she could re-use this story to get Harry to keep her company that evening, the babysitting would be cancelled at the last minute.

Was that the faintest game-on smile from Tabby? Too late Sophie recognised the trap she had walked straight into.

'How about you Harry? There will be some blokes there as

well. We're having a pool table challenge evening. I bet you're a pool expert.' Tabatha, stared, wide eyed, directly at him, her voice oozing an intimacy like they were lying naked in bed together.

Sophie's heart sank, she had been outsmarted by an expert. Harry would at least be honest and say if he didn't want to go, but what if he did fancy a pool tournament, or even worse, a different type of tournament with Tabby or one of her friends that were eyeing him like a late lunch across the room?

'I'm sorry Tabby, I can't, I'm having dinner with a friend on Friday,' he said.

Sophie turned her head slowly to look at Harry, trying not to frown. He was serious, he wouldn't think to be dishonest. Which friend? He didn't have any other friends in Honeyborne, at least not the type he would have dinner with and he would have told her if he had army buddies coming. Surely he hadn't found himself another casual bed-friend, those older women that enjoyed men, but couldn't be bothered with the effort of a relationship. Already? He had only been home a few weeks and for most of that time he could hardly walk let alone *entertain*. Rosie had said yesterday that he was feeling a lot better and was thinking about moving into his flat. Is that why he had been so cheerful all day today? Had he found himself someone to satisfy a physical need with? Why not her? She had made her willingness clear often enough hadn't she? Bitch! Whoever it was.

'Oh well,' sighed Tabatha, picking her glass of wine from the table, 'next time then. I'll give you a call Harry.'

Get your eyes of her arse Harry! thought Sophie as she watched him watch her return to her friends.

'That was quick thinking,' said Sophie under her breath. 'Dinner? It's not like you to tell a fib.'

'What fib? I am having dinner with a friend on Friday evening.'

'Oh, OK,' said Sophie, confused, alarmed. 'Anyone I know?'

'Nina. Dentist Nina. We're meeting here for a drink and then back to hers for what I'm hoping will be some seriously good, home cooked Indian food. I'm going to skip lunch so I can do it justice.'

Sophie frowned again. 'Isn't she…? You know… '

'So gossip has it, yes, but from my limited knowledge of the subject being gay doesn't affect your ability to cook,' he paused in thought. 'Can't think why it would.'

Sophie relaxed. She didn't know much about Nina, apparently no one in the town did, she kept herself to herself outside of the dental surgery, but she definitely wasn't a threat.

Sophie had nearly cancelled her first check-up when she heard the gossip and had been mightily relieved (and perhaps a little disappointed) when Nina hadn't tried to French-kiss her in the treatment chair. At the end of the appointment Nina's knowing wink, as if to say 'See, no snogging', had made Sophie want to apologise for listening to the nonsense tittle tattle.

Sophie found herself envying, enjoying, the woman's beauty, her serenity. Those Asian eyes, those deep, dark, gorgeous pools of invitation could probably disable almost any person on the planet and for a moment Sophie had allowed herself to wonder what it would be like to stare into them as she was being kissed.

Wow! Stop! Back in the room. Nina was definitely not competition and whilst Harry was with her he was as good as under lock and key. Yep, she liked Nina.

'Well, if there's any leftovers make sure you bring me a takeaway, I love Indian, especially those vegetarian potato dishes and the spicy… You exchanged telephone numbers?

You exchanged numbers with Tabatha? How did you get to exchange numbers?'

Harry, lost in the mental mastication of tender lamb in a subtly spiced sauce, wrapped in a tear of warm chapatti, couldn't quite mask his irritation at being dragged away to answer a nonsensical question. 'I don't know.'

'What do you mean you don't know? What *exactly* were you doing that needed her to give you her number?' demanded Sophie, not bothering to try to hide her own irritation. 'What?'

Harry's indifference to questioning frustrated her so she would think about it later. She wanted the evening to be about Harry and her sharing and getting close as adults. She needed him to see her, not just as a good friend, but as an interesting and interested woman. How was she supposed to keep his attention with four very attractive women sitting just behind her, one already having made her intentions very clear. Sophie was relieved when Tabatha returned and hugged her goodbye, they were 'All off to Dorchester for the evening if anyone fancies coming', but then irritated when Tabatha spent far too long kissing Harry's cheek goodbye. At least Tabatha's coat had separated Harry's eyes from her fabulous bum.

Her attempts at small talk were failing. Neither of them were interested in celebrity, reality TV or shopping and at this rate he would soon be bored and make an excuse to go home. He had been impressed with her gym membership in Brighton and her fitness regime, but didn't seem to want to discuss her body tone, so now there were only two options that could guarantee his attention. Galaxies and space travel were far too heavy without alcohol to numb the pain, she had decided on soft drinks to match his fizzy water this evening, which left one other topic.

'What do you think Ancient Egyptian women used for

In the Arms of Giants

make up all those years ago? If the pyramid paintings are anything to go by they were perfectionists so it must have been good stuff. Isn't it strange how thousands of years later women are still doing the same thing? Do you think I'm looking a bit Egyptian tonight? It took me ages.'

The bait, carefully dangled, was snapped up and for the next hour Sophie soaked up his words, his smiles and his glances into her eyes.

Chapter 10

Harry was glad Nina had waved to him to stand on the corner rather than walk up the street to meet her. He could enjoy the sight of her fabulous figure in the late evening sunshine as she moved relaxed and confidently towards him. Her long black ponytail swished an occasional appearance as she feigned silly dance steps to entertain him whilst she walked and he waited. There was definitely an Asian influence in her multi-blue, simple dress, he couldn't quite pick it out, but it managed to communicate modesty whilst still offering a tantalising hint of what may lie beneath. As she drew closer her eyes filled his senses. How could such a beautiful woman not have a partner? Thank goodness there was not the remotest chance of a physical relationship otherwise his strict rule of only being involved with women at least ten years his senior would have been seriously tested.

'Hello handsome Harry,' she said, grabbing his arm and pulling him along as she walked past him towards the Harlequin front door. 'I'm dry as a bone, let's get a drink.'

Harry sat at the table Nina had pointed him to and marvelled at her confidence as she stood at the bar getting drinks. She had insisted on buying the first round because her cousin was in the RAF, she knew 'How poorly paid Services people are'.

'The trouble with not working on a Friday,' said Nina, as she sat back and let the first big gulp of chilled South African Chenin Blanc wash through her, 'apart from not getting paid of course, is that Friday evenings aren't such a relief anymore.'

'True,' Harry nodded. 'To really enjoy the light you first need to come from darkness.'

'Handsome *and* philosophical,' said Nina, in a tone that had Harry trying to guess if it was intended as a compliment, a put down or a simple observation.

The complete absence of sexual tension helped him to relax and enjoy Nina's company as a friend, albeit a beautiful friend. The only feint signals he could detect were of the *absolutely no chance* variety which he guessed were probably for general broadcast rather than aimed at him. He just had to be careful not to look into those eyes.

The light hearted disagreement about whether Egyptian or Indian women first used bold eye makeup to enhance their already disarming beauty earned him a kick to the shin. He managed to redeem himself by telling her about his trip to India and particularly his awe of the magnificence of the Taj Mahal. She seemed really interested and kept prompting him for more, despite having spent her early years just a few miles from it.

A loud grumble from his stomach stopped him mid-sentence.

'Come on, let's gulp and go,' she said, swigging the remainder of her second glass of wine. 'I think you're really going to enjoy what I've got for you tonight.'

The simplicity of Nina's flat appealed to Harry. Clean, uncluttered, functional, and surprisingly spacious for a new build. It was as if she was passing through, nothing in it said *Nina*.

Leaning back in the chair and sighing with contentment he looked across the table loaded with rustic serving dishes, still half full of food of all colours and flavours. She had changed into a simple, pale blue, silk kaftan and with her long black hair roughly clipped up and tumbling down and wearing black framed glasses instead of contact lenses, she looked the perfect host. Did her last glance at him give away a hint of vulnerability, confusion?

'No, really I can't. Another mouthful and I'll explode.' He allowed his eyes to half close. 'Thank you. That was fantastic.

I didn't recognise any of those dishes. Were they all family recipes?'

'Sort of, but don't forget the food you call 'Indian' here is rarely like anything in India. I'm not sure why it's so different... I guess when you went to India you ate in hotels or tourist restaurants.'

Harry nodded.

'If you go again try something more at street level, get someone you trust to take you to where they eat. The surroundings may not be what you're used to, but the food will be an experience you will never forget,' she said enthusiastically. 'That's *never forget* in a nice way of course,' she smiled.

They slumped down at opposite ends of the cream coloured sofa and Nina swung her feet up, pressed her soles against Harry's thigh and modestly pulled the hem of her kaftan down to cover her calves.

'Fab cushion. I knew I'd find a use for you,' she said, in a deliberately silly, satisfied tone, wiggling her toes against him.

Harry sipped his strong, black coffee and returned the dainty cup to the side table that had been fashioned from a stout piece of drift wood and fitted with a glass top that looked like it had found a way to defy gravity. He let himself sink back into the deep, comforting upholstery, resting his head thankfully against the cushion.

'This is just too comfy, kick me if I start to snore,' he sighed. He liked Nina and was glad she had forced him to eat with her this evening. With sex firmly off of any possible agenda he found he was enjoying exploring her personality. Talking to her was effortless, comforting. Was this the real Nina or was she unconsciously using a reassurance skill she used to lure her patients into the treatment chair. She was a very different person now to the blue-tunic clad one that had soothed away his panic at the hiss-whizz of the drill when she had sorted out his filling those weeks earlier.

For several long minutes they sat in comfortable silence then for half an hour shared thoughts of their favourite parts of Dorset. For Harry it was the peace and serenity of the countryside. Nina's number one was the nearby abbey. She impressed Harry when she listed several of the regimental colours hanging there. A frequent visitor to the abbey, Harry knew every one of them and every story behind every one, but remained silent, he enjoyed listening to Nina.

'So, which gossip about me do you believe? There's plenty to choose from.' She prodded him with her toes for attention. 'Most of it's probably true.'

Harry shrugged his indifference. 'Life's too short to waste time on such stuff.'

'It's true you know, I do play cricket with the other team.'

Harry frowned. 'Do you mean... bat for the other side?'

'That's it. Lesbo, dyke and so on,' she looked at him. 'It's true, in case you hadn't worked it out yet.'

Harry shrugged again.

'We'd just had security cameras installed in the practice and naively I hadn't realised they were on during the day as well. They captured me and one of the dental nurses *sharing affection* with each other. It wasn't frivolous, we were... close. I suppose I was on the rebound from my previous, long-term partner, but she meant something to me. The IT operator tried to blackmail me so I told him to go fuck himself. He kept his job, I didn't, my girlfriend moved away and the rest, as they say, is history.'

She stared out of the window at the night sky. One of the things she loved about her first floor flat was that she could keep the curtains open without compromising her privacy. It helped her to feel unshackled. 'I'm over it all now, time to move on, try to build my business up again, but it just felt so unfair.'

'But will you be able to find a partner in a rural area like this? Won't you feel alone?' asked Harry.

'I'm not ready for anything serious right now. When I am I'll have to think about it, but you'd be surprised what's available for a girl like me, even in this sleepy town.'

Nina yawned, stretched her arms above her, straightened her back and pushed her feet hard into Harry's leg, gripping it with her toes.

'I want to go to bed,' she said calmly.

'Oh, yes, right, it's getting late. I should go,' said Harry, starting to lever himself out of his comfortable nest.

Nina poked him in the ribs with her big toe, 'Harry?' Her deep, brown eyes snared him. 'With you Harry... I want to go to bed with you.'

'But you've just said... I couldn't share a bed with you and not...'

'I'm bi-- bisexual, but I find that sometimes worries and confuses people, apparently I'm *neither fish nor fowl*. It's easier just to use the *lesbian* label, everyone seems to understand that, even if they don't like it.'

She eased herself up from the sofa and stood in front of him. Her hands moved slowly under her hair and behind her neck to release the hook of her kaftan. She let it slip down over her shoulders, holding it with one arm to conceal her breasts. She looked for reaction in the eyes locked onto hers. Nothing. She dropped her arms to her sides. The kaftan floated to the floor revealing her nakedness. She raised her eyebrows in question. His heavy swallow answered, but she asked anyway, for fun. 'Yes?'

Chapter 11

Spring

'Screw you, No!' Sophie croaked, straining her neck to get her face away from his again. The effort of trying to push him off was draining her energy. She must stay on her feet, but how could she? Fight, fight, don't give up. 'No!'

'What are you? Some sort of fucking dyke?' he spat out in anger.

His body pushed harder, pinning her against the wall, his excitement clear, even through his jeans. Now he grabbed her head with both hands, she struggled, but couldn't move, no match for his strength. His tongue pushed against her clamped shut teeth, searching for a way in.

She growled defiance and strained again to wriggle free. Her energy drained, she felt helpless, even her jaw muscles were spent. Her growl turned to a soft cry. She didn't understand what was happening, why he was doing this to her.

'No! No!' she whimpered, 'please, no.'

'Hey cock brain, leave her alone,' Victoria shouted from the light of the patio. She strode into the semi darkness of the street beside the bar. 'Leave her, shit head!'

'Go fuck yourself, shag bag!' he panted without turning his head, 'she owes me.' He continued with the collection of what he considered a debt and lifted the hem of her dress groping for her knickers.

Victoria took off a shoe, hobbled closer to him and swung a massive hay-maker to deliver the tip of the stiletto heel hard into his thigh.

'Shit, what the...' he turned towards Victoria, trying to work out what had caused the deep, stabbing pain, 'fucking....'

The brief weakening of his grip let Sophie push him back

just enough to get her thigh up between his legs. She felt the contact, but she had no strength, it hadn't slowed him.

The giddiness that immediately follows a blow to a male groin swept over him and he knew something much worse wasn't far behind.

'Fuck... off... arsehole...' sobbed Sophie, breathing hard, pushing him back a little more before bringing her leg up a second time, now with more power, connecting her knee solidly with him. She panted hard, trying to summon more energy before steadying them both and bringing her knee up again.

'No...' she cried, as she watched him whither, retching and groaning to the ground, 'means no!... Bradley!'

Victoria standing lopsided, her shoe still in her hand, watched Bradley's crumbling descent.

Sophie, still struggling to breath, wiped his saliva from her face and then the tears from her eyes.

'I liked him Victoria, but I've never *ever* led him on, never even let him touch me. Why did he do that?' she sobbed.

Victoria fumbled behind her for her blue suede bag and found a tissue. With one arm around Sophie's shoulder she pulled her close then gently wiped her face.

'Don't worry it's over now.' She pushed a tangle of hair behind Sophie's ear, kissed her gently on the forehead and held here close until the shaking was no more than a shiver.

'But why did he do that? I thought he was a nice guy. I trusted him.' Sophie sounded more hurt than angry.

'I don't know. Some of these gym junkies think because they've got muscles they're irresistible. He was probably looking for a notch for his belt to mark the end of the academic year,' mused Victoria. 'I've never seen you angry like that, you walloped him *three* times. Christ.'

'I wasn't angry, I was scared, really scared. He's so strong, I couldn't move. I was petrified he would come back at me. He didn't seem to feel the first two.'

Bradley's groaning was turning into a squeaky, strangled sob and the girls turned, both frightened they may still be in danger.

They needn't have worried. Bradley was desperately trying to make sense of the world around him. He knew his knees and his nose were the only parts of his body in contact with the ground and guessed his hands were somewhere around his groin. He didn't understand any of the other signals his body was sending to his brain, other than they were carried by waves of uncomplicated agony pulsing relentlessly through him. He desperately wanted to pass out, but his inability to do so added to his despair.

'Well,' Victoria feigned casual disinterest, '…I think he felt all three.' She paused, 'I don't know about you, but I've had enough for the evening. Shall we head home? You'll feel better after a shower to wash the slime-ball off of you.'

'We can't just leave him like this can we? Should we call an ambulance? What if I've injured him?' Sophie was only now realising what she had one. She hated violence in all its forms, she couldn't even watch boxing on the telly and now she felt guilty about Bradley writhing in pain. She had reasoned and pleaded with him, then demanded he stop. What else could she have done?

'Oh, you've injured him for sure, He'll probably have elephant-sized testicles tomorrow,' Victoria giggled, 'but I don't think he would thank you for calling an ambulance.'

'Why?' Sophie really felt she should be looking after her once friend, now attacker.

'Can you imagine the headlines in the local rag? *Muscle man in hospital after having the shit kicked out of him by tiny girl.* I know he's a bastard, but it would make him hate you even more.'

'Good point.'

Victoria walked back into sight of the pub patio and caught the attention of one of Bradley's muscle-bound buddies.

His grin widened when he saw the two girls together, but it disappeared when he realised he hadn't been invited to extensive extra-curricular activities.

'What's up with Bradders?' he asked, looking down at his friend.

'He…' Sophie wasn't sure what to say, or if she could say anything without crying, or swearing.

'I think he inadvertently slammed his todger in the gate there.' Victoria pointed to the opening in the rusty waist high railing separating the road from the adjacent park.

'What the fuck?' Muscle Buddy cringed, as much in disgust as sympathy. 'What was he doing? Having sex with…? That's weirder than I can deal with.' He wasn't sure how much of a friend he wanted to be right now.

Although there was no one else to hear Victoria pulled him close so she could whisper. 'We saw it from a distance. Maybe he was enjoying himself on his own or something, I don't know and it's not my business. Look, can you watch him until he can get up? I don't think you should mention that we were here. It would only embarrass him.' She stepped back then looked straight at Muscle Buddy. 'I think he may need help,' she said solemnly and tapped her finger on the side of her head.

Victoria turned and looped her arm in Sophie's, 'Let's go.'

Sophie, right there and then, was determined to put the event behind her, to forget it, brush it away. Both new it would be a painful and frightening marker in her life for a very long time, probably a lifetime.

After about fifty metres of walking in silence Sophie needed to talk, say something, anything.

'You Victoria, are a prize, crazy bitch!' Sophie forced a giggle. '…One of the many reasons I love you so much.'

Their arms still linked, Victoria pulled Sophie closer. 'Sisters we never had?'

'Sisters,' Sophie nodded.

******

Sophie woke to the early morning sun and stretched lazily, enjoying the feel of the warm duvet against her skin. She trapped the memory of the previous evening and pushed it away before it could occupy her consciousness. Saturday mornings were her favourite time of the week and a cuppa was her favourite start to it. She pulled on the white silk robe Victoria had given her on the strict condition that Sophie recycled her faded, tatty towelling one immediately. On her way to the kitchen she stopped at Victoria's door and listened, then tapped gently before continuing to the kettle. Victoria, not a natural morning person, had asked for a wakeup, she didn't want Sophie to be alone for too long. She knew from bitter experience the next days would be raw.

As Sophie poured her second cup Victoria dragged herself, yawning, into the kitchen.

'Victoria, please… put it on,' sighed Sophie, pointing to the house coat Victoria was dragging behind her, 'the sight of a bare bum doesn't go so well with toast.'

'Oh yeh, sorry,' Victoria croaked, lazily scratching the bum in question. They had been sharing for nearly nine months now and it was the first time Victoria, an only child, had shared anything. Although neither of them were prudes by any stretch of the imagination she was still trying to remember that Sophie had a strong preference for people to be dressed when they ate.

Sophie poured Victoria a cup from the brown earthenware,

charity-shop teapot and pushed it across the table towards her. They both loved to drink their morning tea from real leaves, in real cups with real saucers, it had become a weekend ritual.

'Ooh ta Soph. I'm parched.' Victoria plopped herself down on the dining chair across the table from Sophie and, with elbows on the table, sipped from the pure white, bone china cup. 'Perfect.'

Victoria pushed her hair back and looked at Sophie. 'How are you feeling?'

'I'm trying not to think about it, but I'm flip-flopping between angry and sad,' replied Sophie quietly. 'I just don't get it. Why? We were occasional kissing friends that's all, I always paid my way, then boom, out of nowhere this bastard appears.'

'Have you thought about going to the police? Perhaps you should. You may not be the first… or the last.'

'I did think about it and I know I should, but I can't.'

'Why? You're not thinking about protecting the little prick are you?'

'No. I'm worried about mum. If the police were involved she would have to know and that would just add to her worries. We're already struggling for money and I'm not there to help her in the shop evenings and weekends. She doesn't say anything, but I know she's exhausted. Worrying about me being stupid would be another burden.'

Victoria sat upright. 'Stupid? Stupid? You,' she said firmly, 'were not stupid. You were not even mildly silly. Don't ever think it! The guy is a fucking prick. Full stop!' She took a deep breath. 'I could ask Pop to look into it. He might find a way that doesn't need your mum to be involved. I know he's corporate, but he's got lots of criminal law friends,' she tried to lighten the mood, 'like that silver haired sex-god QC guy who was on the telly last week. *He* could cross-examine me any day.'

'Please don't Victoria. I couldn't keep such secrets from mum.'

'I know. Forget it,' said Victoria, 'but the money thing, you know Pop thinks the world of you. He'd love to…'

'Victoria,' Sophie lifted her hands from the table and lowered her head to stare directly at her cup, 'don't, please.' She rested her hands again and looked up. 'I know he's loaded and would be happy to help, for all the right reasons, and I really do appreciate that, I do, but I can't accept it. For one thing it would alter our relationship. I mean, I already feel like a parasite living in this huge luxury flat rent free.'

Victoria stood and walked around the table to sit next to Sophie.

'Now Miss Pansay, you listen to me. First: Pops didn't buy this flat for rental income, he would never rent it. He's got three more like this: one in France, one in Spain and err, one somewhere else. He doesn't rent them, he lets his *real* friends stay in them for vacations. Two, um…twice, no, second: you do pay your way, you pay your share of the gas, electric and stuff and we split the food bill half and half. Three, and most important, without wishing to induce vomiting: we are friends. You are the first and only person I've actually wanted to be a friend with. My whole life has been about taking, you've taught me how to share and I know I'm the richer for it.' She paused, 'That last bit sounded a bit icky, sickie sweet didn't it?'

'It did a bit.' Sophie half grimaced, half smiled.

It was pointless to correct Victoria on the utilities bills. Every month from the very start of her tenure Sophie had religiously estimated a half share of the utilities costs and sent Mr Bartholomew, care of his PA, a cheque. Sophie was confused when she had seen the first cheque cleared, but then within days the exact amount credited back into her account.

After that every cheque went un-cashed. On three separate occasions Sophie had called to confirm she was using the correct address, but the PA claimed no knowledge of what was going on and promised to look into it. Sophie now had eight months of utilities payments sitting in her account waiting to be collected, a nice little sum by her standards.

'Look, if you're uncomfortable here let's find a double bed-sit, I really don't mind, it's all part of life's experience. It would be fun,' said Victoria.

'Would you?' said Sophie eagerly. 'Like the one I was in when we first met, with the shared shower room, peeling paint and sticky carpet?'

'If you want,' said Victoria, nodding in earnest.

Sophie, tilted her head to one side and frowned in thought, then looked around her at the pristine, modern, very expensive apartment.

'Naah,' she wrinkled her nose and smiled. 'This penthouse palace will have to do.'

Chapter 12

Sophie opened her eyes and enjoyed the comfort of seeing the familiar wall paper. The Brighton apartment was surely anyone's dream, but there was nothing like waking up in your own room, in your own home and your mum within cup of tea distance. Sophie had arrived late from Brighton, the coach had crawled forever through roadworks and then a car-accident hold-up. She had begrudgingly agreed with her mum that it was too late in the evening to knock on Harry's door. Both had thought, but not said: arriving unplanned at a young, single man's door at any time, let alone the late evening, may provide you with surprises you might not completely enjoy.

Finally the number thirty appeared beside the five, she switched off the alarm early and jumped out of bed. It was Saturday and Harry liked the weekend jumbo crossword. There was every chance he would be in the shop as soon as it opened, on the dot of seven.

After a quick shower, very thorough brushing of teeth, over-long gargle and good squirt of the very expensive, citrus notes perfume Victoria had insisted she take, Sophie pulled on her clothes. The jeans were high-waist and perfectly tight and the blouse perfectly short. She took her time to apply the Morello lipstick and very important thick, black eye-liner. As she rushed down the stairs and through the back door of the shop, banana and hot black coffee in hand, she hoped her mum would allow herself a lie in. If Harry came in early enough there could be opportunity to start the summer holiday in the way she would like it to continue, with their tongues spending a lot of time in very close proximity.

Thank goodness the assembly and stacking of the newspapers had kept her occupied and it was good to see the order was up by half. As her mum had said, business was picking up.

It was near enough to seven to open the shop. As she drew back the door bolts she wondered if he would be walking towards her at that very second. Was he hoping to see her this morning? Surely yes? Her mum, after Sophie's considerable nagging, had told him of her impending arrival twice in the last few days. Sophie refused to even consider he could be anywhere other than somewhere within the few hundred metres between his flat and where she stood right this minute.

She stepped out into the cool, Saturday, early morning, the silence broken only by the hopeful calling of songbirds somewhere in the hedge across the road. This was her favourite time of the week and she felt good. She tried hard to look left first, but immediately looked right. Would he be there? Would he be there? Yes?

No.

She forced a casual look in the opposite direction and then over the low hedge and up across the school sports field. If she turned now he would be there, for sure. Would he be there?

No.

It was gone seven, he was always here at seven. Seven, always. She stared up the road, willing him to walk around the corner and when that didn't work she tried to send him telepathic instruction to do so immediately. When that didn't work either she went back into the shop and set about dusting the, as usual, dust-free shelves.

Sophie soaked up the warm greetings and welcome-homes from the regular Saturday early risers. In the hectic and hard work of her first year at university she hadn't realised how much she enjoyed those familiar and caring friends. Right now they were small, worry free islands in a stormy ocean of where-is-Harry waves of anxiety.

She had just given Mrs Walldash a gentle, belated eightieth birthday hug and kiss when a familiar, no-nonsense rumble of an engine coming to a halt outside caught her attention. The clunk of a door closing, like a solid metal lid being reunited with its solid box, set Sophie's heart racing before her brain made the connection. Harry's Land Rover!

With no time to stuff mints in her mouth or grab a quick top-up squirt of perfume she rushed to the door as the tinkling bell announced an arrival. Damn, a hug and quick, hard kiss on the lips would have to keep her going. The customers in line at the till were all happy to wait whilst Sophie came from behind the counter to congratulate Mrs Walldash, Mrs Walldash was considered everybody's granny, but they would surely not be so tolerant of the snog Sophie had planned for Harry. No matter how handsome the receiver or how needy the dispenser.

Harry's warm hands on her bare waist sent something delightful mostly straight to her heart, but also to other parts that quickly signalled tingly receipt, even though those hands were firmly clamped to her and prising her away. The kiss hadn't been as brief as she had planned and she most certainly had not intended to clamp her legs around his waist.

All eyes following her, Sophie flushed crimson as she returned to the counter and a sheltered-housing companion of Mrs Walldash asked politely how long, exactly, he would have to stay away before *he* would qualify for a similar greeting.

Sophie, happily serving what looked like an endless stream of early morning shoppers, smiled as her mum appeared with two cups of coffee. Mrs Pansay, listening to her daughter's questioning, moved to the till and gently pushed Sophie out from behind the counter, chiding her for being nosy. It wasn't anyone's business who Harry had taken to the station this morning.

Damn! Sophie had been trying to think of a clever way to get that piece of information ever since Harry had arrived and explained his lateness, now her mum had shut the door on it. Harry hadn't fallen into Sophie's trap to confirm gender when she had asked 'What train did he or she get?' Sophie was uncomfortable. It was her first day home, the first time she had seen Harry in the flesh in ages, web-cams weren't the same, and now she was confronted with the painful possibility that he had been sharing a bed with someone just a couple of hours ago. Damn. Damn!

When the daily delivery arrived the tantalising smell of the fresh bread swamped the front of the shop and gave her a crumb of hope. She put two of his favourite rolls (according to Rosie) into a paper bag, grabbed him and marched him out of the back door and up the stairs to the flat. Whoever he may have spent the night with, as beautiful as she no doubt was, she wasn't there now and in fact was hopefully travelling away from them at one hundred miles an hour. Sophie had him on her own now and she knew she would have his undivided attention, at least until she served his bacon sandwich.

******

Sophie knocked on Rosie's front door. The day in the shop had gone quickly, catching up with regulars she hadn't seen for weeks had been warming. She hadn't realised how much she had missed them. Now, this evening, if all went well, in the next few minutes she would be snuggled up beside Harry as he tried to fix her computer.

Baggy, flopped like a huge, soft black pudding in the middle of the carpet, opened one eye, looked at her, sighed contentedly and went back to sleep.

As Sophie sat next to Harry, her arm gradually slipping around his shoulder, she peered into the screen whilst he typed away at the keyboard. She remained silent as he made mistakes, she could probably have done it in a quarter of the time he was taking, but she didn't care. She was confident she had double backed-up all of her spreadsheet files before deliberately deleting the application and then calling Harry for help. It was completely true that it had *just disappeared*. Her focus now was when best to gently rest her breast against his right arm.

The sleeves of his dark blue cotton shirt were neatly turned up to mid-forearm. His top two shirt buttons, undone, exposed the powerful and very kissable neck muscles that she had so often imagined straining above her as she lay in bed dreaming about him.

He blanked her probing about the morning station run. Did his guest get to London safely? Was she beautiful? How long had he known her? Was it special? (Sophie immediately regretted asking that last question as the words were coming out of her mouth and was relieved when he didn't answer).

'Where's Rosie? I was hoping to say hello,' asked Sophie.

'London.'

'When will she be back?'

'Tomorrow.'

'When did she go?'

'This morning. I dropped her off just before I came into the shop.'

'You mean…' Sophie realised she had been the victim of a day-long tease. Her first instinct was to pinch him hard, but then she saw the opportunity and leaned into him.

'So, Harry… It's just you and me, two consenting adults, all alone in this house.' Excitement lifted her. He hadn't moved away from her, even after her slight adjustment of where she was pressing against him. She met his gaze. It would be so easy to pull him towards her and kiss those gorgeous lips that were just centimetres away, as she had imagined doing so many times. He was still, silent. Was he waiting for a cue, or deciding how to approach the subject of love between them? Still seated he turned slightly towards her, his left hand moving onto the table.

'That's really nice perfume,' he said, deliberately breathing in.

'I've got all evening,' she whispered.

'You won't need it, it's fixed, all you need to do now is reload your backed-up files,' he said turning the laptop towards her. 'Do you want to test it?'

'Not really,' she said, looking demurely down and away and expecting a first, warm kiss at any moment. 'I'm thinking of lots of other things I'd rather do right now.'

'Me too.'

'Really?' She started to feel warm and a little nervous. They had never been this close to what she wanted.

'Yes.' He closed the computer lid gently. 'I'm meeting some mates for a blokes' darts night in about thirty minutes. I'll drop you home on the way.'

Chapter 13

Excitement cheered Sophie. It was Friday again, she had been home a week and finally Harry was taking her to the pub for a drink. It was a date, definitely a date, she refused to consider it as anything other than a date. OK, they might meet friends there and end up in a group, if she couldn't secretly signal them to go away, but Harry was collecting her in the evening and they were going out together. It was a date. Full stop.

She had let her anger be known last Saturday when he refused to take her along on the blokes' darts thing on the spurious grounds that she didn't qualify because she wasn't a bloke. That had tipped her over the edge. She had punched him on the arm as hard as she could and stormed out, slamming the door behind her. Out of sight of the windows (not that she for one minute thought he would be watching her) she sobbed, cursed him with some completely out of character rude words and walked home. Sod him! She had had enough. It was Saturday night, she would go out on her own and find someone who would be interested in doing all the things Harry wasn't interested in doing. It shouldn't be too difficult, if she wasn't too choosy. Screw Harry!

But she didn't go out. Instead she baked her mum an apple cake with out of date flour and out of date apples. They scoffed at least half of it whilst watching Saturday night rubbish on the telly.

The next day, with Rosie deciding to stay another night in London, Harry invited Sophie and her mum (why did he have to invite mum!) for early evening Sunday dinner. As he fussed over them it was clear to Sophie he was contrite. She was absolutely sure he had no idea what he had done, but at least he had picked up on her frostiness. Even Harry couldn't have missed that. That was progress.

She decided to forgive him, besides, anyone who could cook such a sublime cocoyam and smoked haddock chowder deserved another chance. And his plantain candied gooeys? Well!

She didn't let him off the hook immediately, he had to work for his forgiveness. On the Tuesday afternoon he had taken her to the shopping centre on the A303 where she made him wait whilst she tried on three pairs of summer shorts she knew her mum would definitely not approve of. His opinion, and justification for his opinion, was demanded for each. 'Nice buttons' wasn't accepted.

On the Wednesday morning he had done the heavy lifting at the cash-and-carry and in the afternoon fixed two wobbly shelves in the shop using the bolts Sophie had removed and dropped amongst the cans the night before. With Sophie's mum gratefully accepting the opportunity for the afternoon off Sophie carefully engineered silences for Harry to fill. It worked. After his second cup of tea he told her of his disappointment that he was still signed off of all duties with no idea of when he would be allowed to return. He had been training hard and was almost back to full physical fitness, his regular check-ups had said so. He was ready. Then he muttered something about 'Bloody shrinks', but she didn't press him further. For Sophie this was already a big step, he was sharing a rare confidence.

As a reward for his hard work that day Sophie confirmed he could take her out for a drink on Friday, just the two of them. He had earned it.

Friday seemed to take for ever, but at last it was evening. The solitary, small, solid white cloud looked stark against the pale blue evening sky as it transitioned imperceptibly to a gentle amber in the west. The earlier shower of rain brought a cool freshness to the breeze that caressed her bare shoulders and midriff and somehow managed to find its way through the soft cotton fabric of her loose, cream trousers. Had the birds understood her bubbling emotions and turned out in numbers to serenade as they walked to the pub? The refreshing smell of wet foliage reminded her how lucky she was to live in the countryside. And here she was, on a date, walking side by side, on a date, with the most wonderful man she could ever imagine, on a date. The only man in the world she had ever wanted and was already absolutely certain would ever want. On a date.

'Don't evenings like this make you feel so lucky just to be here?' gushed Sophie as they walked towards town, the intense green of the hedge on the other side of the road adding another colour surge to her senses.

'Yes.'

'Yes? Just yes?'

'Well, yes. It is pleasant, but you know it's the rain that makes me feel alive, on the planet, engaged with nature,' he said softly, in a tone Sophie felt she could reasonably consider as intimate.

Another piece of the never ending puzzle that was Harry. She had often wondered why he seemed so relaxed walking in the rain. Not hunched over with eyes squinting and head turned away from the prevailing wind, but upright, head back and relaxed. How he sometimes went into Rosie's back garden to stand in the rain, as if he was taking a hot shower to warm up. She thought of the umbrella that had been in his Land Rover forever, still in its original packing, that he didn't use because he *didn't want it to get wet*. Her subconscious played back buried memories and pushed forward a now clear conclusion. Another click of a puzzle piece – a rained-on Harry was a happy Harry.

Sophie stopped abruptly and grabbed his arm. They had reached the lamp post where, on one New Year's eve, she had

planned to tell him all, hold him and kiss him and then turn
around and lead him back to his flat, to spend the New Year
together, alone.

Now? Was now the right time? Should she? Was he ready?
Yes! Was it adrenalin making her heart pound? Or unbounded
love? She turned to look into his quizzical gaze. She pulled
him closer.

'Harry, I... I... want to tell you something.'

No response, deadpan, cucumber.

'Harry, I... I want to... I've got a stone in my slipper.'
Bugger! Damn! Bugger!

For the rest of the walk Sophie stayed in her own despair,
the sky, birds and breeze shut out.

She managed to stick to her plan and insisted on turning
right before the Harlequin, the current favourite evening
haunt, and steered him around the corner to the Barrel and
Tap 'For a change', but really to reduce the chance of being
joined by her friends. The Barrel and Tap was her mum's,
Rosie's and Sophie's favourite when a lunch time treat was
called for, the food was always unbeatable (she was addicted
to the fish pie special) and the atmosphere relaxed, friendly
and unhurried.

Sophie settled into her favourite cosy corner, almost
completely out of sight of the bar, with a padded bench
seat that would allow her to quietly move close to her man
and perhaps steal a kiss. She was sure quick kisses would be
allowed in the pub, a snog probably not. She pointed to the
sepia sign attached with a rough spike to what was probably
a several hundred year old wall timber and switched off her
phone. Harry in a rare moment of non-compliance turned
his ringer off and placed the phone face up on the table.

She decided that once they were married they would come
here every Sunday for lunch. She would have the fish dish, he
would have the sausage casserole (her second favourite) and

they would share, half and half, feeding each other.

Harry sipped at his usual tall glass of sparkling water, ice and lemon, the condensation trickling down the sides to darken the olive green beermat. Sophie was very careful not to get carried away with her half pint of local still cider. She loved the chilled, dry freshness, but she wanted to make sure Harry understood she was in full control. She knew he wouldn't entertain intimacy on any level if there was the slightest suggestion of alcohol influencing her. She was careful to place her glass in the exact centre of her beer mat, with the edge of the mat aligned exactly to a natural grain line in the wood, just like his was.

He was pleased to hear about her first year at university and was particularly interested in her classes, what they covered and what she planned for the next year. She told him about the chance meeting with her now best friend Victoria (who was coming to stay with her in Honeyborne in the next couple of weeks), the fabulous apartment and Victoria's lovely dad, Jason. Without saying so directly she let it be known there had been no boyfriends, casual or otherwise and that both she and Victoria had focused their energy on doing the best they could in their first year. She didn't mention that most of the boys in their intake year appeared to be more like kids in grown-ups' clothes being regularly surprised by the effects of excessive alcohol consumption. That is, apart from the few mature students, some of which had been rather tasty, but were so busy with studying they didn't appear to notice that other genders were available.

She didn't mention Bradley. She decided she would liken him to something unpleasant she had stepped in. Vile, but trivial, once you could stop yourself re-imagining the smell.

The evening was going better than she could have hoped for. He was interested in her and what she was saying, looking directly at her, smiling (smiling!) and reading her face. For their second drink she had joined him on fizzy water, she didn't need alcohol, this man was all the intoxication she could handle. Harry was relaxed, not doing his periodic assessment of everyone and everything within sight. He had hardly once realigned his glass on the beermat. Perhaps it was the comfortable atmosphere in the Tap? Was he lowering his defences in readiness to let her in to what she knew was his soft and caring inner self? She had controlled her instinct to chatter incessantly, to give him space to talk. She was keeping it cool, moving gently, she didn't want to frighten him, to burst the bubble. She was going to suggest they go back to his for a cup of tea and late night toast whilst they watched the evening movie, like she and Victoria often did, but he seemed subdued. Or was it worried?

According to her spies (and information unwittingly provided by her mother) he hadn't had much company of any sort for several weeks. The mutual scratching-of-itches relationship with Nina that everyone knew about, but no one mentioned, had apparently ended a month or so ago. Or - a rush of panic - had it simply gone completely under cover? Had Nina also brought him to this very pub? This very corner? A quick pie and mash before a Sunday afternoon of comfort-scratching togetherness? Certainly not in this last week. She had known his whereabouts for the last seven days, she would have spotted it. Oh God! Was that it? Had her watchfulness kept him away from Nina's comforts? Is that why he was quiet? She tried not to think of his appetite, but she guessed it was significant and hadn't been addressed for at least a week. Had Nina, her gorgeous eyes and slim body, popped into his thoughts? Not fair! Sophie was sure she could provide whatever he needed. Heaven knows she wanted to. All she needed was one chance to prove it.

Or was it Tabatha? She was unashamedly eager to share with Harry and lived in a grand house out of town with plenty of rooms to get lost in. Had he been visiting where no one would see him?

She thought back to the advice he had given her when she had once questioned whether she was good enough for university. 'You are as capable as you let yourself be. When you have an objective, never stop, never doubt yourself, always go forward'.

Right! Do it!

'Does Rosie have any of that stone-ground wholemeal bread she loves?'

'What? Err, yes, I think so. Why?'

'Why don't we pinch some and…'

Harry's phone lit up. The single number 5 along with an empty silhouette filled the screen. Did he number his girlfriends to keep them anonymous? Who was 5? What number had she been assigned? Perhaps she didn't even warrant a number and was listed under plain, uninteresting – not-worth-shagging - 'Sophie'.

Harry put the phone to his ear and listened, alert, focused, still.

'Yes.'

He listened more, his body tense.

'Yes.'

He sat upright.

'Yes.'

As much as he ever showed emotion Sophie could see his excitement.

'Now. No. Where are you?'

He nodded.

'Five minutes. I'll see you there.'

He rang off and turned to Sophie, his excitement now easy to see. 'Sorry Sophie, I've got to go.'

'What?… Why?… Who? It's her isn't it? It's her!' she demanded. 'Tabatha! No, it's Nina! She's whistled and you're running to her like a randy dog!'

Sophie didn't try to contain the anger that was exploding inside her. 'You're on a date with me, she calls and invites you for a shag and you go running. What the bloody hell is this?'

Harry looked at her as he stood up and slid between the table and the seat, confused, but determined.

'Sophie, I'm sorry, I need to...'

'Don't... say another word,' she spat out. 'If you go to her now, we are finished.' She spoke the last three words clearly, slowly and so loudly that everyone in the pub turned to look. 'I will never speak to you or even look at you again!'

'Sophie, I need to...'

She stood up, shaking with fury, her arm outstretched, palm flat towards him. 'Just... Piss *off.*'

She sat back down, eyes glazed, staring ahead, not seeing him leave, not seeing anything. She didn't care that almost everyone in the now full pub was staring at her. She didn't care about humiliation or reputation. The man she loved, the only thing she wanted in life, had just gone to have sex with another woman. Bastard! She hated him. Bastard fucker!

******

Harry turned left out of the pub and left again onto the main road, walking briskly, but not fast enough to draw attention. He scanned the cars in front of the terrace of old, redbrick houses on the other side of the road and recognised the green Range Rover at the same time as its side lights flashed on and off once. He skipped lightly across the road, as anyone avoiding traffic might, there was no traffic, but it didn't look out of place.

'Sure about this?' asked the driver, as Harry pulled the

passenger door closed and reached for the seatbelt.

Harry looked at the driver. 'Oh yes,' he said quietly, with a nod and a smile that he shared with only those he was closest to.

******

Sophie had walked home alone, dazed, holding back tears. She kissed her mother goodnight, climbed into bed fully dressed and sobbed herself to sleep. Her mother listened at her daughter's door, her own tears wetting her cheeks.

******

A few hundred metres south of her open bedroom window an early morning, London-bound express train whooshed and shooshed Sophie from her troubled sleep. So many times she had imagined it to be on its way to collect her darling and bring him to Honeyborne, to her arms and kisses, to the start of a life that really would be happy-ever-after. Now it was an arrow, stabbing her with his indifferent rejection.

She opened her eyes and tried to focus on the ceiling. Did that thing really happen yesterday? She played back the events.

Yes.

The pain, emptiness and despair slammed her awake.

Every minute of Saturday hurt. Even the early morning rush to assemble and stack the newspapers then dispatch the paper boy couldn't ease the ache that ran through her from head to toe.

How could her Harry do that to her? Was she that uninteresting, dull, unattractive? What did Nina have that would make him behave like that? Her heart sank, it was a daft question, everything about Nina was beautiful. The summer sun added a lustre to her light brown skin and gave an extra dimension to her already exotic beauty that even Sophie found tempting. When Nina entered a room her presence filled every space to overflowing. But she was supposed to be gay, the story had been in the local paper when her scandal broke. How could that be? Had Harry turned her? No, apparently such things were urban myth. Was Nina experimenting with him? Or having fun thumbing her nose at all those who had judged her and treated her so unfairly? Sophie regretted not paying more attention to how such things worked, up to now she hadn't really cared who did what to who.

Her mum knew something was wrong and Sophie was thankful not to be asked. In the evening she drank her mother's home made pea and leek soup, her favourite and her first food of the day, and simply confided that Harry had been a complete arse and she had told him to get lost. They probably wouldn't speak ever again. Ever.

Chapter 14

Perspiration trickling down her back woke Sophie early on Sunday morning. Damn! She would probably have slept longer if she had kept the window open and told the train to sod off as it laughed at her.

This morning her despair made a more controlled, almost formal, appearance.

She desperately wanted to talk to someone, to someone who could listen and not judge her or offer inane platitudes. Apart from her mum, and Harry's mum, who was definitely now not a candidate, there was no one in Honeyborne. It was surprising how just a few months away at university had put so much distance between Sophie and her old friends.

She really wanted to talk to Victoria. Victoria was worldly wise in such things and would at least help with coping with the pain. But Victoria was on her biannual pilgrimage to visit her mother in Spain. She knew that was an emotional struggle for Victoria and it wouldn't be right to burden her best friend now. Sophie was on her own.

Although tears were close and the pain still suffocating she decided crying wasn't going to improve anything. She thought back to words from the man she now hated. *Never back down, never give up. Never stop until you achieve your objective*, or something like that.

She looked at the clock. Seven. Mum wouldn't need her in the shop for at least another hour or so. She wouldn't give up, she had a plan.

She showered, put on enough makeup to make a difference without being obvious and rummaged through her tiny wardrobe for the soft cotton apricot blouse that had, on more than one occasion, got Harry's rare attention. Victoria's loose, mid-thigh, light olive shorts, modest enough for the early morning, but short enough to show her strong legs, went well. Mid-brown slave sandals finished it off.

Perfume? Just the lightest spray.

The cool tranquillity of the early morning slowed her heart rate from overload to simply pounding as she strode purposefully to Harry's flat. The solitary bird singing from a nearby rooftop soothed her nerves.

They were both adults. Now the heat of the moment was gone and there had been time for reflection they should reassess. She would tell him she was still furious and his behaviour was appalling, but she was his friend and understood that sometimes men inexplicably ceded control of their brain to the contents of their underpants. Rational thought was not always possible when that happened.

They should learn from it, agree it should not be repeated, put it behind them and move on. Be friends again. At that point she was hoping she would have the courage to announce that she was available for sex at any time, particularly right this minute, then unbutton her blouse and tell him to take over.

Sophie felt slightly uneasy opening the foyer door to the block of flats using the code Harry had given her for emergencies. Well, this actually was an emergency, for her at least.

She quietly climbed the slatted oak stairs to the first floor and turned left to the front of the building and the door to Harry's one bedroom flat. Her heart pounded, her mouth was dry and she was in danger of hyperventilating. She should go back? No. Forward, as Harry had told her, only forward. Easy for him to say, he was brave, she was a coward.

Keep going. You want this. Take it!

Stop panting!

Sophie adjusted her smile and rang the doorbell at the same time. Done. It was going to happen, one way or the other.

Movement inside, a door closing, a muffled voice. Was he talking to himself? Or? Shit!

No going back!

Run!

No, stay, you don't know the circumstances, maybe Rosie has come for breakfast. Maybe…

The door opened a crack and then fully.

'Good morning Sophie. This is um, a surprise. What's up?'

The words stabbed Sophie through the heart, everything went white and she wanted to step back, to turn and run.

Nina! Wide-eyed and slightly out of breath, she had clearly been interrupted in the middle of a physical exertion Sophie did not want to imagine. Nina pushed back her dishevelled long black hair and pulled into place a short, skimpy black nightshirt that did almost nothing to conceal her womanhood. She looked impossibly desirable.

'Everything OK?' asked Nina, trying hard to transition from her preoccupation with her previous activities to concern at the silence from the young woman in front of her.

The pain stopped Sophie's brain processing and it went into automatic. She could hear herself speaking, but had no control over the words.

'I'd like to speak to Harry.'

Nina frowned and looked to her left along the short corridor that Sophie knew lead to Harry's bedroom. 'He's not here.' She glanced along the corridor again.

A door closed with indifference and a music player switched on.

'Can I tell him anything if I see him?' asked Nina.

Was there no end to this woman's abilities? Professional, articulate, beautiful, no doubt an expert lover and now a consummate liar. How could she be so convincing when they both knew he was in the next room, probably waving at her to get rid of dull, boring Sophie?

Words came from Sophie's mouth, unasked and unconsidered, 'Yes. Please tell him Sophie came round to deliver another *piss off* to make a matching pair with the *piss off* she gave him on Friday.'

Sophie turned on one heel and walked off. Only after her head dropped below first floor level as she went down the stairs did she hear the apartment door close. Her legs broke free from her control, she stumbled and almost fell, saved only by grabbing the handrail. Then flames of anger flared through her and she considered going back, hammering on the door and going in and punching him, but the flames were almost immediately quenched by the flood of darkness and despair that swept into every corner of every part of her.

Sophie barely remembered how she got back to her room and only when she was in her bed, curled up in a ball with the duvet blocking out all light, did she allow her brain to understand what had just happened.

The man she loved that was truly without doubt, for her, *the one,* had not only unambiguously rejected her, but moved his lover in with him, right under her nose, just a few hundred metres away. Why did he do that? How could he do that? Was she that insignificant as to not even count? What was the point of anything? Of life? She might as well die. If she had that option now, to push a button and go into eternal nothing, she would. Fuuuuck!

******

Sophie didn't have the will to argue with her mother's insistence to do a stock check, today of all days. Usually they would have done it in a week evening after closing. Between them they could easily finish within a couple of hours, but today, with Sunday shoppers to be looked after at the same time, it would take ages. Normally Sophie enjoyed the counting, ticking and tallying, there was something satisfying about confirming expectations or, with discrepancies, explaining and justifying differences. Today though there was no such joy. OK, the grey cloud lightened occasionally as she reconciled the stock room, shelf content and sales on the day, but after each tick on the list Harry or Nina or both made an appearance in her head. Sophie was glad that as the day wore on the appearances were getting shorter and she was glad she had her mum as a friend.

Her mum slid the door bolts closed at four, just as Sophie finished counting the last item. She always left the toothpaste until last, something fresh and minty to finish on. Mother and daughter looked at each other and then hugged tightly. Both had been hurt by the same event, both feeling the pain in different ways.

Her mother walked to the sweet rack, reached up and selected an expensive box of chocolates. She grinned and waved it at Sophie, 'Let's go up and *scoff*. I think we deserve it.'

They curled up at each end of the old, comfy sofa, feet tucked under them, coffees on side tables and the open chocolates in the middle, only the two strawberry crèmes of the first layer remaining. Sophie felt warm and cosy, the pain was still raw, but her mum's undisguised love and patience was a soothing balm. For the first time that day Sophie felt small bubbles of relief bursting up through her pool of hurt. As hard as it was she resolved to move on, wipe Harry from her thoughts, start afresh. He was just one man, there were plenty more and if he could do what he just did to her he wasn't the kind of person she wanted to spend her life with. Sod the little shit!

Sophie was scanning the channels to find a soppy film, something light and unchallenging to veg out on, when the doorbell to the flat rang.

Sophie's mum looked up from the TV page, 'Who on earth can that be on a Sunday afternoon? Probably Mrs Walldash again, wanting a tin of carrots for her tea or something. I'll go. If she's on her own I'll have to walk her home.'

Sophie worked her way through the TV menu options, skimming past the titles she knew were dull and reading the descriptions of others intently, the task made slightly arduous because some of the remote buttons had stopped working. She decided to buy a new one tomorrow, blow the expense, the television was likely to be her main distraction for some time, until Victoria arrived.

'This one looks good mum, it's got…'

'Sophie, you have a visitor,' said her mum quietly.

Sophie's head flicked around to the door. Rosie? She felt sick. What did she want? Surely Harry hadn't sent her to apologise. That wasn't likely, he had made his position quite clear, he didn't care enough to even think about apologising. Rosie and her mum had become close friends and Sophie got on really well with her, she was a straight, honest and no-nonsense woman and easy to talk to. She had probably come to apologise for her son's behaviour. Well, it wasn't needed and she needn't have bothered. Screw him!

'Hello Sophie. I've come to ask for a favour,' said Rosie, taking an uneven breath. 'Harry's hurt and I was hoping you would…'

'Harry's hurt? Harry's hurt? How do you think I feel? What about me? How could he treat me like that? Why? He could at least have told me instead of just walking away and letting me find out.' Sophie's voice grew louder as her anger got the better of her. 'I know he's your son and you think the world of him, but I'm sorry Rosie, to me he's a self-centred swine, he's out of my life now and I don't ever want to see him again. I don't care. Ever! Don't care!' Sophie stared at the floor, took a deep breath and spoke quietly, the pain in her voice touching the two mothers, 'He *hurt* me.'

'Yes, I'm sorry, I shouldn't have...' Rosie said quietly, turning away.

Ilona touched Rosie's shoulder as she turned to go, 'Rosie, what do you mean *Harry's hurt?*'

Rosie's face crumpled. 'One of his friends just called me. Harry's been critically wounded and they say I should get to him as soon as I can, there might not be much.... They're bringing him back in an air hospital, they think he'll be back in British airspace within the hour and by then they should know which medical unit they'll take him to.' She swallowed hard and took a deep breath. 'I'm frightened. Tom said I should bring someone for support and I hoped you would be able to... no, I understand. I know Harry's not easy to...'

Sophie leapt from the sofa and stood in front of Rosie, trying to work out what was happening. 'How has this...? Are you sure it's..., it can't be Harry. I went to his flat this morning and he was there with Nina. I didn't see him, but she was there, with him. They were...'

Rosie, unwilling to risk a frown in case she broke down, clenched her jaws and took a deep breath. 'Nina and her partner have been back together for weeks. They've been living in Harry's flat whilst her own is being repaired after a water leak from the flat above.' Rosie took another deep breath. 'The last time I saw him was Friday, he was really happy and on his way to pick you up. I've come to terms with him disappearing for weeks and months, but a few minutes ago I got the call I've lived in fear of for years.'

Sophie stepped back, lost, confused, then the enormity of the situation hit her. The man she loved was seriously hurt. In all these hours she had been hating and cursing him for something he hadn't done he had been in mortal danger. How could she have been so selfish?

'Yes, anything, I'll do anything. What do you want me to do?' Sophie pleaded desperately.

Rosie and Sophie hurried back to Rosie's house in silence, both numb, Sophie carrying the small holdall her mum had packed as Rosie had shared the little more she knew. As they turned the corner and started up the last few metres of the gentle slope Sophie spotted an unfamiliar scruffy, green Range Rover parked outside of Rosie's house. She didn't recognise the driver, but as he got out of the car she could see he was one of Harry's sort. Expressionless, passive confidence, his physicality suggested an intimidating readiness for anything. Not someone you would want to seek the attention of. Did others see Harry like that? Not Harry, no, he might sometimes look scary, but inside he was warm and gentle.

Rosie deliberately ignored him, she opened the front door and ushered Sophie in then followed, leaving the door open. Baggy growled as the driver closed the door behind him, then heaved herself off of the floor and waddled over to give him a casual sniff.

His deep, gravelly, voice exactly matched his appearance. 'Rosie, I'm sorry,' he said quietly, following her with his eyes. 'I don't know anything more other than they're fighting to stabilise him and they're heading towards Birmingham.' Rosie stared out through the glass of the back door, refusing to look at the man.

He turned his attention to Sophie. 'You must be Sophie, I'm Tom, I'm going to take you to him. Did you bring your passport? I need the number to sort a security pass for you.'

Tom photographed the picture page and sent it, to whom Sophie didn't know and didn't care. Within a few seconds his phone rang and judging by the number of times he said 'Sir' in his responses it was someone very much his senior delivering non-negotiable expectations.

Tom stared at his phone, probably to make doubly sure the conversation was over. 'That was the base commander, he's having a helicopter fuelled and there's a flight crew on their way in. We can get to Harry quickly if you are both OK to fly.'

Baggy lifted the cool atmosphere as she leapt up, yelped with excitement, bounded out of the back door and through the side hedge as Rosie encouraged her with, 'Baggy girl, next door, next door.' Baggy knew that spending time with the neighbours next door meant serious pampering and attention.

Rosie looked at Tom for the first time. 'I'm sorry Tom, I know it's nothing to do with you and I really appreciate your help.' She swallowed. 'I'm scared.'

The Range Rover had purred sedately up out of the town, before turning left onto the main road, Sophie wondering if they really had to stick so strictly to the speed limit. Immediately a blue light flicked impatiently across the interior, the police car alongside them announcing its presence with a short blast of the siren before speeding off ahead.

'Our escort, hold on,' said Tom calmly.

Sophie and Rosie were thrust into the back of the rear seat, their heads thudding into the rests, the engine roaring then screaming in continuous anger as it catapulted the car forward, towards the blue light blinking ahead of them.

In any other circumstance Sophie would have been petrified of such aggressive driving and shouted at the driver to slow down, but one glance at Tom's calmness set her at ease. Just as she had seen Harry relaxed, taking control of situations that frightened her, Tom was in complete control of their world right now. Hurtling at God knows what speed along the dual carriageway, she trusted him. How did they do that?

The police car blocked traffic as they shot through red lights and past the main entrance to the airbase, the Range Rover engine finally calming from its journey-long arrogance to a sedate, Sunday afternoon hum. The blue light had gone and they turned left into a side road. Weren't they driving away from the base? The air museum was well behind them now. Another left turn and then, just out of sight of the road, a barrier and gate house. Were those soldiers carrying…? Yes, they had rifles, and side arms. Sophie was frightened. Guns? In Somerset? She had never seen a real gun, let alone been close to one.

After a stony-faced scrutiny of Tom's pass and then the passengers faces the sentry signalled for the barrier to lift and they continued onto a sterile, grey concrete road running through a sterile green nothingness. A left fork and then… *what is this doing here?* A small, squat, grey bunker building and a tall, serious, steel fence topped with razor wire running into the distance.

Tom pulled on the handbrake. 'Almost there. We need to go in here to collect your passes.'

In the concrete grey room were more guns, more straight-backed guards, more hard faces and a single metal desk. The two women were left in no doubt about what would happen if they attempted to take photographs, use their telephones or leave Tom's supervision once they were through the gate. Tom studied the passes carefully as the women looped the bright red lanyards around their necks. His inquisitive look at the guard was met with a blank stare then a shrug of shoulders. Something wasn't as Tom had expected, but his return shrug was good enough for Sophie.

Apart from the scripted questions delivered in neutral, bored, tones and the women's nervous answers there had been silence throughout the cold, sterile process. It was like interacting with machines with pink faces. This had to be one of the most intimidating places Sophie had experienced, she would do whatever she could to get Rosie to Harry's side, but she really wanted to get out of this place as soon as she could.

As they turned to leave the man of grey metal, who had made it very clear how terrible would be their punishment if they misbehaved, stepped towards them, his greyness suddenly gone. 'Rosie, please tell Harry we're all rooting for him.'

Two more metal men took human form. 'Yes, please tell him.' and 'Yes, he's a tough sod, he'll fight.'

Rosie, who hadn't spoken since leaving the house, other than twice to confirm her name and answer the security questions, turned to the young man. 'Thanks Leonard, I'm sure he knows, but I'll tell him. And, if you're allowed to, please give your mum my love.' Rosie turned to the others, 'Thanks, I know you care.'

The cold, mechanical process and cold, mechanical people had chilled Sophie's mind giving her some small respite from the worry that had brought them here. Now, with the thaw, the pain came back and viciously ripped at her.

Harry, please be OK.

Please.

Please.

Please!

Through the steel fence and a few metres past tall pine trees Tom parked the Range Rover in the exact centre of a yellow box beside a small door into what looked to Sophie like a vast something out of a science fiction movie. There really were buildings this big in the world!

The guard had done a double check of the passes, there was something definitely not right about them, before smiling and opening the door. Was it a smile, or was it pity? Did he know something they didn't?

Inside were boxes, equipment, sacks, bags and all sorts of odd looking things exactly stacked along the sides and on racks. Parked squarely in the corner nearest them were four aggressive looking, open topped, brown and green painted vehicles that looked vaguely like they may once have been Land Rovers. As they walked across the building from one side to the other, it was too dark to see along to the far end, they stepped over taped outlines of squares and rectangles on the floor. Sophie couldn't work out what they represented and couldn't know that the day before Harry and others had spent many hours using them to plan and practice. She couldn't know that as she hurried over the shape labelled with a large yellow chalked "1" she was stepping over marks that depicted a door and the real life thing it represented would soon be haunting her waking and her sleep. Two very different worlds were on a collision course.

As they emerged from the dark, echoing interior the daylight lifted them. Sophie had never been close to a helicopter and the one she was looking at now, with engine whining and rotor lazily stirring the air, was big, very big. Something was niggling her. Did the army do this for everyone who had an accident? Perhaps this was one of the helicopters Harry used in his logistics job, to move his boxes around.

One of the flight crew took the three holdalls from Tom and strapped them into a corner then buckled the two women into their seats. Sophie didn't know what sort of seat she was expecting, but she definitely wasn't expecting to sit in a piece of net tied to the wall. Was this even safe? She glanced across at Tom who had the appearance of someone settling down for a night in front of the television.

The dark green helmets were heavy and cumbersome, but it was a relief to block out some of the machine noises. Both Rosie and Sophie jumped as the pilot's voice came through the headset, thanking them for joining *this rapid reaction training flight*: Harry was stable and expected to land in Birmingham within the hour. Their own flight expected clearance to depart in the next five minutes, flying time would be approximately eighty three minutes and they would be landing at the hospital.

All was delivered with detached indifference, he could have been reading a shopping list. Then softly, 'Rosie and Sophie, Harry is in the best possible hands. He has a huge team of dedicated professionals working non-stop to make him well. I've worked with him many times, he's a hard man, a fighter, he won't give up.' A pause and then shopping list, 'Thirty second to take off.'

Tom must have seen her fear as the aircraft shook and throbbed and she became disorientated as the buildings slid away from under her at a confusing angle. The noise was all around her, everywhere. She grabbed Rosie's arm. Tom's gravel came through the headset, 'It's always a bit scary until you get used to it, now I think it's quite relaxing. Plenty of leg room.' He pushed his legs out in front of him, wiggled his feet and smiled. Tom could smile.

Chapter 15

At any other time Sophie would have soaked up the thrill of her first helicopter ride, in fact her first ever aircraft experience, but she spent the whole flight willing the journey to end. Now, as she stepped back on to the ground, then held Rosie's hand as she stepped down behind her, all distractions of the flight were gone. Harry occupied her whole awareness. Rosie looked straight at Tom and shouted above the still slowing rotors, 'Where is he? Which way?'

Tom grabbed the holdalls, turned to look at the two women and mouthed, 'Follow me.' He strode off towards the hospital, realising he would have to quicken his pace if he was to lead, Sophie and Rosie had already trotted past him.

The high level of security at what Sophie had expected to be a normal hospital surprised her, but at least there were no guns in sight and their passes, although carefully scrutinised, were not questioned. They had entered through a simple side door and waited whilst Tom made a call and asked one question, 'Harry Stone?' Sophie and Rosie watched him for any sign of what he was hearing. How did these people learn to show no emotion?

Tom turned to Rosie, his voice now that of a friend caring for a friend, 'He's been in theatre for about thirty minutes, he's going to be in for some time, no other information. They've directed us to the place they'll take him when he's out. Do you want to get a drink or food before we go?'

'Take me there. Now!' Rosie snapped back.

Tom lead them through a maze of corridors, waiting areas and connecting doors without having to check signs or get directions. He knew his way around. The building was new and the absence of anyone other than nursing staff and people with passes prominently around their necks suggested it was a restricted area. They stopped in a large, bright, open space which looked like a hub for four large doors each with an internal window beside it. A busy workstation against the far wall was the centre of activity.

He ushered them to a row of hard, grey plastic chairs near to the desk. 'This is where they'll bring Harry, into one of those four rooms. Keep your passes visible at all times and you won't be challenged unnecessarily. Just there on the right is a rest area with a television, easy chairs and kettle and cups if you want to get a bit more comfortable. I'm just going to get the details of the sleep room you've been allocated. It's a twin, I hope you don't mind sharing. There's a lot of guests here tonight.' He took his phone from his pocket and pressed a speed dial. 'Sophie, if you switch your phone on I'm calling you. Store my number and if you need me call me.'

'How did you know my... forget it.'

Rosie and Sophie sat side by side, neither feeling the hardness of the plastic, Rosie staring straight ahead, jaw permanently clenched, Sophie watching the growing gathering of blue uniforms and white coats and trying to make sense of the stream of instructions, questions and confirmations.

Doctor Christina Marchand, her security badge and silver name tag the only adornments on her plain white coat, commanded immediate recognition from the team as she strode into the room. Her eyes swept the group, mentally registering the presence of each person and dwelling for several seconds on Rosie's and then Sophie's pass and then ignoring them both. The procession of updates and statuses, none requested, some spoken with raised voice across the room, but all directed at the doctor, were clearly part of a well practiced routine. Sophie marvelled that so many people could work so seamlessly together.

Doctor Marchand checked the clip board handed to her. 'He's going into room four. Somebody check it please.'

'It's already been checked Doctor,' a nervous young nurse volunteered.

'Check it please.' The response was emotionless.

'But it's…'

Doctor Marchand turned to the nurse and handed her the clipboard. 'Name?' she demanded.

'Nurse Lesley, Doctor Marchand,' came the uncomfortable reply.

The doctor's firm voice drilled into everyone, 'Nurse Lesley, you are new to the team. The men and women who come here for our help do what they do for Queen and Country. They do what they do for us, that's you and me. Some come here many times. They give everything, they fight until they succeed or their bodies can no longer respond to instruction. Please look at this man's list of wounds. It is almost certain that he didn't get them all at once, that means that after each wound he kept going, kept fighting, to the next one and the next one. My guess is that some of the blade wounds were first, fighting hand to hand with someone trying to kill him, closer than you and I are now, to someone trying to kill him. Think about that. I don't know about you, but just being that close to someone who wants me dead would paralyse me with fear. Any of the multiple gunshot wounds could have been next, entries and exits tell us they came from different directions, probably at different times. He kept fighting after each one - after each one. Fractured ribs under body armour require a force that would have certainly knocked him off of his feet, deflated his lungs and left him in agony, fighting to breath and trying to work out which way up he was. The blast wave from whatever it was that fired shrapnel into his chest probably hammered into him so hard it finally stopped him and left him trying to prevent his body shutting down. Think about it.'

Doctor Marchand stepped back, her eyes holding the nurse

transfixed. 'I will work every hour I can stay awake, for as long as I have strength, to do whatever I can, to keep this man with us. If I can extend his life by even one breath then every minute of my effort will have been worth it. If, Nurse Lesley, if you don't feel the same please leave now.'

The warble of a desk phone caught the doctor's attention, she took the receiver handed to her, listened intently and then replaced it on the cradle. She dialled a number on her mobile. 'Tom? It's Marchand. Harry Stone, I've just had an update from theatre. You need to get his next of kin here now, right now. Right now! Where are they?' she demanded. She looked over at Rosie and Sophie, checking the passes again. 'No, they are not here! Just a couple of MOD bean counters.' She made no attempt to disguise the contempt in her last words. She listened again then looked behind the red lanyards at the two women staring at her.

The younger woman: face taut with fear, wide eyed, unblinking, tears welling. The older woman, with an expression Marchand had these last few years seen too many times: pain, self-recrimination. A mother punishing herself for not doing differently something, anything, any small thing, that would have turned her child's path away from this moment. Both women no doubt wishing they could, right now, change places with this man they loved. This man with a body so punished the physical was probably looking to the spirit for guidance on whether to try to continue.

Marchand's return, involuntary stare acknowledged their contact and she took a deep breath, 'Oh shit!'

As Doctor Marchand pulled a chair around to sit with Rosie and Sophie Tom rushed in. 'Ah, good, you've found them.'

The introductions were quick. When Rosie, at Tom's earlier advice to avoid next of kin issues, introduced Sophie as her daughter, Harry's half-sister, Sophie recognised the doctor's flit of attention from face to face as an unspoken question.

Rosie had stopped the doctor mid-sentence to make it clear they had no intention of registering a complaint against her and the mix up in communications. They fully accepted the doctor's explanation that because they had special MOD badges, not usually issued to visitors, the doctor had wrongly assumed they were just another unannounced monitoring exercise. There had been many since this secure wing of the hospital opened.

'Tell me honestly, what's happening? What's going on? The truth. I want to know the truth,' demanded Rosie.

Doctor Marchand used what she hoped was a balance of detail and impact that would be least distressing when delivering honest, but frightening news. Harry's wounds were each, on their own, usually survivable. Her concern was that, all together and coupled with his almost complete physical exhaustion and loss of blood, he was in an extremely vulnerable state. Their single biggest worry was a piece of shrapnel that had entered under his arm, grazed a lung and was now lodged against his heart. It had to be removed immediately, there was no choice, they were operating now.

Sophie wanted to crawl into a corner, roll up into a tight ball, close her eyes and put her fingers in her ears, then perhaps none of this would be true. Instead she put her arm around Rosie and held her. Sophie had never felt such pain, she couldn't even begin to understand Rosie's.

Rosie turned her eyes away from the doctor. 'Percentage,' she said.

'Every situation is different, every person's circumstances…'

'Percentage,' Rosie repeated firmly.

Marchand took a deep breath. 'Twenty to thirty,' she said quietly. 'If he survives surgery the next forty eight hours are critical.'

Tom and Sophie convinced Rosie to move to the nearby

lounge where the softly upholstered, deep chairs made them at least more physically comfortable. Tom made them tea in the small kitchen space and persuaded both to eat a biscuit. It was going to be a long night and it was important to eat and drink then rest as much as they could.

Tom's regular fifteen minute spaced trips to the workstation and returns with *No change* were each met with anxiety and then muted relief. That meant not getting worse and Sophie clung to Tom's earlier words, 'Harry's fighting. He's a stubborn, tough bastard. He never gives up. Never stops. Ever.' The words all the stronger for the absence of any 'Everything will be OK' meaningless assurances. At least they were getting the truth, nothing was being hidden from them, no misguided attempts to shield them from reality, no matter how bad that may be. One less thing to try to work out. Thank goodness they had Tom. In just a few hours he had gone from dark and sinister, to be avoided, to what Sophie thought a close family member might be like. Was he old enough to be an uncle? She was short on uncles. His half missing eyebrow, twisted nose and clumsily miss-aligned two halves of a top lip had shifted from frightening to endearing. She shouldn't have let this warmth into her reality of cold, but she needed something to slow the downward spiral of despair. She would close her eyes for just twenty seconds.

Something deep inside her head, or was it her chest, slapped her. She looked at her red, plastic digital watch and then up at Tom standing sentry-like to her left, with a sausage of a finger pressed to his lips. Rosie, who had remained silent for the whole time they had been in the rest room, was asleep, head slumped against the wing of the olive green chair.

The curtains were closed and most of the lights were off. What time was it? Three fifteen. The fuzz in her head stopped Sophie working out how long she had slept, she knew it must have been hours. Ends of dangling threads started to reconnect pain. Harry. She couldn't remember, surely it wasn't as bad as... What was Tom mouthing? *Still OK*.

Rosie stirred then sat bolt upright, eyes blinking wide, her whole body rigid.

'He's still stable,' said Tom quietly. 'They've removed the dangerous shrapnel and finished the work around his heart. The third team took over about an hour ago and...' Tom looked up at the face peering through the window and beckoned the person in.

Nurse Lesley stood self-consciously in the doorway, her mousy hair pulled back into a tight, neat bun, every square millimetre of her earnest face bright red, 'He's just come out of theatre, he's stable and blood pressure increasing. He's doing well.' A single fat tear trickled down the side of her nose and a sob of joy escaped before she straightened herself back to formality, 'Doctor Marchand is with him now and she says she will come to see you as soon as she's finished with him.'

Sophie marked the hour and the minute by the clock on the wall. The forty eight hour count had started.

The nurse gave in to Tom's insistence that she should have a cup of tea with them - because Rosie and Sophie must be tired of his ugly mug and scratchy voice and her company would be more therapeutic than a biscuit. She took her first sip of tea then froze as Doctor Marchand strode in.

'That's a good idea nurse, Tom, is there another one in the kettle?' The doctor's smile and soft tone let everyone know positive news was on its way.

Surgery had been completely successful, Harry's vital signs were better than expected and heading in the right direction. Everything had been attended to apart from a piece of shrapnel still embedded deep in his chest muscle and difficult to get to. It wasn't a risk and they hadn't wanted to make a non-essential incision, so they would remove it once he was stronger. He would be kept in an induced coma for probably forty-eight hours to allow his body to gain strength. Doctor Marchand added with a smile that it would also stop him trying to get out of bed and get dressed.

Rosie and Sophie had taken the doctor's advice and tried to get some sleep. The twin beds of the sleep room had been surprisingly comfortable and the en-suite bathroom, although tiny, had been a god-send when they woke at just after six with furry mouths and tired eyes. Coffee had been all they could manage for breakfast. Tom had answered Sophie's call at the first ring and assured them everything was as expected. Harry had just been moved from recovery to room four of intensive care three, where they had been last night and where Tom was now. Yes, Tom had slept and eaten.

It occurred to Sophie, as she gripped Rosie's hand tightly for comfort, that she had never seen Harry asleep before and now, watching him through the observation window, a light sheet covering most of him, he looked calm, relaxed. She might have been able to blank out the tubes, wires and beeping and chirping machines, but the dressing covering a large part of the left side of his face kept forcing its way back to the centre of her attention.

Although the atmosphere was less fraught than when they had arrived yesterday there was still tension in faces and voices. Nobody was relaxing, nobody was unhurried. Doctor Marchand had arrived as Sophie stood up from the hard plastic chair to take her second look at Harry. The doctor was wearing a fresh, crisp white coat, but her jet black hair with its wisps of grey was escaping haphazardly from its tortoiseshell crocodile clip. Her dark brown eyes begged for sleep, she had been with Harry all night. She assured them that green gowns and masks in Harry's room were normal at this stage as were a minimum of two nurses with him at all times. There was still a long journey to full recovery, but every minute made the journey shorter.

Nurse Lesley arrived an hour early for her mid-day shift and Doctor Marchand asked if she would mind taking Rosie and Sophie to the cafeteria. Tom of course would be good company, but his constant diet of bacon sandwiches and Cornish pasties, although both excellently presented downstairs, may not suit everyone.

Rosie dragged her eyes away from the observation window and surprised everyone with her declaration that she was starving and ready to eat. The calm, considered Rosie that Sophie was used to was back and it lifted Sophie's spirit.

The basement cafeteria, already busy, was bright and clean and its muted blues and yellows décor set it apart from the stark, clinical corridors and rooms above. The lighting was subtle and relaxing despite having no windows and the staff, in their starched, creaseless mustard uniforms seemed genuinely cheerful. It could easily have been a new build restaurant in a city centre flagship department store. The only giveaway was that most customers were in uniform of one sort or another and everyone in the room was wearing a prominently displayed security pass. Sophie tried to enjoy the rare treat of eating in such a place, but the man she loved, somewhere several floors above her, headlined her every thought.

Rosie's bravery was a welcome source of strength for Sophie, but her brain had erected a self-defence barrier stopping her from trying to understand the mother's pain. She knew she should try and she felt guilty, but she just didn't have the courage to go there, she just didn't.

Nurse Lesley introduced herself as Rebecca, ostensibly to them all, but her regular, hoped-to-be-crafty glances at Tom as she sipped her mug of creamy tomato soup let slip the intended recipient. Sophie thought it an unlikely match. The very pretty, but nervous Rebecca, not much above five feet tall, slim and in her early twenties and Tom, probably six years older, six foot plus, wide shouldered, bull-necked, confident, calm and handsome, his scars adding both thrilling menace and bad-boy excitement. Not so different from her and Harry then. Maybe it could work.

'Hi Bekka,' one of the four nurses called across as they settled at an adjoining table. 'You've made the leap over the security wall then. How are you finding it? Talk about in at the deep end. I'm supposed to be on vacation this week, but when I got the alert and called in they said it was big.'

'Hello Ruth, yes it is…'

The male theatre nurse sitting furthest away chimed in, mouth half full of sausage roll, 'Three critical and ten serious, I've never seen anything like it all in one go. It must have been a huge job. Red teams I bet, it must have been at least four teams in one operation. They can't keep that out of the news, it sounds like something went seriously wrong.'

Tom put down the brown sauce bottle and replaced the top of his soft white roll on the crispy bacon. 'One team,' he said, his deep voice silencing every other. 'The operation was one hundred percent successful. All objectives achieved.'

'Oh my god,' the theatre nurse continued, his low voice a mixture of shock and compassion. 'There's supposedly only sixteen in a team, that means… oh god, it must have been horrendous. I bet it was Red Five. If you believe what's on the internet they're a complete set of nutters, and totally ruthless. They always get the job done, no matter what, but look what happens to them.'

Tom twisted in his chair to stare at the nurse, his cold eyes making clear it would be wise to follow his measured words carefully. 'First, I suggest you re-read the confidentiality clauses in the agreement you signed to be allowed to work here. Second, Rebecca and I are having something to eat with the next of kin of one of your patients. We would probably enjoy it more without further internet updates.' Not until the nurse peered intently down at his second sausage roll did Tom unlock his stare and turn back to his own plate. 'Now, where did I get to with my bacon butty? It looks like you're enjoying that soup Rebecca.'

Sophie looked up at Rosie who, with her back to the other nurses, had continued to eat her cauliflower cheese, apparently deaf to the exchange. Did she know what the objective was? What was it that everyone else around Sophie seemed to know that she didn't?

As they approached the window to room four Sophie looked at those around the workstation, searching for any suggestion of worry. One of the nurses looked up, smiled and gave a thumbs up. Sophie breathed out. Lying there, the white sheet draped loosely over him from the shoulders down, Harry looked so relaxed and calm, like he might open his eyes and jump up at any moment. Was he really hurt? Maybe she had misunderstood the last twenty four hours, it was all a silly mistake and really he was just badly bruised.

The two busy people behind her, organising, questioning and answering said otherwise. The two green smocked and masked nurses in the room with him, constantly checking equipment, constantly checking him, adjusting here, peering there, said otherwise. Rosie's urgent gaze following the nurses' every movement said otherwise. Sophie's stomach pushed bile upwards, of course he was really hurt.

Rosie accepted Tom's offer to 'brew' whilst they slumped in the easy chairs of the rest room. She looked like she may be able to sleep and Sophie hoped she could follow.

Rosie stared through the mug of tea being offered by the ungainly fist. 'What Tom?' she asked quietly, not moving, 'what *objective* is so important that you can consider it fully *successful* when my son is lying there with his body so torn he's unlikely to see out the week?'

'Rosie, I can't…' Tom stuttered, his voice quivering as his brain searched desperately for words to explain to a mother why the politicians' assessment didn't consider the probable loss of her son significant.

'What? Exactly? Exactly… fucking… what?' shouted Rosie, as Tom recoiled, her anger piercing him.

'I'm sorry Tom,' Rosie apologised softly as she took the tea from the two hands of the now kneeling, misty-eyed man. 'I know the Service means more to you guys than us non-warriors can ever understand, but we still have to deal with what happens, even if we can't make sense of it. You soldiers aren't alone in this world, people love you.'

Tom smiled, visibly relieved that he didn't have to continue explaining within a context he had little experience of. He had never known a mother or father and Rosie was the only non-military person in his life that had shown him warmth and caring, if you didn't count the numerous compliments and tenderness in the children's homes that always turned into anger and beatings because he refused sodomy. He trusted Rosie, she would never lie to him. If she said he was loved then it was true. That felt good.

The classic ring of Tom's phone broke the tranquillity of the moment. Both women held their breath and Sophie, having already sprinted across the room and grabbed the door handle turned to look back at him.

'It's not about Harry,' he said to Rosie before listening for a few more seconds and then hanging up without speaking a word to the caller.

'OK. I'm not allowed to give you any information about Harry's activities, you know that, but I do know there's a news flash on all the major networks which you may want to listen to,' said Tom. He picked up the television remote. 'Shall I?'

The flat screen flickered into life and Tom adjusted the wall bracket so the television faced directly at Rosie and the now kneeling Sophie.

A clumsy, child-like graphic of a map of West Africa filled the screen. Sophie recognised the outline of Ghana and the two cities Accra and Kumasi. The third, Tamale, she couldn't remember. She didn't know if she was absorbing information from the news reader or the bottom of screen news-ticker. It flooded in.

Unconfirmed reports… Twenty five diamond mine hostages freed and safe… thirteen British, seven American, five French… unharmed… four day ordeal

Dawn raid… multinational… Ghanaian and American supported British ground assault force… heavy British casualties… critical injuries, all back in Britain

Notoriously brutal Galamsey Gang … Russian, Nigerian… illegal diamond mining… child slave labour

Hand to hand combat… withering fire-fight… at least fifty bandits dead

Keep you updated

Rosie and Sophie, all four hands clasped together, stared unseeing at the anti-wrinkle cream advertisement that followed the news bulletin.

Tom cleared his throat. 'From what I've seen on the internet they parachuted in overnight, in position by four, went in at first light - around five fifteen, first contact at five thirty one, all hostages away by five fifty six, our team clear of the fire zone by six eleven. American helicopters north to Tamale. Last of the extraction aircraft left Tamale by eleven hundred. You know the rest.'

'So, completely successful then,' said Rosie quietly, as she picked up her mug of tea from the hard, woven carpet beside her chair. 'All we need now is to see the butcher's bill.'

Sophie couldn't understand how Harry's logistics job got him caught up in all this. It didn't make sense, but now wasn't the right time to ask. She would corner Tom on his own and ask and if she didn't get a satisfactory answer she would write to the Defence Secretary and the Prime Minister and demand an explanation and assurance it wouldn't happen again. People whose job is to move stuff around shouldn't be put in such danger.

******

The minute hand of the ward clock shuffled lazily past the end of the forty eight hour marker, but it brought no relief. Harry was still lying there, unconscious, unmoving, being attended to day and night by busy, green-smocked staff.

Through the observation window she could hear machines beeping and chirping, questions being asked and answered. Dials were checked, scales checked, charts checked and then all checked again, endlessly. It comforted Sophie that so many professionals were focusing all of their expertise and skills on her Harry relentlessly, minute after minute, hour after hour, day after day. Their dedication and determination, obvious with every word and every action, humbled her and she willingly accepted her sense of inadequacy and her position of watcher. Their honesty helped her feel a part of what was happening, they didn't hide their concern that he was still in a very vulnerable state.

At the end of seventy two hours a visibly weary Doctor Marchand, who never seemed to go home or sleep, let them know the drugs keeping Harry in a coma would be withdrawn. It was time for him to wake up, possibly tomorrow.

As the clock ticked on the regime gradually changed. Green smocks disappeared, the checking of things was less frequent and usually only one nurse was in attendance – although he was never alone, and the curtains on the observations window were closed more often as Harry was bathed and turned and his dressings changed. Tubes and wires gradually reduced.

At the beginning of day five, after careful scrubbing of arms and hands, Rosie and Sophie sat either side of Harry as he slept. No one apart from Sophie seemed worried that he hadn't woken. Every minute of the last days had felt like an eternity, every second hoping, willing him to be better, pushing the possibility of the alternative aside, but never managing to get it far enough away to stop it banging back into focus whenever she relaxed. She glanced at Rosie. What strength was this woman drawing on to hold her face calm and emotionless as she listened to every word the doctors and nurses said? Cold and detached, she asked for explanations and clarifications, whilst every second she waited to see if her only child would see the next second, her haunted eyes the only give-away.

With him now, holding his hands, they chatted to him, perhaps their voices would wake him. Surely this change to his regime, them being in the room, touching him, must mean he was on the mend? Rosie's hard steel hadn't changed. Had the doctors told the mother something Sophie didn't know? Were they keeping something from her? The lump returned to her stomach.

Rosie had gone back to their sleep room to rest after lunch and Sophie, having worked out how to nod off sitting on the hard chairs in the ward, closed her eyes and sank into an uneasy, but welcomed darkness.

'Only next of kin I'm afraid.' Rebecca's voice woke Sophie with a start and she looked up through gritty eyes to see a woman looking through the observation window at Harry, one hand pressed against the glass, the other holding her heavily pregnant belly. Was she Ghanaian? Her crisp white maternity dress was trimmed with a kenti design, the colourful, traditional, handwoven cloth Harry loved. The tears and the pleading in her voice made it clear Harry was important to her.

Pregnant? A different question gripped Sophie as her imagination played out scenarios of explanation, none of them comforting. The woman certainly knew Harry and Sophie felt an urge to help her, but she couldn't, she was frozen in silent guilt to the chair. The woman's short, carefully plaited light brown, Rasta-style hair accentuated her long, slim elegant neck and dark, flawless skin. Sophie guessed she was in her early thirties and there was no doubt she was beautiful, she radiated beauty, and love.

After extracting a promise from Rebecca to pass on a message that Akua had come to see him the woman waved goodbye to a sleeping Harry. Her pale blue sandals, no doubt chosen to match the dominant colour of the kenti trim on her dress, slapped softly against the soles of her feet as she left. Even in sadness she looked stunning.

Only next of kin, so they weren't married. If the child was his he would have planned, Sophie was sure of it. Maybe... maybe he didn't know and Akua was coming to tell him.

Sophie added shame to her wretchedness. How could she let jealousy cloud her judgement? Whoever Akua was she cared for Harry, the gentle, quiet Harry Sophie wished every good thing for. If she saw Akua again she would speak to her. If it was convenient.

******

As Rosie and Sophie walked back to room four after their early evening meal in the cafeteria they looked down the long, soulless corridor to see Rebecca jumping up and down, waving and grinning like an excited child. 'He's awake, he's awake,' she shouted.

'You go in, I'll wait,' said Sophie at the door, but Rosie grabbed her wrist and pulled her along.

'I'm afraid I have to stay,' apologised Rebecca, standing in the furthest corner.

Rosie ran her hand over Harry's close cropped hair and gently kissed his forehead. 'Hello big fella,' she said quietly, for the first time in days a smile warming her face. 'You gave us quite a fright.'

'Sorry mum,' he croaked, through dry, chapped lips, returning the gentle squeeze of her hand. 'Had a bit of an accident.'

'Look who's here to see you. Come on Sophie, grab a kiss whilst he's defenceless.'

Sophie wiped away her tears with the heels of her hands, bent over and kissed his cracked lips. Relief flooded through her, here was her man, alive, awake and getting better. Her tears wouldn't stop and she moved her head to one side to stop them dripping off of her nose onto him. 'Harry...' She looked away.

Rebecca cleared her throat as another nurse joined them, 'I'm a bit late with his checks...'

'Oh, yes, OK, well I'm going to have a lie down and rest. Sophie would you keep an eye on him for me?' asked Rosie with a wink.

The seats were no longer hard and the ticking clock no longer mocked her. Sophie wanted to dance and sing and hug everyone in sight, surely she would burst with happiness. Harry had been returned to her and now, no matter how long it took, she would be by his side helping him to recover, doing anything and everything that was needed.

The curtain on the window opened and the second nurse left the room smiling, 'All washed and fresh. All ready for you.'

Sophie stood up and deliberately ignored the clock. She hadn't realised how much she hated that clock. Screw that clock!

Rebecca was smiling and happy as she chatted with them. 'He's been awake two minutes and already causing problems,' she tutted. 'I'm supposed to give him a suppository and bed pan, but he won't let me unless he can use a proper loo. Well, we'll see what Doctor Marchand has to say.' She straightened the light bed sheet. 'I can tell you her insertion technique is far less gentle than mine,' she giggled. As unprofessional as it was she couldn't hide the affection she had for her patient.

Talking to Rebecca was calming, it added a relaxed normality to the situation. She was on her third boyfriend since Christmas, the first two couldn't put up with the shifts and emergency call-ins and she didn't think the current one was happy about it either. She had thought about looking for someone in the army, but all the ones she had met were *troublesome* she said whilst making big, staring eyes at Harry.

She came to work on a moped, but didn't like it at all, especially in the winter, and her dad was going to help her with some money to buy a car this autumn. It would probably be a small, old banger, but at least it would have four wheels and be dry and warm. Perhaps she should look for a mechanic for a boyfriend.

Sophie worried for her new friend. Most of the boys she had met at university would have been delighted to take advantage of this warm, quiet, mild mannered girl. It was easy to see how her gentle, easy way would be appreciated by her patients, but it was an open door for testosterone fuelled predators to stomp through and up their bragging scores.

'Oops, what happened their?' said Rebecca calmly, as an unscheduled beep caught her attention. She touched each dial and control as she checked the monitors and equipment.

Nothing. Then another unexpected beep. The professionalism took over. She pulled back the sheet and quickly checked the wires and connections on Harry's arms and chest. Sophie hardly noticed the purples, browns and yellows of the bruises across most of his left side.

'Sophie, I think you should wait outside for a while,' said Rebecca firmly.

More unexpected beeps, and now silences and an intermittent, irritating whine. Sophie didn't know what the monitors were saying, but Rebecca's worried look as she scanned them told her something was wrong.

Rebecca's attention fixed on a small grey box with green display and another row of numbers in red. She touched the numbers and then the screen, saying the readings from each out loud, then she repeated it, confusion in her voice. 'That's not... How can that...?' She followed the tube from the equipment along the support frame to the bed then glanced at the monitors again. 'How...?'

Then a flutter of different pitched, louder beeps followed by another, louder, fear inducing, whine that Sophie instinctively knew meant something very bad. At the same time Rebecca's attention refocused on the rows of red and green numbers. 'Shit!' she cursed as she grabbed the tube and ripped it and the needle out of Harry's arm leaving the fixing tapes dangling. She banged a large red mushroom button on the wall, immediately setting off an urgent, loud alarm, then grabbed a piece of equipment on wheels and dragged it to the bedside.

'Sophie, get out now!'

Sophie was numb, she couldn't move, she half heard Rebecca over the cacophony of alarms, whines and beeps. She heard 'Charging' and 'Clear!' then nothing. Rebecca's eyes flickered across the defibrillator, checking by rote. 'Charging' then 'Clear!' then nothing.

'Fuck!'

Sophie heard running feet then the door flew open and two nurses burst in.

'Cardiac arrest, defibrillator's broken, Susan – go and get another one, Grace – get her out then come back.' Rebecca rattled off the orders, confident, in control, unflustered. As Grace parked Sophie beside the window more nurses and white coats sprinted up the corridor, piling into the room until one stood holding the door open, but keeping new arrivals out.

Sophie fumbled for her phone and dialled. 'Please Rosie, come quickly, come quickly, heart attack,' she shouted to a Rosie coming very rapidly out of a deep sleep.

What was Grace doing? She had just punched Harry on the chest. Rebecca shoved her aside then, with both hands clasped together and arms outstretched above her head, brought a heavy blow down onto his ribs. Then another, this time Rebecca's feet almost left the ground. Whatever they were hoping for didn't happen. Rebecca barked another order, repeated by the nurse at the door. 'Get another defib unit.' Two nurses waiting outside sprinted off in different directions. A man in a white coat moved to the bedside and delivered another blow. Nothing. People in front of monitors called out their readings, in sequence, over and over, the controlled urgency and tension in voices clear, incessant, increasing. Someone shouted 'Two minutes'.

Rebecca looked frantically at the monitors then hitched her dress up to her waist and in one movement vaulted onto the bed to kneel astride Harry. Again she brought her joined fists down on his chest, her body taught, transmitting her whole weight into the punch. …Nothing. Her fists raised high above her head, then crashed down again. …Nothing. Rebecca was tiring, her chest was heaving, trying to suck in air. Again her fists rose above her head, this time rocking back, sitting on her heels, her thigh muscles bunched. Screaming through clenched teeth, she launched herself forward, her fists coming down in a wide sweeping arc, slamming into him. Harry's whole body shook. Desperation in her face, she raised her fists again, gulping air, preparing for one more. Then a beep. Two quick beeps, a pause, then a regular beep, beep, beep.

All in the room froze, staring at the monitors, then a solitary, muted 'Yes!'. The calling of readings from equipment fell to a relaxed mundane with the callers' relief only partially hidden. Most filed quietly from the room and away, returning to their earlier tasks chatting casually about sandwiches, rosters and an unfair football decision, as if they had just attended a scheduled meeting. Those staying with Harry went busily about things Sophie didn't understand. Two men in white coats were looking at the grey box Rebecca had focused on. One of them cursed loudly and the other picked it up and moved it to a trolley in the far corner of the room then wrote something on a piece of tape he had stuck across the screen. The defibrillator got the same treatment.

Rebecca, having clambered exhausted from the bed, stood with her back to the window adjusting something on Harry's arm. Another nurse walked around and pulled Rebecca's dress down to cover her pants and then gently squeezed her shoulder and whispered to her. Sophie scanned faces, everyone seemed relaxed.

Rosie, she should call Rosie. Sophie started to dial and then saw Rosie running frantically towards her.

'It's OK, he's fine, he's fine, he's OK,' Sophie shouted, running to meet her.

As they reached the window Rebecca left the room and Sophie grabbed her, hugged her and kissed her. 'Thank you Rebecca, thank you, thank you. Rosie, Rebecca saved Harry, got his heart going again.'

'Well, I think a lot of people were involved in it,' said Rebecca shyly. She looked at her red and swelling hands and laughed, 'I think I might have added to his bruises.' She took a deep breath and exhaled slowly to steady herself. 'I am sooo glad I wore good knickers today.'

Doctor Marchand appeared within the hour, her white coat squeezed closed over what looked like a vivid yellow ball gown. Sophie guessed that at some point that evening she would have been wearing something other than the plain black ward shoes she had on now. 'Perfect timing thank you Harry, you've saved me from the most boring evening of my year. My Husband's works' annual dinner and dance. I just feel a little guilty that the poor man's got to endure it on his own.'

After apologising, even though Harry insisted none was necessary, Doctor Marchand explained that a piece of equipment intended to deliver a carefully chosen set of drugs had malfunctioned and started pumping huge, random quantities into him. It should have failed-safe, but instead carried on with no notifications. It had been nurse Lesley's rapid, structured analysis that had prevented the situation deteriorating further and apparently her bed-top athletics had brought it back to normal. As for the defibrillator, that had been the third one to malfunction in as many weeks and the hospital administrators had finally decided there was a need to revisit the supply contract.

'Hey Rebecca, you certainly know how to get to a man's heart,' Harry called across to the nurse who's face, already flushed, now turned strawberry. 'By the way, Tom knows a lot about cars. I think you should *definitely* ask him.'

******

Sophie poured tea into the three cups, she was elated.

Doctor Marchand had assured Rosie no damage had been done, apart from a bit of extra bruising, and there was no reason to delay his discharge sometime in the next few days. Rosie sighed in relief and sat back in her chair. Now here they were, less than an hour after the panic, in the cafeteria to discuss his care. Stitches would soon need to be removed, antibiotics taken, dressings changed, pain killers carefully managed, regular check-ups attended. It all sounded quite straight forward. Then the doctor's tone changed.

A psychologist colleague had published a study paper on the impact of violence on the mental health of specialist forces. She shared it with Sophie via a phone connection and recommended she read it. Some governments, in addition to the special forces everyone hears about on the news, were developing small groups of people specialising in narrow, specific tasks, many involving high levels of violence and danger.

'Let me summarise it for you. It would be easy to find enough psychopaths to do everything required, but these very clever users of people worked out that, perversely, the most successful outcomes were from using young men that are naturally non-aggressive, then trained to deliver what's needed.

'They select normal, young people, train them in unimaginable ways of violence, instil iron discipline into them, then put them into truly terrifying, horrific situations and tell them to do terrible things. Their sense of duty becomes all-consuming and their bonds with colleagues unbreakable.

'The programme worked well to start with, very high success rates, apparently in part by the bad people hearing rumours of hell-hounds on the loose, but then the military noticed the growing losses of their expensively trained assets.

'The paper suggests that for these naturally non-aggressive people to do what they do they have to block out their normal feelings, suspend their humanity, work within a limited cold frame of reference. Unpleasant as it is, it's not a problem in itself, but what appears may be happening is the more they work within the cold frame the more painful it is to go back to their normal self and so they stay there, in the frame.

'The longer they spend in there the more detached from the warm world they become and the more indifferent they are to their own safety. It took a while to work out, and longer to admit it was a problem. The beasts, discovered, harnessed and trained in each of them, were now fully awakened, broken free of their leashes and running in an ever more self-destructive pack. Their injuries become more and more serious and now the mortality rate is heading off the scale. It sounds comic-book, but I can't think of any other way of describing it.'

The doctor sipped her tea. 'I'm not suggesting that applies to anyone upstairs, that would be completely inappropriate, but it may be worth considering if you can see any parallels in your own experiences.' She put her cup back on the saucer and looked directly at Rosie. 'I think it would really help Harry if you could get him away from everything, away from his normal environment where he sees his duty as resting his body then going back.' She smiled, 'As Harry would say – press his reset button.'

The doctor looked at Rosie again, then Sophie, bit her bottom lip, then lightly slapped the table, her internal struggle over, she had made a decision. She lowered her voice, 'Right, this is against all the rules, but I'm going to say it anyway because it's my duty to my patient... I've seen too many fine young men broken on the rack of rigid military regulations, all for the want of a little common humanity. I work for them, but I'm not one of them... This is confidential and I'm trusting you not to speak of it beyond this table.' She took a deep breath. 'This is not the first time Harry's been in my care and, if things don't change, it's my guess I'll keep seeing him until he's no longer with us.' Then, as an afterthought, 'And Sophie, I know Harry doesn't have any sisters.'

Rosie turned her head away and stared into space. Stiff fingers wiped her cheek.

Doctor Marchand sat back and looked at Sophie, measuring her next words. Sophie braced herself for an argument. She would *not* leave just because they weren't related. She would *not!*

The doctor's voice softened. 'I've also known, long before these last few days, that someone called Sophie is special to Harry, he just won't admit it. I don't know what your relationship is, I'm guessing you'd like it to be a lot closer - it's not my business, but I do believe having you near him over the next weeks could be very important for him.'

Sophie sat upright. 'Rosie, let me take him to Brighton, please. I can be with him every day and look after him for the whole summer. Please?' Sophie begged, stretching across the table to grip Rosie's hand.

Chapter 16

Harry's body clock woke him as usual on the dot of five a.m. At five a.m. and four seconds his brain provided its usual, automatic situation report: threats, status, position, next actions. This was only the fifth day in Brighton with Sophie, but he noticed he was already able to pay less attention to it. He felt relaxed enough not to need to fully evaluate it, to only register that nothing needed immediate reassessment or attention. It could just be that the shrinks weren't all complete dick-heads, perhaps taking a holiday was actually beneficial for a soldier. This was the first time in five years he hadn't spent every day of his leave preparing to get back to duty. He couldn't shake the guilt of not being there for his unit, but let's face it, it was going to be a good few months before his body was fixed enough to be of any use.

Was it the wonderful Brighton sea air, the removal of all things military from his environment or his real friend Sophie, who had taken it upon herself to selflessly help him through his difficult patch? She would do well in the forces, she had all the raw materials: courage, determination, focus, quick thinking and above all, loyalty. He could imagine her excelling in many key roles where size and strength really weren't important. Even her occasional preoccupation with sex wouldn't be out of place, several of his own unit seemed to be the same. The big difference between them and her was that *they* didn't invite him for intercourse.

In the first dim light of morning he folded his bedding and placed it in a neat pile on the sofa. The chair bed folded silently and smoothly back ready for its day role and the black silk panel decorated with subtle grey Chinese-like brush strokes that had screened his sleep from the rest of the lounge clicked confidently flat against the wall. This kind of quality cost serious money. How many apartments had a laundry room and a guest shower for goodness sake?

How Sophie had found herself here he had no idea, but nothing she did now surprised him, she was something special. It was amazing how these few months at university had transformed her from a goofy, awkward girl to a strong, confident, driven woman. He wondered how long they would remain close friends once she finished her education and set herself loose on the world. Once that world recognised her worth there would be no shortage of opportunities and people, especially men, wanting a part of her.

What sort of man would she end up with? He would need to be her equal, that's for sure, and Harry didn't think there were many such men around, not of her calibre, not if she sustained this huge rate of development. Some of his women friends had said the only important thing is love. Love cuts through all boundaries and if you have love you have everything. He wasn't so sure. It wouldn't be long before Sophie realised he didn't have much to offer her world and left him far behind.

Harry eased himself down carefully onto the sofa, beside his bedding. As he was waking up, so were his wounds. They were reminding him that they still had a long way to go before he could ignore them.

He wondered what would have happened if he had taken a different route, gone to university instead of joining up, got a regular job. Although he wasn't sure if he was smart enough or had the patience for a degree. Or the personality come to that. Not that it had been an option. He had signed up to the Navy at sixteen, as soon as they would have him, to get away from home and set his mother free from his obnoxious, bullying, parasitic father. And then the Navy had let him go to Lympstone. It had taken just days into training to prove to himself he wasn't the *useless, stupid prick* his father told him he was whenever they were alone. There was no challenge they could throw at him that he didn't meet head-on and not just succeed at, but excel at, especially in the combat skills that let him channel his anger.

Then active service wasn't enough and he got caught once too often seriously damaging opponents in underground fight clubs. The unexpected visitor to his police station cell hadn't been in military uniform, but seemed to know everything about him. The offer had required just three sentences, Harry had taken three seconds to accept. He walked out of the cell and into something that felt a perfect fit, Programme Red.

The brotherhood, discipline, structure, planning and, yes, the violence and addictive, fear driven flood of adrenalin. He needed fear. Then the satisfaction of success in the debrief. They had done what had been asked, what needed to be done, and no one needed to know. This was him, exactly him, all he needed.

Then he saw Sophie.

If they hadn't ordered him to go home on leave he wouldn't have been in the shop buying a paper and wouldn't have seen her giving him a weird look across the counter. Was it really possible to fall instantly in love with someone you had never met before and never spoken to? What was she, sixteen? A child. Probably never been out of Honeyborne. What was all that love bollocks anyway?

Now here he was just a few metres from her as she slept and more or less in her care. Could he have been a candidate for Sophie's affections rather than just her physical curiosity? Most surely not, but he allowed himself to enjoy the absurd thought of her wanting him for more than just sex. He thought back to that New Year's kiss that had taken him to a place he had never been to before, or since. Why had she done that? Had she felt sorry for him? Was she taunting him? He had never wanted a woman like he had wanted her that evening and still wanted her now. Whatever it was he had forgiven her, she had been only seventeen and couldn't have understood the effect she had had and besides, he couldn't stay mad at Sophie for more than about three seconds.

And what was the sex thing about now? She didn't push herself on him, it was more relaxed, more of a *I'm here and happy to have sex with you, if you want. It might be fun* sort of attitude. Perhaps she'd had an active relationship during her first university year and needed something over the summer holiday to fill the gap. (He tried hard not to visualise himself as active in the unintended pun). If only she knew how difficult it was for him to keep saying no perhaps she would stop. It might be just fun-sex for her, but he was scared to think what it would mean for him. God, she was beautiful.

He snapped himself away from that warm place. What-ifs don't help anyone, he reminded himself, life is about the what-is. His what-is was that for this last five years he had been trained to do one thing and one thing only and he did that one thing very well, efficiently, ruthlessly. Regularly. Like everyone else in his welded unit, he had realised that the more effective he was in shutting down unnecessary emotions, dehumanising his adversaries and himself, the more efficient, proficient, machine-like he had become at his job. Once he had found out how to turn off the self-preservation switch it had all become less stressful. In fact he was beginning to feel more at risk in the company of Sophie than he did on operations. This was not good, he needed to sort it out. The sooner he was back with his unit the safer he would be.

Despair flashed through him. He rested his elbows on his knees, his head in his hands and breathed in. If she knew what he had done, what he was capable of, what he would no doubt be called on to do many times again, she wouldn't want to have anything to do with him. It was no comfort that they had been promised all official records of his activities were locked away, not to see the light of day in his lifetime.

He would never break his oath of secrecy, but she should know what his job entailed. If he didn't tell her he would be deceiving her, he couldn't carry on like that, she deserved better. If he did tell her it would soil her view of life and she would no doubt walk away from him anyway, her consciousness tainted by him. No, the only fair thing for Sophie was to just get out of her life, whilst she still liked him.

The shower had perked him up and he sat down at the end of the large glass table with a mug of strong tea and yesterday's newspaper. He always saved the crossword, sudoku and word puzzle for the following morning, to try to partially fill the gap left by not being able to go for an early run. Right now he could hardly walk, running was some way off.

It would probably be another hour before Sophie stirred. He had readied the teapot and caddy beside the kettle and her teacup and saucer and the milk were set on the table at the chair next to his. She would, sleepy-eyed, drink her first cup of tea, then shower and dress and then they would walk slowly to the bakery around the corner to buy croissants, or muffins or some other still-warm breakfast treat. Despite the guilt he allowed himself to imagine her now, her soft, warm body, relaxed, sleeping in the warm bed, her shallow breathing the only sound, the sheets holding her sweet smell. Just a few metres away. It would be too easy to let her use him, but he wanted more than that and he knew he could never be a contender. No. Stop. Forget it.

Thank goodness the pain in his leg, ribs and shoulder weren't quite as bad as previous days, he must be on the mend. He set himself a target over the next two weeks: to be able to walk to the pier and back.

Harry looked up from his crossword as a bedroom door clicked closed. They were so well engineered you never heard them open. Then the slap-swish, slap-swish of sleepy, bare feet on the polished teak floor as they padded across the dining area towards him.

Her hair was tousled from sleep, her eyes still closed and her right arm raised straight above her, the hand wriggling, trying to find the sleeve of the black silk gown which on first sight looked like she may be waving as some sort of trophy. An unhurried yawn followed by a mild curse of the robe for being uncooperative was the only indication that she was actually awake. The robe, staying stubbornly mostly above her, did little to cover her otherwise naked body.

'Good morning,' said Harry, 'you must be Victoria.'

Victoria's eyes opened wide then blinked closed and open again trying to focus on the stranger sitting at her table before looking down at her body to confirm her fear that she was indeed without clothes.

'Agg!' was all she could manage as her left hand shot across to cover her groin and her right arm came down to cover her breasts, dragging the billowing robe over her head and shoulders making her look like an upmarket Halloween prank for consenting adults. Blinded by the festoon of black silk, but realising her dignity was probably not fully restored, she corkscrewed down and to her right. Her left hand flicked around in a vain attempt to hide some of her bottom and she waddled duck-like towards where she thought the doorway to the bedroom corridor should be.

Victoria realised her spatial awareness wasn't all that she hoped when she head-butted the wall.

'OK... calm,' she said assertively, taking a deep breath. Standing up straight she abandoned the guard over her buttocks and used both hands to pull the robe from her head. Finding her nose almost touching the wall, a good metre from the doorway, she scuttled sideways to the corridor. Then, head held high, she strolled towards her room.

In the Arms of Giants

'Would you like tea?' Harry called after her.

'Yes please,' she half sung.

The tea had just brewed when Victoria returned, this time with hair brushed and wearing a huge, fluffy pink towelling robe that hid all evidence of the female attributes of the body inside it.

'Good morning, you must be Harry,' she said, straight-faced as if at a business meeting, standing erect and shaking his hand confidently.

'I am indeed,' he said starchily, maintaining the formality.

'Oh shit, I'm sooo sorry Harry,' she said, with a grimace, 'I'd forgotten you were coming. I got back from mum's late and I haven't eaten since yesterday morning. Hunger pangs woke me up. I was on my way to Sophie's secret biscuit stash.'

'No problem,' he said indifferently, but then with a mischievous tone, 'I've already decided - that's my favourite way to meet someone for the first time. I feel I know so much about you already...'

He gestured to the extra place he had set opposite Sophie's. He tried to have Sophie to his right whenever he could, so she didn't have to look at the ugly mess on the left side of his face. 'The tea's just brewed, let me find Sophie's secret bics.'

'Damn! Custard Creams, my favourite,' said Victoria, peering into the white and multi-coloured polka-dot tin, trying to talk about anything that could get her mind off of her embarrassment and the other very obvious topic of conversation that needed to be addressed, but she didn't know how to even begin.

As Harry sat down again he could see her discomfort, her eye movements gave her away. Why had he suggested she sat to that side of him? Stupid! Damn! He felt guilty for putting her in this position, perhaps being in Brighton hadn't been such a good idea. Best to get it out into the open, to make it as easy on her as possible.

'I'm sorry about my face,' he said quietly, 'I know it must look pretty revolting. I can put a dressing on if you like, it's just that it heals quicker without one. He put his hands on the table ready to ease himself up, 'Let me move to the other…'

Victoria's right hand shot across the table and rested on his left hand, holding it firmly down. She looked at the eight centimetre wound that ran from the top of his ear downwards towards the corner of his mouth.

'That looks… painful.' She continued her examination. 'I've never seen a real, serious wound before. Does it hurt?'

' Not too much now. The stitches are beginning to itch a bit and they pull if I laugh.'

'So…' she said thoughtfully, 'if I get angry with you all I have to do is tickle you.'

'Yes,' he smiled, 'ouch!'

Thank goodness. Victoria had worried that Sophie's Harry might not like her, find her shallow or vacuous, but he had put her at ease and he was so easy to talk to. She had allowed Sophie some leeway, it was natural to exaggerate the attributes of someone you were crazy about, but he was indeed everything Sophie had said. No doubt he had a flaw somewhere, everyone did and men of course had many, but she hadn't spotted any of his and she wasn't going to look. No, in knowing him for just a few minutes she knew she liked Harry and she knew she had found a second real friend. And Sophie, she thought, you are right, he really *is* drop dead gorgeous, you lucky bitch!

Harry carefully avoided describing how he had got the injury, batting it aside with a flippant comment about trying to occupy the same place as something sharp. (Victoria would have to ask Sophie what on earth a space-time continuum was). He hadn't wanted to talk about his other wounds either, so she didn't press him, but she guessed it was pain that caused the short interruptions to his conversations

- slight stutters, the occasional tightening of his lips, quick, short pants of breath and the tiny adjustments of posture.

She let him not so subtly steer the conversation towards her and told him about her twice yearly visit to her mum in Spain, how she couldn't resist pigging out on the fabulous paella and was probably two kilos heavier than when she went. Then she asked how his first days in Brighton had been and what bits he liked so far. They agreed that lungs full of cool, early morning, crisp sea air were one of those physical pleasures that helped start the day well.

Victoria admitted she had dreaded spending another summer alone in the apartment so was really happy when Sophie had invited her to Honeyborne once she got back from Spain. Sophie had tried to apologise in advance that they would have to share a bed and their flat above the shop was tiny, but Victoria had stopped her. If you are with friends who cares was her view, anyway, they were practically sisters in every way, other than DNA.

When Sophie had called her in Spain to give her the daily update on Harry's situation and to ask if it was OK for Harry to spend some time in the apartment Victoria hadn't hesitated and only after Sophie's insistence had Victoria cleared it with her father. His only house rule up to then had been no men in permanent residence, apparently Pops had a rather low opinion of the average male student's ability to understand the basic concepts of hygiene. 'You'll never get rid of the smell' he had said, only half joking. As soon as Victoria had mentioned it was Sophie's 'Army' Harry, wounded in service, Pops had gone into overdrive and rattled off a list of instructions. Victoria was to: Phone his PA and book a car to collect Harry, move in with Sophie so Harry can have Victoria's room to get good rest and 'Get in some proper food for goodness sake', definitely no student pots or packets. Pops had sounded a little surprised when she mentioned Harry would probably be sharing with Sophie, Sophie having achieved almost angel status in her father's mind, but he quickly decided it was none of his business.

Victoria didn't tell Harry that she had been in a cab on the way to the airport and the hospital minutes after Sophie had first called in tears. She had turned back only when Sophie explained the hospital's next of kin rules and they had both decided there was no point to her being there. Victoria's mother hadn't understood why Victoria was so upset about a man she had never met or, for that matter, the bond between Sophie and Victoria. There was very little in fact that she did understand about Victoria, but when Victoria burst in to tears and grabbed her she knew it was important. She had been overwhelmed that her sometimes distant, often judgemental daughter was sharing her pain, a daughter seeking solace from her mother. After moments of holding and silence her mum had gently disengaged and disappeared into her room, returning, arm outstretched, offering something to Victoria. It was Victoria's old, battered bible from prep school which she hadn't seen in probably ten years and was more worn than she remembered. Seeing Victoria's confusion her mum had said it was OK if Victoria didn't believe, she wasn't sure if she really believed herself, it was though the only thing she could think of. Her mum had done something then that Victoria had never seen before, hadn't even considered her capable of. She had knelt at that spot, on the cold, hard ceramic floor tiles and prayed. She prayed earnestly for a man, a woman and a mother she had never spoken to, never met. Victoria knelt facing her and, holding the bible between them, they pleaded together for them all.

Victoria looked at Harry again then glanced over her shoulder. 'Relegated to the sofa? Have you two had a falling out already?' she said nodding towards Harry's neatly piled bedding.

'To be honest I'm never entirely sure when I've had an argument with a woman, but at this time I don't think so. We're friends, good friends I think, we're just not sleeping together friends. That's all.'

Sophie! thought Victoria, frustrated that her darling friend hadn't got herself what she knew she really, really wanted. Don't be polite, don't give him a chance. Grab him for goodness sake. Victoria couldn't help herself, she had to intervene.

'Harry, I know it's none of my business, but you know she wants to, don't you? You know she wants you?' Victoria paused to let the message sink in. 'If you were to climb in beside her now, right this minute, she would be very happy, and I wouldn't be in the slightest bit offended to be left in mid-conversation.'

A bedroom door clicked closed.

'Ah, good. I see you two are getting to know each other,' said Sophie, as she walked bare foot across the dining area, wide awake and excited.

'I feel I know so much about her already,' said Harry, with as much of a smile as his stitches would allow.

'Oh god, Sophie, I'm so sorry, so sorry,' Victoria apologised again, 'I forgot Harry was going to be here and I stumbled in half asleep and half undressed. As usual.'

'Well,' said Harry, 'I don't think waving a housecoat above your head really counts as being partially dressed.'

'So shall we say naked then?' asked Sophie. 'As in naked, butt naked, nude, sans a stitch, au naturel, birthday suit city?'

Victoria nodded with wide eyed shame.

'Well, I suppose it could have been worse,' sighed Sophie, shaking her head.

'How... exactly?' asked Victoria.

'Well, you could have been wearing your tatty old Santa sleeping shorts.'

'Mm, good point, so not a complete disaster,' agreed Victoria.

'Those I have to see,' said Harry.

'Never,' replied Victoria, '…ever.'

Chapter 17

Sophie sank down onto the metal chair and stretched her
legs under the table to rest against Harry's, giving a long,
caressing nudge so he knew it wasn't accidental. The soft,
sea-scented, occasional breeze cooled her bare shoulders and
the early evening sun rushed to warm her again. This was
one of his favourite places, he relaxed here, he loved to sit
looking out over the water. The ten or so simple wooden
tables, set back from and about two metres above the road
gave a clear view of the beach. Similar seating inside and a
well-staffed bar meant there was rarely a crush and service
was quick. The wall of doors, concertinaed open, allowed a
single, unbroken calming space. Sophie guessed that it was
an evening assembly point for those planning to eat in the
splendour of the hotel next door.

She imagined the surrounding low murmur of conversations
was from couples falling in love or exploring new found love.
How could it be that this man in front of her, everything
she could possibly want, appeared completely oblivious, or
worse, indifferent, to her feelings? She wanted to lean across
the table now and tell him, commit herself to him, give
herself to him, but she was sure if she did he would walk out
of her life forever.

She would even settle for just sex, she had made that clear
to him enough times, in a relaxed, jokey way, in the hope that
it would develop into something deeper, but he had gently
turned down every offer. What man would, could, do that?

Thank goodness Victoria had agreed to play gooseberry
again, otherwise she would probably mess up the evening by
saying something really stupid.

'One pint glass of ice, lots of sliced lemon and a large bottle
of Scottish sparkling water for Sir, two glasses of ice-cold

South African Chenin Blanc for the ladies,' said Victoria, as she carefully moved the drinks from the dark brown metal tray decorated with a cartoon of a toucan. 'Have you two actually said a single word to each other since I've been at the bar?' she asked as she sat down next to Sophie, frustration edging into her voice.

'Not really. I've been too busy imagining all the disgraceful things I'd like to do to his body with my body. Thank goodness you're back, I'm about to slide off of the chair.' Their giggles all the more enjoyed when Harry's face remained unmoved.

'Well,' Victoria started in a stage whisper, 'you'll have to…'

'Harry? Is that… good God. What are you doing in beautiful Brighton?'

'Elizabeth?' Harry stood up quickly and Sophie twisted in her chair to watch him stride across the patio to hug the tall, slim, red-headed woman, almost lifting her off of her feet.

Sophie's heart pounded as she saw the returned affection confirm a strong bond, a close history. He had never hugged her like that, never held her close and kissed her cheek like that.

The pale, almost translucence of Elizabeth's flawless skin suggested the red hair was natural. How did she look so attractive without makeup? Was she a model? She certainly made her supermarket jeans and trainers look good. Even the end-of-day creases in her calico blouse with casually strapped up sleeves made her look natural, effortless. The bright red nail varnish was the only suggestion that she had taken any time to present herself. Sophie guessed late twenties, just about within the lower range of Harry's apparent woman preferences.

Damn! How could she even begin to compete with this poised, self-assured beauty. Was she an 'ex', or worse, a 'not-ex'? Here in Brighton? There was something very strong between them. Had they…? Would they…? Damn! Sophie's confident teasing from a few minutes ago was now completely erased from history.

No! He was holding her hand, leading her to the table, inviting his 'Very good friend Elizabeth' to sit with them. No! Sophie felt helpless. Thank goodness Victoria was there to support her.

'Hi, I'm Victoria, nice to meet another friend of Harry's, there don't seem to be many of us about,' Victoria smiled, offering her hand across the table to the now seated Elizabeth. 'Can I get you a drink?'

'No thanks, I can't stay long,' said Elizabeth, shaking Victoria's hand then picking up Harry's glass of iced sparkling water and taking two good swallows before replacing it carefully in the dead centre of the beer mat, where Harry had put it with precision a few moments before.

Sophie stifled a whimper as she looked at Harry's glass and Elizabeth's stark finger marks in the condensation. Elizabeth had helped herself to his drink as if they were husband and wife or long-term lovers, and he hadn't even registered anything unusual.

Ring! Elizabeth was wearing a wedding ring! Surely Harry would never… Not a married woman. Or were the two of them actually…? That would explain so much.

'And this is Sophie, we're all sharing a flat just up the road,' said Victoria cheerfully.

'Hi Elizabeth, nice to meet you,' Sophie managed to offer, with what she hoped was convincing pleasantry.

Elizabeth turned to face Sophie directly, one eyebrow slightly raised. 'Sophie?' she asked with a curiosity that didn't quite fit the situation.

Sophie sensed an unasked question and saw it repeated as Elizabeth turned to look at Harry. Although Sophie didn't see a response Elizabeth's faintest hint of a smile said there had been one. Had Elizabeth known him so long she could see through his carefully maintained front? In a tone that Sophie could only interpret as warm and with no suggestion of competition Elizabeth said, 'I'm very pleased to meet you too.'

Sophie was confused. Had that been a smile of genuine warmth, or was it a confident signal of competition? She was beginning to think Elizabeth already knew a lot about her, much more than she knew about Elizabeth, which was nothing.

Why hadn't Elizabeth commented on the two prominent wounds on Harry's face, one just a few weeks old? They were certainly good friends so it wasn't through politeness. Had she already seen them? Sophie tried to think back to when Harry would have been out without her in the days since his leaving hospital. Or had Elizabeth actually visited him in the hospital whilst Sophie had been asleep or in the cafeteria? Next of kin were allowed in.

Surely Harry wouldn't have set up this chance meeting?

At Harry's prompting Elizabeth briefly explained that her mum and dad had moved their bakery business to Brighton. Two of the big supermarkets had opened convenience stores just a few minutes from their previous shop on the outskirts of Durham and the bank had then quickly called in their overdraft. It had been hard to up-sticks after thirty years of building a business, transport the whole family to the other end of the country and leave behind half a lifetime of friends, but they could see no alternative. Fortunately Justin, her son, had taken all of one day at his new play-school to decide he really liked their new house and the 'lots and lots of nice, nice toys' the school had in the 'big, big' cupboards. She had been lucky to find a job as an office manager in a publishing company just a ten minute walk away. It was busy, if not challenging and the money was modest, but much better than anything she had earned in Durham.

'How's Chip, is he with you?' asked Harry, 'I haven't spoken to him for a while, I think I may have an old phone number.'

'Yes, he's here with us. It's taking him a while to adjust.'

Whatever 'Adjust' meant Sophie saw the word hit Harry hard. The involuntary twitch of his usually expressionless face said so.

'Is Chip your husband?' asked Victoria casually.

Elizabeth stared at the unused beermat in front of her and took a deep breath. 'No, Chip's my brother. Chris, my husband, died,' she turned to look at Harry, 'three years ago.'

Harry nodded and held Elizabeth's gaze before both turned away.

'Oh, I'm sorry,' said Sophie and Victoria, almost in unison, both regretting the question.

Elizabeth's shrug signalled that she wanted the conversation to move on. 'How did you two gorgeous women manage to get saddled with this ugly lump?' she said, using her thumb to identify Harry, just in case there was any doubt. Her smile invited humour.

'Care in the community,' Harry responded with his usual dead-pan face. 'They've taken it upon themselves to make sure I realise how important it is to avoid accidents in the future.'

Elizabeth turned to look at Harry, her face cold. She clamped his jaw hard between her fingers and thumb and yanked his head around so she could see the raised tracks of scars on his left cheek. She took her time to survey the still red swellings before twisting his head away from her and turning to look away from him, dismissing him.

'Judging by the state of that mess they've got an uphill struggle. Get a new job Harry, or one day very soon they'll be delivering you in a box to the people that love you.' Elizabeth looked up to the sky and closed her eyes, struggling to control her voice, 'Like they did with my Chris.'

Sophie's confusion grew. In a matter of moments Elizabeth's relationship indicators had flipped from possible secret lover to a mother losing her cool with a persistently errant child. Was that guilt that zipped briefly across Harry's face?

'The stitches should have come out ages ago. I'll get Chip to dig out his medic kit tomorrow, let me give you the address,' said Elizabeth to no one, indifference now replacing her earlier see-saw of emotions.

Sophie's sense of helplessness was compounded when Victoria invited them all for breakfast the next morning. Sophie wanted to see less of Elizabeth, not more of her and now Elizabeth's family were being thrust into her life. What was Victoria thinking? Within a few short minutes of meeting Elizabeth was taking over and now the waiter Elizabeth had waived to earlier was coming to the table with a bag in his hand and a beaming smile all over his face. What now?

'Master Justin's special order of Thai fish cakes and Luigi has added two small South Coast Crab Cakes which he would like Master Justin's opinion on before he considers them for a new menu item,' grinned the waiter.

Elizabeth thanked the waiter and confirmed she would bring the pies and pastries delivery as usual at seven tomorrow morning.

As she stood to go Elizabeth apologised to the girls for darkening the moment, it had been a long difficult week, but she shouldn't have let it get the better of her, it was just that sometimes, as they had no doubt already discovered, Harry can be infuriating. She thanked Victoria again for the breakfast invitation and she, Justin and Chip would be knocking on their door at about seven-thirty tomorrow morning. Justin loved doing the Saturday morning deliveries with her although she would have to keep the breakfast a secret until the last minute otherwise he would be awake all night with excitement. Chip would no doubt be grumpy at being dragged to a social encounter, but it would do him good to talk to someone other than family and anyway, if Harry needed help even chains wouldn't keep her brother away.

Chapter 18

Sophie's stomach churned as she pressed the foyer-door release button to let in the smiling visitor. Seven thirty on the dot. Of course any friend of Harry's would be governed by an internal clock of atomic digital precision. Of course they would. Harry would appreciate that. Sophie had hardly slept all night and now felt puffy and decidedly unattractive.

Holding open the apartment door, and standing over the threshold Sophie practiced her welcome smile. It wasn't easy. The footsteps held a quick, steady skip up the five flights with no suggestion of slowing. At the sight of the shock of soft red curls bouncing upwards from the floor below Sophie sighed inside. Gorgeous hair *and* fit. Bugger.

Victoria's idea that getting to know your competition was better than avoiding them still wasn't making sense and Sophie decided that once the morning was over she would, as promised, strangle her flatmate.

This was going to be more of a challenge than she thought. Elizabeth was a likeable person and Sophie had been able to greet her with a genuine warm hug, although her smile had to struggle its way past gritted teeth. This beautiful, poised woman unpacking Harry's favourite pastries from the eco-friendly brown paper bag, (a small mercy she hadn't brought bacon rolls), was a perfect match for him. She probably didn't even have to work to keep that fabulous body tone. Sophie's self-perception, in the short walk from the door to the table, had gone from puffy to bloated and finally settled on a faithful representation of an overfed juvenile donkey. Even the smell of the still warm croissants and freshly brewing coffee couldn't lift her. Bugger. Bugger. Bugger!

Sophie invited Elizabeth to sit at the table and poured them both coffee from the steaming glass jug. 'Harry's just dragged himself into the shower. He overstretched himself again on our morning walk and had to sit for a few minutes. I don't know why he always has to push himself to the limit of his pain endurance.'

She was dreading Harry joining them. How would she react to his inevitable affectionate hug, lingering cheek-kiss and soft worded greeting for Elizabeth and the chummy smile-nod for herself.

Elizabeth sipped her coffee and *mmmed* in appreciation, then sat back in her chair, looking like a glossy magazine picture of the perfect available woman in a perfect home waiting for the soon to appear perfect available man.

It was like getting ready to watch the final scene of a love story where the beautiful heroine appears at the last minute to snatch up the gorgeous, but until then deluded hero and save him from the clutches of the unworthy, self-centred, frumpy, dull, uninteresting third character. Sophie's donkey-nose itched as it continued its transition to being even more donkey-like.

Elizabeth examined the chunky, squat, white coffee mug and then looked straight at Sophie, her voice calm, determined. 'Sophie, I've learned the hard way life's too short to beat about the bush so I'd like to tell you two things you need to know.' She took another sip of coffee and placed the mug dead-centre on the coaster. 'First. There are two Harrys. Human Harry, the warm, soft, caring, funny, good-company Harry we all love and enjoy being near. The one almost any sane woman in the world would want in their bed and in their life. The Harry you've fallen in love with.' Sophie's attempt at indignation didn't work and no words came from her open mouth. Elizabeth continued, 'Then there's Machine Harry, hopefully a Harry you'll never meet, driven by duty to Queen and Country, forever striving for perfection in the execution of the unspeakable things he is trained and tasked to do, unshakeable in his bond with those he works with. Those two Harrys can't co-exist, one will kill the other and personally... I hate Machine Harry, I want him gone, dead.'

Sophie didn't attempt to hide her anger and steeled herself to defend Harry, but somewhere in her subconscious more pieces of puzzle were clicking into place. 'What gives you the right to...'

Elizabeth continued, steady, determined, she spoke over Sophie, 'Because the machine in my Chris stole the man I love from me. The machine in my Chris robbed my son of his father. The machine in my Chris fed and fed off the machine in Harry, Chip and every other fucker in Red Fucking Team Five. And now the man I love and the father of my son, is in pieces, in a box, in the ground.' She took a crumpled tissue from her pocket and wiped the tears that were escaping down her cheeks then held the hand Sophie had slid across the table to her.

'Sorry about that. I still can't shake the pain away and sometimes it helps to let the anger out. Let's talk about something nice, it's the start of the weekend.'

Sophie smiled and squeezed Elizabeth's hand gently, 'I'm almost too scared to ask what the second thing was.'

'Oh yes,' said Elizabeth, calming herself and looking at Sophie again, 'I'm not competition. Although I expect you've guessed that.' Elizabeth smiled, 'And... Harry, Chris and Chip have... had, been close for several years and sometimes they forget I'm listening in. So I know somebody called Sophie has been inside Harry's head for a long time. He doesn't say much and men probably don't pick up on it, he probably didn't even realise the signals he was giving, or what this *Sophie* means to him, but I knew exactly what they meant. When I met you yesterday and looked at Harry's face I immediately knew you were *the* Sophie.' Elizabeth gently squeezed Sophie's hand. 'There's no doubt he wants you, but that horrible part of him is blocking you out... and I know only one of the two of you wants those bedclothes there,' she said pointing over her shoulder at the neat stack on the end of the sofa. 'If you want my advice, if you wait for him to ask you, you'll wait for ever. Grab him, don't give him a choice. To hell with convention, grab what you want and don't let go.'

Sophie glanced towards the bedrooms. A door had clicked closed and Harry, looking gorgeous in his dark green, soft cotton shirt and dark blue jeans, walked towards them.

'Don't let go of what?' he asked.

'Mind your own,' said Elizabeth, dismissing him, winking obviously at Sophie and then turning to receive a kiss to her cheek. 'Don't you know it's rude to kiss just one friend when there's others present? But I suppose that could be quite time consuming in the army.'

'But Sophie and I...'

'Kiss!' instructed Elizabeth impatiently, gesturing casually to Sophie.

Sophie's view of Elizabeth did a one-eighty flip now she recognised she had an ally, not yet another eager offerer of services to meet Harry's physical needs, the needs Sophie desperately wanted to be the sole provider for.

Sophie didn't know if the jolt of pleasure was due to Harry's obvious surprise or the sensation of touch as she turned her head and caught him, lips to lips. 'That's not really a kiss Harry, but it'll do for now,' she said, trying to sound indifferent.

'And to be absolutely clear Harry,' said Victoria, as she walked in, half asleep, having watched the event in silence from the doorway, 'adopted sisters only require cheek-kisses and only on birthdays and New Year.'

Victoria greeted Elizabeth and flopped onto the chair next to Sophie. 'Are we coffee-ing this morning? Good, my body's not used to functioning at this time on a Saturday. Be a darling Harry and get your little sis a mug please.'

After Elizabeth had expressed her envy of the *fantastic apartment*, Victoria had *mmmed* at the warm, comforting, buttery croissants and Harry had said he felt like he had somehow found himself in a Shakespearean scene involving three women stirring a very large pot, Elizabeth explained her brother's absence.

Chip had had a difficult few days. Volunteering part time at the nearby stables had helped a lot, and the dark clouds were less frequent, but he still wasn't free of them. As much as he tried he couldn't always hide them from Justin. Yesterday evening the four year old had climbed onto his uncle's lap, snuggled in under his arm and declared, in a tone strikingly similar to that often used by his ever-present grandparents, that what was needed was 'An ice-cream breakfast, and as soon as possible'.

Elizabeth laughed that right now the pair of them were probably sitting outside at Luigi's restaurant with her son force-feeding his uncle a large helping of double choc chip smothered in Luigi's homemade raspberry sauce, which by coincidence was also Justin's favourite. The little one had somehow worked out that his mother's strict healthy eating regime could sometimes be compromised when his beloved uncle Chip was involved.

'I've got his medi-kit, do you want me to do the stitches? They need to come out soon or some of them will be difficult to find,' offered Elizabeth.

'Yes, if you don't mind,' said Sophie, talking over Harry's attempt to speak, guessing he would try to delay. 'Should Victoria and I disappear for a while?'

'No, I think you should watch, if you're OK with such things,' replied Elizabeth, talking over Harry's attempt to speak, guessing he would prefer them not to be there. 'Feel free to ask questions. You may one day find yourself doing the same thing, if Harry keeps going the way he is, if he stays alive.' Elizabeth hoped those last words had their intended impact on all three.

'Ladies, you are witnessing an excellent display of pure bravado,' said Elizabeth, as she gently tugged a cheek stitch from under its overgrowing skin. 'I know it's hurting because his pupils are dilating, but being the macho warrior he is,' sarcasm crept into her voice, 'he's pretending it doesn't. I have no idea why he thinks he needs to do such a thing.'

Harry, sitting on the dining chair he had carried to the window, *for better light,* said nothing.

Once Elizabeth was sure the number of stitches in her small plastic bowl corresponded to the count on the written record Harry had been given on his discharge from hospital she flipped over to the next sheet.

'Right,' said Elizabeth, scanning the page, 'shirt off next please.'

'Do you think the girls should be here for the rest of it?' asked Harry with discomfort.

'Hey! You've seen me butt naked, I demand at least partial reciprocation,' said Victoria, with mock indignation. Then, seeing Elizabeth's raised eyebrows and realising some sort of explanation was needed, added, 'This was before I'd told him we are to be adoptive siblings. It was an accident, but he didn't even have the decency to check out my bosoms.'

Harry sighed. 'One centimetre diameter light brown birthmark on your left breast, pierced belly button with no adornment.'

Victoria couldn't hide her surprise. 'That doesn't prove anything, Sophie could have told you all that,' she defended.

'Oh yeah, for sure. I can't get him interested in my own boobs so I'm hardly likely to be bringing your magnificent rack to his attention,' said Sophie quietly, to no one in particular, shaking her head.

'Appendix scar, probably six-ish years old,' droned Harry, like he was reading from a tedious instruction manual.

'She could have told you that as well!'

'Blue butterfly tattooed on your right buttock, male avonius quercus is my guess,' continued Harry.

'And that!'

'Hollywood,' Harry paused, 'recently maintained.'

Victoria remained silent, her bright red face answering for her.

'OK, I'm definitely *not* going to be discussing *that* with him,' said Sophie firmly. 'Well done Harry. I'm not sure we need any more proof. And you…' she said, reaching over and giving him a light cuff across the top of the head, 'shouldn't be so damned observant!'

'Exactly. Shirt off please!' said Elizabeth tersely.

Victoria stepped closer, Sophie understanding the tilted head and puzzled look. Elizabeth lifted Harry's arm above his shoulder so the fading yellow, brown and purple colouring across a large part of the left side of his torso could be seen. 'This is what you get if you're lucky enough to be wearing body armour that can stop a high velocity, heavy calibre bullet when it's trying to smash its way through your insides and out of your back,' said Elizabeth, with indifference. She looked directly at Harry to make sure the next sentence was received as an admonishment rather than a question, 'Three ribs?'

'Two broken, two cracked,' he said quietly.

'And if he hadn't been wearing it?' asked Sophie, trying to swallow the lump growing in her throat, already sensing she wasn't going to like the answer.

Elizabeth looked through the window, into the distance, 'Then you and I would probably never have known each other, other than perhaps through a glance across church

In the Arms of Giants

pews, both wearing black, each wondering briefly who the other was. Plus of course half a square metre of a field in a foreign land being briefly enriched with…'

'I was wearing it, I'm here, it's a lovely Saturday morning, can we talk about something else please?' said Harry. 'How about getting back to breasts for instance?'

Sophie cuffed him again, thankful that Elizabeth's answer had been cut short, but deeply troubled because she knew Elizabeth was trying to tell her stuff she wasn't sure she wanted to understand. During her time sitting with Harry in the hospital the staff had kept his wounds covered whenever they could, but when his heart had stopped most of the light sheet had fallen from him. His scars, wounds and bruises, fresh and old, had hardly registered, her attention had been on his face as she willed him to breath, but they had become more and more vivid as her subconscious, against her struggles, replayed and reprocessed the scene over and over again.

Sophie and Victoria watched, wishing they could turn away, as Elizabeth systematically removed stitches, compared the numbers to the list and gently touched and massaged each wound. Humour gone, no one was able to joke as Harry complied with a hand gesture from Elizabeth to take his trousers off. Elizabeth said little. She asked what had caused the *mess* at the top of his left chest ('Something hot and sharp had found its way through') and then pointed out that he needed to keep an eye on the three blade wounds on his leg, one of them looked like it could be infected.

Elizabeth straightened her back as she stood up from attending to the leg and started checking the list against the wound sites, pointing to each list item and site in turn, mentally ticking them off. As she surveyed his back, he was sitting sideways on the chair, she stopped and stared at the back of his left shoulder.

She touched what looked like a long healed scar with the

tip of her tweezers. 'Is that…?' she asked quietly.

'Yes,' replied Harry.

'She stared at it, turned away as if trying to ignore it and then turned to stare at it again. 'Can I… touch it?'

'Of course,' said Harry.

Sophie didn't understand. Elizabeth's hands had been all over Harry's injuries without seeking approval, yet now she was asking permission to touch an old wound. Sophie had felt only envy for the woman's sure-handed, confident actions, no jealousy of what she thought now was a non-existent competitive relationship. The tip of Elizabeth's index finger lightly traced the full length of the ten centimetre jagged, lumpy scar tissue, then she rested the outstretched fingers of both hands directly on it.

Only when tear drops tumbled down Elizabeth's cheeks onto Harry's shoulder did Sophie realise that Elizabeth was crying. She instinctively put her arm around Elizabeth's shoulder. Elizabeth turned and accepted the touch before stepping back and wiping away the tears with the heels of her hands.

'Sorry, sorry. I slipped there.' Elizabeth took a deep breath and stared at the ceiling for a few seconds to gather herself together. 'My Chris did this stitching,' she pointed to Harry's shoulder, 'a few minutes before he died.' She looked at the scar, her hand moving to touch it again, but pulling back. 'Harry was with him. They won't tell me when, where or how, let alone why, but judging by the mess Harry was in when he got back, it wasn't a friendly place.'

Harry winced, a rare emotion across his face, 'Elizabeth… you know we… I can't…'

'Yes, yes, I know, Queen and Country et cetera. Whatever. I know it's not you Harry, let's get back to the here and now.'

Elizabeth took a deep breath to steady herself then waved the list at Sophie and Victoria, a theatrical grimace showing her teeth. 'Now girls, believe me when I say you do *not* want to watch the last bits. Bum stitches. No girl should have to peer into a man's butt-crack, especially if you have to share a flat. It could scar for life.' She looked directly at Sophie and winked, 'And double-especially if you have ideas about sharing more than that.'

'All over!' said Elizabeth, as she gave her hands a soapy scrub in the kitchen sink. 'I could do with a cuppa, poking around in the nooks and crannies of a hairy-arsed squaddie is not my favourite way to start the day.'

'Thanks Elizabeth, I wasn't looking forward to the trek back to Yeovilton and you know how it is with rumours if I'd used a local surgery. Confidentiality isn't always what it should be,' said Harry.

'Please Harry, just think about the ones that love you,' said Elizabeth, knowing no other words were needed.

As the four sat around the table sipping tea in silence Victoria decided to lighten the mood. 'So Sophie, you should know that, for men, a woman's bosom is a bit like the tempting red jam on a custard doughnut.' She paused until she saw two curious frowns and Harry's nervous glance. 'As soon as it's got their attention their focus immediately switches to planning how to get their tongue, as quickly as possible, into that creamy crevice.'

Sophie, wanting desperately to laugh and unable to swallow her mouthful of tea, or control its passage of ejection, ended up returning it to her cup via her nose. She gulped air haphazardly as the sobs of laughter racked her body. The two other women joined her, not knowing if Victoria or Sophie was the funnier.

Sophie, finally managing two reasonably close consecutive gasps, tumbled out some words, 'Victoria! Bloody hell! Why did you say it when my mouth was full?'

'And… getting your mouth full is their second objective,' Victoria shoved out before the three women, all now struggling to breathe, collapsed again into belly-aching laughter.

Harry, allowing himself a soft smile, sat back and soaked up the sight of his three good friends laughing and happy together, enjoying especially that it was at his cost. Too late to shut it out, he let the warm glow seep deep into him. He couldn't remember the last time anyone had found him funny, or the last time he had felt like this – happy and close.

Chapter 19

The three women had decided Harry would cook jollof rice for a late lunch and now the apartment was full of mouth-watering smells. Elizabeth hadn't been able to judge how her brother was feeling when she called him so she had asked to speak to Justin, under the guise of delivering a treat. Knowing Harry was in town and wanting to have lunch with him Justin would plead to be taken to his 'Big buddy' and Elizabeth knew he would only have to ask once. Whatever Chip's frame of mind, bringing a smile to his nephew's face always lifted him. *Each devoted to the other* wasn't an exaggeration.

Victoria's early interest in meeting Chip had been dampened when she sensed all was not well. She had enough problems of her own, she decided a long time ago she didn't have spare capacity to offer others. Nevertheless, a friend of Harry's would always be welcomed.

Victoria held open the apartment door and watched the little boy prise himself free from the strong arms keeping him safe then scramble with excitement up the last few stairs to stand, staring past her into the room. He turned to look up at her, his big brown eyes rendering her defenceless. In his haste to get his words out Justin's tongue wriggled around his mouth. 'Hello. I'm Justin pleased to meet you. Yes please. Thank you very much. I hope you are well. Don't mention it.' He took a deep breath. 'Do you have my Harry in there please? In there?' He peered past her again, crouching, arm outstretched, pointing into the room.

Victoria resisted the urge to scoop him up and smother him in hugs and kisses. 'You know, I do believe Harry *is* in there. Would you like to go inside and find him?'

Justin turned towards his uncle, saw the nod of approval

and shot past Victoria, into the room. 'Hello Harry, Hello Harry. Harry? Where are you Harry? It's me, Justin.'

Chip stood at the top of the stairs, being careful not to encroach on anyone's personal space, whatever that was. Two metres should be enough. 'Hi, I'm Chip. Sorry about that, he hasn't seen Harry for a while. He made me force-march all the way here and apparently I'm *getting old and slowing down*. He's going to be desperate for a wee, I'd better catch him and get him to the toilet before he floods the place.'

Victoria was embarrassed at her disappointment, she immediately knew Chip wasn't her type. He wasn't really what she could describe as handsome, he was plain at best and there was an obvious limp which he didn't try to hide. OK, he was clearly fit, articulate and emotionally mature, but that didn't explain why she didn't want to stop looking at him.

'Hello big fella,' Harry called out softly as the little boy ran into the lounge.

At his mother's one word instruction 'Shoes' Justin hurriedly removed his still buckled sandals, placed them neatly, side by side randomly in the middle of the floor and rolled himself sideways up onto the sofa, then quickly crawled along beside Harry.

Sophie couldn't take her eyes from the pair, she had never seen Harry like this. His iron control was abandoned to happiness as little arms around his neck pulled tight to press two slobbery lips and a runny nose into his cheek.

'Missed you Harry, where've you been?'

'I've missed you too fella. Have you been good for your mum?' asked Harry softly.

''Corse I have.'

Harry's nostrils flared as the little boy snuggled into his damaged ribs.

As Victoria introduced Chip Sophie found his scrutiny of

Victoria slightly disconcerting. What was he thinking? Surely she hadn't upset him, they had just this minute met. Sophie decided he must be in a bad mood. Harry and Chip were supposed to be very close and you wouldn't give a friend you hadn't seen in months a cursory nod and then sit at the other end of the sofa without a word.

Chip finally broke the silence that only Sophie and Victoria appeared to feel uncomfortable with. 'Food smells good, when's it ready?' he asked casually.

'In about nine,' replied Harry, relaxed and still enjoying Justin's hugs. 'We'd better eat soon or this little man's going to be asleep.'

Sophie couldn't see anything in the body language of the two men that would suggest friction yet they were hardly talking. It looked more of an indifference than deliberate ignoring, there was no animosity or frostiness that she could see. She was uneasy.

Justin, with a beaming smile, wiggled his bottom excitedly into the pile of cushions. He had been allowed to sit at the table between Harry at the head and uncle Chip to his right. His mother sitting opposite him had happily relinquished feeding supervision to the two men. Victoria, having quietly nudged Sophie to the far end of the table and now seated opposite Chip, looked everywhere except at the man she had already whispered to Sophie she thought 'a bit odd'. Sophie's discomfort had, if anything, increased as, with sideways glances, she watched Chip, wrists resting squarely on the table, stare silently at his place-mat. He was giving it the same detailed, close-up attention he had given a small patch of blank wall for a full minute or more just before his sister had called him to eat. Something wasn't right, but Harry and Elizabeth were relaxed so she decided she should try to be as well.

Harry's fragrant Jollof rice smelled delicious and looked

truly tempting. Bright orange pieces of carrot, vivid green slices of bean and occasional slivers of golden fried onion all vied for attention, but lost to the deep brown, crispy edged chunks of lean lamb emerging from the tomato-ey rice. Harry had presented it impressively in the large, blue, earthenware serving dish he had found at the back of a cupboard, probably its first ever outing and then, alongside it, plonked the microwaved spinach in a cereal bowl. The baked beans, still in their microwaveable container, and bottle of Worcestershire sauce, both a special concession to Chip, looked completely out of place. *Typical man* thought Sophie, identifying a good list of Harry's rough edges she should start to smooth as soon as possible.

After the first few mouthfuls had been enjoyed in silence, apart from the occasional clanking of cutlery on plates and appreciative *Mmms*, the complements started to flow. To ease Harry's discomfort Sophie let them know the recipe was from their favourite cookbook, written by a Ghanaian lady who was as beautiful as she was accomplished at African-Western fusion cooking.

'And we nearly missed it,' said Justin, after first chewing and swallowing everything in his mouth. He was hoping for seconds and didn't want to give his mother any excuse to say no. 'Uncle Chip was a bit slow, he's got a sore toe.'

'Can you believe a horse stood on his f…' Elizabeth stopped mid-sentence and looked up at Chip and then Harry before reluctantly finishing the last word, 'foot.'

Sophie, sensing tension, carried on with her explanation of how the author presented her own versions of classic African recipes and encouraged readers to make adjustments to suit their own preferences.

'A horse? What sort of horse?' asked Harry.

Sophie continued, saying how important it was to get the stock and sauce just right as a basis for so many Ghanaian dishes.

'An ordinary horse,' Chip responded, with a slight edge of defiance.

'Once I've finished university I'm going to save up and take us both on one of the courses she runs in Hertfordshire,' Sophie continued, as if a parallel conversation wasn't happening.

'One of those horses about eight foot high at the ears?' asked Harry again.

'Yes, one of those,' Chip responded.

'And weighing about half a tonne?'

'Yes. Half a tonne.'

Elizabeth looked at both men, shook her head and continued to eat.

Sophie's discomfort returned. Harry appeared to be baiting Chip, she had never seen him behave like this before and Chip's responses suggested he was irritated. Chip was a guest and this was wrong. Once she got Harry alone she would tell him his behaviour simply wasn't acceptable.

'Apparently it's a one day course and a lot of fun. We're really looking forward to it aren't we Harry?' said Sophie, in a tone she hoped he would recognise really meant *shut up*.

'One of those eight foot high, half tonne horses that makes a sort of clip clop clip clop noise when it walks?' said Harry, now with apparent superficial interest.

'Yes, one of those,' replied Chip.

'Clip clop clip clop clip clop,' repeated Justin, enjoying emphasising the last letter of each word.

'Eat please Justin,' said Elizabeth wearily.

Harry sat back in his chair and finished chewing. 'It's easy to see how an eight foot high, half tonne horse going clip clop could sneak up on a specialist in jungle warfare and tread on his toe,' he said, nodding.

Sophie froze in her seat and Victoria stared for the first time at the man opposite her as he carefully placed his knife and fork on the sides of his plate and stood up. At first Sophie thought he was going to walk out, but when he walked around to stand behind Harry she feared trouble. Surely they wouldn't come to blows? There was no way anyone in this room would be able to separate them. Her chest tightened.

Harry, relaxed, continued to eat. Chip, quiet and calm, reached from behind and placed his flat right hand over Harry's eyes. With his left hand he took the fork from Harry, held the large piece of tender lamb on it between his teeth and then returned the empty fork to Harry's grip.

'Just like you didn't see that coming,' said Chip, before going back to his chair, picking up his cutlery and making a noisy show of chewing his prize.

'And that,' said Elizabeth calmly to her son, 'is bad behaviour, by naughty boys, at a host's table. Never ever copy that silliness by your uncle and Harry.'

Justin, ignoring it all, continued to concentrate on his food. 'I don't know, always the same, will they ever stop being naughty?' he asked, tone and words again borrowed from granny.

The two men looked at each other, grinned and then laughed, the warmth between them now easy to see. Sophie and Victoria relaxed, the strength of relationship revealed, the depth not understood.

'If the last five years are anything to go by, I don't think they will,' said Elizabeth in a stage whisper to her son before she too returned to her Jollof.

Chapter 20

'Are you sure about this?' asked Sophie, 'it's a long way to the end of the pier and you're walking quite fast. Shouldn't we slow down, or not go so far or something?'

Over the last two weeks Harry had gradually increased the distance he walked every day and slightly increased his speed. Getting to the end of the pier was quite a bit further than yesterday, but he was sure he could do it. His head was clear and he was managing the sharp discomforts by taking only ibuprofen instead of the painkillers he had been issued. This time next week he should be able to walk to the end and back twice. At his last check-up they had signed him off duty for another three months, but they were wrong as usual, he intended to report back for duty in four weeks.

They strode along Madeira Drive enjoying his favourite part of the city, especially in the early morning, with the smell of the sea and the sound of waves crashing against the shingle cleansing his senses. There was something calming and serene about the sea here, it made him feel whole, comfortable, relaxed, washed. He liked to think that if humans had never walked the earth the sea, the shingle and the sounds would probably be pretty much exactly as they are now.

His ribs had started to ache from the more deliberate breathing and he could feel another cramp creeping through his left shoulder. He didn't understand how the wound under his arm, or was it the shard of mortar shell still in his chest muscle, could cause cramps, but they were just a nuisance and he was going to ignore this one. His left leg was also nagging, not surprising given the sudden increase in distance and pace. He knew how to manage pain and he would simply work through it. As soon as he reached the Ferris wheel he would up the pace again for the last few hundred metres to the pier end. Pain and gain, pain and gain he kept reminding himself.

Sophie had been with him on every walk and her fitness had improved with his. Striding comfortably alongside him, breathing easily and enjoying the exertion, she was sure their closeness was growing with every day. Looking at him sideways she worried if he was ready for this extra effort, maybe his stitches had been taken out too early.

She was relieved when they reached the furthest point of the pier where they could lean against the side rails and look down at the water. They stood unspeaking, gazing at the waves smashing effortlessly up the shingle beach, enjoying the rattle of pebbles tumbling over each other as they tried desperately not to be left behind by the whooshing retreat of the water. Sophie sometimes felt like a pebble. Harry had so many times rushed into her life, engulfing her, flooding her whole existence, then just as quickly soaking away, leaving her to tumble after him, never catching up to him.

Staring across the water to the Marina in the distance, Sophie spoke softly, 'Why won't you share my bed Harry?'

She waited, she wasn't going to let him off the hook, as she had so many times before, by breaking the difficult silence. He would either have to speak or ignore her.

'Sophie, you know I think the world of you, I care about you deeply,' he replied quietly, 'you are more of a friend than I could ever hope for. Look at how you're caring for me now, I really, really appreciate it, I do, but if we get together in that way it will change our whole relationship.'

'Sex Harry,' she said turning to look at him, 'Say the word sex, because that's what we're talking about. Not a betrothal, not a marriage, not a lifelong binding of our souls. Simple sex!' She took a deep, calming breath, she was close to having a rant and knew if that happened this exchange would be another waste of time.

'It might bring us closer, it might not change anything, who knows? What I want to know is why I'm excluded when you've obviously been going at it hammer and tongs with your previous not-girlfriends? I feel excluded Harry. Not good enough for you, like you can't be bothered or there's something wrong with me. What is it? Why? Is there something wrong with me? Tell me.'

'You know I'm never going to talk about other women Sophie, it wouldn't be fair. All I can say is that they were all, hopefully still are, good friends.'

'Good friends? What, like me? And you don't need to talk about them, it's always very obvious. You may be an expert at cargo, or camouflage, or concealment or clandestine operations or whatever it is you do in logistics, but you're absolutely useless at disguising where you're keeping your willy warm on a windswept winter's evening.

'I mean Nina for instance. It couldn't have been clearer if you'd taken pictures and posted them on social media. You thought you were covering it up by pretending to be casual acquaintances in public? Don't they teach you anything about body language in the army? Maybe they should teach you some basics about women because you clearly don't know a great deal.

'It was obvious to just about everybody that you two were in rabbit mode. I mean, Christ, if Nina hadn't got back with her girlfriend there's every likelihood you two would have shagged each other to a standstill!'

At first Sophie had regretted mentioning Nina and tried hard to stop talking, but once it was out it had become therapeutic and the words kept coming. She was going to get everything off of her mind.

'Then there was the Welsh woman at the check-out in the hardware store, that didn't last long and Lucy Wilson - Wilson Shoes. She must have been a good fifteen years older than you? Poor Lucy.' Sophie shook her head in honest sympathy. 'It may have been *good friends* for you Harry, but you broke the poor woman's heart when you did one of your disappearing tricks. She loved you, probably still does, wherever she is.'

Sophie returned Harry's stare. What were his eyes saying? Were they pleading with her to stop? Was he finally understanding that not everyone thought about relationships in the one-dimensional way he did and maybe he was causing damage to people he cared about and who cared deeply about him? Was it possible she had found a chink in his thick, self-serving, cold-steel armour, a way past the emotion-free zone that he used for protection? She knew it was a construction of his own making. She knew the real Harry, the Harry she wanted, was in there somewhere. She was close, she was going to find her way in. And she was going to have him, all of him, every single bit of him.

'You know I can't tell anyone where I go or when, very often I don't know myself. That's just how my job is. I thought Lucy understood. When I got back I looked for her, but she'd gone,' said Harry, more to himself than Sophie. Sophie thought there was something unusual in his voice, the normal quiet confidence wasn't there.

'Of course she'd gone. What did you expect? One minute you're playing warm-the-secret-sausage and the next minute you've disappeared without trace, not a word for six months! Not a text, no email, nothing!'

Sophie had liked Lucy even though in her early smitten days she considered Lucy as competition. They were friends, as much as a woman in her late thirties could be with a schoolgirl. Long before Harry had disrupted her life Lucy had always had a smile and a wave for Sophie. She would call Sophie in to the shop just before the sales and give her first choice, often adding an extra 'Clear out old stock special discount' which Sophie knew was really a *Sophie* special discount because the shoes were always recent stock and she wouldn't have been able to afford them otherwise. Lucy was simply a plain, honest-to-goodness nice person and Harry had crushed her.

'Somehow she knew there was a connection between you and me and kept asking if I'd heard anything. Can you imagine what it must have taken for a mature woman to ask a girl if she knew where her lover was? In tears? She cried Harry, really cried, you broke her. In the end I wasn't sure if she believed me. I had to ask your mum to explain to her that this was your usual behaviour and you'd probably be back in another few months, but no one would know when, until the next time you got off the train.

'Then one day, six months after you had left, she came into our shop to say goodbye. She had put her business up for sale with a broker and was heading North, possibly Manchester. That was it, she was gone.'

Was that worry creeping across Harry's face? Was he counting months? Should she tell him, or give him a taste of what it's really like not to know? She waited.

He started to speak. 'Did she…'

Sophie spoke over him, 'No, she wasn't pregnant.'

Harry was blank again, no messages. Could he have felt something special for Lucy? Was he relieved or disappointed that Lucy hadn't been pregnant, she wasn't sure. Had Sophie woken something that otherwise would have slept and eventually disappeared? Would he try to find Lucy, even after all this time? Suddenly Sophie didn't feel so confident.

'So back to my original question,' said Sophie bringing him back to the here and now, to them. 'What's wrong with me? Why am I excluded?'

Harry looked back across the water to the marina. The sun was low on the horizon and warming him through. For many it would be another perfect day.

'There's so much I want to tell you, but I'm not allowed to. Stuff that might change your mind about me,' he said.

'I get it Harry. Your job is your job and you have to do what you're told. If it's not illegal I don't care. I accept I might not like it, but I really don't care. Let's shut that line down and move on,' she said with impatience.

'When you were with me in the hospital you heard a lot of speculation about where I'd got these wounds, how my absence had coincided with the diamond mine thing.'

Sophie listened intently. There had been so much talk in the hospital, much she shouldn't really have been privy to, and it painted a different picture to her understanding of logistics. Lots of things didn't make sense and she had quickly stopped trying.

Harry continued, he wanted to pour it all out, tell her everything, but he knew he couldn't. 'The press said there were seventy three or so hostile deaths and four injuries. No hostage or rescue team fatalities. That suggests that the rescue team were efficient and ruthless in their execution of the operation. They didn't just neutralise, they destroyed, to make sure nothing got in the way of success.'

'Harry, I get it. I get it. You work as a team and sometimes people die. I know any death is dreadful, but it's part of what the Armed Forces sometimes have to be involved with, although what part logistics plays I don't know and don't really want to know. I don't think any worse of you for being caught up in that stuff,' she said softly, hoping to put him at ease.

'Lucy, I'm trying to expl...'

'Lucy?' she exploded. 'Who the *fuck* is Lucy now?' Sophie stamped her foot and rounded on him. 'Right. I'm going home. You can follow me if you like, or you can wait to see if *Lucy* or any other of your fuck-friends show up.' She turned and strode off, noting from the corner of her eye that he was following, hobbling slightly, but following.

She had surprised herself at losing her temper and swearing. She rarely did either, but right now it was a release. She was hurt and *angry*.

Walking briskly, but not too briskly, she shouted at him over her shoulder, not looking back, making sure he knew she didn't really care if he heard or not.

'I'm Sophie. My name is Sophie. So-phie. I'm the one that stayed with you in hospital. I'm the one that's dropped everything to look after you these last weeks. I'm the one who's constantly watching over you to make sure you're OK.' She slowed her pace slightly in case he was struggling to keep up.

'And in case you're still confused, *I'm* the one you are *not* fucking. You may have me mixed up with one of the dozens you *have* fucked and for all I know are *still* fucking.'

The swearing wasn't helping any more, it really wasn't her, and hurt was pushing anger aside.

'If you want Lucy go and find her. Get on the bloody train and head north, just don't keep me dangling like a puppet. If you damned well don't mind!' The shouting and anger had all but drained her emotional energy. 'How can you treat me like this? Why do you treat me like this? You can't really think it's fair on me.'

She walked on, slower now, the pain in her heart sapping the little energy she had left.

'It's not fair Harry, you know I care deeply for you, please be straight with me. When I saw you in the hospital and they said you may not survive I didn't know how I'd cope if you weren't in this world with me.' Oh god she was pleading now. What the hell, she decided to go for it.

'You know I love you Harry, I've loved you since the moment I first saw you. You know that. Knowing you were with all those other women really hurt me, my only consolation was thinking you didn't love them, but do you love Lucy? Have I lost to her?' Why couldn't she stop talking? Her mouth was out of control.

'I love you Harry, I want to be with you forever. I want you to father my children.' Shit, where did that come from? Oh Lord, it's true.

'That's it, all out, now you know, I love you,' she sighed. 'Say something, anything, don't ignore me,' she said, turning to look at him for the first time since walking away from the pier end.

'What? Where?...' she stuttered. Where was he?

She looked back along the pier. The swine hadn't even bothered to follow, he was sitting on a bench staring at the deck. Swine! She felt sick. She had forced him into a corner, forced him to make a decision and he had made the wrong one. He had probably called someone, probably another woman, to come and collect him.

Wait. Was that Harry? It must be him, but how could it be? Harry always sat up ramrod straight and this person was slumped forward. She started to walk back up the pier. It was him, something was wrong, she started to sprint.

'What is it? What's wrong?' she shouted as she got close, her vision blurred.

He half turned and forced a smile.

'I'm OK,' he mouthed.

She crouched in front of him, panting, looking at a man in serious pain.

'I had another cramp in my shoulder and it set everything else off all at once. It's beginning to loosen a bit.'

Sophie walked behind the bench, pulled him gently to sit up straight and started to massage his left shoulder. The muscles were in spasm. 'Wow, they're as solid as a block, all the way from your back to your neck.' She worked steadily along the muscle group pulling, pressing and stretching as she had learned in one of the short massage sessions a mature student had run during her first semester.

She could feel the muscle and the man relaxing. She had never heard him make any noise whilst in pain so she knew his quiet moan was from pleasure. Ooh, what was happening? She was feeling her own little bit of pleasure as well.

'I've done something a bit stupid,' he said quietly.

'Let's not start a list,' sighed Sophie, her anger evaporated, 'or we'll be here all day.' Then, emboldened by her earlier release, 'No, let's start one. What can we put at the top of the list? Let me see... Hmm, I know, Harry's stupid thing number one, not shagging Sophie, even when she puts it on a plate for him.'

'I didn't take my pain killer this morning before the walk,' he said.

'Ah, that might explain things, it's not like you to forget. Luckily I have some of your antibiotics and pain killers in my back pack and a bottle of water.' She rummaged around the numerous emergency items in her small brown canvass haversack and handed the tablets and water to him over his shoulder.

'I took the antibiotics, I deliberately didn't take the pain killers. I don't like the dreamy, light-headed way they make me feel. Now I think I'm going to need to take two.'

'Yep, that does count as stupid, almost up there with list item number one,' she said.

She continued the gentle massage, moving her finger tips steadily deeper into the muscle and felt him relax as the tablets kicked in. She so wanted to hold him, Lucy or no Lucy. She let her left hand slide down over his warm chest to his stomach and leaned forward to gently kiss the side of his head. He smelt so good. She expected his hand to move to hers then move both away. She took the moment to enjoy her lips on him and the warmth of his body, her inner arm enjoying the touch of his chest.

His right hand moved across, but simply pressed her hand onto him. His left hand came up and, pulling her head carefully down, he twisted and kissed her lips, full and gentle. A flash of brilliant white pulsed through her. Everything she wanted was her, now. His deliberate breathing thrilled her.

'What are we doing?' he asked quietly, pulling his head away, but then moving it back to rest his lips on hers again.

This time she pulled away, slowly brushing her lips across his stubbly cheek, then his still angry scar, before gripping the lobe of his ear with her lips and gently tugging it.

She knelt on the bench beside him and kissed his temple. 'Harry Stone,' she whispered in his ear, 'I think you enjoyed that kiss and… in this moment, I think you want me. Now… I have to decide when you can have me.'

She leaned back, 'Come on, let's get you home, before the pain killers have you floating off into the clouds.'

Forcing him to take a cab would have done more harm to his ego than good for his now vulnerable body so as a comprise, for the first time, Sophie set the pace walking home, making it clear that any attempt to speed up would be severely dealt with. She was as eager as him to get home, certainly for very different reasons. She had to pace him, she didn't want him pegging out half way.

Harry wouldn't admit it, but he was enjoying this slip of a girl taking charge and he knew why. He would have to bin those damn painkillers as soon as she wasn't looking.

Sophie relaxed at the satisfying, solid clunk of the apartment door as it closed them in. She held his shoulders from behind, steering him away from the sofas and towards her bedroom.

'You need to lie flat, in a proper bed, with a proper pillow, scrunching up on a sofa is not a good idea.'

She manoeuvred him to the window side of the bed, the

spare side.

'Kit off and in,' she instructed with deliberate indifference.

Her decency gene made it quite clear she should look away as he undressed, but her smutty gene barged it aside. *Sod it – I'm watching*, she thought, involuntarily licking her lips and enjoying the tingling elsewhere.

She wondered at the discipline that made him, even in his current physical mess, fold every item of clothing into a neat rectangle as he took it off. Each rectangle exactly the same proportions, stacked one on the other with the biggest item at the bottom and the smallest at the top, placed dead-centre on one of the two padded grey stools by the bed. Who else would fold socks? According to the oldie soldier films she had seen a flamboyantly moustached sergeant major should march through the door about now and inspect the geometry of the pile with a stick designed especially for that purpose.

Harry – you have a serious bod, she thought. Toned and in perfect proportion, not gym-junkie, more business-like, efficient, almost intimidating, dangerous. Even the fading yellow and purple bruising around the broken ribs made him look slightly exotic, special. She started to feel a little light-headed as she fought hard to slow down the lungs that were pumping large amounts of oxygen into her system.

Why on earth did he have to wear those green army pants? He looked so much better in his bum-hugging boxers.

Damn! He was leaving them on.

Harry pulled back the cover and lowered himself carefully down. He lay flat, savouring the sensation of the soft mattress supporting his full length before using the light summer duvet to cover his lower body. That felt good, really good. Why was she staring at him? He couldn't think what he might have done wrong or was it the scarring and bruising that was making her uncomfortable? He had been right to leave his pants on, bullet holes through the butt cheeks were enough to make anyone queasy.

His ribs protested as he reached down to pull off his underpants then drop them by the side of the bed, he hated sleeping in them, but now he would have to deal with them not being folded.

He breathed in deeply, the smell of her in the bedclothes immediately swamped his senses and he couldn't stop himself imagining her lying beside him, pink, warm, soft, naked. Oh shit! His lower body started to react, out of control, the duvet offering minimal concealment. He should have left his pants on.

'Close your eyes and sleep,' she said softly, 'I'll sit here for a short while, until you nod off.'

Chapter 21

Harry floated slowly upwards from the satisfying depths of a deep, fully embracing, comforting sleep, gradually becoming aware of the soft bedding, the pillow caressing his neck, then the smell of her. He breathed deeply, and sighed. The aches and pains had almost completely gone, he felt good and was looking forward to her company again now the nonsense of the pain killers was wearing off. He was back in control.

From the intensity of the sun streaming through the window and onto his still closed eyes he guessed it was around nine, he must have slept for a solid hour. He should get up, find her and make sure she understood how grateful he was, how important her friendship was to him. He had no idea how he was going to explain the Lucy name slip up, it was just a clumsy, but understandable mistake. Hopefully she would know that men just aren't so good with names and after all, both names ended in an 'e' sound.

'Good morning sleepy baby.'

Sophie enjoyed his startled look and the blinking as he tried to focus, then the double take as he noticed she had swapped her charcoal walking hoody for the loose, pale apricot, cotton blouse. She enjoyed his sideways glances when the loose buttons fell undone to the middle of her tummy, as they often did. The blouse tended to make her almost shapeless and she wondered if he was imagining going in search of hidden treasures. This morning the buttons were done up to the top, for now anyway.

'Don't worry,' she tutted, 'I'm dressed, I was just tired and didn't want to leave you alone so I sneaked in this side.'

She adjusted the duvet around her chest and propped herself up on her elbow. She tucked stray strands of hair clumsily behind her ear, the same strands that she had just a few seconds earlier ruffled over her face to make her look sleepy. She had read somewhere that men felt attracted to women who looked sleepy.

'Thanks for looking after me this morning,' he said, 'I really appreciate it. I can't believe I was so stupid. And then taking the double dose of pain killers was ridiculous, you saw what effect they had on me, totally out of character. I'm sorry about that as well.'

'Forget it,' she said quietly. 'You know it really frightened me seeing you like that, I was scared for you.' She counted three seconds in her head. 'I'm still a bit out of shape, can I come for a hug?'

'I'd love to Sophie, but I don't have any clothes on, it's probably not a good idea. I don't think...'

'Well I'm fully dressed,' she spoke over him, then with mock tedium in her voice, 'and... I promise I won't touch your *thingy* unless you absolutely beg me to.' She batted her eyelids. 'Please,' she whined sweetly.

'OK, but no funny stuff,' he said, immediately thinking it was a bad idea as he lifted his left arm straight across the pillow so she could snuggle in close.

She shrugged the duvet further up over her shoulders and quickly wriggled across to him, one sneaky tug opening all of the blouse buttons as she went. Her left leg shot across the top of his thighs, squeezing their lower halves together, her left arm slipped quickly across his chest so she could bury her hand under the other side of him. There! They were well and truly clamped.

'Mmm,' she sighed contentedly, nestling her cheek against his shoulder and kissing his neck lightly, 'this is nice.'

'Err, Sophie,' he said without emotion. His left hand, flattened and stiff, hurried under the duvet dabbing her side down to her hip, then her bottom, rather like he might be checking a kettle to see if it had just boiled.

'Sophie,' he sighed with irritation, 'you are naked.'

'Mmm.'

'We've been through this so many times,' he said, his voice not as even as he wanted it to be, 'we've discussed it so many times, each with the same result.'

'Well, that is true,' she admitted softly, 'but each time we've discussed it we've always been standing up, at least two metres apart and fully dressed. I thought this time we should discuss it lying down, close together and without clothes on.' She kissed his neck again, then wriggled to make sure as much as possible of her naked body was touching his own warm, muscled nakedness and her left breast was resting, not pressing on him.

He pulled his head away to look at her, then moved it back so they were almost nose to nose. 'You… are stark raving bonkers,' he said softly, smiling as much as his scarred cheek would allow.

She looked into his eyes as she moved her left thigh up and then down again across his groin. 'And judging by what's going on down there,' she said, surprised at the huskiness of her own voice, 'I think we might get a very different result this time.'

His deliberate breathing excited her. Was now the time to tell him? Her secret? She had always promised herself she would, before they did it, but how would he react? Perhaps it was too late, she had let it go too far. If she told him now he may feel deceived, be angry and turn away, forever. If she didn't tell him he would guess, he would certainly work it out pretty quickly. Then what? Tell him now! Just blurt it out! No! Wait! Keep quiet! It wasn't her fault, everybody's different, it wasn't as if she had really been given a choice.

His right hand rested softly on her shoulder, his fingers tracing small, light circles on her skin, caressing. His lips pressing gently on hers removed any thoughts of speaking, the decision had been made for her.

Then all moving things stopped, frozen. His hands lifted away from her and he jerked his head back on the pillow. Was it her breath? No, it couldn't be, she had brushed and mouth-rinsed extra thoroughly, then freshened her bits before sneaking in beside him. He had guessed! He had guessed her secret, but how? Some sort of extra sensory signalling that men pick up on?

He seemed to be having a conversation with himself, or the ceiling. 'What the hell are you doing Harry?' he asked another Harry who was apparently somewhere in the room. 'What are you thinking of? You can't do this to her. Where's your discipline?' he said shaking his head. The other Harry responded sharply, 'She's driving me crazy, this woman. She's beautiful. I'm only human!'

Sophie wasn't sure if she should be listening to what appeared to be a private conversation and glanced around the room, checking to see if someone had actually sneaked in to save her. She didn't need saving thank you! Bugger off!

Harry, turning to face her, took a deep breath and breathed out slowly.

'Sophie, you're a wonderful, beautiful woman, I've tried, I can't resist you any more, I give up,' he said quietly.

The warmth of his gentle kisses, his hands moving lightly over her body, took Sophie to a place of happiness she had never visited before. She felt giddy, she abandoned herself to him and whatever he would do next.

Harry stopped moving. Again. Sophie dragged herself back from the semi-conscious, pleasure induced state she had lost herself to. Surely, even if he had discovered her secret, he couldn't turn away now. Could he?

'Slight problem,' he said, trying to slow his breathing.

'What? What is it?' she said with the same breathing challenge.

'I wasn't expecting… I hadn't planned… I don't have any condoms.'

Sophie relaxed, his caring was yet another tick on her checklist of his perfection.

'I'm on the pill,' she said matter-of-factly into his cheek. She didn't bother to explain her mother had agreed to it a long time ago, to help stabilise her otherwise distressingly disruptive cycles. 'And, I happen to know I don't have any diseases, infections or other such unwanted things in the areas we're interested in right now.' She kissed his neck lightly, 'And, as you've just come out of a military hospital, where they no doubt check you from toe to head for everything known to man, I doubt you have either.' She moved up to kiss the corner of his lips, 'And, if you're still not happy,' she said, reaching under the pillow, 'we can use these *Ultra-sensitive, extreme pleasure, ribbed condoms for lovers.*'

Harry took the packet from her, looked at it, looked at her, then flicked it over his shoulder. 'Let's keep them for later,' he said, returning to his exploring, what the military part of his brain was subconsciously categorising as a territorial familiarisation.

Sophie couldn't find her way back into her semi-stupor of pleasure. Something wasn't quite right. She had enjoyed every moment, every leisurely new touch of every new place, and every leisurely re-exploration, but she was getting worried that he hadn't ventured to the one place she so wanted to share with him. Could it be… no, she was fresh, she had made doubly sure of that. Was he nervous, having second thoughts? No, 'nervous' and 'Harry Stone' never appeared in the same sentence. He must have been in lots of dangerous places, this wouldn't worry him at all.

But actually, for the first time ever with a woman, Harry was just that, nervous.

Sophie wasn't prepared to wait any longer, she was about

to burst. She took his hand and pressed it on to her hip then slid it firmly behind and down. Finally fingertips found their way to where she wanted them to be.

'Ooooh.' The air rushed from her lungs.

She pressed every part of her body hard against him, gripping him, then staying still, the only way she could think of to let him know he was getting it very right. Her breath came in short, sharp pants.

Then everything was a heady blur. She remembered abandoning all thoughts and pushing her tongue as far as it would go into his mouth, his own forcing its way past hers, in an apparent desperate quest for her tonsils.

Her knee had somehow appeared on his side, she hadn't noticed him turn to face her, and his hand had stopped delivering its magic.

For the first time she recognised the frightening, brute strength of the animal holding her. Harry was gone and this animal that gripped her, snorting like an enraged bull, every muscle hard, taught, moved her body about like a rag doll. She abandoned all control over what would happen next, he would decide how he would use her. She was both petrified and ecstatic. She would tell him now, tell him she loved him, then tell him her secret.

The first thrust silenced her. The short, sharp pain, already a somehow-memory, forgotten in the mind-numbing pleasure and satisfaction that swept through her and reached every part of her.

At first every movement, hers and his, was almost angry, punishing, uncompromising in their search for maximum contact and its ensuing spikes of pleasure, every other sense numbed, ignored. She wanted it to go on for ever.

She was relieved when he recognised her nearing exhaustion and lowered them both, still entangled, to rest. Then gentleness, swaying, reciprocation, each taking pleasure from knowing they were joined to the other.

Sophie felt her own animal fighting its way to the surface, making her movements more abrupt, quicker.

Then Harry stopped moving. Again.

That wasn't what Sophie was expecting. 'Have you…? Have we…?' she asked trying to sound relaxed, but appearing far from it. 'Are we done?'

What happens next, what should she say? She should say something, oh yes, 'That was very good Harry, you were wonderful,' she cooed.

'Ribs,' he muttered, 'I think I might have set them back a bit, I have pain.' Then as an afterthought, 'Trying to keep up with your wild antics.' He laughed, which made his ribs hurt more.

'I can breathe OK, but you'll have to do the rest of the work.'

Sophie's heart sank, she would have to tell him. She desperately wanted to keep going, but he would guess immediately.

'I'm not sure… I'm not sure what to do. How do I…? I've… never had sex before.' There, it was said, her secret was out, anyway it was old news now, Harry had made it old news.

Harry searched her face for some sort of April Fool smile. 'You're joking, right?'

'No,' she said quietly, searching his face for reaction. 'I'm a virgin, or was until about ten minutes ago.' She thought humour might ease the situation, 'and about a million hard strokes ago.'

Harry didn't move. She needed to break the silence. 'Don't be angry Harry, I was going to tell you, but I, we, just got swept away. It doesn't make any difference, does it? We still want to be together. Don't we?'

Another silence and still she couldn't read him, although

she took reassurance from there being no deterioration in the status of the physical connection between them. She could feel his pulse.

'Just when I think you can't surprise me any more you come up with something else. Extraordinary,' he said flatly. 'Of course it makes a difference.'

Was he in pain? Had she hurt one of his wounds? His eyes seemed to be watery.

'A beautiful, intelligent, articulate, warm woman who could have just about any man she wanted, like this,' he clicked his fingers, 'and you give this gift to *me*. Of course it makes a difference.'

He blinked his eyes clear, pulled her close and kissed her forehead, her eyelids, her nose, her lips. 'More of a difference than I know how to cope with right now.'

Sophie gave her bottom the wriggle she had been dying to do since they started talking. 'In the meantime can we get on with it,' she demanded, matron like.

Sophie suddenly found herself on top and astride him, still connected. How did he know how to do that?

His hands clamped firmly to her hips, he pushed her backwards and forwards. 'Keep doing that until we both collapse.'

Oh yes, oh yes, oooh yes, this is definitely working. She started to feel less of an amateur. Until her enthusiasm disconnected them.

Several backwards thrust bore no results, apart from one that would have, if she had not shot forward, resulted in another type of first-connection she was definitely not ready for.

'You have to steer,' said Harry urgently, 'with your hand. Steer.'

'Ah, OK.' She reached behind her, then stopped. 'Wait… A promise is a promise. You have to beg.'

'What?!'

'I promised not to touch it unless you begged.'

'Sophie! OK, please!' There was urgency in his voice.

'That's reeeally not begging Harry,' she said, her voice husky and deep.

'Oh shit! OK please Sophie, please, please, please. Please grab hold of it and stick it back in. Please!'

'OK, if you insist.'

The intensity and acceleration of her pleasure surprised her. She had lost all capacity for rational thought. Whatever was driving her was beyond control. She looked down at Harry through unfocused eyes, he was looking as desperate and out of control as she felt.

'Breasts,' she gasped breathlessly, 'grab my breasts. Squeeze.'

'Beg.'

Without breaking her punishing rhythm, she wrenched his hands from her hips and rammed them onto her chest.

'Now!'

'OK.'

Their rhythm turned to shuddering, desperate squirms until they jerked and groaned to spent stillness together.

She didn't need to be told the encounter was complete, but the soppy, soggy disconnection confirmed it.

She flopped exhausted onto her back beside him, enjoying the flood of emotion, enjoying the closeness, the confirmation of the bond between them. He, Harry Stone, was hers, at last. And she was most definitely, without question, his.

'Harry, that was wonderful, I've never felt so close to anyone,' she said quietly. She took a deep breath. 'I need to tell you now Harry. I love you, really, really love you. I've loved you since I first saw you. I want to be with you, be yours, forever.'

Harry responded, with a low, contented snore and a few moments later another.

(

Chapter 22

Victoria, glanced up at the sound of footsteps coming into the dining area, but without diverting her attention from the important task of getting the tea right. It was builders tea this morning, but builders tea required the same care as the best Earl Grey.

'Morning Sophie, good timing, a fresh brew.'

'Good morning.'

Victoria stopped in mid-pour and, still holding the kettle, turned to look directly at Sophie.

'Well, look at miss cat-who's-just-had-the-cream,' she smiled, 'something's made you very happy. C'mon do tell, please.'

Victoria finished the pouring, abandoned the kettle and carried the steaming tea pot to the dining table, setting it down in its appointed place beside the three bone china cups and saucers and milk jug. She had forgotten the pot-cosy, but who cared, something good had happened to her dear Sophie and she wanted to hear. As they say – 'A happiness shared is a happiness doubled' – or something like that.

Sophie stood holding the chair back, across the table from Victoria. Was she so easy to read? Or was it just that Victoria knew her so well? She had crept out of bed, leaving Harry to sleep, to recover from his hard work and it had taken all of her control not to burst into song in the shower. Normally she was frugal with the shower gel, it was ridiculously expensive, but this morning she had taken a triple squeeze without care and enjoyed the thick, fragrant suds caressing her weary body. She had grinned as she realised it would soon be Harry soaping her all over and then it would be to hell with counting the squeezes. Her tummy tingled - exactly how tired might he actually may be right now? Perhaps...?

No, better let him sleep.

'Well?' Victoria prompted impatiently.

'Harry and I, we...'

'What? What? Cuddled? Held hands? Kissed? He kissed you? He *kissed* you! What?' Victoria was almost beside herself with excitement at the thought of Sophie getting closer to the man she so obviously loved.

'We did it.'

'What? Did what?' Victoria didn't like guessing games and she started to wonder if this was a joke. Then she understood Sophie's smile, the contentment in her voice. 'You had sex? You and Harry screwed?'

Victoria was already on her way around the table as Sophie nodded shyly. Victoria enveloped her in a smothering hug and kissed her hard on the cheek. 'Wonderful, wonderful, wonderful,' was all she could say.

'Now,' said Victoria, pouring the tea and pulling her chair closer to Sophie's, 'tell me everything. No, on second thoughts. Brother, I have to think *brother*, Harry is now my brother. Darn! That would be weird. Just tell me how you got together.' Victoria watched Sophie like a child watching a favourite dessert being dished up and willing the portion to be big.

Sophie shared everything, in detail, up to the first physical encounter. The argument, the swearing, Lucy, the pain killers, the massage, Sophie's worry for Harry's well-being, the slow walk home. Victoria thought Sophie's sneaking into bed with just a blouse on was a master stroke and begged her to repeat that bit of the story.

'I'm just a bit worried I may have done damage to his wounds,' said Sophie. 'He pretty much fell asleep as soon as we finished.'

'They all do darling,' sighed Victoria, 'I think men have some sort of hard wiring between their testicles and the sleep centre in their head. As soon as they ejaculate they go unconscious.'

Victoria poured more tea as they giggled. It was only warm now, but she wasn't ready to get up and make more yet.

'So tell me Sophie,' asked Victoria, with a serious frown of concern, 'knowing about his multiple knife, bullet and shrapnel wounds, broken ribs, general physical exhaustion and obvious pain, at what point, did you think *How can I improve his situation? I know, I'll fuck his brains out!*'

They collapsed together laughing. 'Bloody hell Sophie, if you ever trained as a physiotherapist,' Victoria gasped for air, trying hard to control herself, tears streaming down her cheeks, 'your patient mortality would be off the scale, but you'd still have them queueing around the block for your services.'

Victoria could barely breathe for laughing now and decided making tea may calm her down. Sophie was sprawled over the chair, legs outstretched in front of her, laughing without care. She felt wonderful.

Victoria returned with fresh tea and fresh cups and breathing almost normally.

'So,' asked Victoria, nodding downwards, 'how are you down there?'

'Bruised and stinging a bit.'

Victoria rested her hand on Sophie's. 'To be expected,' she said, 'I'm the same if I've been out of action for a while. I know exactly what you need, I'll pop to the chemist shortly and get you some. I'll leave it on my dresser. Use my bathroom to apply it, you don't want a man to see you putting medicine down there. They can't cope with it. It upsets them.'

Sophie frowned. 'I'm a bit worried about what we're going to talk about when he does surface. What if he doesn't want that sort of relationship? What if he thinks I tricked him into it? He seemed OK with the virginity thing, but it's always difficult to tell with Harry.'

'I've seen how he sneaks peeks at you Sophie, his pupils dilate to saucer-size every time he looks at you. I don't think you need to worry,' Victoria reassured her.

'Just stay cool, don't gush and smother him. If it was me I'd take the stance – *It was nice, I enjoyed it, I'd like some more, but it's not the end of the world for me if you're not interested.* And remember men deal with things in priority order. First it's their dick – you've well and truly sorted that out this morning by the sounds of it. Second is their stomach, he'll be thinking about that next – there's fresh bread rolls in the bread-bin, make his favourite bacon sandwich, extra bacon, that posh brown sauce and a cuppa. Third is usually football or cars. For Harry I think it's crosswords and sudoku. I didn't see the newspaper before I went to the shop this morning, so I brought one back,' she pointed to The Times lying on the sofa, 'make sure he's got a pen to hand and, hey-presto, you're on a safe bet.' Victoria nodded, convinced of her assessment.

******

Sophie flicked through the newspaper for a second time, trying to find something to focus on, but, at around the third sentence of each article, her mind always wandered to Harry. Victoria had gone to the shops, promising to stay out for at least a couple of hours and Harry hadn't stirred. She guessed he wouldn't be much longer, he never usually slept in the day, in fact he didn't seem to sleep much at all, so it was probably the effects of the pain killers keeping him under.

At last she heard the click of a bedroom door closing and she tried to become enthralled with an article about wheelie bins. She might get away with it if he didn't ask her for details.

'Hi.'

She looked up smiling. 'Hiya. You've had a good sleep, you must be rested now.' The banality made here cringe inside.

Harry rested his hands on the back of the chair at the opposite end of the table. His hair still wet from the shower, he was wearing jeans and a loose, light blue cotton shirt. He looked like something seriously edible out of a men's casual-wear catalogue. Apart from his scar. His face said nothing.

'What happens now?' he asked. His eyes, fixed on her, left no doubt the question needed an answer.

Sophie met his stare, her heart pumping, was this a brush-off coming? What had Victoria said – play it cool.

'What would you like to happen?' she returned evenly.

The silence was awkward, painful. Sophie wondered if he was going to say something really crass like 'Sorry about just now, it was a mistake' or 'It must have been the tablets'.

She glanced at the teapot, saw that it was within reach and decided that if any such words started to come out of his mouth she would fling it at him. Sod cool!

'I'm hungry, do you mind if I fix something,' he said.

'I was about to make a bacon sandwich. Fancy one?' she asked, getting up from the table and putting the teapot into 'safe' mode.

Harry nodded with a child-like eagerness that made her want to shout 'I love you'. Instead she busied herself with the detailed precision of assembling tea related paraphernalia around her and flicked on the kettle, hoping he hadn't spotted her discomfort in walking.

From the corner of her eye she saw him move towards her.

'Can I do anything?' he asked.

'Not really. Why don't you sit down at the table? Today's paper's there.'

He disappeared from view and she reached for the tea caddy, so far so good, but you never knew what Harry was going to say until he said it.

'Or...' Sophie jumped as his hands gripped her hips, 'I could put my hands here.'

'Then I could...' His hands slid to her lower stomach, his arms pulling her against his hard, flat body.

'And when you've finished playing Chinese Checkers with those tins...'

Sophie slammed the caddies against the wall and slapped her hands flat and still on the cool granite worktop.

'I could perhaps nibble just... here.'

His teeth gently gripping and pulling her ear lobe sent an electric shock straight to her groin, somehow managing to change the stinging to a different, altogether more pleasant and suddenly urgent sensation.

She was a fraction of a second too late to stop the groan escaping from deep down in her, although she did manage to convert it to a strangled gurgle.

Sophie struggled to believe this was really happening to her. Harry and her? Was it some sort of mistake? Was it just a bit of fun for him, a short interlude to relieve his boredom? She wriggled around to face him, really glad she hadn't worn a bra, wondering if her rock-hard nipples pressing through her soft cotton thigh-length vest onto his chest were affecting him the same way she was being tormented by his strong hands gently squeezing the base of her bum. She guessed the already high hem of here vest must now be up around her brand new knickers. Was he going to...? How could she steer him to the sofa? Here on the worktop? Surely not, but... maybe...

She eased him away and looked into his eyes.

'Shall we...? Do you want me to...?' she whispered, hooking her hands into the top of his jeans.

''I think so, yes,' he said slowly, gazing back at her, squeezing her hands gently. 'You do the bacon and I'll do the rolls. One or two? I'm starving.'

******

'This is never going to work,' sighed Sophie, as, for the fourth night in a row, she grabbed the pillows that she had placed between them a few minutes earlier and threw them to the bottom of the bed. 'We're going to have to be in separate towns if we're going to keep our hands off of each other.' She was still in wonder at the transformation of this man who, for how many years, had ignored her advances and kept her at arm's length and now accepted her every initiation and once in a while made his own.

She snuggled herself up against him into the position she knew would leave him unable to resist providing everything she wanted.

'We should start learning more about each other, stuff that only lovers share. Every night let's ask each other one question and the other has to answer honestly. You go first,' she said poking his arm. She poked him again and then a third time, silence was no longer going to be an option for Mister Stone.

He took a deep breath. He recognised the subtle, but *I'm not joking* tone in her voice and knew the question would have to be deep and meaningful or he'd have to ask another, it could go on for a long time. 'OK, OK. So… the other morning was your first orgasm?'

'Why do you think that?'

'Because you said you'd never had sex before.'

She frowned and then reached up and flicked the tip of her outstretched middle finger rapidly side to side across the tip of his nose. 'I said I was a virgin, not an angel.'

It was his turn to frown, then, 'Err… Ah.'

'Now my go.' She propped herself up on her elbow and leaned over until they were almost nose to nose. 'Do you remember the other day after Elizabeth took your stitches out and we were all laughing whilst drinking tea and talking about what boobs mean to men?'

'Y…es,' he wasn't sure where this was going.

'Well, I've been wondering… when do we get to do the custard doughnut stuff?'

Chapter 23

'Good morning Arajoa,' said Victoria cheerfully, as she walked up to the reception desk, 'this is Harry, he's thinking about signing up. What's the best deal you can give him?'

'Good morning girls, nice to see you both again. Good morning Harry,' Arajoa welcomed, 'let's get some details and see what we can do for you.'

Harry didn't understand why so much personal information was needed for temporary membership of a gym, he kept his answers brief. Being identified as his landlady was uncool so Victoria insisted all three should be identified as flatmates. Sophie watched in admiration as Victoria argued, albeit unsuccessfully, for Harry to be added to her father's family membership.

'Not to worry, I'll be happy with three months of the standard package,' said Harry, pointing to the price card on the counter and showing his credit card in the hope of bringing the conversation to an end.

Arajoa ignored him and pointed out sympathetically to the girls that the two allowable family concessions were already used up by Sophie and Victoria.

She liked them, they were down to earth and fun and if Harry was their friend he would surely be the same. She glanced over her shoulder at Woody, the manager, in his glass-walled office. His crew cut and huge, muscular frame looked completely out of place sitting at the simple, metal-legged, virtually empty desk. A mid-forties man of action with a serious countenance, he looked like he had been somewhere else, doing something bold and manly, then magically and unexpectedly transported to materialise in front of a keyboard.

'Let's see what the boss says,' she said gesturing over her

shoulder with her thumb and leaning into the PA system mike.

'Mr Greenwood to reception please, Mr Greeeenwood,' said Arajoa, in her best artificial officialdom, grinning as her voice boomed through the building.

Sophie guessed from Woody's palms-up, mock reaction of exasperation, he was sitting probably only three metres away from them, that he secretly enjoyed being on the receiving end of Arajoa's teasing as much as Arajoa enjoyed dispensing it. Neither tried to hide the chemistry.

'Victoria, Sophie,' Woody nodded with a smile as he left his office, 'nice to see you back. Ready for another programme?'

The girls held him in awe. His gravelly, quietly confident voice barked and cajoled them through punishing regimes, he had a presence that suggested he should not be disappointed. Most of all he seemed to know the shape they wanted, how to make them look good, and he had got them there in just two weeks and then kept them there. This huge gorilla of a man understood women!

'Victoria was wondering if there were any membership concessions for Mr Stone,' Arajoa continued in her official voice.

'He's our flatmate,' Victoria chimed in, 'and I'm about to file papers next week to adopt him as my brother and Sophie's going to make him marry her in the near future.'

Harry looked at Woody and shook his head, 'A standard membership will do me fine, really.'

'Well, I'm not sure...' Woody started, but Victoria spoke over him.

'And he's a really good friend of Chip, known him for years.'

Woody stepped towards the desk, picked up the calendar and flipped one month back. He frowned, working something out in his head, then looked straight at Harry, focusing directly on the scar.

In a rare moment of openness, he'd had to talk to someone, Chip had confided in Woody that a close friend had been critically wounded on a recent operation. Woody was surprised that Chip would even admit to having a friend and felt honoured to be his confidant and then humbled when he learned of some of the situations he and his friend had been through, side by side.

'A friend of Chip?'

Harry nodded.

'That wound looks about… five weeks old?' asked Woody quietly, looking at the calendar again.

'Pretty much,' replied Harry.

Sophie saw the recognition, acceptance, a bond or unspoken understanding, as if the encounter had enabled each to now connect into the other's thoughts.

Woody offered his hand, 'Steve Greenwood, Woody, ex Two-para.'

'Xtwopara?' asked Victoria, puzzled. 'Is that a computer game level? You're a gamer?'

'Second Battalion the Parachute Regiment. Finest fighting force in the world,' sighed Arajoa in mock, repetitive boredom.

'Present company accepted,' said Woody, recognising Harry with a nod of the head.

'Woody! You're a parachuter?' asked Victoria, excited.

'Yes. No, *was* a paratrooper. Fifteen years.'

'Oh my goodness Sophie. Our personal fitness instructor is a paratrooper!' she said with unrestrained glee. 'Who can I tell? Who can I tell?' Victoria rarely attempted to hold the little girl in when she was excited.

'Harry Stone, Two Seven Commando, Royal Marines,' replied Harry quietly, hoping Victoria wouldn't hear in her excitement. No such luck.

'Wait. What? Harry, you're a commando? I thought you… A commando?' asked Victoria. 'Why didn't you tell us?'

Victoria looked at Arajoa and pointed to the computer screen, 'Flatmate, *definitely* flatmate on that record please.'

Victoria grabbed Sophie's arm, 'Our flatmate is a commando. Sophie, you're sha… you know, with a commando!'

'Mr Stone,' said Arajoa, placing the credit card machine on the counter next to Harry and feeling slightly uncomfortable at the direction of the conversation, 'if you could just put in your card and PIN please. Three months standard membership.'

Woody reached over, picked up the card machine, pulled Harry's card out and passed it back to him.

'My apologies, the machines not working, we can set up your membership now and sort out the payment later,' he said, passing the machine back to Arajoa.

'No, it's working, I've just fixed it,' said Arajoa confused, giving it a good shake then squinting into the card slot.

Woody sighed. 'No Arajoa, it isn't,' he said in monotone, 'please put Mr Stone on the same class of membership as Chip.'

'Ah, yes, I can see now, it's not working, silly me,' said Arajoa mechanically.

Nobody noticed that Sophie was quiet, still, staring at Harry. She had shared Victoria's excitement in discovering Woody's military past. Looking at him, his fitness, his clean-cut confidence, his ability to communicate, to lead, it all made sense. You wouldn't need many like him in an army to have a very good chance of winning.

At first she thought, then hoped, Harry had made a mistake or was joking when he said Marines. The clear, unspoken communications between the two men said something else. From what she could remember Marines went to dangerous places and did dangerous things, they got shot at, people tried to kill them. And they shot back. That couldn't be her Harry, her quiet, gentle Harry, he moved stuff about, he was in logistics. He was. How could anyone want to hurt him? *He* would definitely not want to hurt anyone. She was quite confident he certainly wouldn't shoot at anyone. Never.

She thought back to the hospital, Harry's near mortal wounds and the quiet conversations the MOD security badge had allowed her to overhear. The chat with the doctor in the canteen that hadn't made much sense. The Red Teams that were spoken of with respect and admiration and sometimes a hint of fear. What had the nurse said about Red Five and being crazy? What was Red Five?

She thought back to the odd encounter with Rory the photographer, on the hill overlooking the church. All his gibbering of dangerous people and Red Teams again. He had been a bit scary at first, but his fear seemed genuine so she guessed he had some sort of harmless personality issue.

She thought back to the argument on the pier. Harry had been trying to tell her something and she had refused to listen. Was she really not interested, or was she frightened of finding out?

How had the photographer known about Red Teams?

'Can we drop the *Mister* stuff now, I would prefer *Harry* if that's OK?' asked Harry.

'Let me give you a quick tour, then I can put together a personalised plan for you. Any particular focus?' asked Woody.

Harry tapped his left thigh. Woody nodded.

'Right, this way please,' Woody gestured to the glass door in the floor-to-ceiling glass wall that separated the reception area from the gym and its huge selection of steel, chrome and matt black, very business-like equipment.

Woody briefly pointed out the obvious equipment groups, certain that Harry was already familiar with exactly what they did and knowing that the two women had been using it for months. The most exciting part of the tour had been how to work the lockers. He had asked Sophie and Victoria to join the tour because he wanted to show them his latest expansion, a significant investment he would have to work very hard to meet the loan repayments on.

'Wow!' said Victoria looking at another wall-to-wall glass partition, marking the start of the new area, 'it's doubled in size.'

'And there's as much space again behind that,' said Woody, pointing at the new end wall, 'it's just a question of finance, as always, and finding the right management team. Or partners.'

Standing in the middle of the cavernous, almost empty room and pointing to the padded floor areas he explained his hopes for encouraging martial arts groups and offering self-defence courses.

Harry remembered Chip mentioning he had been asked to give self-defence classes, but Chip didn't think it was viable because, with genuine discomfort and no humour, he reflected that up to now most people he had defended himself against had finished up rapidly dead.

'What are those body shaped things in the corner?' asked Sophie, still struggling to blank out her earlier worries for Harry.

'Once we get the screens delivered they'll be hidden from day to day use. I didn't want to hold up the opening whilst we wait. They're a type of punch bag, for specialist combat training – body guards and the like. To be honest it probably involves a type of aggression most casual gym users wouldn't be comfortable with.'

Woody walked over to the matt black equipment, picked up a pair of fingerless leather gloves and held them up to Harry. 'You or me?'

Harry really didn't want to, but the little girl in Victoria was whining, insistent. Sophie seemed indifferent.

After a dozen or so slow, but technically perfect punches and kicks, just heavy enough to make business like thuds, Harry stepped back and handed the gloves to Woody.

Well, thought Woody, he's definitely not trying to impress anyone. If he was right about Harry's past he could probably have separated the equipment from its fittings with a violence that would have frightened everyone else in the building, including him. Did these two young women, little more than earnest, fresh-faced kids, really know who, or more to the point, what, they were keeping company with? *Not my business.*

Sophie and Victoria looked at each other, both had been taken back to the episode with that *vile bastard Bradley.*

'We want to sign up for the self-defence course,' said Sophie, with a determination Victoria understood, 'when does it start?'

Woody grinned. 'I was hoping you'd ask. Let's talk about that.'

He took them up to the new cafeteria on the mezzanine overlooking the exercise areas and got them very good cups of freshly ground coffee from the brand new, ridiculously expensive, rental coffee machine that had, at long last, been plumbed in. If it didn't start earning its keep soon it would likely be taken away. He didn't want to think about the alternative - a kettle, jars of coffee and teaspoons.

'OK,' said Sophie, sitting down at the round, glass-topped table, '*this is nice.* Steel and glass everywhere and quality gear. It has that open, fresh, outside feel. I love the see through chairs. Serve the right stuff and this could be a lucrative business on its own.' It was odd how she could hear her mum's analysis as she spoke.

'Have you considered sponsorship?' asked Victoria. 'Like

an organisation promoting women's equality paying to have their name associated with a women's self-defence course?' Ever since she had shared her relationship problems with Pops, try as he might, he couldn't hide his pain at his daughter's hurt and had become an active promoter of women's empowerment. She had no doubt he would be able to find someone to put money into this.

Sophie and Victoria sat back in their chairs, their brains both galloping in the same direction.

'Of course,' Sophie added with a wry smile, 'you'd be marketing to women, but where there's fit women men will always be sniffing around close behind.' She winked at Victoria.

It took a split-second glance between Sophie and Victoria for them to agree they would accept Woody's offer of free training in return for assistance with a marketing campaign. It wasn't the waiver of fees, Victoria knew the only money challenge would have been convincing Sophie to accept another sub from Pops. What they were excited about was being involved in a real commercial activity.

'Done!' they said in unison, offering their hands across the table for Woody to shake.

'Done!' Woody responded, cupping their two hands together in his massive clams, in one enthusiastic three way contract.

'Christ Harry, how do you keep up with these two? They've only seen this two minutes ago and they're already three streets ahead of me,' said Woody, now slightly less stressed about his overdraft than when the day had started.

'I don't even try.'

Victoria didn't understand why working with a friend of Chip's had popped up as a plus point in her mental equations. Chip was harmless enough, but very withdrawn and a bit strange. He hardly spoke and what was all that staring at walls thing? Dull, not her type at all.

Sophie also felt a sense of gain. Whatever this link was between Harry and Woody, a respect, a bond between two people that had just met, it was obviously important to both. Working with Woody could get her closer to Harry, the man she loved, shared her body with and just a few minutes ago realised she knew next to nothing about.

Chapter 24

As soon as Harry and Sophie arrived in Brighton Rosie had started working almost full time in the shop with Ilona and refused to be paid. By all accounts they were supporting each other and so Sophie's early guilt at not being there for her mum quickly reduced. Besides, Sophie was still doing the accounts, stock control and ordering remotely. Thank goodness for bar-codes.

Harry's recovery was going well and these summer days must be the closest anyone could get to heaven. Sophie was sure of it, she thought she might burst with happiness.

She was deeply in love with Harry. She loved his quiet, calm gentleness, the deep pool of his emotional intelligence that allowed him to understand her, even when she sometimes didn't understand her own self, and of course his debilitating good looks. Even his scarred face added a wild scoundrel element to his persona. (Could she call it luck that with one scar so close to the other it looked like a single wound?). She couldn't believe this man wanted her and was sharing himself with her.

Now, as they explored each other, he allowed her to discover facets she had never known existed.

His sense of humour was wicked, often dry and always made her laugh and she enjoyed his teasing. His deadpan explanation of the Schrödinger's Sock phenomenon had sucked her in completely. The hypothesis, where one of a pair of socks in a full load of washing mysteriously disappears from the machine, had her enthralled. Until the bit about the said missing sock spontaneously re-materialising as a blue plastic food container lid, without its matching bottom, in the back of a rarely used cupboard. He had accepted his punishment bravely, perhaps because it was delivered over a long Sunday afternoon, under a duvet.

Harry's preference for music was *interesting*. Sophie had popped out for fresh granary bread one Saturday morning and returned to find him wearing headphones and doing what looked like ballet steps in the middle of the lounge. Unaware of her presence, he continued his practised, graceful movements, engrossed, lost in his own world, physically expressing a level of emotion Sophie had never seen in him before. Where had he been hiding that elegance? Pointed toes? She drew breath between her teeth as her love for him squeezed her heart. Chip, reading the newspaper at the table, looked up at Sophie and shook his head, 'Highland Sword Dance, be thankful he's not making us listen to it.'

Harry had once mentioned a Scottish grandfather and spent, what Sophie thought then, was a very long time explaining the origins of the tartan of his scarf. As they walked back from the Harlequin one blustery winter's evening he had, unasked, wrapped the scarf gently around her neck. Smelling of him, still warm from him, it was all Sophie could do not to wrap herself around him. Then his denim jacket had protected her from the worst of a sudden, lashing squall. Walking to the weather side of her to shield her from the worst of the sometimes horizontal sheets of rain, sleeves rolled up, water plastering his shirt to him, he had looked like a man of granite, treating the weather with casual indifference. He was challenging it to do its worst and enjoying its inability to cower him, as he spoke with pride of the long, hard history of the people of his clan.

At least now Sophie knew Harry liked music and had a favourite group, even if it was the Royal Scots Dragoon Guards Pipe Band. Uncool as it was, *The Gael* had let her discover a new emotion and, whatever she was doing, she would stop to soak up the mid-track tinkling of *The Ceilidh*, eagerly anticipating the following crashing avalanche of excitement.

Along with *Ashley's Thinning Napper*, her favourite, she had quietly bought them and sneaked all three of them onto her fire-me-up play-list. She soon gave up blaming Harry and had to admit that she loved the pipes and drums. For sure they would have to move north, so their children could be born in Scotland and lay claim to this heritage.

His choice of a pet, in a pretend scenario of unlimited money, surprised her the most. She had guessed something like a thoroughbred horse or at least some sort of sleek, efficient hunting dog. She hadn't expected, after repeatedly checking he wasn't joking, he would choose a cow. A farmyard cow. Apparently they were intelligent, friendly, affectionate and above all curious. She couldn't remember anything else from the full fifteen minutes of his justification. So, that explained his reluctance to drink milk, or *cow-squirt*, as he called it, but he fully agreed his passion for West Country Farmhouse Cheddar, Somerset Brie and rich British butter was completely unexplainable.

Every day seemed to bring something new and usually curious. And he was hers, all hers.

God, she loved this man.

Sophie woke early every morning, the only man she had ever wanted lying next to her. In the half-light she would watch his chest gently rising and falling, listen to his low breathing, feel his warmth, breath in his intoxicating smell. She always made sure she was touching him, if not in full spoon then perhaps with the side of her hand, a part of her leg, even a toe or the back of a finger, anything, as long as they were connected.

Did he love her? He must surely do. The way he spoke to her, touched her, held her, so gentle and caring in their joining, always careful to be sure of her satisfaction before taking his own. Yet that word never passed his lips. What did love mean to men anyway? Did he feel for her the same bottomless, painful longing she felt for him?

She had tried not to talk about it, in case he turned away. So many times she had been close to telling him, always managing to hold back, but one night she couldn't keep it to herself anymore.

In the tenderness of the early moments, before the physical overwhelmed them, she whispered her love close to his ear. Without pausing he had turned and gently kissed her lips and gently squeezed her, but no *word*.

What would happen to them once he was fit for duty? She couldn't consider the thought. After his last two visits to Yeovilton for check-ups he hadn't been his usual relaxed self, he had been quiet, withdrawn for a while. Depressed? He wouldn't talk about it so Sophie didn't know if he was upset because he hadn't been given the all clear or if he had been passed as fit and would soon have to leave, and leave her behind. Chip's recently more frequent and always welcomed visits had helped. Sophie had left their quiet conversations uninterrupted, their positive effects on Harry were clear. Victoria had also recognised it and kept her distance. Despite her professed concern at Chip's silences and prolonged close staring at inanimate objects Victoria always seemed to be in his three metre orbit, always with subtle makeup and always ever so slightly revealingly dressed.

Harry was still warm and attentive and Sophie convinced herself the shift in his demeanour wasn't an early sign of his tiring of their relationship. His recent daily walks alone to 'Clear the head' were understandable, their closeness was something new for both of them. Although she definitely didn't need any head-clearing time for herself she didn't want to smother him, so every day she kissed him goodbye and kissed him hello again. At every gentle greeting embrace she enjoyed breathing in his smell, it sent something warm to her heart. She was most definitely not checking for unusual perfumes. Besides, he was only ever gone for an hour or so, certainly not long enough for an encounter, not the way Harry *encountered* anyway.

Sophie's relationship fears and uncertainties surfaced and sank randomly. She didn't think Tabatha was much of a threat now although Akua still made occasional appearances in her worry space. Who was she and why had she been so desperate to see Harry? Nina was surely out of the picture. Wasn't she? Elizabeth?

Whatever her worries Sophie had absolutely no doubt that Harry was the one, the only one ever, for her. He had opened himself to her, let her in to his warm, gentle, soft self. She loved him with everything she had and she knew it was only a matter of time before he felt the same about her. Of course it was too early to plan, they were still getting used to each other and it was certainly too early to share her ideas with him about their first child six years from now or whether they should wait a year or eighteen months to start on their second. She was ready to face the ups and downs of life with him, side by side, thick and thin, rough and smooth. She had no doubts that she had found the perfect, warm, caring, gentle human that would be the centre of her life, for the rest of her life.

Until the phone call.

The phone call that changed nothing for him.

The phone call that would change everything for her.

Chapter 25

Sophie always marvelled at the silent precision with which the huge television screen appeared from its hiding place in the ceiling and slid exactly into position, centimetres from the ceiling to floor, wall to wall windows. With the sofas tugged round at an angle the room was now more like a home cinema than a living space. She was still trying to come to terms with the speakers all around her.

Sophie snuggled her back comfortably into Harry's warm chest and rested her head on his shoulder. With her feet up on the sofa she was looking forward to being close and sharing the evening with him watching his favourite sci-fi blockbuster movie. It couldn't get much better than this.

She glanced across at Victoria clicking away on the keyboard to get to the movie whilst Chip blockaded himself with cushions to provide her with a backrest. Sophie smiled, it would be only a matter of minutes before Victoria's wriggling would have the cushions on the floor and her bare shoulders sharing their warmth through Chip's thin cotton shirt. She was putting a lot of effort into getting close to someone she thought strange. For his part Chip seemed completely confused by the whole thing.

'Do you want me to pause it?' asked Victoria, as Harry struggled to take the buzzing phone from his pocket. It was the first point of high tension in the film, the hero was walking into an obvious trap, to be confronted by the hideously looking, immediately hateable, slime-ball alien bad thing.

'No, carry on, unless it's mum I'll tell them to call back.'

Sophie, peering over her shoulder at Harry's telephone, knew it wasn't Rosie, her picture wasn't smiling out at him. His upper body tensed, she knew immediately something wasn't right.

'Yes,' was all he said to the caller in quiet affirmation.

Sophie caught the last few words of the short one-way conversation. '… check your email.'

Harry gently eased her away from him and carefully settled her against the back of the sofa, propping her up with cushions before standing up and moving to the kitchen area.

Victoria, enjoying Chip's hands suddenly on her shoulders, wasn't happy when she was left similarly propped up and alone. No words had passed between the men, yet they had moved as one.

Victoria paused the film with an irritated stab to the keyboard, the cacophony of zapping laser guns and other futuristic killing mechanisms silenced in time to hear the last words of advice from Chip. '…it's in the public domain, don't wait, face it up now.'

Both women recognised the men's greyness, something was wrong. As Chip searched for a web address using the television keyboard Harry turned to Sophie, held her hands together in his and kissed them. 'Sophie, please remember this is my job, this is what I'm trained to do, what I'm sent to do. After you've seen this I'll still be the same man that was holding you a few moments ago.'

Stomach-burning fear surged blood to her head. This wasn't the usual calm Harry, was he trying to say goodbye to her? She would not let him walk out on her! What the hell was going on?

'If this is some sort of silly joke stop it now you two! It's not funny, you're frightening me,' demanded Sophie, her voice quivering.

Chip spoke like he might be reading a television review from a newspaper. 'Someone's hacked into military systems and stolen a ton of operations videos. I don't know much more, but it looks like they've published interesting highlights

In the Arms of Giants

of Harry's last op. It's on the internet now. Public.'

The first few minutes were a blur for Sophie, she heard an American voice talking about murderous America and its murdering allies, 'In our name... the world hates us... *Charlie Two* thinks this is the answer...' Then she recognised Harry sitting in what looked like an aircraft. The picture was in low light, but she saw a few seconds of him checking a rifle, oblivious to the camera. The black smears across his face made him look aggressive, menacing, ruthless. OK, she could deal with this. The thought of him handling a gun made her uncomfortable, but as he said, it was his job. He probably never fired it.

The scene cut to a small, bare walled room, bodies on the floor, blood everywhere, a woman huddled into a ball on a table, naked. Apart from her gentle sobbing there was silence. Sophie knew it would be Harry with his back to the camera struggling with someone. He held the man's wrist above them, a huge cutlass thrashing wildly in the man's hand. It was like a replay of the fight at the shopping centre except that this time Harry didn't drop his opponent to the ground. This time as the man fell Harry wrenched his arm behind him and up, the man screamed in agony. Then Harry, emotionless, face towards the camera, half knelt behind the crumpled man and gripped his head. A violent twist, a crack and the body slumped lifeless to the floor.

Then Harry's voice, calm, cold, disinterested, factual, 'Charlie Two, five hostiles cleared.'

Sophie knew she didn't want to see any more, her head was spinning, bile burnt her throat, but she couldn't look away.

'This is some ridiculous spoof? Right? Stop it now, it's not funny, stop it!' Sophie demanded.

'It's real, it happened. No one would joke about this,' said Chip.

The video cut to an outside scene, looking along the barrel

of a rifle. A dreadlocked, sweating man in a grubby, torn tee shirt rushed screaming towards the camera, a cutlass held high above him. He was no more than four metres from the camera when his head exploded, then another man, then another.

Harry's voice, calm again, no sign of tension, 'Kojo, I'm five rounds to empty.'

The video cut again, this time Harry was in full frame, bodies surrounding him, blood streaming from a gash down his cheek. He hit a man across the face with the butt of his rifle and as he fell Harry spun the rifle around and thrust his bayonet deep into the man's stomach then yanked it upwards. A sickening scream filled the lounge as Harry stared directly into the camera, then smiled.

Sophie's head was spinning, anger and loathing swept through her. Half blinded by tears she stumbled to the kitchen and just reached the sink as her stomach ejected its contents. Victoria ran to help, to hold Sophie's hair behind her.

When Chip explained in his usual disengaged tone that these were surely edits and the video most certainly didn't tell the whole story, Victoria turned to glare at him, incredulous. 'You mean there's more? Fucking hell! I don't want to see it!'

Harry went to hold Sophie to comfort her, but stepped back when Victoria shook her head.

'Perhaps I should go,' said Harry quietly.

'Get out of my fucking sight!' screamed Sophie into the stainless steel sink.

Chapter 26

On the third night exhaustion finally brought the release of sleep and the next morning Sophie had to agree with Victoria that after two days it was about time she showered and brushed her teeth and ate something. Sophie couldn't work out if what she felt was physical or in her head, but it was still hurting now as much as when she first realised the man she loved, had loved, was a monster, a bastard, a vile, murdering bastard. She had seen it with her own eyes. She shuddered and tried again to wipe away the image of him using a knife on the end of his gun on an unarmed man. He had stared directly into the camera as if to claim ownership. What sort of person did that? No government would ask anyone to do that. He should be tried in court and rot in jail.

Chip had come round the day after the video to collect the few things Harry hadn't taken that night. It wasn't much, Harry travelled light, but it was gone now. Sophie stripped the bed and gathered up everything he might have touched and shoved it into the washing machine. Hot wash, double soap, to hell with colours.

She looked at her bright pink body in the full-length bathroom mirror. The scrubbing in the hot shower must surely have removed any trace of his touch, his DNA. She looked at her wide open mouth in the mirror, at least that was... Oh god! She spat into the sink, mouth rinse, she needed mouth rinse.

'Here we are my darling, a good thick slice of stone-ground, wholemeal toast with a seriously thick spread of our favourite Cornish butter. Ger yersef an th' ooside or thit and tings'll look a lot berrer,' said Victoria, as she kissed Sophie on the forehead then poured her a mug of steaming builders best tea. Victoria's attempts at mimicking accents usually involved several counties in one sentence and this morning, as always, it brought a smile to Sophie.

The unexpected smile and the comforting taste of creamy butter on her tongue sent a brief couldn't-care-less through Sophie. Maybe if you actually loathed the man you thought you had loved then you hadn't actually lost any love. That just left the bitter taste of deceit and if you could manage to view with contempt the little shit that had deceived you in the first place then you were almost back to normal.

It must surely be the bitterness of being fooled that was causing her pain, it couldn't be the losing of love.

So what if Harry (according to Victoria's conversations with Chip) was sharing a loft bedsit with Chip on the top floor of their family house, just above Elizabeth's two bedroom flat. Elizabeth who must have known the sort of work Harry did, knew how to manage him and was still able to like him and care about him. The beautiful and shapely, red-headed Elizabeth, the widowed parent of a young child who Harry adored and who adored Harry back. The Elizabeth who may well be open to considering another partner. So what! So what?

The cool, salty, early morning sea breeze in her face refreshed her, but it didn't make her feel alive like it used to, just like it didn't yesterday, or the day before. Victoria was, as usual, right, getting out of the apartment for an early morning jog was flushing something out of her system and making her body feel good. It wasn't reaching the parts that really hurt though, that pain refused to budge.

Something else wasn't quite right either, she was uncomfortable. She slowed her jog and turned round to run a few steps backwards. Yes, there he was again, in the distance. Could it be coincidence? Lots of people jogged in the mornings, but this lumbering, tree trunk of a man seemed to have chosen exactly the same route and time as her, three days in a row. This morning she had missed out the pier and continued running along the front. So had he. Sophie was pretty sure he had also been outside of the wine bar last night when she and Victoria had made less than a half-hearted and completely unsuccessful attempt to go out 'On the pull'. His curly mop was distinctive enough to convince her. She turned and sprinted as fast as she could for as long as she could and then slowed to run on the spot to catch her breath before stopping and leaning against the railing to look out over the beach.

He hadn't quickened his pace and as he passed behind her his easy stride and unhurried breathing told her he was used to exercise. It must be pure coincidence. She would not let Harry add paranoia to the hurt he had done to her. She would jog home without stopping and not look behind her once.

But she enjoyed running backwards! Harry would not control her. On the way home she slowed, turned and ran backwards again. Not that she cared, but there was no curly headed huge person anywhere to be seen. The young man in khaki shorts and vest some way behind her and who had been running up from the far end of the pier as she passed its entrance, must live near to their apartment, she had seen him stretching in the mornings as she set off, (Maybe Victoria should get her running shoes on). He must take a different route, he was always on the pier first.

Tree Trunk man knew that at this altitude, temperature and pace he could run for at least two hours before dehydration had to be managed. He also knew he had been spotted. As soon as his speed-dial was answered he hung up and watched a more nimble, less conspicuous runner leave the pier and fall in behind the bobbing blonde ponytail.

Chapter 27

The warm shower relaxed her and the fragrance of a new, different shower gel reminded her of a new start. As expensive as it was she had thrown out the one she had enjoyed Harry soaping her with.

Sitting at the table in a baggy white tee shirt and pale yellow shorts, combing her damp hair, she couldn't hold back the memories of him sitting opposite, serving her his fantastic cooking. Everything she looked at, everything he had touched, even the dining table, reminded her of what she thought she had had. Sophie's swamp of despair rose up to engulf her again and the fetid stench of betrayal, or whatever it was Harry had done to her, burnt deep inside her nose. It hurt.

Sophie's lips trembled and she looked at her friend. 'Victoria, I loved him with everything I had. Everything. I would have died for him. What sort of man could take everything knowing he could bring nothing?' Only when her tears were tickling her chin did she wipe them.

Victoria took Sophie's hands and held them between her own. 'Sweetheart, hear me out, let me finish before you speak. You know I love you and wouldn't do anything to hurt you.' Sophie looked up confused, but thankful for the warmth, the touch. She couldn't, didn't dare, share this with her mum, it would be too much of a burden, she worried enough about Sophie as it was.

'Before you decide what to do, and I will support and not try to influence whatever you decide, I think you should get as much information, as painful as it is, to help you understand what happened.'

Sophie nodded.

'When you were asleep yesterday evening Chip came around

to try to explain. It does look like whoever stole the videos from the military did heavily edit them to paint a picture. Apparently there are hours of footage of this operation and we saw a few seconds of it. Now it looks like another version has been released adding more to what we saw, but telling a very different story. Chip doesn't know who released it, it could be a government, a military, anyone who could get their hands on it. No one really understands the politics as far as I can tell.

'I won't lie, some of it's far worse than what we saw together and I couldn't cope with a lot of it, I had to turn my head away. But there's a lot more around the bits you've seen. I still don't understand how one human can do such horrific things to another, but I do now understand why Harry did the things we watched him do.

'I think you should take a look at those bits. I don't think Harry's a bad man, he's beyond anything I can understand and, I'll be honest, he frightens me now. You may not be able to love him again, but I think you may able to stop hating him.

'Please Sophie, not for him or me or anyone else, for you and your own peace. Please?'

Sophie refused, she had seen Harry killing, slicing open, an unarmed man then gloating into the camera. How could Victoria possibly see anything different? Again the memory played itself vividly in her mind and her stomach heaved. She wanted to cry.

Sophie spent the morning dusting, sweeping and polishing already pristine surfaces. Only after Victoria had finally tempted her with two soft poached eggs and a slice of soft wholemeal bread plastered with more Cornish butter, did she finally agree to watch the video that evening. Hating was a destructive emotion and if she could just downgrade her feelings to contempt for the little shit it may help numb the constant pain. What actually was causing it? It most certainly wasn't love, she hated him.

******

Chip gulped his tea as he waited for the video to download from the memory stick. He was careful to make clear this was his edit of a very small part of quite a bit of newly released material. He had tried to be even-handed and complete the stories of what they had seen. There was a lot of other stuff he hadn't included, a lot of it they may find difficult to watch.

The two women agreed Chip should talk them through it so they could try to understand and look away any time they felt the need. Sophie's chest tightened. She so wanted to see something different, perhaps she had imagined the dreadful things she was remembering.

Sophie immediately found herself defending Harry against Chip's comment that in the plane Harry was wearing his frightened face. She was certain Harry had no fear of anything until Chip pointed out that Harry openly admitted he was 'Shit-scared' of jumping out of planes and would probably have preferred to cycle across the Sahara rather than parachute. Night jumps into darkness, or even worse into trees in darkness, had him shaking. They usually went out in four sticks of four and Harry was always allowed to be the first man in the first stick so there were fifteen others behind him ready to kick his arse out of the door if he bottled it. Chip explained that a stick was a bit like a conga dance in the sky. You left the aircraft staying grabbed tightly one behind the other until the last minute, then opened your chute, so you landed close together. It was a standing joke in the team that Harry being first out also meant the others didn't have to worry about his grip developing into a bear hug, all the way to the ground.

Sophie tried to ignore an unexpected emotion. Surely she couldn't be feeling sympathy for him?

The next part was of Harry and three others outside of a closed, shabby, dusty door. Their short, abrupt hand signals seemed to be agreeing a pattern of next actions. Then Harry patted his shoulder and swapped places with one of the others. In the audio she heard men laughing and someone screaming, Sophie knew exactly what was happening to that desperate woman. Why were Harry and the others still outside the door? Why weren't they doing something to save her? Get in there for Christ's sake!

'*Charlie* are the spearhead of the assault. They are the four door openers and take a room together, taking it in turns to go through the door first, the most dangerous position. There could be someone waiting inside with a bloody big gun or something similarly unpleasant. The fourth stays at the door, the least risky place, so he covers their backs and has the best chance of surviving to call in status if something goes wrong. Harry should have been fourth, but signalled a problem with his comms. He should have swapped with one of the others, but changed with Kojo, to be first through.

'The next part's messy, but it's important to understand what happened.'

Sophie nodded. She guessed they were watching through Harry's head camera as the door flew open and the wearer darted into the room. Before Harry turned to the left there had been a glimpse of many frightened people sitting on the dusty concrete floor, cross legged, hands behind them, a wall of grubby, peeling, once pink paint their backdrop. Five still grinning, but startled men looked up from their manhandling of the petrified, screaming, naked woman held spread-eagled on the old, wooden desk.

A handgun with what looked like a silencer appeared in the frame, steadied, then kicked three times as three shots spat out and three of five heads sprayed pink and red from behind. Then a click and nothing.

Harry's matter of fact voice broke the silence, 'Gun jammed.' Sophie was paralysed with shock, she could hardly register Harry's four metre sprint towards the fourth man. Then blood gushed from the man's throat and she saw a dagger buried deep into the side of his head.

The fifth man, open mouthed, howled in rage and slashed a long high downward chop with a cutlass, missing Harry by millimetres. Sophie and Victoria both screamed and jerked their heads backwards. As the blade rose for a second blow Harry darted forward.

'Mistake,' said Chip, pausing the film. 'You've seen the rest of this bit, where Harry snaps his neck, so unless you want to see it again I'll fast forward.'

'What was a mistake?' asked Victoria.

'Hostile five should have slashed on the upward stroke as well, instead he left neutral time. If you make a mistake like that when you're facing the likes of this lot there's only ever one outcome.'

The video restarted with Harry's camera quickly panning the room. The audio was full of voices talking calmly, reporting status, some of it over crackly radio static. A gentle Welsh voice somewhere near said, 'British Army, we're taking you home.'

A woman whimpered. Harry's camera turned from scanning grotesque dead faces to the naked, shaking form hugging herself into a ball on the desk. He stooped and took her dress from the belt of one of her attackers where it had been tucked as a trophy, then wrapped it around her and hugged her close. 'We're with you now. We won't leave you,' he said softly.

His words grabbed Sophie's stomach.

Chip paused the video, freezing the frame of Harry with his arms around the young woman as she desperately gripped him tightly, her white knuckled fingers clawing at him to pull him closer. The picture burned into Sophie's consciousness. She didn't try to hold back her tears for the young girl. She couldn't - didn't dare, imagine her fear, the helplessness, the desperate clinging to safety.

Anger surged through Sophie. How could those vile animals do such a thing? How dare they? How dare they! She hated them. Without thought she abandoned her rigid belief that justice should always be through courts and rule of law. The fuckers deserved to die. Justice had been dispensed there and then. Good!

And Harry had dispensed it.

Chip continued to explain. One of the two American helicopters hovering out of site to the east had been called in to the rendezvous point, a sheltered hollow just south of the abandoned school buildings where the contact had taken place. As the four bodyguards, *Bravo*, shepherded their priceless charges towards the extraction aircraft a drone circling overhead had picked up an unexpected convoy of three trucks carrying hostiles and moving rapidly towards them. Harry and Kojo had moved out towards the trucks, to engage them head-on and slow them down.

Victoria looked confused, 'So the *two* of them were running out to attack *three lorry loads* of bad people? Does that even make sense?'

Chip shrugged his shoulders, 'No alternative.' He explained that the four snipers, *Alpha* and the four sweepers, *Delta*, would normally have moved to support Kojo and Harry, engaging the hostiles in a three pronged assault. Ten against about fifty was usually doable in that scenario. Unfortunately two hostiles with RPGs – rocket propelled grenades - had appeared from nowhere and Alpha and Delta had to focus on closing them down to protect the helicopter, so Kojo and Harry were on their own.

Sophie marvelled that Chip thought the single word *unfortunately* was adequate in the context and she was pretty sure she knew what *closing down* actually meant. Now she was feeling sick with fear for Harry and for Kojo - a man she had never met.

The video started again with the calm voice of what must have been Kojo. 'Charlie One - Alpha, things are getting difficult here. As soon as you've sorted the RPGs some help would be appreciated.' He was looking towards an overturned truck with men shouting and waving cutlasses running towards him.

'What are all those wiz-wiz sounds?' asked Sophie.

'Incoming rounds – bullets fired at Kojo and Harry.'

Victoria looked at Sophie, then Chip and then back at the screen.

Harry told Kojo he had five rounds left, Kojo's camera jerked around to point at Harry then stayed still. Harry, on one knee, was aiming and firing steadily.

'Empty, reloading,' Harry droned then looked at Kojo. 'Kojo's down, head-shot. Fuck!'

There was no panic in Harry's last word, but there was emotion, strong emotion. Pain.

Harry had moved to stand beside the still Kojo and was firing rapid single shots. 'Ten seconds to overrun. Reloading.' The video had switched to Harry's camera and, as he spoke furious, sweating, screaming men in ragged, filthy clothes were almost on top of him.

The video switched back to Kojo's camera. Harry, in full frame, was on one knee removing his empty magazine when he jerked backwards.

'That was the tracer he took to the shoulder, I bet that hurt.

He probably smells like a poorly seasoned beef burger right now,' offered Chip, with no hint of humour.

Sophie watched through her splayed fingers as five men swarmed into the shallow dip in the ground. Two jerked sideways and fell to the floor, still. Harry clubbed a third in the side of the head with his rifle butt and slashed another across the throat with his bayonet. Harry jerked his head backwards avoiding the worst of a slash with a cutlass, but it opened his cheek, exposing pink and then red. He twisted his head, just avoiding a second slash.

'Some say that if you look into the eyes of a man fighting to the death, you can see into his soul,' said Chip with indifference.

Sophie recognised the face staring out at her, but not the man. This wasn't the quiet, tender lover that had wrapped himself around her heart every time he was near her, every time he spoke to her, every time he touched her. Looking out at her, eyes cold, face rigid in its determination, wasn't a machine either, but a giant. There, in this moment of mortal reckoning, plainly visible to her, was his soul, an unleashed, unwavering beast, taking on monsters on the terms of their choosing. Never stopping, never giving up, never turning away from the ever nearing abyss. Now, at last, she understood the man, she understood his unchanging answer when asked why he was in the military – *Standing up, being counted.*

Sophie remembered what was coming next and desperately wanted to look away, but she stared transfixed as Harry sliced open the man in front of him.

Harry turned to the camera, his face blank, then smiled. 'Kojo's still with us, he's got movement.'

This man, who had just been shot and slashed and fought frantically for his own life, face to face with men determined to kill him, could only feel happiness at seeing his friend was alive. What bond was this?

'Alpha three Charlie two. The RPGs are cleared, we're back with you. The third truck is still moving, weaving between the rock outcrops, and we can't get a good shot. There's a fourth coming from the north. A clapped out old yellow bus.'

A crackly, static laden voice thrust itself irreverently over the business-like, disciplined exchanges. 'Hey you Red Five Wankers. It's me, Kwaku, I'm in the yellow bus, don't fucking shoot me. And it's not clapped out it's retro, I've just painted it. I'm going to take out the third truck. I've got four jerry cans of petrol strapped to the front, that should warm things up. Don't fucking shoot me. Although I dunno why I'm worried, none of you fuckers could find your own dick if you didn't have a zip to give you a clue. You tossers!'

Chip smiled. Kwaku had been in the core of Red Five before he was medically discharged because of, in Kwaku's words, *some missing bits*. He had moved back to Ghana to start a transport business with his yellow buses, or trotros as transport like the old TJ Bedfords with locally made wooden cabins were called in Ghana. In this early morning Kwaku and his cousin had picked up the team from their drop zone and transported them overnight the ten miles to get them within sneak distance of the target. A trotro, complete with huge sacks of charcoal strapped to the roof and passengers wrapped in blankets against the cool night wouldn't attract attention. Kwaku may no longer be a part of the British army, but, as he willingly confessed, *a piece of his heart would always belong to the Crown*. Harry had seen to it that the goody bag exchanged for this bus service included two sets of body armour and new boots and a radio set so they could listen in on the action.

Chip wound the video forward and pressed play. 'You may want to see these next bits as well, they're from the chopper cameras. They needed to get Kojo to a medic asap and that meant Harry getting him on to the first chopper with the hostages.'

People, wide-eyed with fear, ran towards the aircraft doorway, their hair and filthy clothes rattling in the downdraft of the thumping helicopter blades. Relief relaxed their faces as each willingly submitted to be being picked up and launched bodily into the back of the hovering machine by two Bravo men that had been screaming at them to *move, move, move*.

A soldier, half running, half staggering, struggling to hold up the heavy load across his shoulders, ran towards them. Harry knew the pilot would diligently follow the usual standing instruction in such operations, to focus only on the primary objective and take off as soon as the cargo count was complete, regardless of what else was happening in the field. For this flight only the cargo of hostages was of primary importance, everything and everyone else on the ground was disposable and Harry had been certain to confirm that instruction to the aircrews. Now, if he didn't get to the helicopter before the last hostage was on board, Kojo would have to wait for the second lift and very likely die.

'How can he be so calm, look so relaxed?' Victoria shrieked at Chip, whilst hugging a cushion for protection.

'He's not relaxed, pulling faces takes effort. He's probably running on empty, channelling his last grams of strength into putting one foot in front of the other, focusing on his goal. You're seeing a man stripped naked, nothing exists in his consciousness other than getting Kojo on the chopper.'

Harry stumbled and staggered to his left, stumbled again and ran on. 'That's where he got shot through the backside,' offered Chip, with no emotion.

One of the aircraft crew, in a calm, deep Southern drawl, mechanically counted the boarding of their passengers, ' Twenty-one... Twenty-two, estimate thirty seconds to loading complete.'

Sophie, sitting on the edge of the sofa, her fists clenched, screamed at the television, 'Run Harry, run for God's sake. Please!'

Harry's top half, now life-size, soaked in sweat, covered in red dust, filled the screen. His chest heaved as it tried to pump oxygen into his starving lungs, dead eyes from his camouflage painted face stared into the camera, blood from the wide gash on his cheek covered the left side of his face and neck.

Two clean pairs of hands reached down and pulled the dead-weight from his shoulders.

An American voice droned, 'Twenty four... twenty five plus one. Loading complete, clear for departure.'

Harry waved away the already departing aircraft. The high pitched engine whine and determined hammering of the rotors filled Sophie's head.

Harry stood, gulping in air then jerked backwards propelled by some invisible force, arms and legs trailing squid-like.

Sophie screamed. 'What's happened? Why did they leave him? Bastards! Why didn't they take him? They must have had plenty of room!' she shouted at the screen. 'He's not moving!'

'Something heavy calibre just broke his ribs and deflated his lungs. He probably doesn't know where he is right now and he's trying to work out how to breathe.'

'But why didn't they take him?' demanded Sophie.

'Part of the standard ops plan. If they'd pulled him on board he would have jumped off. None of the team would leave without the others. The next bit is from a few minutes later, the second chopper extracting the team.'

The film jumped to the inside of the second helicopter. Soldiers were sitting, lying or crumpled on the floor, some slumped against the aircraft side, some not moving, staring into space, blood everywhere. One was on his hands and knees vomiting, another strapped a clean, white dressing onto his own leg, over filthy, blood soaked trousers, another signalled a medic he was OK as he pinched together a gaping, pumping gash in his arm whilst grubby fingers sack-stitched it closed. Another went from soldier to soldier doing something to their guns. Harry lay to one side, on his back, crisp-uniformed, bare armed medics kneeling either side of him. One was frantically cutting a trouser leg open, another pushed a drip needle into his arm. A third finished clipping something onto Harry's bleeding face before hurdling over strewn soldiers to the back of the aircraft, reacting to the one screamed word, 'Medic'.

Sophie knew not to ask why two of the aircraft crew were ignoring the desperate trauma all around them and stood unmoving, staring out of the open doors on either side, their hands gripping the huge hanging guns.

This was nothing like she had seen in the cinema. This was the reality of what happened when determined people tried to kill each other.

Chip spoke quietly, 'Harry got caught in the blast from a mortar, god knows how he managed to climb on board, but he's lost a lot of blood and his body's exhausted, hammered, shutting down. The American medics are excellent at dealing with battlefield trauma, from this point on he couldn't be in better hands. They kept him going until they got him on to one of their flying hospitals waiting on the runway at Tamale. No one does that stuff better than the Yanks.'

Being comforting to adults wasn't natural to Chip and he wondered if he was getting it right. He felt clumsy and changed the subject. 'The guy in the helicopter with the multi-coloured shirt is Kwaku, a civilian now. He broke his ankle jumping from his bus just before it crashed into the third truck and set it and most of the occupants on fire, Alpha took care of the rest of them. He's smiling now, but wait till he remembers he's just written off half of his entire transport fleet.'

'How come you know so much about this Chip?' asked Victoria.

Chip breathed in slowly then out, taking time to consider his words. 'Kwaku, Kojo, Harry and me served together.'

'You did stuff like this?' asked Victoria, gesturing to the television, careful to give no hint of her feelings.

Chip paused again, 'The four of us were Charlie in Red Five for quite a while.' He smiled, 'I've had to push Harry out of a lot of planes.'

'But you don't do it anymore?' asked Victoria, her voice still carefully unemotional. Chip shook his head. Victoria leaned towards him and rested her hand on his thigh. 'I'm glad,' she said softly with relief, 'I couldn't bear the thought of anyone trying to hurt you.' The need to blink her eyes clear confused her and she pulled her hand away and sat back.

Chip didn't know how to hide his clumsy uncertainty of what had just happened so resorted to his usual strategy of being blunt. 'The army doesn't want me anymore, apparently stuff's gone missing up here,' he said tapping his temple.

Sophie reached over, took the remote from him and turned the television off. 'Why Chip? What was it all about? What makes people do these unspeakable things to each other?'

She wasn't surprised to hear that money was at the root of it all. The unexpected discovery of diamonds to the north of Kumasi, they had only ever been found to the south-east, had sparked a crazy scramble. Local, quick-footed opportunists had been almost immediately, ruthlessly displaced by what Chip had called *drain-slime from across the world*. The Russian led mob had included the worst foulness from places like China and North Korea with foot-soldiers mostly African-from-who-knows-where.

The local security forces, initially taken aback by the violent, shocking tactics of murder and mutilation, quickly responded with their own harsh sanitising. International watchers were confident the situation would be resolved by local forces, to the satisfaction of their diamond trading needs. In fact the episode had caused a spike in prices so it looked like a useful no-lose situation from their business perspective. The Ghanaian military were taking heavy punishment, but were relentlessly moving forward and were expected to sort it all out within weeks. They knew what they were doing, their success was not in doubt. It didn't even warrant a mention on late night news channels.

The game changed when western hostages were taken whilst several western heads of state were seeking re-election. Here was a chance for candidates to demonstrate strength and leadership or do favours, but it had to be quick. These bandits were operating to their own rules, probably despised by their own nations, they had little to lose and no homes to go to. They had already been careful to establish and maintain their reputation for indifference to life. Slaughtering of westerners could only enhance it.

Despite the offers of assistance that flooded in, all knew there was only one choice. The one group that could fully engage on the ground within forty eight hours, that continually trained across West Africa, knew the Ashanti lands better than many locals and certainly much better than the bandits, and locally were spoken of in hushed tones, in case they heard and paid a visit.

******

Late on a Friday afternoon, as Sophie had been getting ready for her evening with Harry, the British Prime Minister strode into Cabinet Office Briefing Room A and looked at each one of the assembled faces in turn then locked eye contact with the man in the crisp, brown uniform. 'I have just received a request from the necessary authorities for assistance in the release of the hostages held north of Kumasi. Please provide it. All-zeroes is approved... Get them out.'

******

'But why did they send Harry? He was on sick leave. The army has thousands of people. Why him?' asked Sophie.

'He's a very particular type of specialist, in a tightly bonded team of specialists, trained to do one specific job and you've just seen him do it. It's not part of what you would recognise as the military, I bet he hasn't saluted anyone in years.

'Politicians ease their conscience and deny knowledge of them by calling it a triple zero situation - zero other options available so deal with it with zero negotiations and zero compromise. What it really means is set loose a Red Team to locate and retrieve the objective and, at the first sign of resistance, deliver a cascading shit-storm.

'You saw what was about to happen to that young woman. They would have shared her with their friends for a few hours and then taken her outside and had fun killing her. Most of them are so out of their heads on drugs and alcohol they're crazy. Why else would a man with a knife think it's a good idea to attack a man with a gun? The ringleaders keep them stoked up, but away from firearms, in case they shoot each other.

'Harry wasn't ordered to go, like all the others, he volunteered.'

Sophie started to feel a different sickness, a different anger.

She was sure she recognised some of the other faces in the dim light of the aeroplane hold. 'Can we look at the bit on the plane again please Chip? I think I saw someone else I know. Mike, I met him at a funeral in Honeyborne.' Had those warm, gentle, quite men been on the plane with Harry?

Chip looked at Sophie. 'It wasn't Mike.'

'Let me see, I'm sure I saw someone with a piece of his ear missing, I'm sure it's him.'

Chip took a deep breath, 'It wasn't Mike. Mike died a week before this.'

Sophie flopped back onto the sofa, her head spinning. Shy, gentle, polite Mike, dead? What was happening to her world? Harry, the man she had loved with her whole being she then hated for the vile things he had done. They had been relaxing in a cosy country pub on a warm summer's evening when he had left her sitting alone and furious. In the next thirty six hours, whilst she was feeling sorry for herself and loathing him, Harry had flown thousands of miles, confronted so many of his own fears and, face to face, taken on merciless evil and violence. Those sixteen men had put their lives on the line for each other and for the love of people they had never met, didn't even know.

She was stupid! Arrogant! Self-centred! She had refused to believe that the real world could be different to the comfortable story she existed in. That somehow the dreadful things she saw on the news, before quickly changing channels, didn't actually happen or were at most nothing like as bad as they were made out to be. It was just a few fools, a long way away, being difficult. Putting a few coins in the next charity box to be shaken at her would resolve it all. Having to wear a thick jumper in the flat in the winter to save on heating was what she had thought was really tough.

Her belief that every bad person could, should, be brought to justice in a court of law now staggered her. She had judged and convicted Harry according to the expectations of her own little, self-righteous social media circle. A different reality now stared at her. The real world was horrible, frightening and unfair, but it was just that, the *real* world, for most people.

Old certainties stripped away, her pain turned to fear. Fear that her own stupid arrogance may have robbed her of the one thing she most wanted and so very nearly had.

She had let Harry's work, his skills, his sense of duty – *to stand up and be counted*, define him. That's *what* he was. It wasn't *who* he was.

Memories of Harry, the feelings of warmth and closeness, gentleness and caring, came like a foaming, cleansing wave towards her, sweeping away the wall of loathing she had erected to shut him out. Of course she had never stopped loving him, she had just hated him because he hadn't conformed to her view of right and wrong or matched her abhorrence of violence. Or rather their sense of right and wrong was probably closely aligned, how each thought the worst transgressions should be dealt with was where the gulf had been.

The video had opened her eyes and it frightened her that such things could happen in this same world at the same time as she was in it. Knowing that people like Harry and his friends were willing to do what they do made it a little less scary.

Her voice quivered, 'What have I done? Chip, I need to talk to Harry, I need to apologise to him. Do you think he'll listen to me?'

Chapter 28

On Victoria's advice Sophie and Harry had agreed to meet in town for a morning coffee, neutral ground, so neither would have to walk away from the other if they couldn't immediately agree. Sophie slowed her pace. She would be ten minutes early, even so she knew Harry would be there waiting. Would they be kissing and holding each other within the hour? She had to hope so, she loved him. What she had done was stupid, but an easy mistake to make. Surely he would see that. She would be straight and honest, admit her silliness, ask his forgiveness and suggest they give it another try.

Harry waved to the waitress and nodded. 'I took the liberty of ordering your usual cappuccino, I hope that's OK.'

Opposite or beside? Opposite or beside? Damn, she hadn't planned where to sit. He pulled out the chair beside him. He had chosen one of the tiny, round tables, he must want her within easy touching distance, a good sign, Harry didn't do random.

They sipped coffee in silence. He looked calm and relaxed in faded blue jeans, his dark blue cotton shirt making him casual-sexy tempting. As usual Harry remained silent, if she didn't say something they would quite possibly finish their coffee and go their separate ways without exchanging a word.

Sophie stared at his black coffee as she explained what she had felt and why she had reacted the way she did. At the time everything had been terrifying, she had never seen anything real like that and couldn't cope with the horror of it, didn't know what to think. She didn't see how two so very different people could be together. She saw now she had rushed to judge, how her expectations had been crazy. Looking back, he had tried to tell her so many times and she had refused to listen.

Sophie stopped talking and waited, her heart pounding. Perhaps now she had apologised she could, in the right moment, suggest they had a fantastic future together. Maybe he would brush it all aside and suggest they should try again. He always looked to the future, 'What's done is done, learn and move on' was his response to 'Sub-optimal situations'. His body language said nothing until he reached across the table to hold her hand. His warm, soft grip sent ripples straight to her heart. Was he receiving the love she was sending back through the touching of their skin?

He spoke quietly, the affection reaching deep into her. 'I know it must have been horrible for you Sophie. Who could watch that stuff and not feel shock, revulsion? Only the coldest heart wouldn't be affected. I often feel physically sick when I watch these things in debriefs and I've seen plenty of them. You shouldn't feel guilty about your reactions, it's normal. I'm so sorry you had to see it, but at least now you know what I am.'

Sophie struggled to control her excitement, within minutes she would be holding him, they would walk back to the flat hand in hand talking, touching, kissing, planning.

Harry kissed her hand, touched it to his cheek, then let go and sat back in the chair, his voice still warm, 'Don't punish yourself Sophie, it's not your fault, I agree with you. We are so very different, we live in very different worlds and I'm truly sorry I've tainted yours. There's no hope we could build anything between us. You had the courage to stand up and say so and I admire you for it. You're a wonderful person, you'll always be special to me, you already know that.'

Sophie froze, her lips started to tremble.

Harry sipped his warm coffee. 'It's not all bad, thanks in no small part to your caring and attention I'm hoping to get cleared for duty in the next weeks and then I'll be off for a year or so. At least I won't be here to remind you of my awfulness.'

Chapter 29

Victoria held her best friend. She listened intently as Sophie sobbed out the morning's pain.

'I love him Victoria and I didn't have the courage to tell him! What's the matter with me? I walked away. In a few weeks he'll be gone forever. I know he won't come back. It was in his voice.'

Victoria eased herself away, sliding her hands down Sophie's arms to hold her elbows. 'What does he always say? Never give up? Don't let anything stop you achieving your objective? Well, time for the cavalry, or reinforcements or backup – or whatever it is his type say. We're not done yet!' She was furious with the man. At least he hadn't used the truly murder-inciting words, 'It's not you it's me', which men for some reason thought was acceptable code for 'That was nice, now fuck off'.

Harry hadn't returned Victoria's voice messages or texts and now she could see Chip's physical discomfort at being summoned 'To talk'. Sitting beside him it looked like he had been warned the seafront bench may catch fire at any moment. She estimated his emotional sensitivity for this morning may be borderline 'Plank', completely incapable of recognising there could be emotional connections between a man and a woman beyond agreeing the merits of a decent meat pie. In this situation that was good. She was confident he would pass on the exact message without trying to filter it through his own interpretations, which at the very best could only be that of a man's. She was surprised that Chip felt at ease repeating the instructions and didn't appear phased by saying words like 'Love', 'Caring', 'Passionate' and 'Lifetime'.

Victoria was also in no doubt the short response Chip recounted, on the same fire-risk bench the next day, was unfiltered Harry. *It was in Sophie's best interests that she moved on and found someone worthy of her.*

'Twat! Right! Is he at yours? Yes?' demanded Victoria. Chip nodded. 'I'm going to see him. Don't follow me,' she warned as she grabbed her bag and marched off.

Chip stood up and wandered further along the front to find another bench, in the opposite direction to the storming Victoria. As beautiful and articulate… magnetic as she was the woman was crazy. She was one of the few humans that frightened him and it was clear she only tolerated him because of his friendship with Harry and by extension Sophie. At first he had accepted her subtle flirting as good-natured teasing of his social clumsiness, OK, his complete inability to interact casually, but it started to be hurtful after a while. He sat down and poured strong, black coffee from his small stainless steel flask into its small stainless steel cup. He was going to enjoy sitting alone on this empty bench, under an empty sky, looking out over an empty sea. He tutted. He wished he had had the courage to sit closer to Victoria just now, or even look at her.

The distant wail of what he guessed was a police car siren stirred him from his thoughts, then a second siren. Not long ago he would have felt compelled, eager, to head in their direction to see if he could help. It had been a struggle, but he had put all that behind him now, those things were no longer what he did. It hadn't been easy, he didn't understand social skills, whatever they were supposed to be, but he was out of the frame and firmly back in the warm world. Nevertheless, the state had paid to give him combat skills so he felt morally obliged to keep them polished as best he could, like one might shine a deactivated firearm, for the appreciation of its engineering.

A third siren, something significant was happening. He worked his way through the calming steps the shrink had given him.

A metallic clunk and vibration announced the arrival of a text message with a video link. Victoria. He shook his head, she couldn't bring herself to talk to him now. Well, a message from Victoria was better than nothing at all. He pressed play. He paused it. Was this a wind up? He searched Victoria's frozen expression for a tell-tale indication of poor taste. He watched to the end, adrenalin igniting a furnace of reactions he had spent so long trying to extinguish. He played it again, resisting the destructive anger, but allowing everything else. At the end of the third view his pulse was elevated, but steady, his breathing deliberate. He was back in that space he had fought so hard to leave. Should he deal with this alone? No. He pressed a speed dial on his phone. 'Harry?'.

******

'English! I can't understand a word of Obble-Gobble or whatever it is you commy fuckers speak,' the voice from the back seat of the stolen Mercedes barked.

'Sorry boss, I was defending you,' the shaven headed, front passenger said apologetically. He waited a few seconds before continuing, *'Igor reckons you English don't bath and smell worse than a pig. I defended you, I said it wasn't true, I said you smell about the same as a pig.'*

'Very funny Rasputin, let's revisit this conversation when it's pay-out time shall we? Now shut up and keep your eyes open, our spotter says she's left moron-man and should be walking just up ahead. Wait, that looks like her... Yes, it's her, now don't get excited and don't fuck this up.'

******

Sophie's need to answer the door in case it was Harry overrode the urgent message from her bladder. She peered into the screen and her heart sunk. What did *she* want? Had she come to deliver a 'You should know I've got him now' message? Or gloat? She wouldn't, surely not... 'Hi Elizabeth, I'm bursting for the loo, I'll leave the door on the latch.'

As she left the bedroom she took a deep breath, things couldn't get much worse, so what the heck.

A man's voice, not one she recognised.

As she walked into the room he was standing at the kitchen island. He looked up at her, his eyes scanning her from head to toe before returning to the open drawer in front of him. Sophie knew she had been assessed, for what she didn't know, but it had been expert.

Sophie's heart raced. She immediately recognised the massive, brutish frame filling her vision, the head of tight sandy curls making his angular jaw almost cartoon square. The tree-trunk of a neck disappeared into impossibly heavy shoulders. At least six feet four he dwarfed the two women. But it was the expensive, light tan, leather bomber jacket that gave him away. Her heart raced and she felt sick. It was him, the nutter that had been following her these last days and nights. Shit!

He must have forced his way in behind Elizabeth, who was standing at the other end of the room, staring at her, worry clear on her face. Think! Quick! What would Harry do? Show no signs, get yourself into position then attack with everything you have. Sophie looked at Elizabeth and put her finger to her lips for silence. Her heart thumping and acidic fear burning her throat Sophie walked casually behind the lump as he ignored her and rummaged through a second draw. Was he looking for a knife to stab them? Surely he wasn't here to steal cutlery?

She picked her favourite, heavy-based, non-stick, stainless steel frying pan from the draining rack, held the handle with both hands, raised it high above her and smashed it down with all her strength on the back of his head. He must have moved at the last moment. The pan landed with a promising 'Clung', but skidded off to one side. She remembered Chip's words about attacking on the upswing and levelled the pan for a chop to his ear, but he was too quick. Spiralling down into a half-crouch, he clamped her upper arm in vice-like fingers to hold her facing away from him. From the corner of her eye she saw the battering ram fist heading for her side and braced herself for the inevitable agony.

Nothing. No punch. No pain. Instead she was engulfed from behind by two iron arms that lifted her off the ground.

Her arms pinned, she flailed her bare feet pointlessly. 'Run Elizabeth! Run! It's that crazy that's been following me for days! Run,' she screamed. Elizabeth frozen to the spot, stared back.

'Merde! Sophieee! What the…?' the French accented voice bellowed back in stung amazement. 'You English women are crazy. Harry said you were fiery, he didn't tell me you were a head-case. Merde!'

'Sophie?' Elizabeth finally managed to squeak out past her utter amazement. 'This is Frank – Françoise. Harry's asked him to come here, they're good friends. He's not here to hurt you, he's here to keep you safe.'

'Then why has he been following me?' Sophie demanded, feeling slightly absurd wrapped in two huge arms, thirty centimetres between the ground and her still thrashing toes.

'Because Harry asked me to keep an eye on you, he was worried about you in case there was a backlash from the video. I said to him, "Look at me Harry, do I look like an undercover operative? No. Do you think I blend into the background? No. Do I stick out like a Christmas tree on the beach? Yes". Although I do feel proud you didn't spot me for the first days.'

Only after Sophie had put the frying pan down on the work surface and Frank had moved her out of grabbing distance of anything heavy or sharp did he lower her gently to the floor. She turned to face him, flushed with embarrassment and definitely nothing to do with being held by a Frenchman's warm arms, against a Frenchman's warm chest.

'He also didn't tell me about your beautiful, warm, firm yet soft, full body,' said Frank, to himself more than the others.

'Victoria's in trouble, somebody's kidnapped her,' Elizabeth blurted out, amazed at Frank's lack of focus, or dual focus anyway.

'What?'

Frank unpacked wires and clips from his metal briefcase as he spoke. 'It sounds like it was supposed to be a warning to her father, something about a money laundering case, and they would have released her, but it's gone wrong big time. Someone spotted her being bundled into a car by two men and called the police.'

'That's good isn't it? Now the police are involved?' asked Sophie earnestly.

'That's bad. These are probably second-rate contractors, five or more, brought in for a scare job and expecting to be away again tonight with a wad of cash. Now they're being hunted they'll do whatever they need to do to get home. Victoria has gone from a person they've been paid to frighten to a bargaining chip, to be disposed of as soon as she's of no use.' Frank plugged a lead from his case into a power point on the kitchen island.

He pointed to the smashed casing of the door intercom and video and the small black tube he had attached to it dangling from five coloured wires. 'Sorry about that, it's a new security key type and we don't have time to enter it elegantly.'

He flicked a switch and six small screens inside the case lid crackled into life. 'Now we can see all the entry door cameras and we have enough backup power to keep the door locks enabled, even if they take the building power out.'

Elizabeth held Sophie's hands, 'Sophie, the police have stopped them down near the pier, near the roadworks. They're armed.'

'But that must be good then!'

'Chip and Harry are on their way down there now. The police won't work with them, that's for sure, so they'll take these people on themselves. You know what that means, they won't stop until Victoria's safe, or…' said Elizabeth quietly.

'…or they're both dead,' Frank, without emotion, completed Victoria's sentence.

Sophie pulled her hands away from Elizabeth's, 'No! No! No! Stop him. Let the police deal with it, they're the experts. Frank! Call him and tell him to stop, to come home right now. The two of them against five with guns? It's stupid!'

'My money's on the two, I wouldn't want to face that pair with a dozen contractors,' said Frank, with what Sophie thought was a really insensitive chuckle. 'Anyway no one on the planet can call them off now, they won't stop, they won't abandon a friend.'

Elizabeth spoke firmly, 'Sophie, you've seen the video, you've seen what they'll do for people they don't even know. They'd fight their way into hell and chase down the devil for Victoria.

'Victoria… and you, are part of something you can't control, can't opt out of now. And there's dozens, hundreds more like them ready to do the same, for you, for Victoria. If Chip called up support there's probably ten or more just like them racing to get here now.'

'He did, there's three on their way, six waiting for instruction, but they won't get here in time, it's going to be all over within the hour, one way or another,' said Frank.

Sophie fumbled with her phone.

'He won't answer your number,' said Frank calmly.

Sophie stared at him. 'But he'll answer yours! Call him and let me speak to him,' she demanded.

Frank handed her his phone. 'Speed dial four seven, but think about it Sophie. If you *could* persuade him to walk away Victoria will probably be dead before the afternoon's out and he will hate both himself and you forever. Could you live with any of those outcomes?'

Sophie stared at the phone then slammed it back into Frank's waiting hand.

'But why aren't you down there helping them? He's your friend. What are you doing here?' demanded Sophie, pointing at him desperately.

Frank's calmness counterbalanced Sophie's near hysteria, 'First question: because Harry asked me to come here and in such circumstances I will do *whatever* he asks me to do. I have complete confidence this is where he wants me to be. Your safety is one less thing for him to think about now... Second question: if anyone comes through that door without an invitation... I kill them.' He pulled open another drawer, 'Now, where's the rolling pin, I hope it's not one of those heavy marble things.'

******

Sophie flicked the television from news channel to news channel and refreshed her laptop browsers pointing at newsfeeds. Cricket? Why so much damned cricket? It was worse than football! Why so damned much of it?

World upside-down described, literally, how Sophie felt, like she was seeing everything whilst doing a head-stand. Nothing was making sense and the pressure on her brain was confusing, horrible.

The man she had loved and then hated she would give her life for right this minute, right now, without a thought. She loved him so much it was physically hurting her insides. Whatever he was, whatever he had done, she loved him, without reservation, even though that love was no longer returned. He had loved her once, maybe just a little, but it was love, she was sure of it. Why hadn't she given him more of herself? She had given him everything she knew how to give, but she should have given him more. More. She should have opened her soul to him and said *This is yours*. Perhaps then he would have loved her more.

She couldn't even begin to understand her feelings for Victoria, it was like each was the other's daughter, each the other's protector, each the other's cherished responsibility. Two very different people from two very different worlds, joined by an invisible bond, each knowing and nourishing the other.

Chip. What was Chip? Odd, quirky, peculiar, mostly silent, distant, indifferent, unfathomable, a solid rock of unshakeable, dependable calm. Cold, until you understood him, then unending warmth. Close, effortlessly inside her defences, caring for her. A good man in this world and she was blessed to know him.

Treasures, they were her treasures in life and no one could take them away from her.

Except someone could.

Chapter 30

The young man wiped his sweating palms on his new, immaculately pressed, blue uniform trousers. He wasn't sure why the sarcastic sergeant Atherton, who usually gave him the shittiest jobs, always with a smile, always taking great delight in the emphasised pronunciation of the first syllable of his name, had put him on the outer cordon. There had been no sarcasm today, the sergeant's whispered warning to *be very careful* had been paternal and the constable was glad to be as far away as possible from the centre of anything that involved Armed Response.

Standing alone in the quiet side street, fear crept upwards. The two heavies, even from thirty metres out, had already trampled over every lesson of his assertiveness training. Their running had slowed to a walk as soon as they saw him and as they approached they split apart, as if stalking for a kill. A metre from him they stopped and waved two unusual identity cards in his face. He needed a toilet.

The one with a limp and less frightening eyes had given him two pieces of information and coolly instructed him to call in the second first and the first second. The cold, silent menace oozing from the one with the scarred face made it clear there was nothing open for discussion. Trying desperately to control his shaking hand on the radio button he read the two identity numbers to the control centre along with the explicitly demanded words *in theatre*. He was uncomfortable as he passed the second piece of information and, despite his frantic waving, the two men walked past him and down the street.

The authoritative voice of the operator crackled over the radio. 'Please repeat that last,' she requested with a hint of confusion.

Then sergeant Atherton's unmistakeable, irritated growl, 'So Peabody, this elephant loose in Bridge Street, did they say what *colour* it was?'

******

'Looks like it hasn't gone according to plan,' said Chip dryly, as he joined Harry crouching beside the rear wheel of the almost pristine, bright yellow digger, abandoned a few minutes earlier at the bottom of Duke's Mound by the panicking driver.

They had already agreed with Frank that this was a frightener, a warning for Victoria's father, gone wrong. Most likely they had intended to abandon her, bound, gagged and petrified, in a second car in one of the secluded carparks en-route to Newhaven Ferry or the A26. Probably a third car in another carpark would have allowed them to torch the first. The game had changed and, if these people were as amateur as they looked, Victoria was now at best a pawn, very soon to become an unwanted liability and unlikely to survive a long, drawn out police negotiation.

It was possible the plan could have survived a concerned citizen remembering the fake number plate, convinced he had witnessed an abduction. Maybe the woman was joining friends in the car and the police would have given it a low priority if the real owner of the registration hadn't been involved in a road traffic accident two hours earlier, five hundred miles away. It should have been an easy gig.

******

*Ronny regretted hiring in the four East Europeans to save
money. They had panicked at the first sign of a significant
police presence and, instead of carrying on sedately to the ferry,
had taken a screeching sharp right, down to the sea front and
straight into roadworks and concrete barriers, heavy machinery
everywhere. Igor and Rasputin (or whatever his name was) had
produced guns. Ronny had insisted on no guns, he'd made that
clear. All they had to do was pick up a girl, give her a message,
squeeze her tits and then let her go. Now these cowboys were
turning it into a western, but the cavalry, which was growing
larger by the minute, was on the wrong side. And who were those
two behind the digger? Why were they heading into the middle
of it whilst everyone else was running away? Perhaps they were
after a really cool selfie, there was something unsettling about
their lack of fear. Oh shit! What was Igor doing? He's pulled the
girl from the car and heading towards the beach, holding a gun
to her head. Surely the dickhead wasn't going to swim for it?*

Ronny shook his head. You got what you paid for.

******

On Chip's nod Harry swung the yellow, half empty,
twenty five litre oil drum and heaved it into the centre of
the junction. As it clanged its first contact with the ground
they sprinted from behind the water tanker and in opposite
directions around the red and white plastic barriers. The first
shots found their mark, the drum spewing oil from the bullet
holes.

Harry was racing towards a dirty, orange road roller when
he heard two rounds pass close behind him then, in the
silence of his absolute focus, the unmistakeable click of an
empty chamber. He didn't know if it was instinct, training or

something else that controlled him in such situations, he had been unaware of any decision process that found him now turned ninety degrees and sprinting towards the shooter.

Startled at Harry's banshee howl the gunman had looked up and fumbled the insertion of the new magazine. As Harry launched himself headlong over the barrier, stretching with his fingertips to just nudge the gun to one side, he felt the first shot tug at his thigh. The second went wide. Harry was confident that smashing the man's head against the rusting steel digger bucket had killed him, but he took three seconds to snap his neck, to be sure.

He picked up the gun and, crouching behind the heavy steel bucket, allowed himself three steadying breaths. Ahead and to his left he heard the crack of a handgun, probably firing in the direction of where Harry expected Chip to be. He saw movement between two tall dark blue oil drums. An easy target, but he couldn't see who it was. Harry stood up and fired a shot to skip across the tops of the oil barrels. A gun appeared and fired four shots randomly in his direction. OK, definitely not Chip, definitely not Victoria, Harry fired three rounds into the gap. A long, low whistle signalled the target was cleared and Chip had remembered his combat communications.

Harry sprinted to his right, towards pallets of pale yellow bricks, knowing Chip would already be amongst the drums.

'Hey English pig, the beautiful and sexy Victoria has a message for you,' the heavily accented voice shouted out sarcastically from beside a big, clumsy looking machine covered in black shiny stuff and reeking of bitumen.

'He… he wants you to stand up. He's got a gun pointing at me Harry, a gun… at my head.' It was unmistakeably a very frightened Victoria.

'Easy English, easy now. My finger is very tight on this trigger. Eject the clip and then drop the gun down that drain beside you. Easy now,' the grinning Russian purred, his head pushed hard against Victoria's. The clip clattered into the road drain and Harry, holding the grip by his fingertips dropped the gun after it. 'You English are so easy. We Russians would never sacrifice ourselves. Now instead of a dead whore, we have a dead whore and a dead pig.'

Harry shrugged his shoulders and tapped the centre of his forehead, 'Take your time, one clean shot.'

The Russian aimed the gun at Harry, leaning backwards slightly to counterbalance his outstretched arm.

'Mistake,' said Harry.

'What mistake?' sneered the Russian confidently, moving his head further back in smiling arrogance.

Harry leaned to his right just before he saw the pink spray from the left of the Russian's head and heard the single shot. Then, as the body collapsed backwards it twitched as two more shots reported. A year out of active service hadn't affected Chip's marksmanship either.

Harry ran forward and held the silent, shaking Victoria. 'We're with you now Victoria, we won't leave you,' said Harry gently, as he wiped the Russian's brain spatter from the side of her face, 'you'll be OK.'

'I'm out,' said Chip, as he ran his hands over the body, searching unsuccessfully for ammunition. Then, offering Harry the dead Russian's gun, 'There's two more somewhere, take this, I'm going to flush them out. It needs to finish here or she'll never be free.'

'I've got a better idea, you look after Victoria, I'll go for them,' said Harry, pushing the offered gun aside and gently easing the shaking Victoria into Chip's arms.

Chip stared at Harry. 'She needs to be free Harry... it finishes here.' Few would recognise the absolute commitment, the unbreakable bond of duty to a friend, in Harry's almost imperceptible nod.

Harry's one-eighty degree scan to the east, towards the marina, revealed little opportunity for hiding. A few oil drums and small equipment. There had been no one in the parked coaches further along, no opportunity for hostages. He headed west, towards the pier. Being unarmed, up against one or possibly two guns was a challenge. Being under the careful and cautious scrutiny of police officers lining the railings on the roadside above was going to make what he had to do next difficult and he needed to do it quickly, before Brighton's finest decided it was safe enough for them to engage.

The alcoves to the right had been netted off for building work and there was a clear view down the road. That left the green containers and the builders yard. These clowns had really screwed up, he couldn't think of a worse situation to end up in if he was trying to make an exit. The big grey shed in front was locked and on previous morning runs he'd seen there was no back entrance. What was that to the right of the yellow truck skip? A body in a pool of blood by the look of it.

Harry ducked under the barrier.

'One step closer and you get one between the eyes,' said the smug cockney voice.

'I think we both know that if you had a loaded gun you'd have already taken the shot,' replied Harry calmly, as he continued his walk towards the skip. Good, the shed would stop anyone standing on Marine Parade above seeing what happened next.

'Very good. It's you and me then, let's hope you're more of a challenge than that pointless commie twat. He's been a mouthy pain in the arse from start to finish, no respect. I was glad to get rid of him.'

Harry cleared thoughts of the frightened Victoria from his head. Anger was dangerous, this needed to be clinical. And it almost was. The blade, glinting in the morning sun, came from high, diagonally down in a wide slash, missing Harry's face by a centimetre. The immediate horizontal return swing, with no adjustment for distance, would have been equally ineffective if Harry hadn't leaned into it allowing the tip to slice across his chest. Strange how the cutting sensation brought no pain.

Harry allowed himself to relax into his combat head. He must have practiced this exact scenario in training thousands of times. He clamped the right wrist with his left hand then, with his right, hammered his first two knuckles into the solar plexus, the throat, then the solar plexus again and the exercise was over. But Harry had a promise to keep and it needed to look realistic. With his DNA on the blade edge this was self-defence. Five unhurried, practiced, targeted strikes collapsed both lungs and did irreparable damage to multiple other internal organs. It wasn't needed, but to be doubly sure, for Chip's sake, he fired a sixth to smash the larynx, sending what was left of it into terminal spasm.

Harry lowered the body, in its last desperate twitching of life, to the ground, making sure the switch blade stayed clasped in the fist.

No carotid pulse. Propping himself up against the skip and gulping in air, he had channelled every gram of his power into the blows, he waited sixty seconds and checked again. Nothing.

By the time the police arrived with their guns, helmets and body armour, looking like something out of a B rated Sci-Fi comedy movie, the body was cooling and releasing.

******

Chip left Victoria being checked in the back of an ambulance and walked over to Harry in the back of another, enjoying the attention of a bossy, very attractive, and obviously ex-military paramedic. Harry's slight nod answered Chip's unasked question.

'Your friend's lucky to be alive, but I can make him *all* better,' announced the paramedic, with an inviting intimacy that only military could appreciate in the circumstances and making Harry actually feel better with every word.

'I doubt luck had much to do with it,' muttered a watching, worried Sergeant Atherton.

******

Sophie waited impatiently for the clock at the bottom of the television screen to turn to a new minute. Right, that was three now. She turned to ask him again, for the sixteenth time. As calm and patient as Frank was she didn't want to irritate him. He was her only link to what was going on, he was her whole world right now.

How was Elizabeth staying so silent, detached? Her brother was in danger and so was Harry, a close friend - possibly by now her lover, and she hadn't moved from the television or said a word.

'Nothing yet Sophie,' said Frank, before she spoke.

'What do you think? It's been fifty one minutes now. What might be happening?' pleaded Sophie.

'Sophie, I know it's hard on those that wait, but believe me those two are very good at what they do and this *is* what they do. They're not a couple of random blokes getting into a pub brawl, they've worked together for years, they're masters of their craft. I've seen some of their debriefs and the pair of them frighten the shit... Anyway.'

And Sophie decided she didn't want to hear anymore. Not because she didn't want to know, but because she only wanted to know what Harry wanted to tell her. That would be good enough for her from now on. She prayed there could be a *from now on*.

'Here we go,' said Frank, breathing in, straightening up, readying himself and touching something in the briefcase. His right hand reached out and adjusted the position of the one-piece stainless-steel vegetable knife lying on the marble top beside him.

Sophie and Elizabeth stared as the quiet caring of the man evaporated leaving something alien and mechanical, crackling with aggression. Now he was frightening them.

'What?' asked Elizabeth.

'OK, good, wait a minute,' he said, visibly relaxing, the aggression disappearing under the return of the warmth.

The strangled screech of the broken door security buzzer on the wall was joined by a sharp double beep from the briefcase.

'What's the password?' Chip's unmistakeable voice asked from the briefcase.

'What do you want it to be?' Frank responded.

'How about… French wanker?'

Elizabeth sat back on the sofa, tilted her head back and whispered something to the ceiling.

'Good enough mon ami,' said Frank with a grin, releasing the door lock.

'If Sophie's there, Harry's fine, he's just gone to the hospital for some fixing up, nothing serious, he should be back within the hour,' said Chip.

'He's OK Sophie, he's OK,' shouted Victoria.

Sophie stood up, sat down and then stood up again. 'Thank you God. Thank you, thank you,' she said, her wet eyes squeezed tightly closed.

******

As he parked, the black-leather clad rider knew he had attracted attention. The sleek, stunning lines of his Triumph motorbike always did, he considered it a thing of engineering beauty. The other two would be here soon. On a job, especially dark-grid, they were always careful not to ride so close together that they may look like they were in convoy.

All three had received the "Wait" instruction and then the "Stand-down", but he called in to confirm, to be sure. A pity.

Perhaps they could salvage something from the journey and on the way back stop off at Portsmouth and blag a tour around one of the new warships. And off load the hand guns they each had hidden under their fuel tanks.

******

Sitting close to chip Victoria rested her elbows on the dining table, gripping her mug of steaming tea with both hands to reduce the shaking. 'I called Pops, he wanted to come down, but the police told him it's better for me if we stay apart for the time being, until they've swept up any more dross hanging around. He reckons that once word gets out about what happened to those bastards any others will be running in the opposite direction.' She put the mug down and gripped Chip's forearm with both hands. 'Chip… I… Thank you… I…' She looked across the table at Sophie, 'You know, if Chip and Harry hadn't… I can't think about what would've happened if they hadn't known how…' She bit her bottom lip, fighting back a sob.

Chip sat bolt upright, staring at an empty spot on the table.

He had been uncomfortable when his sister had hugged and kissed him then Sophie had flung her arms around him, kissed him long and hard on the cheek and declared she would love him for ever. He had been completely destabilised when he had had to sit on the toilet seat lid with eyes clamped closed as Victoria showered and dried herself. Now her hands holding his arm made him feel seriously peculiar.

Frank, cleared his throat, 'It might be good if you tried to sleep for a while. You're probably emotionally exhausted and in shock, it happens to most people who go through this stuff. Things will look a bit less scary after a good rest.'

Victoria took a deep, wobbly breath. 'Yes, I think you're right.' She pulled Chip's arm closer to her. 'Come on let's go, you need a rest as well.'

'What?' frowned Chip.

'You can't expect me to sleep on my own and Sophie needs to be here when Harry gets back. You can lie on top of the covers, come on… please, I need you to be close,' pleaded Victoria.

As they stood Victoria pulled his arm around her waist and leaned against him, trying to keep in the here and now. She sniffed. 'And you need to take a shower before you slide in to the soldier-shaped space in my bed. In fact… I've got several soldier-shaped spaces that need your attention.'

Chapter 31

So, this is Chip, thought Jason Bartholomew as he sipped from his mug of tea and looked across the table at one of the two men leisurely enjoying doorstep bacon sandwiches and arguing between themselves about the merits of two brands of brown sauce. Calm, clean-cut, polite and gentle now, it was difficult to believe they were both expert and willing in the delivery of extreme brutality. He had only ever read about such people, or faced them across a court room whilst they were restrained and under the control of guards. This early Saturday morning, sitting unprotected, vulnerable, his discomfort was calmed by the knowledge that they were the product of British tax payers' money and, thank god, they were all on the same side.

Their skilful avoidance of Jason's carefully concealed questioning, designed to learn by stealth, had been worthy of any court. Their training had involved a lot more than just the physical. They frightened and warmed him equally.

'I can't think of words to tell you how I feel, which is a pretty damning admission for a barrister. All I can say, sincerely, is thank you so much, both of you.' Jason took two stiff, plain brown envelopes from his jacket pocket and put them on the table, one in front of each man. 'I hope you can accept these. It's all above board, the cheques are against my personal account, all legal.'

Harry licked his thumb then used a square of kitchen roll to wipe away the remaining melted butter. He picked up his envelope and ran his fingertip along its sharp crisp edges. 'That's a serious envelope,' he said in admiration, passing it to Chip before picking up his second sandwich.

Without looking at either, Chip added the envelope to his

own, aligning one carefully, edge to edge, on top of the other, before placing them back in front of Jason. 'We do what we do for those we care about because we care about them, that's all. It's not for sale. Your thanks are more than enough,' he said whilst trying to decide which part of his butter-dripping sandwich to bite next.

Sophie looked up from her coffee and stared at Chip, then Harry, then Chip again, her stomach churning. Chip, always so careful with his words, careful never to mislead, painfully pedantic in not setting an incorrect expectation, wasn't using past tense. *We do what we do…*

Victoria, sitting next to her father, turned and rested her hand on his forearm. Chip's use of *Care* finally liquidised the last remnants of her insides that he hadn't melted with his words and touch over the previous days. 'Pops, since the… you know, Chip and I are… you know.'

'Know? What do I know? I don't know anything,' said Jason, picking up his mug with disinterest and grateful for the breaking of the awkward silence.

'Together, we're together,' she said, the need for approval in her voice.

Jason turned to his daughter and smiled. 'Well, finally, thank goodness for that. How many of our calls over the last weeks have been about what Chip did or didn't say, what Chip did or didn't do? Chip, Chip… Chip, Chip, Chip.'

'Did I?'

'Yes, you did. And don't misunderstand, I love hearing about anything you want to tell me, any time, but a little variety maybe?'

Jason sipped his tea, time to change the subject. 'I'm particularly interested in the transport business investment you spoke of. What's that about?'

Kwaku, explained Victoria, had served with Harry and Chip before leaving the army to start up a transport business in Ghana. It was struggling to expand because one of his two trucks had crashed. (She didn't say how it had crashed, but Jason had trawled the internet. It hadn't taken long to understand what had happened in the diamond mine hostages operation and how important this Kwaku's involvement had been. Chip's words about doing things for those you care about finally explained why Kwaku would have committed such a selfless act).

Victoria and Sophie thought it would be a medium risk investment. The Economy was growing at an impressive rate and the potential for agriculture and light industrial was significant. Sophie and Victoria had already built and were managing Kwaku's website for him (on a shoestring budget provided by Harry) and there was more business than could be serviced. Victoria was managing the marketing and Sophie the business processes, accounts and the like.

Jason looked at Sophie to his left, then Victoria to his right. Yes, he was sure. He picked up his battered, soft, brown leather holdall, pulled out two stiff canvass portfolio folders and placed them in front of him. 'I don't have the time to manage that kind of investment, it needs to be constantly monitored and adjusted. It's a lot of work, even if you do understand the sectors, which I don't. So I've set up a small investment company with modest, but useful capital which I'm hoping you two ladies will manage for me. When you've got time take a look in here and if you like it sign the forms so that I can make you directors. I don't aspire to be a venture capitalist, but I do want to see viable business and measurement plans before we invest.' He pushed the folders towards Victoria and Sophie. 'You could start with the transport and I also like the sound of Greenwood and his gym if that's still available.' He picked the two brown envelops from the table. 'If you two gentlemen prefer not to take these I'll add them to the investment fund, they'll add budget for Kwaku maybe.' If Chip and Harry wouldn't accept a direct reward he would at least get it to someone they cared about.

It was the first time Victoria could remember not wanting to go shopping, but as everyone else had agreed, it was important for her to get out and about as soon as possible, to push those horrible events into her past. She set off to the town centre, arm in arm with Chip and her father. She didn't understand Chip's discomfort at the thought of being in a crowded place, but it was real and his willingness to go with her was already making her feel stronger.

Sophie and Harry hadn't spoken since that dreadful day - he had come from the hospital to check with Frank what security was needed. They had agreed the twenty-four hour police guard on the apartment was enough and Chip staying the night, although no doubt preoccupied, was a bonus. When Harry's local anaesthetic had started wearing off Sophie suggested he could rest in her bed, she would have the sofa and then he wouldn't be alone in Chip's bedsit – just in case. Sophie's dismay was complete when Harry had said, apparently without any sign of understanding the impact of his words (but, Victoria had suggested later, with strong evidence of being a thoughtless dick-head), *Elizabeth will be around to sort me out if I need anything.*

Now, to Sophie's surprise, as the three left for the shops, Harry accepted her request to sit back down at the table whilst she made more tea. She wasn't sure what she was going to say. She definitely was not going to follow Victoria's hurriedly whispered advice to *grab him by the lapels, drag him to the ground and pummel his body with soft punches until he agreed to love her forever, then rip his clothes off and ravage him.*

Sophie cleared away the mugs and plates, brought two clean cups and placed the pot of fresh tea on its stand, careful not to have it as a barrier between them. Her outer calm perfectly hid the mad panic in her brain and the thumping of her heart. This was all last-minute, nothing was planned, no strategy, no carefully considered groups of phrases to fall back on. What was she going to say? How did he look? Anxious? Irritated? Vulnerable? (if only!). Bored, he looked bored. Too polite to leave, but knowing, like sitting on a delayed train, the journey would sometime be over - precious minutes of your life had been stolen from you, but you would soon be free to get on with the rest of it, without the bloody train, or Sophie.

'How's Justin and Elizabeth?'

'OK I think. I don't see Elizabeth much. Chip and I have spent most of our time with Woody designing course contents. His place has the potential to be something special.'

They looked at each other in silence. Despite the clear signal that Elizabeth wasn't competition Sophie still felt helpless. She had to get words out quickly otherwise it would be his next opening that shaped the rest of the conversation. He sipped his tea. Of course, he was comfortable in silence, he could happily go all day without saying a word. She swallowed hard at the lump in her throat. No tears, no tears, she must not cry. Where were her words? She bit her bottom lip. Something in his face moved. Was he getting fed up? He looked at his watch. Words, she needed words. She gave up control of everything and set her mouth free. It took full advantage.

'I love you Harry, I love you. I want to be with you. I don't care what you've had to do, what you might have to do. I'm sorry I was angry, I was frightened, I didn't understand. I was childish and self-righteous without knowing what was outside of my own little bubble. I love you Harry.'

Harry looked at her and sat back in his chair. 'I'm sorry you had to see it, but there's no need for you to apologise, I've told you that, I understand. I'm just glad you know and I'm

In the Arms of Giants

not living a lie any more. You're a good person, a wonderful person, Sophie, I wish my world was full of people like you. There's a lot to be said for bubbles, the only problem is that once it's burst it's gone, forever.' He looked at his watch again. 'I really need to go, I've got a lot to do and then I promised to take Justin to play crazy golf.'

No! He was giving her the brush off. She'd said everything she possibly could, she couldn't make it any clearer. He was walking out of her life, right this minute he was walking away. Should she get up and grab him, force him to kiss her? It wouldn't work, but it was all she had now. She put her palms on the table ready to spring up.

He drained his cup then looked at her, curious at her posture. 'How are you with a putter? Fancy a game?'

She hadn't expected that. Harry was like a doting uncle where Justin was concerned and to be invited to share time must mean something. Was it because he thought Justin might enjoy her company (that would be good) or was Harry, in his often almost emotionless mind, offering her a way back? Or was he just being polite and expecting her to be polite enough to decline? She had no idea. She should back off.

'Well, perhaps I shouldn't…' she looked at him. *Never ever stop, never give up*, his words. She had to know. Screw it! Go for it!

'Will you let me win?' asked Sophie.

'Sorry, that's Justin's position.'

'Oh yes, of course, can I come second then?'

'Yes.'

'Can I have an ice cream?'

'Yes.'

'Can I have a big bag of those candy covered chocolates?'

'Yes.'

'Can I have a kiss?'

'Yes.'
'Can we have a shag?'
Harry looked at his watch. And smiled.